THE STATE WE'RE IN

What are the odds that the stranger sitting next to you on a plane is destined to change your life? Especially when they appear to be your opposite in every way.

She's a life-long optimist, looking for her soul mate in every man she meets; he's a resolute cynic – cruel experience has taught him never to put his faith in anyone.

People can surprise you. In the time it takes to fly from London to Chicago, each finds something in the other that they didn't even realise they needed.

Their pasts are such that they can never make one another happy and it's when they get off the plane, that their true journey begins . . .

'Adele's well-crafted tales of modern life always pack an emotional wallop, and she's on fine form here. The intoxicating tale of strangers and absolute opposites bonding on a long flight is beautifully done, with a final, gut-wrenching reveal that will have you weeping away on the floor' *Star* magazine

'The story is completely mesmerising, and the ending heartbreakingly epic. Adele has created a cast of characters that completely cover the moral spectrum. *The State We're In* is a superb triumph' *We Love This Book*

'This book made me laugh, caught at my heart and then broke it. The story is clearly building to something but I didn't know what – I won't spoil it but this is definitely not one for public transport' *A Case for Books*

'I very much recommend you should pick up *The State We're In*, it was amazing. Adele Parks is such an amazing writer and managed to keep so many different plots and characters up in the air with ease . . . It was a magnificent read with twists and turns at every avenue. My one piece of advice to you is to just read it' *Chick Lit Reviews*

'A perceptive insight into family life, both idyllic and dreadful, and the individuals that are part of it. The characters are all people that you can believe in . . . and the ending? It's an absolute stunner!' *Our Book Reviews*

'A cleverly written and tragically beautiful story filled with empathy and regret, that will stay in your thoughts for a long time, *The State We're In* is a story of love, family, abandonment and putting ghosts to rest. A haunting tale that will leave you in floods. This truly is Adele Parks at her best, I can't recommend this book enough' *Handwritten Girl*

'This novel has been tenderly and beautifully written and will stay with me' *A Lover Of Books*

By Adele Parks

Playing Away
Game Over
Larger Than Life
The Other Woman's Shoes
Still Thinking of You
Husbands
Young Wives' Tales
Happy Families (Quick Read)
Tell Me Something
Love Lies
Men I've Loved Before
About Last Night
Whatever It Takes
The State We're In

Adele PARKS

THE STATE WE'RE IN

headline
review

First published in Great Britain in 2013
by HEADLINE REVIEW
An imprint of HEADLINE PUBLISHING GROUP

First published in paperback in Great Britain in 2014
by HEADLINE REVIEW

5

Cataloguing in Publication Data is available from the British Library

ISBN 978 0 7553 7139 6

Typeset in Monotype Dante by Palimpsest Book Production Limited,
Falkirk, Stirlingshire

Printed and bound in Great Britain by
Clays Ltd, St Ives plc

Headline's policy is to use papers that are natural, renewable
and recyclable products and made from wood grown in sustainable forests.
The logging and manufacturing processes are expected to conform to
the environmental regulations of the country of origin.

HEADLINE PUBLISHING GROUP
An Hachette UK Company
338 Euston Road
London NW1 3BH

www.headline.co.uk
www.hachette.co.uk

For Jimmy

Prologue

'So you know all about love, do you?'

'I know enough.'

'Well, I know nothing. I don't know anything about aliens, or ghosts, or any other empty phenomena either.'

She laughed, as though she thought he was joking. The laugh flew out into their history. It was a strong, heartfelt laugh; bigger than her. He wriggled in his seat, uncomfortable that he found himself intrigued by her nonsense.

'Why *wouldn't* you believe in love?' she asked, unable to hide her incredulity.

'Oh, the usual. I think it brings nothing but pain,' he said, pulling a well-practised, neatly deflective hound-dog expression. He mocked himself so that she wouldn't guess how serious he was.

'Hating isn't exactly a bag of laughs either, though, is it?' she pointed out. 'I've never met a happy cynic, or a miserable optimist, come to that. So obviously being an optimist is the way to go. Open-and-shut case.' She beamed, content in her own reasoning, and he slowly moved his head from side to side, bemused. Amused.

Interested.

1976

1

Eddie

Eddie stood on the step of his terraced house in Clapham and drew a deep breath. He took in as much of the chilly blue-black night as he could; slow, calming breaths that he hoped might rinse away some of the smells of good times that Diane was very likely to object to. Smoke on his clothes, whisky and beer on his breath; he'd need to shower to remove the scent of woman. As he paused, he noticed that the people next door were now also ripping up the black and white Victorian tiles that decorated the front steps. Eddie had got rid of theirs as soon as they'd inherited. They'd pulled out the old bath and replaced it with a more sanitary plastic suite, in avocado green. They'd installed central heating too, done away with the mess and inconvenience of real fires. He'd felt unshackled. Out with the old, in with the new. Progress. Looking forward, that was what it was all about. Not looking back. That had never been his style. Never would be.

Diane hadn't wanted to make the home improvements. She'd gone on about original features, insisting that they would one day come back into fashion; she hadn't wanted to change anything from the way her mum and dad had had it when she was a girl.

'Yeah, but when we want something bigger and need to sell

5

on, no one will look at this dump in its current state,' Eddie had explained. Frankly it irritated him a bit that she had no idea that everyone else in the world actually enjoyed living in the twentieth century. She'd become upset and unreasonable, which was often her way nowadays, especially after a glass of wine.

'We don't need anything bigger. We can't afford anything bigger!' she whined. Her voice was always whiny or screechy. Had been for a few years.

It was true that they struggled to pay the bills on this place, but even so Eddie regretted Diane's lack of ambition. Anyway, it was his house, even if they had inherited it off her parents. Law of the land. If he wanted to sell it, he could do just that. He found the old panel doors, parquet floors and stone sinks depressing. He'd told her he wasn't going to live in a museum. So they'd all gone.

Eddie sighed as he recognised that he hadn't done much in the way of redecorating for over a year; he'd discovered that no amount of orange plastic chairs could turn number 47 into the home he wanted.

He tentatively pushed open the front door and forced himself over the threshold; he was immediately hit by the smell of regurgitated breast milk and steeping nappies. He wanted to turn and run.

Diane appeared in the hallway. She had a distinctly unwashed vibe. Her hair hung in greasy curtains about her face. She was wearing grubby jeans and a T-shirt stained with perspiration. That said, Eddie could not deny she still had a cracking figure, despite having given birth twice. He noticed it anew every time he looked at her. Even though she was feeding, she still had small breasts and so she never bothered with a bra; her tiny hard nipples were nearly always provocatively visible. She had long legs and a trim arse. It bemused Eddie how she could resist progress when her body seemed to be made for this decade. She'd have struggled in the sixties to warrant a second glance, because back then, men wanted something to grab on to, but her lithe, elongated body made her a goddess in this decade. Or at least she could be a goddess, if she ever washed.

Wordlessly Diane thrust the baby into Eddie's arms, causing him to drop his script on the floor. The sheets scattered like petals from an overblown rose; he regretted not numbering the pages. Diane shrugged indifferently and stomped straight into the kitchen. Words were no longer a nicety that either of them regularly bothered with. Eddie didn't need Diane to tell him that she'd had a bad day; that the baby was teething and had been difficult to settle, that her nappies had been exceptionally pungent. Diane had said as much, often enough, with this baby and the boy, when he'd been younger; it seemed to be the same story every day. Over and over. Eddie could not help. Diane thought that he wouldn't. Eddie barely knew whether there was a difference any more.

Thoughtlessly he hoisted the grumbling baby on to his hip and leant his forehead against the hall wall. He was a little flushed. That would be the whisky. He should have stuck to pints. He shouldn't have allowed himself to be tempted into drinking spirits at lunchtime, but it was difficult to resist. She was such a fun girl. Frivolous. Game. Plus, he knew whisky made her dirty. There was nothing better than a free and flippant afternoon in the sack, other than, perhaps, a filthy and risky one. The hall wallpaper was a smooth, cool vinyl; brown squares on a slightly paler brown background. The floor was covered with cork tiles. Eddie had picked them both out but now regretted his choices; momentarily, he felt like he was inside a cell for the mentally ill, but there was no padding.

Eddie forced himself to look at Zoe. She was a fat baby. When old women peeked into her pram they oohed and aahed and swore blind that she was a cherub, a bonny baby, a *proper* baby.

The women who gave these compliments had been mothers during the war and so liked fat kids. Eddie didn't like the way his daughter looked. He wished she wasn't quite so opulent. This child seemed to burst out of her nappies and smock dresses; hats popped off her head, tights wouldn't quite pull up over her chunky thighs. Her brow melted into her nose and she had no neck at all. Dean was the same. Eddie had thought that once he was running around a bit, he'd slim down, but he hadn't. He was five years old but he had to wear clothes for eight-year-olds; the bottoms of his trousers were always covered in mud because Diane was too idle to hem anything. Idle or incapable. Still, at least with a boy you could tell yourself he was stocky and hardy, you could console yourself with the thought that he might make a rugby player. It was 1976, for God's sake. Lithe meant affluent, fashionable, desirable; chubby meant, well, the opposite.

Eddie was a writer for the BBC; people expected certain things from him in terms of style and presentation. He was part of the *it* crowd. He knew people who would, no doubt, one day be described as iconic. It was assumed he would wear his hair inches past the collar, and he needed long sideburns; he had to wear corduroy trousers that fell dangerously low around his groin, with unforgiving polo-neck jumpers, which did not allow for an ounce of spare flesh. People presumed he would indulge in recreational narcotics and free love, that he'd have a wife who had once dabbled as a model but now was a little bit too dependent on Valium and vino; every night was a party.

No one expected kids, but if there had to be kids then they should be skinny, whimsical types. They ought to wear fancy-dress costumes all day long and have long blond hair that made it difficult to discern gender. Scandi or American kids were the role models; Dean looked as though he was getting his vibe from Billy Bunter. Eddie blamed the copious amounts of tinned rice pudding, Angel Delight and Findus Crispy Pancakes that Diane spooned into him. He knew why she did it: kids couldn't cry when their mouths were full. Lazy cow.

His mother had warned him that Diane would not make a proper wife. That she couldn't cook a decent meal, or sew or clean. He'd agreed; it was her improperness that he'd fallen for. He thought she was like him. Bold and irreverent. Selfish. And that had been attractive. Now it was just inconvenient.

Eddie followed his wife into the kitchen. For a moment he allowed himself to hope she might actually have cooked something for supper. It was a ridiculous thought. Even if she had been the sort of wife to have his dinner waiting for him, he'd arrived home two hours later than he'd said he would, so it would be cold or burnt to a crisp by now. Anyway, there was no hint of home-cooked dishes; the kitchen smelt damp and dank, a mixture of drains and stale food. The only thing Eddie could ever taste in the kitchen was sour air and neglect.

Diane always had the radio droning on in the background. She turned the volume down low so as not to disturb the baby presumably, but this irritated Eddie. How was he supposed to enjoy the tunes or follow the news stories at that volume? He snapped the radio off and the silence was only interrupted by the sound of the hot tap dripping. He'd been meaning to get that fixed for a while. He doubted he ever would.

Eddie thought it was bizarre that despite the lack of industry that occurred in the kitchen, the room was invariably a mess. The lino on the floor was sticky; it was like wading through a sea of Blu-Tack, his shoes making a strange squelchy sound as he walked about. The circular plastic table was crammed full of dirty pots and condiments, left over from the kids' tea, lunch and breakfast. His critical eye noted the open packet of butter that was turning rancid. There were gummy jam jars, a bottle with souring milk, a gunky ketchup bottle and plates covered with greasy smears suggesting that Dean had been fed fried eggs tonight.

They'd get mice again if she wasn't more careful. They rarely sat down as a whole family at the table. Eddie didn't care that they didn't eat together on a Sunday – the family gathering for meat and two veg was bourgeois and staid, something the last generation valued – but he would have liked it if she'd sometimes made pasta or curry, neither of which was bourgeois because they were foreign; pasta and curry were cool. He'd have liked to invite friends round for supper. They could use the fondue set and drink red wine; they'd bought a carafe when they'd been on honeymoon in Spain. Where the hell was it? Eddie wondered. How come nearly every pot and pan they owned was left on a kitchen surface but he'd never laid eyes on the carafe? Had she put away all reminders of their honeymoon? It was only six years ago, but it was a lifetime back.

The wooden clothes horse was a permanent fixture in the poky kitchen, a never-ending stream of damp clothes hung on it, draped in a way that always put Eddie in mind of dead bodies. There were two plastic buckets by the door that she used for steeping the fouled nappies. Dozens of mugs and glasses were dotted around the kitchen; they each had their own bioculture growing inside, and around them crumbs were scattered like confetti. Diane ate ten Rich Tea biscuits a day; with two apples and a couple of glasses of wine, she could stay under the thousand calorie mark and ensure that her hip bones continued to jut. Recently she hadn't bothered with the apples but had had the odd extra glass.

The room could do with an airing, but the window was jammed.

The kitchen was Eddie's Room 101. Not a cage of rats put on his face, like in the George Orwell novel, but death by domesticity. In this kitchen they did not talk about the strikes, David Bowie's music or even the perm or the Chopper bike. The sort of conversations Eddie and Diane limited themselves to (if they spoke at all) were ones about this child having taken a fall and got bruised, the other having a funny rash, or Diane would moan that she needed a few more quid to buy a new breadbin, her aunt had been round, her aunt thought they needed new curtains, her aunt wondered when he was going to get a job that was better paid. Depending on how much she'd had to drink, Diane might yell that she wondered as much too. He was a graduate, for God's sake. He had a degree, why was he wasting it being a writer? Writing didn't pay. She should have married an accountant. That was what her aunt said; that was what she thought too.

Eddie knew men who hit their wives. He never had. That wasn't his thing. Hitting your woman didn't sit well with reading the *Tribune*. But sometimes when she went on and on and on and on, he could imagine grabbing one of those dirty tea towels that lay screwed up on the kitchen surface and shoving it into her mouth. He didn't want to choke her, not exactly. He just wanted to stop her going on.

He glanced down at his fat gold wedding ring. This wasn't how he'd imagined it would be. He was suffocating.

1982

2

Clara

Clara snapped off the TV with impatience. There was never any good news; just bombs, kidnappings, the threat of strikes. She only watched the news for the bit at the end when they told you what the Queen was up to. Had she visited a public garden, or perhaps some youth centre? Clara would never know, because she'd switched off before they got to that bit today. They were saying there were three million unemployed now. Three million! Couldn't someone find them something to do? They should, because nothing good ever came from idle hands. The thought stung. She knew how destructive boredom could be. She'd said to Tim that perhaps they should make these doleys join up. The soldiers and sailors and what-have-you were being so brave out in the Falkland Islands right now. They were doing a fine job, but no doubt they'd welcome a helping hand, a few more buddies. Clara didn't really know what was going on out there; in fact she hadn't known exactly where 'out there' was until she'd checked in the atlas, but Neil Todd's father at the school gate said she wasn't to feel bad about that, hardly anyone did know. All that was clear was that there was a lot of bombing and burning and young men coming home with shocking injuries. Thinking about it, maybe the doleys were better off at home after all. Clara sighed. She didn't know what to make of it; she didn't like to think about it.

Instead she turned her attention to how she should kill the next few hours before she had to start the school pick-up. What should she do with her afternoon? Had she anything on video to watch? It was her guilty pleasure to watch recorded episodes of *Dynasty* when the children were at school. She had tried, but found it was impossible to give the TV her full attention in the evenings. The children would invariably squabble their way through an entire episode, or worse, they pestered her with irritating or inappropriate questions. Normally, she was a very patient mother. She was quite prepared to answer endless enquiries about Barbie dolls and Danger Mouse (no, she did not know that Barbie's full name was Barbara Millicent Roberts, but yes, she did think Barbie Millie was cuter, and yes, she did believe Danger Mouse had trained with James Bond; certainly the same school, if not the same year), but it was significantly trickier explaining the saga of the wealthy Denver family who had made their money in oil.

'Does Daddy have much to do with oil?' Joanna had asked thoughtfully, when they'd last watched the programme together.

'No, stupid. Daddy is a banker,' Lisa had replied, harshly dismissing her younger sister. Although there was less than two years between them, the gap seemed wider, as fourteen-year-old Lisa had now clambered into the teenage world that allowed access to DM boots and black eyeliner, while twelve-year-old Joanna was quite innocent, still content to dress up her dolls.

'Perhaps he should do more with oil, because then we'd have a house as big as Krystle's,' Joanna had added, her childish lisp not quite hiding her fully formed ambition to marry well. Joanna lived for the Cinderella fairy tale.

'We're very lucky as it is, darling,' Clara had reminded her

16

daughter, as she often reminded herself. 'We live in a much bigger house than nearly all our friends.'

'What does Krystle *do* in that house all day anyway?' Lisa had demanded as she'd turned back to her homework.

Joanna had shrugged, unconcerned by the glittery woman's inertia. Then a thought struck her. Horrified, she'd asked, 'I don't understand. Why has Blake been married to two ladies?'

Clara had tried to explain. 'Well, Krystle was his secretary but now she's his wife. Alexis was his wife before.'

'What is she now?'

'His ex-wife.'

'What does that even mean?' Jo had asked, stricken. In her protected world – the leafy suburbs of Wimbledon – it meant very little; she had no idea that divorce was run-of-the-mill in other postcodes. In Wimbledon, people stuck it out. Clara, more than anyone, knew that.

'She's not just "his ex-wife", she's the boss of an enormous multimillion-, possibly billion-dollar company,' Lisa had muttered, rolling her eyes.

'Which wife do you like best, Mummy?' Joanna had pursued.

'Krystle. She's so patient, serene and composed,' Clara had replied, even though secretly she was sure Alexis had all the fun. The insipid second wife wasn't half as exciting as the feisty first one, who had a string of younger lovers, but Alexis Carrington wasn't a role model Clara Russell could openly aspire to. Not openly.

'Why didn't they look more for Adam? If someone kidnapped me, would you look lots?' Mark, her youngest, had asked fearfully. He'd hopped on to Clara's knee, and she'd enjoyed his warmth and chubbiness.

'Yes, darling, I'd keep searching until the end of time and as far as the end of the world.'

'The world is round, so strictly, it doesn't end,' Lisa had pointed out.

'He's five, Lisa.'

'So you shouldn't fill his head with rubbish.' Lisa had nodded pertinently in the direction of Joanna whilst continuing to glare coldly at Clara. Clara knew that Lisa firmly believed that Joanna needed to be weaned off the romantic fairy tales she'd been allowed to believe were gospel, and that Lisa did not consider Clara a particularly good role model for dreamy Jo.

Was she a let-down? She had tried so hard. Nearly always done the right thing. Even though doing the wrong thing was so much easier, so much more fun. Clara was confident that she was a superb homemaker. That wasn't up for debate. The house was spotless, their food home-cooked, their clothes carefully ironed (even nighties, petticoats and Tim's underwear), but Lisa would no doubt have preferred it if Clara was a career woman; the sort that wore shoulder pads and carried fat, impressive Filofaxes. When Joanna had started school, Clara had worked, briefly. Through an old school friend she'd found a rather fun position at the BBC; it was mostly typing and filing but it had got her out of the house for a couple of hours a day and she'd met such exciting people. Too exciting. Dangerous. So after that foray, Tim wouldn't hear of her working again. He said that working was not for women like her, ones with children and a husband, and he had a point. Tim rarely got home before nine most nights of the week; sometimes he was much later. How would it work if they both had careers?

Clara often felt uncomfortable under Lisa's gaze; literal and metaphorical. She suspected that Lisa knew much more than she should. Did she know, for example, that Mark was a patch-up baby, after, well . . . Clara's difficult period at the BBC? She'd insisted on him, she'd *needed* him to anchor her. Did Lisa know that, despite trying not to have favourites, Clara enjoyed the company of her son far more than she enjoyed the company of her daughters? It wasn't that she liked one child more than the others. Not as such. It was just that he was so easy. He was confident, independent and somehow 'other'; the girls seemed to be mixed and meshed with Clara in a more fundamental, primal and confusing way. It was probably something to do with the endless comparisons people made between mothers and daughters. The girls were said to be either funnier or not as funny as she had been, prettier or not as pretty, more confident or not quite so. She felt a burdensome responsibility towards them that for some reason did not extend to her son.

Besides, by the time Mark came along, she'd been significantly less innocent and pliable; perhaps that helped her to be a more confident mother. After all, she'd only been nineteen when she'd had Lisa. Still a child herself.

Attempts at watching her favourite show with the children were brought to a definite halt when Joanna asked, 'Why doesn't Steven have a wife? Does he want to marry that man? Is that allowed?'

After that, Clara had bundled the children straight up to bed.

So. How to fill the afternoon? Clara had nothing left to do. She'd prepared chilli with jacket potatoes for tonight's supper. She'd made it relatively mild, but to further induce the children to eat it, she'd also baked a chocolate fudge cake. They knew that pudding was only allowed if they could show her a clean plate. Rita, their cleaner, had changed all the beds; the sheets were hung on the line right now, snapping in the wind. Tim thought Clara was insane, but she liked to keep her hand in with the domestic duties around the house, even though she could have left everything to Rita; it gave her something to do. So she'd dusted all her Lladro figurines – there were twenty-eight of them, so this was no small task – and now she glanced around her sitting room wondering whether there were any other outstanding chores to tackle.

It was immaculate, dust-free and the height of fashion: a mass of pastels, cream, peach and salmon hues placed side by side, swirling and morphing. Her father-in-law had once said that coming to their house reminded him of visiting a French brothel. She'd chosen not to dignify his comment with a response. He couldn't have visited a brothel ever, could he? Perhaps he had; parents were people too. Her father-in-law had a tendency to be very coarse; Tim didn't take after him at all.

The carpet was a pale beige colour. She'd quite fancied cream but hadn't thought it practical, not with three children utilising the patio doors to the full. They were constantly running in and out of the garden, trailing mud, so she had settled for beige. She'd taken a risk with the floral pastel three-piece suite, though; one spilt glass of orange squash and it would be ruined, so she didn't allow the children to bring drinks into this room. The wallpaper was another floral pastel design, but it was a slightly smaller, tighter flower than the suite. The paper stretched just halfway up the wall; there it met with a very impressive – almost regal – border. The top part of the wall was painted peach and then ragged with an iridescent gold paint. Clara was very proud of the ragging; she'd done it herself, even though Tim had said she could get decorators to do the job. It had been a challenge – by the time she was finished, there'd been as much paint on her overalls and hands as there was on the walls – but every time she looked at it, she felt a swell of satisfaction, knowing that she was responsible for it.

Hung on the wall above the television was a picture of a river and some hills. Clara didn't know the name of the artist, but she had seen the original painting in the National Gallery and then bought the print in the shop. The colours were more muted on the print compared to the real thing, but that didn't really bother Clara, because the paler colours matched better with everything else. There were two brass chandeliers, and other than the dark, dreary bar in the corner (Tim's folly), the room was perfect. It was exactly the sort of room Clara had always imagined she'd preside over as wife and mother. It was everything she hoped she'd have as a married woman.

She hated it.

Clara sighed and picked up the *Radio Times*. She combed it carefully as she always did, scouring for his name. She'd spotted it twice in six years and she'd seen it on the credits of three different TV programmes. Each time it had caused a small spark to flicker deep between her legs. Wasn't it strange that a name, written down in print, could have that effect? She didn't regret her choice. What would be the point in regretting? Her lover was trouble. Her husband was kind. She preferred kindness to trouble; it was as simple as that. Yet there were always the sparks.

Clara was delighted to find an article about Harrison Ford. Goody. She hadn't been able to get the man out of her head since that first *Star Wars* film. It was the way he wore his gun slung so low. The thought made her smile all over her body. She'd seen *Raiders of the Lost Ark* twice. Once with Tim but the second time she'd gone on her own. She'd never let on to Tim. He'd have thought she was silly but it had been such fun. Sitting in the dark, alone with her thoughts and fantasies. Little secrets were fine, harmless. Little secrets were allowed. She'd bought popcorn but had hardly been able to eat it; Harrison certainly could wear a fedora, and a whip in *his* hands, well, my . . . Yes, she'd jump to it.

She read the entire article but it was in fact quite dry; Harrison wasn't prepared to say whether that amazing on-screen chemistry with Karen Allen was for real or not. But then he wasn't the kiss-and-tell sort. Real gentlemen weren't. The challenge was working out which were the real gentlemen.

Clara carefully put the magazine back in the rack and wondered whether it was worth changing into her new top before she went to pick up Mark. Yesterday, she'd bought a shimmering silvery shirt from the brand-new store, Next. It had big puffed sleeves that were brought into line by a neat row of fabric-covered buttons running the length of her forearm. It was quite a dressy shirt, intended for a restaurant or even a nightclub, but Clara didn't get out that often nowadays and so she figured she might as well wear it at the school gate. After all, it never did any harm to look your best, especially on a Thursday. On Thursdays Neil Todd's father did the pick-up. He was such a friendly man. Very attentive. She wondered what he'd look like in a fedora. Would he be able to pull it off?

WEDNESDAY 20 APRIL 2005

3

Dean

'Dean, there's a call from overseas.'

'Is it Rogers?' Dean grinned. A flame of excitement and aspiration licked his innards.

Dean was a board account director at a huge international advertising agency, Q&A; however, the Chicago branch of the agency was unofficially viewed as the younger brother to the New York arm, and this was something that chafed at Dean's keen sense of ambition and professional pride. The two offices were equally large, expensive and state-of-the-art. They each serviced approximately the same number of clients. The creative teams were similarly innovative, award-winning and obnoxious, but in the final analysis, when it came down to the numbers (and it always came down to the numbers), there was a sizeable difference between the revenues each office managed to pull in. The New York arm had been more profitable than the Chicago office for many consecutive years. Dean wasn't sure how many exactly, but it was all the time he'd worked for Q&A. It irked, but he was sure that was all about to change.

Rogers was the international marketing director of an extremely large confectionery company. For the last five months Dean had been leading a team of twelve in a pitch to win the company's advertising campaign. The ad spend would be approximately $132 million. That sort of income would catapult his agency and his career; the board account director in New York would have to eat his dust. Dean knew he was on a shortlist of three agencies; success was within his grasp. Success was everything to Dean. He valued it over popularity, friendship and even love. Confectionery wasn't normally what he considered to be his area of expertise – he was stronger on cars or gadgets – but he'd been pretty sure that his strategy was groundbreaking and the creative concepts he'd presented were bold and exciting. Off-the-fucking-wall was how he'd described them in the pitch. Rogers was in London right now, discussing the pros and cons of the various agency pitches with his international team; he'd assured Dean he would call as soon as a decision was reached. Dean was not an unreasonably arrogant man; in fact, he was a realist. He'd led a harder life than anyone would imagine when they met him now, clad in Armani, driving an Audi TT. It was because he'd had more than his share of disappointments that he'd learnt how to judge carefully. His optimism was always curbed, but still he hoped, and almost expected, that the decision Rogers would reach would pan out in his favour.

If Q&A Chicago secured the business, there might be a healthy bonus. He would treat himself to a trip to Vegas. Uncomplicated tits and ass, fun clubs and gambling, what was not to love? He deserved it. He had worked hard to win this pitch. Besides the endless hours needed to develop solid strategy and tease out some crazy concepts, he had invested a lot of time developing a relationship with Rogers. The promise that Rogers would call the moment a decision had been reached was elicited in a strip club that Dean had taken the marketing director to. Turned out that Rogers had never been to a strip joint before; Dean considered that a sin.

'Get out of here!' he had said, laughing and slapping Rogers on the shoulder.

Rogers had initially appeared a little reluctant. 'The expenses for tonight won't turn up on the bill for the pitch, will they?' he'd asked fearfully. Dean had pitied Rogers for his inexperience and slightly despised him for his inability to be a fearless man.

'No way. This, my friend, is on me. Man to man. Buddy to buddy.' Rogers had been flattered; it was clear that he – like most corporate marketers – thought the agency guys were where it was at. Especially Dean. Dean was quite a guy. Everyone said so. He was funny, a wisecracker, full of killer one-liners. And he was tough. Worked out. Fast, determined. He'd completed the Chicago marathon every year for five years, and although he was, obviously, getting older, he always improved on his time. He was the sort of guy people invited to their parties, and if he couldn't make the suggested date, they would postpone the celebration. He was the type of bloke who might hold the lift for a woman and then ask, 'Are you going up or down?' and the woman would beg to tattoo his phone number on to her breasts. He was a man who other men dreamt of becoming.

Dean could almost hear the slot machines pounding. *Ker-ching*. Viva Las Vegas!

'No. No, it's not Rogers,' his PA, Lacey, replied. 'It's a hospital. A UK hospital. Queen Anne's in London. I didn't catch the state.'

'We don't have states in Britain,' said Dean with a sigh. His PA was hot but not sharp. He might have to reconsider his recruitment policy. 'I'll take it in my office.' He hoped to God his sister Zoe and her kids were all OK.

'Mr Dean Taylor?'

'Speaking.'

'I'm Kitty McGreggor, a nurse at Queen Anne's Hospital, Shepherd's Bush, London.'

'Is it my sister, Zoe, or the kids? Are they OK?' he demanded.

'Actually, I'm ringing on behalf of Mr Edward Taylor.' The

nurse had a gentle Scottish lilt to her voice. She sounded no-nonsense; firm, calm and in control.

For a moment Dean could not compute the information he was being given. It was not the Scottish accent that was confusing him. It was the name: a dim and distant memory, not to be whispered, let alone said aloud. The words *Edward Taylor* struck fear and loathing into the core of Dean Taylor, the way the word *Macbeth* – said during rehearsals of any show – struck actors; it was sure to bring bad luck.

'I'm sorry to have to inform you, Mr Taylor, but your father has pancreatic cancer. It's unfortunately spread to other parts of his body and . . .' She paused, tenderness creeping into her voice. 'And I'm afraid it's terminal. In fact, he doesn't have long left. It's only right that you should know.'

'There must be some mistake.'

'We're estimating a week or so, perhaps less. Perhaps days. There is no mistake.'

'I'm not talking about the diagnosis.'

'You *are* Dean Taylor?'

'Yes.'

'Son of Edward Taylor?'

'I suppose.'

'Then there's no mistake.'

'The mistake is him asking you to call me.'

4

Jo

'I just can't believe that in seventy-two hours Martin will be married. *Married!*' I drag the words out of my dark and dingy subconscious and throw them on to the table for my big sister to examine closely, but Lisa is so obviously far more interested in the dessert menu. I understand: she's a working mother of three children and so nights out require military-precision planning; she's keen to have a good time, which includes ordering something lovely and indulgent for dessert. We've only managed to pull off this evening because I'm temporarily living with Lisa, and Lisa's husband views the idea of getting me out of the house (with or without Lisa) as one less obstacle between him and the remote control, so he offered to babysit.

'What do you think, chocolate soufflé or tiramisu? I think I'll go for the tiramisu,' says Lisa, closing the menu with an air of finality. She's taking advantage of the fact that I'm her sister; she'd never order such an unfashionable dessert in front of her City analyst friends, but with me she can even drink Baileys in her coffee if she wants; sisters are forgiving about such things. I love her, but right now she's driving me nuts, as she's clearly reluctant to engage in the subject of my ex's imminent nuptials – the only thing I can think about. I bang home my point. 'Less than three days. Seventy-two hours, to be precise!'

'But are you being precise? Is it seventy-two? Technically I'm not sure, what with the time difference and everything. I mean, Saturday afternoon in Chicago is different to Saturday afternoon here, isn't it?' points out Lisa. 'Theirs is later, isn't it? I think you are looking at about eighty hours.'

I glare at my sister. 'I think you're missing the point.'

'Am I?' Lisa replies. She takes a sip of her white wine and feigns innocence. 'What is the point, then?'

It's clear from her face that she regrets the question the moment she's asked it. I'm aware that the entire evening's conversation has an awful sense of déjà vu rumbling around it. I know that as well as she does; that's exactly why I need her to indulge me.

'It should have been me,' I wail dramatically.

'No, it shouldn't,' Lisa states emphatically. Not really grasping the concept of indulging.

'Yes, it should. He asked me first.' Even I know I sound like a kid in the school playground bagging her place in the dinner queue: *I got here first!*

'But you didn't want him,' says Lisa.

'No, not then, maybe not. But now. *Now*,' I insist.

When I say that this evening has more than a hint of déjà vu, that's because three months ago – when I first received the stiff gold-embossed cardboard invitation to Martin's wedding – Lisa and I had a similar night out; one where I poured out my heart to her and she accused me of rewriting history. That night, like this one, was steeped in indignation and self-pity. During that evening I'd initially tried to say all the things that I knew were expected of me. I pretended to be delighted that Martin had 'moved on' and met someone else, someone he cared about so deeply that he wanted to marry her. Then, when I'd had a glass or two of wine, I swapped the words 'cared about' with 'settled for' and 'wanted' with 'prepared'. The third time I repeated the story (after I'd finished the vast majority of the bottle of Shiraz), I commented on the 'indecent haste' with which he'd rushed into this 'unsuitable match' and repeatedly muttered the words, 'Clearly rebound'.

'Well, it's been nearly five years since you two split up. I don't think that is *indecently* speedy in terms of recovery,' Lisa had pointed out calmly (and somewhat irritatingly).

I'd glared back. 'Yes, but Martin only met this woman eighteen months ago.' That piece of gossip had crawled all the way from America to London through a network of friends that we still shared. 'It takes eighteen months to book a high-quality venue. His fiancée must have placed a deposit the night they met,' I'd snapped.

'Some people just know straight away that they want to be with one another for ever and don't see any reason to hang around.'

This is usually the sort of point I make, so it was difficult to argue; instead I'd suggested we buy another bottle. The night ended very badly. Drunk, I'd telephoned some other, less signifi-cant, ex and dashed over to his place for a bout of consolation sex. Lisa had been very concerned as she helped me into the cab that was to take me away.

'There's something about you that's making me think of Paddington Bear,' she'd commented.

'Cute expression? Doleful eyes?' I'd suggested, hoping I was hiding my slur pretty well.

'More the helpless and confused stance, I think,' she'd sighed. 'I'm tempted to attach a note, *Please look after this bear. She's slighted and worried about dying alone, therefore vulnerable.*' Lisa had tried to smile, but I knew that what she was saying was serious.

'No point. I'm not sure if all my ex-boyfriends can actually read,' I'd joked. It was a sad joke really, because I think both Lisa and I know that since Martin, my standard in boyfriend selection hasn't been too rigorous. Lisa once described my preferred sort of men to be 'boorish, almost animalistic'. Certainly, I didn't have the type of ex-boyfriends who'd care about my motivation for turning up on a booty call; they'd simply want to take advantage of the fact I'd done so. That night turned out as you'd expect. I'd had careless sex with a careless man and woke up feeling worse, not better. Bruised. Not physically but emotionally.

Lisa interrupts my thoughts now by saying, 'Jo, you have to remember that *you* dumped Martin.' She reaches for my arm and squeezes it. 'You weren't in love with him,' she adds baldly.

'Well, no but . . .' I can't bring myself to admit that now I'm thirty-five, almost thirty-six years old, practically staring forty in the face, I might not be so fastidious. So much has happened in the five years, two months since I split from Martin. Right now, all I can think of is the fact that I've attended seventeen weddings and currently have invites to three more. All I can say is, 'Martin was kind and solvent, and tall.'

'And dull. You were always going on about how you had nothing in common.'

'I could have learnt to enjoy his hobbies,' I insist.

'I bet you can't even remember what his hobbies were. Before you received the invite to his wedding, you hadn't given him a thought in ages.'

'I send him a Christmas card every year.'

'You send all your exes Christmas cards every year. Honestly, I don't know how you do, let alone *why*. You must have to start writing your cards in October.'

'Ha ha. Funny.' Her point is, I've clocked up an above-average share of exes in the past few years. Different people have different views on that; some of my friends who have been married for a dozen years or more think it's exciting, others think I'm slutty. My mother thinks it's disappointing. I think it's heartbreaking.

'I can't imagine why he's invited you,' adds Lisa.

'To gloat?' I offer miserably. 'Or maybe his fiancée has a string of exes that she's inviting and he wants to prove he had a life before her.' Depressed, we both stare at the highly polished table between us; neither reason is particularly heroic or appealing. Suddenly I'm struck by a more cheering thought. 'Maybe it's an SOS.'

'A what?'

'A cry for help.'

'You think he wants *you* to help him?'

I try to ignore her astonishment. 'Why not?'

'Because—'

I don't allow her to finish. I won't want to hear it. Lisa and I don't think alike on matters of the heart. At least not *my* heart. I beam, warming to my idea. 'Maybe he wants me to go to the wedding so I can stand up in the church and object to the thing going ahead.'

'Stop it, Jo. You're scaring me.'

'It's possible.'

'But not *probable*. Look, I might have found that theory hilarious under other circumstances, but as it's my sister talking, this situation is fast becoming tragic rather than comic. Get real. Just accept it. Martin has moved on.'

I glare at her. I think her words are sharp and nasty; she probably thinks they are sensible and necessary. She pulls her gaze away from mine, embarrassed for both of us, then reaches for my arm again and gives it another little squeeze. I move away, not allowing her the satisfaction of comforting me. She takes a deep breath and then slowly, carefully adds, 'Jo, I hate it that I have to dole out the yuckiest medicine, but the fact is, nothing has changed. Just because Martin is about to marry someone else does not mean that he's any more suitable for you than he was before. That just doesn't make sense. Obviously, if anything, he is *less* suitable. He's in love with someone else. Can't you be happy for him?'

Can I? Am I still capable of truly revelling in other people's happiness?

As hideous as I sound, no, I don't think I can. If I admit as much to Lisa, she'll be disgusted with me, probably make me pay for my own dinner, so I bite my tongue and pretend to be a better person, more like the person I was until endless, fruitless dates took their toll. I notice Lisa's own wedding ring glinting seductively in the dark restaurant. Lisa has been married for fourteen years – happily married; some might say smugly – so I know she just can't understand what I'm going through. She already had two children and was pregnant with her third by the time she was my age, and she never even expressed any particular interest in getting married when we were growing up; for her it was all about her school work and then her career. She has no idea about loneliness or grief or remorse, which are the emotions that haunt me. She most certainly does not think of her life as one long corridor of closed doors – marked *Missed Opportunities*, *Regrets* and *Lost Chances* – along which she dawdles aimlessly. I feel as though I've wandered up and down that particular corridor, alone, for ages now. I can't explain it to her. It's too harsh. It's too humiliating.

She doesn't think I'm due any sympathy, because I threw over Martin. I dumped him. But honestly, sometimes that makes things harder, not easier. The regret is sharper, more poignant. I messed up. He was a great guy. Marrying material. The sort of man women want to marry. Should marry. I see that now. All my friends are married or living with someone, and once they have settled partners they're no longer interested in coming out and meeting new people. (Oh OK, what I'm talking about specifically here is coming out to meet new men – obviously.) My horizons are narrowing. When I was younger, I used to meet new people by the dozen, every week: at uni, in bars, in nightclubs and then at work. As the years have passed, opportunities have diminished. My friends from uni are now far-flung and most of them are happily coupled off and wouldn't dream of going on a pub crawl and chatting to total strangers like we once did. I can hardly go to bars on my tod, and I could never go to a nightclub now, even with a battalion of supporters; those places are frequented by women who are literally young enough to be my daughters. I'd have to fight the urge to encourage them to wear a coat or button up their tops to cover up their smooth, plump skin. The biggest irony is that I work for a bridal magazine, which besides being a constant taunt is, as you might guess, an entirely male-free zone.

I have tried to find other places to meet people, I really have. I am not a quitter. I'm a member of a gym, I've joined a night class to study French (as everyone knows it's a very sexy language) and I go to a salsa club to practise flirting, every other Tuesday at the town hall in Wimbledon. Afterwards I stay at my parents' house. I know a sleepover at the parental home probably does reduce my chance of wild nights of passion, but my mum makes unparalleled lasagne and it's hard to resist. I have made some new friends through these channels, but no men friends, no *single* men friends, which is the aim; the classes are largely populated by other women who are also looking for romantic leads. While I'm quite good at making new friends and these women are smiley and usually up for a glass of Bordeaux or a margarita after the class, it seems my new friends are invariably more adept at finding life partners than I am. They keep getting married. One after another. Hence the obscene number of wedding invites I receive.

These other women make looking for love seem so easy. It appears to be the case that no sooner have they decided they are ready to settle down than they do exactly that. Then, inevitably, a ritual is observed. Initially the newly-weds invite me to join them on double dates or they set me up on blind dates with their friends and colleagues, but for one reason or another, I've never stumbled upon my soulmate, and while I maintain the friendship with the new bride, the invites for double dates eventually dry up. We settle into girl-only evenings, where we spend the night picking over my disastrous dates, and when that's just too depressing, we pick out kitchenware for their new homes.

What is wrong with me?

I have a good sense of humour (it says so on all my singles profiles but it is also true). I'm generally caring, thoughtful, sympathetic, and I'm known to be generous. I'm fun, I think, as far as anyone can ever judge this about themselves. I know I'm lucky to have a number of interesting, amusing and committed friends – friends I've secured through my resolute loyalty and ability to remember their kids' birthdays – but the fact is I also have an endless trail of faithless, irresponsible or arrogant exes which I'm all too aware that I've acquired because my growing desperation has led to a terrible lack of discernment.

I do look younger than my thirty-five years. I could pass for thirty-three in dim light, younger still from behind, as I make an effort to eat sensibly and dress well in an attempt to defy gravity and the facts. I have long dark hair and huge brown eyes that are framed with thick lashes. I used to think my eyes were my best feature but I'm not so sure now, as there are depressing crow's feet showering from them. I'm considering Botox, although whenever I dare to hint as much to my friends or my sister they howl with laughter and tell me not to worry for another decade. 'You're still a baby,' Lisa often says, but I'm never sure if that's an out-and-out compliment.

I'm not a baby, though, am I? Next birthday I'm thirty-six, literally in my late thirties. That's just maths. No denying it.

The issue is, I have always wanted to marry. Some people

hate the idea, think it's an outdated institution, restrictive, unrealistic, etc., etc., but it's always been something that I thought would be part of my life plan. My parents have been happily married for thirty-eight years this weekend; they're the gold standard – well, technically closer to the ruby standard, I suppose, but you know what I mean. They are happy, fulfilled and inseparable. Lisa and Henry have been together forever, as I mentioned. Even my younger brother, Mark, is happily married and has been for three years. Divorce statistics are trumpeted in newspapers; the pessimists like to present the UK as a country falling apart at the seams, populated with people unable to maintain a relationship for as long as they maintain a hairstyle, but that isn't my experience. I sometimes think I *only* know married people.

I've been actively trying to get married for over half my life. When I was sixteen, I begged my parents to let me attend a sixth form that had only just started to accept girls so that I'd meet lots of boys while doing my A levels. I only settled on a university after carefully studying the male/female quota of not only the university itself but my subject in particular. Naturally, I wasn't daft enough to think I'd meet men at *Loving Bride!*, but I was engaged to Martin when I took the job; I wasn't on the lookout then. Deal done. Or so I thought. Considering all my effort and vigilance on the matter of meeting a mate, it does seem a bit weird that I've mucked it up and I'm still alone.

I have made mistakes. Perhaps I have a tendency to pursue the wrong sort of man; not necessarily the marrying kind. I'm fatally attracted to the wilder sort of guy; the sort with chiselled cheekbones, cool clothes and eyes and a heart to match. I'm drawn to exciting, sexy, unobtainable men. Damaged or divorced men. Worse still, married men who 'forget' to mention the existence of their wives until the said wife makes a phone call or – in one humiliating and heartbreaking case – finds me in her bed. Like metal shavings to a magnet I cling to bad and bold men;

the sort of men who can undress women with a glance. Acutely improper and inappropriate men.

It is an issue.

Improper and inappropriate men tend to last only a matter of months or even weeks. My problem is, I don't see my potential boyfriends in such bleak terms as I approach the relationships. Of course not. I date each man I meet with renewed optimism. I'm a hopeless romantic. Lisa says I'm just hopeless and old enough to know better; I should learn from past mistakes but I don't. I hear her, I respect her view, it might even be advice I'd give a girlfriend, but I just don't seem to learn. If I meet a new guy, who is reticent when questioned about his romantic status, I never assume he's married with two kids. Instead, I have a tendency to construct an elaborate excuse for his monosyllabic responses and his reluctance to give me a landline number. I mean, it *is* perfectly possible that he's grieving for a tragic lost love; maybe his last girlfriend died, or maybe he's never dated because he's been nursing his terminally ill relative, or maybe he loved his last woman dearly but she turned lesbian . . . You do hear of such things. Maybe not often, but there's a shopping list of reasons why a man might be reticent.

I suppose I am inclined to spend a great deal of time and energy imagining how I might save him, how I – and I alone – could draw him back into the land of the living, fill his world with love once again, a love that would be better, deeper, more meaningful than anything else he's ever encountered. I don't believe I'm the only one who does this.

I always start with sex.

It's an odd thing to admit to, but I think I'm pretty safe in saying I'm good at sex (lots and lots of men have given me the thumbs-up; well, not thumbs exactly, but you know what I mean). And men like sex, so sex seems an ideal place to start. Experience never seems to teach me that relationships that start with sex usually stay with sex.

Martin was different. He isn't a bold and bad man. He is a steady and solid man. I dated him for four years; it was a proper courtship (to use my mother's term). We took things slowly. We were really happy in the beginning, or at least content. There's nothing wrong with Martin, and that alone sets him apart from my other exes. Martin is handsome (my mother was always saying as much, although my personal preference is dark hair and light eyes and Martin has blond hair and brown eyes). Unlike many of my other boyfriends, before and since, he had a good job; in fact during the time that we dated, he shot up the career ladder. He was promoted from analyst, to manager, to senior manager in the management consultancy firm he worked for. Lisa was always telling me that it was unreasonable to resent the long hours he worked and the way he appeared to always put his work ahead of his relationship. Of course the marrying kind often do that; they know the importance of being successful and creating financial security. I just wished that sometimes he'd get home when he said he would, that he'd take a day off work on my birthday or that he'd simply turn off the damned mobile phone when we were in bed.

Still, everything was on track. After dating for two years, we moved in with one another; after a year of living together, on my twenty-ninth birthday, Martin proposed and I accepted. Our plan was to get married on my thirtieth birthday. Well, the day before actually, so then I could say that technically I'd married in my twenties. We went at the wedding planning full speed ahead; me, Martin, my mother and my entire office. It was going to be a fabulous event, one with white doves, chocolate fountains and ice sculptures. I thought I had everything I'd ever wanted, until one day I realised I wasn't in love with him.

I loved him.

Probably.

I *certainly* liked him. But he didn't make my heart (or any part of my anatomy) leap. The realisation came to me during my final dress fitting, just two weeks before the big day. Timing has never been my strong point.

But now, *now* I'm considering the fact that maybe I got it all wrong. Those four years that we were together were important, defining years. When I stepped into the relationship, I'd been a carefree twenty-something; by the time I returned the unwanted wedding gifts I noticed that practically everyone I knew had married and started families. Not to mention the years since. Where has the time gone? I have been left behind. Maybe Martin *was* my One, and what I experienced when I gazed at my reflection in the bridal shop wasn't horror, it was nothing more than pre-wedding jitters. It's a reasonable assumption, as I've certainly never met anyone I've liked more since. Well, at least not anyone I've liked more who has been available and suitable and has liked me back.

As I sit in the cosy restaurant with my big sister, sipping wine and eating tiramisu, the alcohol sweeps around my brain and shimmers through my limbs, and it strikes me that I've blown my best chance, *ever*.

I've urinated on my happily ever after.

THURSDAY 21 APRIL 2005

5

Dean

'Do I hate you?' Dean murmured the question, his lips close to the sleeping old man's ear. He'd always thought he'd known the answer to this one. For as long as he'd been aware of the question, he'd been sure. Yes, he hated Edward Taylor, known as Eddie. Yes, he hated his father.

But now?

Now, when the old man was dying, his breath rasping and lumbering through his heaving chest, his skin grey and waxy like sweating cheese, his eyes closed, Dean was surprised to find that it was impossible to summon up the necessary passion to hate. The wizened old man who slept in the hospital bed looked nothing like the father of Dean's memories. That man had been virile and healthy. And cruel. The father he remembered had had long raven-coloured hair, almost blue black. This Edward Taylor was practically bald, and the bit of hair that remained was as white as the hospital sheets. Whiter. His head was blotched with age spots; it looked vulnerable.

Dean seemed to remember that Edward Taylor had always been vain about his hair. He *thought* he could remember that his father had a habit of checking his reflection whenever the opportunity arose: in the hallway mirror, the wing mirrors in the car, shop windows and shiny teaspoons. He was almost sure he could *actually* remember this, but it might have been something his mother or his great-aunt had told him a very long time ago and he'd allowed it to morph into a make-do memory.

It might have been something he'd made up.

In the absence of any sort of a reality – a presence, or even letters or phone calls – Dean had resorted to filling in the blanks. He'd done so for many years, and over time, the wishful thinking, the fantasies, the false memories had all solidified and now had a hardness to them that suggested fact. It was tricky to know anything for certain. Edward Taylor wasn't a presence at all, just an absence. Dean always thought it was ironic that he'd been tortured with feelings of missing an absence. How was that possible? Or fair? He had grown up with no idea whether his father smelt of cigarettes or aftershave. He'd not known if his voice was gravelly, stern or soft. He had only been able to guess which football team he supported. As a boy, he had decided it was Fulham, because all of his mates' dads supported Fulham. He went through a stage – it lasted two, two and a half years – where he used to avidly watch the Fulham games on TV, scanning the crowds for a glimpse of someone who might, just might, be his dad. He strained his eyes, expecting to see a mop of dark hair, stubble and tight designer cords, even though fashions had moved on and his father, by then, was probably wearing ratty oversized jumpers and ripped jeans in a grungy homage to Nirvana.

Eddie Taylor had once been so big, broad and strong. Not dependable, never that, but massive. One of the few memories Dean was certain was real was the one where his father's broad shoulders practically touched both sides of the door frame as he walked out of it for the final time. When he'd opened the door, the orange glow from the street light had flooded into the hallway, splattering across the floor, but then his bulk had blocked out the light as he crossed the threshold and left the family home. He'd been in a hurry. He hadn't even checked his reflection in the hallway mirror. Dean had watched the exit from the top of the stairs.

Dean was having trouble reconciling the shrivelled physical presence of this old man in front of him with the stories, hopes and hates that he'd carefully cultivated for a lifetime. The shadowy threat was a dying human being. There was no sign of horns. Dean resisted the urge to edge up the hospital sheet and check for claws or a tail, or any other physical manifestations of the Devil.

As he'd turned from boy to man, Dean had stopped hankering after his father in the same pointless, heartbreaking way. He had been left with a void that he couldn't fill with small details, so instead he stuffed the hollowness with the one big fact he was certain of: Eddie Taylor had left his wife, son and daughter and never contacted them again, not once in twenty-nine years. The longing had turned to resentment and then congealed into pure hatred.

What was he doing here anyway? If Dean hated Eddie Taylor, it made little sense that he was here. If he didn't hate him and was now indifferent towards him, it made even less sense. He hadn't meant to come. It was all down to his PA, Lacey. After that nurse had called, he'd put down the phone and then sat at his desk intending that business should carry on as normal. Thank you for the information, but the life or death of Edward Taylor was of no interest to Dean Taylor.

But Lacey, terminally bored with her job, had latched on to the crisis and made it into a full-scale, high-cost drama. She'd dashed into his office the moment the line went dead.

'I listened in,' she'd stated, without any embarrassment or apology. Lacey was tiny; less than five foot. Everything about her was diminutive: her waist, her legs, her arms, the two notable exceptions being her big green eyes and her huge boobs. She was a walking, talking Manga cartoon, a doll every man wanted to play with, and as a consequence she'd never had to pay too much attention to details such as rules or propriety, as she was always met with indulgence. Indeed, Dean would have given her a quick go himself, if they'd met anywhere other than work. 'I heard that nurse say your pop is, like, dying. I'm really so, so sorry.' Her eyes had stretched an unfeasible fraction wider. Dean felt caught in headlamps.

'Right.'

'That is so awful.'

'If you say so.'

Lacey paused; she'd watched enough trashy reality TV shows to recognise this moment. She hurried back to her desk, returning to Dean's office just ten minutes later.

'OK, I've booked you on today's 16:05 flight out from O'Hare. You'll arrive at Heathrow at 5:55. I didn't know which hotel to book. The usual one in Covent Garden, or would you like something nearer the hospital? Where is the hospital anyway? But England's small, right? London's even smaller. Wherever I book for you is going to be reasonably convenient, yeah?'

'What?' Dean had gawped at his PA in bewilderment.

'The 16:05 gives you plenty of time to go home now, throw a few things in a holdall and get over to the airport.'

'I'm not going to London.' Dean had turned purposefully back to his screen, no longer able to hold Lacey's gaze.

'Of course you are. Your father is dying.'

'He doesn't need me for that.' Dean could not stop himself adding, 'He didn't need me for living.'

If he had thought about it for a moment, he might have guessed that Lacey would relish this insight into her boss's more sensitive side. She knew more about his private life than was strictly professional; she'd often had to take calls from disappointed women who had hoped Dean really would call them as he'd said he would. She knew he was an aloof prick when it came to women and relationships, a classic love-'em-and-leave-'em type. Hopeful and hopeless women regularly turned up at the office pretending they were just passing (oh yeah, in their Christian Louboutin red heels – of course). They were hoping to have a word with him, maybe grab a sandwich lunch; Dean always told Lacey to get rid of them. Those were his words. Get rid of them. Lacey had made and cancelled enough dinner reservations on Dean's behalf to know that he dated regularly. She'd frequently been sent out for a fresh shirt and therefore knew that he was stopping over regularly too, but never with the same woman, at least not for longer than a couple of weeks.

Lacey hadn't yet been able to work out exactly why an otherwise decent guy – seemingly intelligent and a good brother and uncle – would behave this way. It was 2005, for goodness' sake; relentless variety was out of fashion and there was a trend in serious relationships. Didn't Dean know this? The trashy reality shows repeatedly insisted that there was always a reason behind why an emotional cripple became an emotional cripple. Lacey was actually glad to hear this first hint at trauma in Dean's life; she hadn't wanted to believe her boss was simply a douche bag. There was a father issue and he'd admitted as much! Lacey felt that such a declaration was clearly a cry for help. A cry she was compelled and determined to answer. Despite her size, she was a force to be reckoned with.

'I've already told the CEO that you are going out to see Rogers. That he wants you to meet his international team. The flight is business class and on expenses. By way of a thank you, you could pick me up a bottle of L'Interdit by Givenchy in the duty-free store. It's quite hard to come by over here.'

In the end it had been easier to go along with Lacey's plan, rather than unpick it. Dean's CEO had been extremely excited that the chances of winning the pitch appeared so promising; Dean couldn't find the energy to explain the reality.

He'd had no intention of visiting his father. He thought that perhaps he would swing by and see Rogers. It couldn't hurt. It might be the thing that would indeed clinch the deal; besides, he should cover his arse in case anyone ever checked up on him. He'd also go and see his sister, Zoe. That would be a treat. He'd look at this as a bonus break, a reward for the numerous late nights he'd clocked recently. He was not going to be burdened with grief or tempted by curiosity about a man he hadn't seen in twenty-nine years. Edward Taylor could go to hell. Most certainly he *was* going to hell, and he could go there without a final chat with Dean.

And yet . . .

Dean's flight had arrived in the UK on time, he'd passed through immigration with unprecedented ease, there were no queues snaking the length of the concourse and then he'd caught a tube that effortlessly transported him into central London. He was surprised to discover that his hotel could accommodate an early check-in. He'd taken a shower and a walk to try to beat the jet lag that was likely to hijack later in the day. He'd set out aimlessly. Perhaps he'd drop by the smart Paul Smith store in Covent Garden, or maybe he'd grab a coffee and a croissant from Patisserie Valerie on Bedford Street. He'd had no intention of getting on a tube again, and certainly not pitching up at the hospital in Shepherd's Bush.

He'd been stunned to find himself outside the large red-brick building at ten in the morning, but told himself that just because he was there on the street didn't mean he had to go in. He didn't need to officially make himself into a visitor; he could remain a passer-by. Hospitals were like warrens anyway; it would probably be impossible to track down Eddie Taylor. Then a chilly spring breeze had bitten the back of his neck. He'd turned up his collar and gone inside.

The more Dean looked at this man, the more confused he became. There was nothing, nothing at all, about him that was familiar. For a moment Dean panicked and considered the idea that he might have been directed to the wrong bed. This might not be Eddie Taylor after all. He was probably in another ward. He would have a nurse sat on each knee and another giving him a head massage. Wouldn't he? Wouldn't that be the case? Because wasn't that how he had always been, at least in Dean's imagination and in his mother's stories? The serial philanderer. The womaniser. The commitment-phobe.

The bastard.

Dean rushed to the end of the bed and snatched up the patient's notes. There it was, typed up in black and white: Edward Charles Taylor. Proof. The other thing it said was that the patient has requested no more resuscitation, no life-prolonging drugs, nothing other than medication to ease the pain.

'I'm sorry, visiting hours don't start until eleven a.m. I'm going to have to ask you to leave and come back then,' said a nurse, with a polite efficiency that didn't quite mask her exhaustion. 'The patients need their rest.'

'He's asleep,' Dean pointed out. He felt a mix of relief and frustration about this. If his father slept he wouldn't have to talk to him, but on the other hand, if his father slept he *couldn't* talk to him. Which did he want? It was a deep sleep, but not restful. Eddie Taylor's pupils darted left and right – the movement could be detected through his thin lids – and his chest rose and fell with a shuddering violence. This was not how Dean had imagined a death scene would be. It seemed wasteful to sleep through your last hours, but then maybe it was fitting. He and his father had wasted so much time, their entire lives. What did it matter if they wasted just a little bit more?

'Visiting hours are eleven until one and then three until five and seven until nine,' the nurse replied firmly.

'A little longer. Please.' Dean wasn't sure why he'd asked for more time. He didn't want to be here. He didn't think he should be here. He couldn't remember when he'd last been inside a hospital. During his twenties he used to visit various A&Es on a fairly regular basis on a Saturday night; in fact, a stag weekend wasn't really considered to be a total success unless someone broke a limb or needed stitches. His company had insisted he take a medical, for insurance purposes, but he hadn't had to visit an actual hospital, rather a luxurious consultant's practice on the second floor of a swanky Chicago office block. He couldn't remember ever visiting anyone in hospital. Sitting by a bedside. Watching, waiting, festering. When his sister had her babies he'd been in the States and so he'd met the newborns once Zoe was safely back at home, surrounded by soft toys, piles of disposable nappies and welcoming flowers.

The hospital was bleak, rammed with blatantly baffled patients who drifted through the wards and corridors. There appeared to be an infinite number of anguished or sorrowful souls propping up the walls or slumped on the bedside chairs. Some were no doubt anticipating news about their friends and families; others had already received it. Dean sighed. This was not his sort of place. He liked attractive, successful, resilient sorts. He liked to be cushioned by the lucky and the charismatic. He worked hard to surround himself with luxury, decadence and delights. Now he was surrounded by skinny hardback chairs, tubes, trolleys and a faint smell of disinfectant.

Dean didn't want to be sitting on one of the uncomfortable chairs by Eddie Taylor's bed. Why didn't he simply leave? It was true that he was anti-authority and it was possible that he wanted to negotiate extra time just to prove that something as petty as rules regarding visiting hours didn't apply to him, didn't tie him.

Maybe. Or maybe he actually wanted to stay by this man's bedside.

He wasn't thinking straight. He probably needed some fresh air.

'Sorry, I didn't know the rules.' He treated the nurse to one of his grins. He flashed this particular grin regularly. It was practised, perfect, showing off a line of teeth that had had the benefit of a top Chicagoan orthodontist. He used this grin when he needed a shop assistant to accept his returned item even though he had failed to retain proof of purchase; he used it when he needed a female maître d' to find him a table, even though he'd failed to make a reservation, and he used it when he needed some hot woman to drop her morals and her knickers. It never failed.

'Are you family?' The nurse was already looking for a way to allow this man to stay until official visiting hours started, even though she could get into trouble for doing so.

'I'm his son,' said Dean, turning back to glance at his father, as though he too needed confirmation that this was the case.

'Eddie's never mentioned a son,' pointed out the nurse, unaware, or at least unconcerned, about any potential hurt her comment might cause.

'No, he wouldn't,' admitted Dean with a sigh. The sigh seeped like an ink stain on to the hospital sheets. 'I think I'll go and call my sister. I'll come back at the proper hours.'

'Oh, he has a daughter too?' The nurse turned toward Eddie Taylor and beamed, clearly pleased for the sick man. 'How lovely.'

'Yeah, lovely.' Dean turned away quickly so she wouldn't see his glower.

'Hi, Zoe.'

'Dean. Is everything all right?'

Dean wondered whether there would ever come a day when his sister would simply pick up the phone and be pleased to hear from him. He doubted it. She'd probably always assume that he was the bearer of appalling news. Their exposed and lonely childhoods had taught them to expect the worst. They both made a valiant effort to pretend that this was not the case; they'd clawed their way out of their inheritance and become decent, hardworking members of society, but the fact was, they lived with an awareness of the world's underbelly.

Zoe was the epitome of upright and reputable. She drove an old but reliable estate car to toddler dance classes and to resident association meetings; she dressed in White Stuff jumpers and bought her jeans from Gap. She usually carried a cotton shopping bag; ordinarily it was filled with responsibly farmed produce which she made into delicious meals for her family. Most people would probably peg Zoe at a little older than twenty-nine; she had dashed towards being an adult, as childhood wasn't a place either sibling had wanted to linger. But if anyone watched her striding through the cobbled streets of Winchester, where she lived in a small but cosy house, they would never guess that she wet her bed until she was thirteen and that she still couldn't sleep without leaving a light on.

Dean had pulled off an even more stupendous transformation. He was a wealthy and extremely successful advertising executive, who oozed charm and composure. There was nothing about his expensive and elegant style of dressing, his confident swagger in the boardroom, his affable generosity when buying rounds at the bar that suggested that as a child his wardrobe was limited to charity shop purchases and second-hand clothes donated by well-meaning do-gooders. Nor was there anything to betray that he had been treated by a child psychiatrist for anger management until he was sixteen. They had managed to construct convincingly respectable, balanced personas for the benefit of almost everyone else they knew. It was trickier with each other; they couldn't hide the truth of their histories from one another.

'Hey, don't panic,' he said soothingly.

'It's just that it's so early for you. Ten fifteen here means it must be just four fifteen your time. If you call in the middle of the night Chicago time then of course I'm going to assume that something is wrong.'

'Actually, I'm in the UK.'

'Are you?' Dean could hear Zoe's relief and pleasure. 'You never said you were coming over.'

'Yeah. It was sort of impulse.'

'Great! Will you get time to squeeze in a visit to Winchester and come and see us before you have to fly back?'

'That's my plan.'

'I know your work is always hectic, but we do love seeing you. The kids have grown so much since you last saw them. You won't recognise Hattie.'

'I'm not here on work as it happens.' Dean paused, searching for the right words. He wasn't sure he'd ever find them, so he just blundered on. 'It's our father.'

'Our father?' Zoe sounded stunned.

'Edward Taylor,' added Dean, just in case she didn't know who he was talking about.

'Is he dead?'

'No.'

'More's the pity.'

'Come on, Zoe, you can't mean that. You're too lovely to think that way.' Dean thought that way but he considered Zoe to be the more compassionate of the two of them.

'I really do. I am lovely, except when it comes to him.'

'He's dying.'

'And?'

'And I thought you'd want to know.'

'You thought wrong. I'm not interested.' Dean could hear her breath down the phone line; it was increasingly rapid, as though she'd just completed a ten-kilometre run. She must be wondering why he'd called her about Edward Taylor. Why had he brought this to her Thursday morning? She was probably just on her way out to take the kids to the park, walk their dog. She didn't need this. 'How do you even know?' she demanded.

'He got a nurse to call me.'

'How did he know where to find you?'

'I don't know. I can't imagine I'm that hard to find.'

'Yet it took him twenty-nine years.'

Dean ignored the interruption and carried on. 'I've never been missing. He was the one who disappeared.'

'Oh, so you do remember that much.' Dean did remember that much. Every day of his life.

'Zoe, I'm as angry with him as you are.'

'No, you clearly are not, or else you wouldn't have come from Chicago to be by his bedside. I'm assuming that is why you are here. You're planning on visiting him.'

He couldn't lie to her. 'I'm actually at the hospital right now.'

'You've spoken to him?' Her fury and disbelief caused her voice to crack, and she squawked down the phone. Zoe had always suspected that Dean nurtured a secret need to forgive his father; she did not harbour any similar compunction.

'No, he is asleep or maybe unconscious. I'm not sure.'

'Why has he got in touch after all this time? Does he want a vital organ?'

The thought hadn't crossed Dean's mind and now he felt stupid. It was possible. 'I don't think so,' he mumbled.

'What *are* you thinking?'

'They said he only has days.'

'I don't care. I don't know him.'

'That's my point.'

'You think you are going to get to know him in his last few days?'

'Maybe.'

'You're an idiot to visit him. A bloody idiot. Has he ever visited us?'

Silently the siblings began simultaneous but independent mental tallies of the times that they had waited in vain for Edward Taylor to come and visit them, maybe even rescue them. For the first three years after he'd left, Dean had believed his father would turn up at his school sports days; he'd hoped for this with all the energy and commitment that a young boy could muster. His size had given him an advantage and he'd always been a good athlete, but there was never anyone to cheer him on or witness his victories. What was the point of romping home a good ten metres in front of the other boys if there was no one to feel proud? Dean would be shocked to know that Zoe had harboured similar secret fantasies until she was much older. Right up to her wedding day she'd dreamt that maybe her father would turn up out of the blue to give her away. But he didn't, of course, underlining the fact that he'd already done so, many years previously.

'We had each other.'

'Only because there was no one else around.'

'Still, it was enough, wasn't it?'

They both knew it hadn't been, but neither could insult the other by saying so. After a brief pause Zoe added, 'Well, I'm not interested. I don't want to know anything about him. I don't want details. Don't talk to me about him again. Not until you call to tell me he's dead.'

'Zoe,' Dean pleaded.

'Don't make me hate you too, Dean. Not you too.'

'That's not what I'm trying to do. I don't want to disappoint you but I couldn't hide this from you. I don't want to fight.'

'I have to go. The dog is going to pee in the kitchen otherwise.'

Dean knew the chocolate-brown Labrador was perfectly well house-trained; Zoe just wanted to get off the line.

'OK, sis, I'll call you when—' He didn't get to be specific. Zoe had hung up.

6

Jo

This is the start of something big. This is important. Well, it could be. It *might* be. I'm not an idiot – well, not all of the time. I've had enough false starts, my hopes have been raised more than enough times, for me to be aware that true love – whilst certainly in existence – isn't easy to stumble on. But still, I cross my fingers.

I lie awake and concentrate on not moving. I don't want to disturb and wake Jeff. We only fell asleep at twenty to three this morning and the smart, enormous aluminium clock on the wall says it isn't yet six a.m. But I can't go back to sleep. Emotionally, I'm too full. Too charged.

I try not to fidget or wriggle, but staring at the ceiling is boring. It's entirely blank; there's no impressive coving, no offensive polystyrene tiles, not even a patch of damp that would suggest a financial struggle or a lackadaisical neighbour who might have forgotten to turn off the bath tap. The ceiling tells me nothing at all. I slide my eyes around the room. The decoration is immaculate; I can smell new paint. I wonder whether Jeff might be the sort of person who has professional decorators in every couple of years to ensure that the place always looks spick and span. Some people do live like that, don't they? Well, my parents do, obviously, but other people too.

I can imagine living here, with Jeff. I know, I know, I'm getting ahead of myself. I'm just saying, *if* things panned out, this would suit me very well. At least it would once I conquered my concerns about breaking something or messing everything up. This really is an exceptionally clean and tidy environment. Slowly my confidence picks up and I dare to move my head from left to right. I don't want to wake Jeff yet, but I need to get my bearings. Last night, I was too drunk on wine and lust to take in much. I remember him fumbling with a massive bunch of keys and then, once the door slipped open, I flung him against the hall wall. We had exciting, wild, uninhibited sex, right there and then, followed by a second round in bed; that time it was slower, more meaningful. Twice! Ha, that is something I have on my married friends. How many of them can say they have sex twice in one night? Most of my friends hint that twice a *month* is average. It is a mystery to me how I can be privy to such information but still be more than keen to join their club.

Jeff's bedroom is gorgeous! So modern and comfortable. He has great taste. The prints on the wall are dramatic black and white photos of a beach in winter time. It's unusual for a man to appreciate throws, candles and cushions, but Jeff has them all. I glance around for photographs that might give a sneaky insight into my new boyfriend's world. I can't remember any of the details he told me last night, not specifically. We didn't do that much talking about personal stuff really; there wasn't time. I gleaned that he liked going down to Bude to windsurf; I remember that, and the fact that he works nearby, in Hackney – we discussed the joy of a short commute. Although I can't quite remember what he does for a living. Did he say? He has a brother, or it might be two. The details are patchy.

There are no photos to help fill in the gaps, nor are there any books or clutter that could give clues. Wow, this man is a neat *freak*. If I ever moved in here I'd have to buy one of those jewellery trees because my necklaces are always getting tangled and I have a feeling he isn't the type to appreciate puddles of jewellery littering up the place (or discarded clothes and stray shoes come to that). I'd also have to buy a set of those laundry boxes that say 'Whites' and 'Darks'; it's clear that Jeff is the sort of guy who likes a system.

I turn my head and drink in the sight of my new boyfriend, who is sleeping peacefully beside me. Exhausted. Spent. He looks a bit like Mark Wahlberg, or maybe Ryan Reynolds. Like them, he's sort of boy next door but better. Tighter, more taut and toned. Properly hot. He has a great jawline, dark eyes, dark hair, plump, pink – let's face it – sensual lips. I wonder how old he is. It's quite possible that he is a year or two younger than I am, maybe three or four. I'll have to take care not to let him see my driving licence, at least not too soon. That's not the sort of thing I want to lead with. This properly hot guy will undoubtedly be in demand; he could choose from a queue of women. Younger women, taller women, prettier women, funnier women, women with more successful careers. All of the above. The thought causes my breath to quicken. It is tough out there. It is busy and predatory; twenty-first-century dating rituals are like being continually embroiled in the first day of the January sales. Elbows out.

Still, he is here, right next to me. I am here, in his bed. I push a long, slow breath out into the word. As I do so, I try to let go of my panic and worry, just as advised by the yoga teacher on the DVD I bought myself last Christmas. I can take this slowly. We have time. Obviously not years and years. I am thirty-six next month, for God's sake (back to that again!). But we have *some* time. I could skive off work today and then we could stay in bed. In fact, if I rang in and said I had a stomach bug, I could play truant on Friday too. Then we'd have four whole days of uninterrupted loving. Who knows where those four days might lead. To weeks? Months?

OK, I'm going to stay optimistic. Imagine we did fall in love; how would the timing work? Let's say six months' dating, followed by a six-month engagement (whatever I said about Martin's 'indecent haste' I've now conveniently blanked); this time next year Jeff and I could be drawing up a wedding gift list in one of the smarter department stores. Then we could have a year enjoying ourselves as a married couple, three months trying to get pregnant, nine months pregnant and then the first baby by the time I am thirty-eight. It is just possible to have two before I am forty. Just. A tight schedule but it isn't unimaginable. I have a tendency to think in double negatives; it's the closest I ever get to a positive these days.

But this time, *this time* I think there really is something to get excited about, because there is one thing I remember with crystal clarity from last night. Something he whispered to me after the second bout of lovemaking. He said, 'You're just the sort of girl I should marry.'

Men don't say that sort of thing lightly. He has to have meant it.

And the sex. The sex was phenomenal. I really have never, ever experienced anything like it. Just thinking about it causes a fleeting spike of excitement between my legs. It was so . . . I search for the exact word to describe the marathon session we enjoyed. My head is still a bit fuzzy. What *is* the perfect word? It was so . . . energetic.

I really need to pee. Carefully I inch the duvet aside and edge out of the bed. I glance around, hoping to locate his robe so that I can cover up. No matter how acrobatic I was last night, in the cold light of day my body demands sanctuary. I can't see a robe, nor is there a jumper or hoodie flung across the back of the bedroom chair. I have no alternative but to dash naked into the bathroom.

The bathroom is a delight! It looks like it has sprung from a magazine. He must have a cleaner. He can afford a cleaner! I know it is shallow to care, but the idea of having a boyfriend with an income that allows him to employ a cleaner is fantastic. I've spent far too many 'dates' cleaning the homes of various exes. To start with it is always smart restaurants and a club, then a couple of weeks down the line it's often a trip to the cinema and a bag of popcorn, and before I know it, I'm lucky to be watching a DVD from the sofa. I try to tell myself that dates that consist of me scouring ovens or defrosting freezers are intimate and domestic, part of a real relationship, but in my heart of hearts I know that I'm simply being taken advantage of.

The towels are sharply folded and stacked in a precise tower on the shelf near the enormous walk-in shower, there are tea-light candles lined up like soldiers along the basin and the end of the loo roll is folded into a triangle. I have only ever seen that done in hotels before. This place is amazing! I want to hug myself. Instead I pee, and as I wash my hands I force myself to confront my reflection. There was once a time when a long night of sex meant that I sparkled the next morning. Nowadays, such antics are more likely to lead to bulky blue bags under my eyes. I splash water on my face and look round for some cleanser or soap. There isn't any. In fact, there aren't any bottles of lotions and potions at all. Not lined up on the windowsill or stashed in the cabinet. There is a cabinet but it's empty, pristine.

Pristine like the candles that have never been lit. I quietly make my way through to the kitchen. Something about this place is a bit off, a bit weird, but without coffee I am not up to puzzling it out. The kitchen-diner is as immaculate as the bathroom. The laminate floors and all the surfaces shine; the taps and windows twinkle and the many scatter cushions are plump and smooth. There is a full set of gleaming crockery set out on the dining room table, as though Jeff is waiting for imminent dinner guests.

The room makes me think of Miss Havisham's wedding breakfast, except these dishes are clean and polished rather than covered in cobwebs and vermin. But who is Jeff expecting?

I need coffee to think. I open the cupboard above the kettle, but it's empty. I'd expected a jar of instant coffee granules and a box of breakfast tea bags, at the least, though the apartment is so stylish I wouldn't have been surprised to find coffee beans, filter papers and three different herbal teas.

'We'll have to go out for coffee, of course.' I jump at the sound of Jeff's voice. Despite the intimacy of last night, I don't recognise his tone. I turn to face him; he's standing naked in the doorway. I am naked too. Suddenly, rather disconcerted, I think that there seems to be too much nudity in the kitchen. I suck in my belly. My thighs and bum are towards the high-gloss kitchen units; I really hope they aren't so high-gloss that they reflect my cellulite back out to the world. It is always so much harder in the cold light of day.

'Are you out of coffee?' I ask.

Jeff doesn't reply; he just grins and then walks towards the bathroom.

I seize the opportunity to dash back into the bedroom and dive beneath the duvet. Thank goodness he hasn't opened the curtains; daylight is sneaking through the drapes but it is subdued rather than exposing. I listen to him pee and flush; he comes out of the bathroom without washing his hands. I try not to dwell on that thought but it does bother me. Why don't more men wash afterwards?

I expect Jeff to jump back into bed, but instead he stoops down and snatches up his discarded clothes. 'Sorry, lovely lady, we don't have time for another helping. We have to get up and out of here before anyone spots us.'

I am so busy trying to tell myself that he really does think I *am* a lovely lady and that's why he's used the endearment – it isn't because he's forgotten my name – that initially I don't compute the significance of the second sentence.

Spots us? What does he mean? Who might spot us? Why does it matter? 'But I haven't had any breakfast. Not even coffee.' I really do need a coffee; my hangover is beginning to take effect, as though it has awoken with Jeff.

'Well there's nothing to eat here.'

'I can go out and buy something, if you like. While you take a shower,' I offer.

Jeff is buttoning up his shirt, but he pauses. I wonder whether he is offended that I suggested he shower. Does he think I am commenting on his personal hygiene? Well, in a way I am. Who makes love all night and then gets up and goes to work without a shower? Standards.

'I can't shower here, the other agents will notice, and we can't eat here for the same reason. Come on, get a move on. We have to make the bed so you can't tell anyone has slept in it. There's an iron. I just plug it in and iron the wrinkled duvet *in situ*. I'm getting pretty good at it.'

I stare at Jeff, bemused. 'Agents?' What is he on about? 'Isn't this apartment yours?' Then an explanation strikes. 'Do you share it?'

'I'm trying to sell it. I told you, last night. This is a show home, I'm an agent. Wow, how drunk were you?' Jeff is by this time fully dressed, except for his socks. He sits on the end of the bed and starts to pull them on too. 'Come on, get up.' He taps my leg through the duvet, but it isn't an affectionate caress and there's an edge of impatience in his voice that I didn't hear last night. Then, his tone was all about desire and persuasion; now, it's distinctly sergeant major. 'We really have to be out of here by seven thirty, or I'll be fired.'

'You're an estate agent?'

'Yes. What sort of agent did you think I meant? A secret agent?'

Oh, an estate agent, that does ring a bell. I am disappointed that this beautiful apartment doesn't belong to my boyfriend – mentally I'd already started to arrange my books and trinkets – but I take a deep breath. I'm not going to show my disappointment. Obviously he brought me here because it is exciting and sexy. Lots of men like to do it on their desk, or their boss's desk; it means that the next day, during office hours, the flashbacks provide entertainment. There is nothing wrong with that. I wonder what *his* flat is like. 'Remind me, where do you live?'

'I never said.' I wait expectantly for Jeff to fill in the blank now. He stands up and then picks my dress up off the floor. He tosses it at me, but before it even lands I somehow sense the next sentence. 'It always seems a bit weird talking about my home and stuff. A bit disloyal to my wife. Now, come on and get dressed. Like I said, there's nothing to eat here and I really need some carbs after last night's performance. I wish there was a café around here. I could kill a fry-up.'

'Wife?'

Jeff glances at his watch, then shrugs apologetically. I have a terrible feeling that he is apologising for the lack of a café rather than the presence of a wife.

I can't remember him mentioning a wife yesterday. I know I would have remembered that, no matter how many shots we'd downed. I am always particularly careful to listen out for talk about long-term girl- (or boy-) friends, fiancées and wives. Especially wives. It isn't something I could overlook. No, he certainly did not mention a wife. *Wife* is a stop word for me. Unequivocally. No matter how much I want a husband, I don't want someone else's. I would never, ever have let it get this far if I'd known he was married.

There's only one explanation: clearly he didn't mention his wife last night because she isn't a wife in the true and absolute sense. They are separated. Divorcing. I'm not too squeamish about that. I've long since reconciled myself to the thought that I am most likely going to be someone's second wife. It's just a numbers game. Thirty-five-plus still hunting equals divorcee. An ex-wife isn't a problem. A man that looks a bit like Ryan Reynolds is bound to have an ex-wife. He's too handsome not to have been nabbed in his twenties.

'So when did you and your wife split up? Was it recently?' I ask.

'What?'

'You *are* separated.' But my confidence in my assertion is already beginning to dwindle and fade. There's something about Jeff's rather arrogant and bemused face that tells me he certainly is not separated.

I pull the duvet cover a fraction higher up my body.

'Awkward,' he sings sotto voce. 'I thought you knew I was married.'

'How would I know that unless you told me? You didn't tell me. You're not wearing a ring,' I point out. But as I look at his tanned hand now, I can just about make out that whilst he isn't wearing a wedding band, there's a ring of paler skin that shows that generally he does.

'Wow, thanks for reminding me.' He fishes about in his trouser pockets, retrieves a platinum ring and slips it on to his finger. I suddenly feel extremely tired. Weary. 'So do you want something to eat or not? There is a corner shop, at least, and they sell veggie samosas.'

'Do you do this sort of thing often?'

'Eat breakfast?'

'Have sex with women other than your wife.'

Jeff looks unabashed, a bit bored. 'Yeah. Yeah, I do, when I can, you know . . .'

'Know what?'

I don't know anything. I feel sick. I have never, ever come across such casual cruelty. I have been ditched many, many times; I've even done some ditching of my own, I've snuck away in the early morning before the guy has woken up, but this! *This* is a new all-time low. The young, hard face in front of me (how did I fail to notice its sharpness last night?) is unapologetic, unrepentant. Unavailable.

'You said I was just the sort of girl you should marry,' I protest.

'Did I? Are you sure? I think I might have said you're just the sort of girl I should've married. It was a joke. I was joking about what a fun slut you are. I'd never really marry someone like you.'

'Like me.' I don't mean it to be a question, but Jeff interprets it as such and chooses to be explicit.

'Well, older and so available.' I leap out of bed and start to struggle into my dress. At the same time I hold up my hand, trying to stop him from saying anything more. I do not want to hear what else he has to say. It's all too much already. Too painful. But Jeff isn't looking at me. He's staring at his reflection, running his fingers through his hair, and so he carries on. 'I mean, you came on to me pretty strong last night. I didn't do the chasing. You practically threw your sister in a cab. She wanted you to go home with her but you said you'd make your own way back. I distinctly remember you saying you were a big girl and you could look after yourself.'

'I lied,' I say with a sigh.

'What?'

'I don't think I can look after myself. I lied,' I admit a little louder. He has no idea how momentous this confession is; how sickening this thought.

'Well, *I* didn't lie to *you*,' he adds self-righteously. 'You never asked if I was married. I sort of thought you must have known but just didn't care. You kind of had a predatory look about you.'

I am tangled in my dress. It is tight-fitting and I fight to find the sleeves. I ought to have stepped into it, but in my haste I yanked it over my head. Angrily I turn to face Jeff, but I can't see him because my head has not yet emerged through the neck hole, and as the dress has stuck on my hips, my muff is exposed. Even though I'm fastidious about waxing, this is undoubtedly a humiliating stance.

'Predatory, as in cougar?' I demand as I finally pull the dress down over my thighs and pop my head out of the neck hole.

'I didn't say that, it's not a nice word.'

I wonder whether he thinks 'fun slut' is a compliment, but I am sick of being on the back foot. I decide to go in for the attack. 'I can think of a few other ugly words that might apply to our situation. Adulterer, fornicator, bastard.'

'Hey, there is no need for that. I'm not going to fight with you. I don't even know you. We had a great time, Jill, but—'

'Jo.'

'Sorry?'

'My name is . . . Oh, never mind.' The fight in me vanishes. There's no point. No point at all. I begin to collect up my belongings – tights, panties, handbag and jacket – strewn like scars on the show home's bedroom carpet. I want to get out of here. I want to get as far away as possible from the scene of the crime, before we are caught and further exposed. This is humiliating enough; it doesn't need to be heartbreaking too.

'I pity your wife,' I mutter, as I stand in the doorway.

'My wife has nothing to do with you. She would not want your pity,' replies Jeff. He's ironing the duvet, as I have refused to help.

'Maybe not, but she has it anyhow.'

7

Eddie

I open my eyes. I'm not dead yet, then. Strangely, I feel a bit disappointed that this is the case and am shocked by my own disappointment. I don't long for death or anything oddly morbid like that, but I can't be arsed to fight it either. This indifference is depressing. Indifference to my own death is the most clear and compelling evidence, if more evidence were needed, as to how completely and utterly I've screwed up my life.

It isn't so much that I am despairing – nothing so dramatic; I am, frankly, bored. Bored of being sick. Bored of the pain, the discomfort, the long days. And before the cancer? Well, I was bored then too, for quite some time. Getting older hasn't suited me. I was good at being young. I had a penchant for irresponsibility, wildness and a predilection for living in the moment, carefree and careless. It's tempting to imagine it would be better just getting it over with now.

But then what? Recently, I've started to think about churches. Church and God and the afterlife. I'm trying to work out what to expect next. I can't remember when I was last inside a church. It was probably someone's wedding. Thirty, maybe more years ago? It might even have been my own wedding. I've never given religion much thought, beyond that it's a convenient excuse for lots of wars and lots of hate, but since I've had to organise my own funeral, I've started to give the whole idea a bit more consideration.

I don't believe in the type of afterlife I was taught about in primary school. I cannot accept a heaven, located in the clouds, where a bearded guy with a halo mans the pearly gates, much like a bouncer at a nightclub. I can't imagine St Peter stood with a list of the names of those who have earned access to heaven, shaking his head (with a mixture of smug arrogance and fake regret) at those who had sinned and are going to have to wander along to hell to spend eternity there instead. It doesn't make sense. There are practical considerations, such as how do the rejects get from the cloud to hell once they are denied access? Is there some sort of invisible fireman's pole that they have to slide down, or a rubbish chute that they are shoved down? Why wouldn't the evil guys just storm the gates of heaven and demand entrance? Bad guys aren't normally known for accepting rules and limits; isn't that the point? What could one old bloke do (saint or not) against a crowd of murderers, thieves, paedophiles, warmongers and mercenaries? They'd have him. And at the opposite extreme, why would the Devil be up for torturing the villains when they go to hell? Aren't those guys the ones who have been out doing his work, in which case wouldn't he welcome them with open arms? *Come on in, Idi Amin, take a seat right there between Stalin and Hitler. No, not that one, we're keeping that for Kony.* Why would he burn them in eternal fires? Unless I've got that wrong. Maybe I wasn't listening properly at school. Maybe God is in charge of hell too, but if that's the case, how come the Devil pops up to earth so frequently? Is there an open-door policy for him? Why doesn't God just keep him locked up?

I don't question why God might torture the evil. That bit I get.

But I'm not dead yet. I know as much because I can see the

other patients lying in the beds opposite and next to me. There's the bulky, hard-faced nurse who has let herself go, slouched by the doorway, and there is my bedside table. Unlike all the other bedside tables, it's not cluttered with get-well-soon cards and flowers; all that my table accommodates is a plastic jug of water and a plastic beaker. I am still inside my life, such as it is. Besides, I know I'm alive because of the pain. The excruciating pain that has soused my body for months now pounds with an angrier intensity. My throat is so sore and dry that it feels as though someone has ripped out my tongue. But no, it's still there. I edge it carefully on to my lips in a doomed attempt to moisten them. It feels like sandpaper ripping against wood.

Someone is sitting next to my bed. The man stands up and reaches over me; he picks up the plastic beaker and brings it to my lips. I take a sip and then ask, 'Who the hell are you?'

The man doesn't answer. I eye him suspiciously. Is he a doctor? He isn't wearing a white coat, but then some of the senior consultants don't. He needs to shave, which suggests he might be a doctor shoved up at the coal-face end, too busy for personal grooming, but this man does not seem to be in a hurry. The air surrounding him is still.

'I'm . . .' The man hesitates.

Pain has eroded away what little patience I ever possessed. 'Don't you know who you are?' I demand crossly.

'Don't you?'

I pause. I look carefully at the man's face, his hair and eyes, the arc of the eyebrows, the width of his nose, and I recognise every feature.

'Hello, son. Thanks for coming.'

8

Jo

I smell. I smell and I ache. I reek of sweat, alcohol and disappointment. My thighs throb with exertion and my eyes sting with exhaustion. I pinch the top of my nose, but however hard I squeeze, I can't squeeze out the thought of what I've done in the past twelve hours.

I know that I should probably find my way back to Lisa's, shower and change before I head into work; my colleagues are the type to notice if someone is wearing the same outfit two days in a row. In most offices you might expect walks of shame to be a legitimate source of gossip and teasing, but in the *Loving Bride!* office (a shrine to the happily-ever-after), they're actively condemned. It's a little like it was in the 1950s: unplanned sleepovers are only considered acceptable if the perpetrator ends up marrying the man in question. Obviously there's no chance of that with Jeff. I sigh as on some subconscious level I acknowledge that there wasn't a chance with Mick (my fling from three weeks ago) or Darren (a guy I had a brief thing with a few months before that) either. My walks of shame happen with reasonable regularity, and I'm concerned that, while congregated around the water cooler, people might have started to comment that at best I show a lack of judgement and discernment; at worst I'm a ridiculous, desperate slag.

If I go to Lisa's to shower and change, I'll avoid being subjected to more knowing looks from the scandalmongers. However, I run the risk of bumping into my family. I can imagine that encounter with awful clarity. As I sneak in the back door, I'll find the children buzzing around the kitchen (which will, as usual, be full of delicious smells like buttered toast and fresh coffee), and if I manage to make it upstairs, then I'll no doubt meet Lisa or Henry on the landing (which will ooze the scent of Lisa's shower gel) and they'll throw me that look, the one that is a mix of disappointment and concern; it's the concern that embarrasses me the most. I can't imagine my strained and stinky body in amongst their warm, domestic, sweet-smelling environment. No one would actually say anything too cutting, of course, but arms would be folded across chests in a way that would be clearly condemning. The thought makes me freeze.

I pause for a moment and consider which is the lesser of the two evils: being exposed in front of my colleagues or my family? It's a bleak choice. I'd care less if I could brag that Jeff and I had enjoyed a croissant breakfast together and that we'd made plans to meet up and catch a film this evening, but as the situation stands, it is pitiless and brutal. I could lie – simply tell everyone I've had a night of unprecedented romance and it's the start of something special – but I'm not quite that pathetic. Not yet.

A spring breeze nips meanly at my legs. It reminds me of my mother's infrequent but sharp smacks during my childhood when I'd done something extremely naughty. It seems fitting. I didn't have time to put on my tights; besides, they're most likely laddered, as last night they were removed in a hurry. My hands shake. I feel a bit like I did when I fell off my bike last autumn and had to go to hospital to have my head glued. The nurse said then that I was in shock.

I try to get my bearings. I look left and right but don't

recognise the street I've tumbled out upon. We travelled to Jeff's show home by cab and so I've no idea which part of London I'm in. A red double-decker bus hurls by; the number 43 to London Bridge. It doesn't help much. I could be anywhere between the old Friern Barnet library and Guy's Hospital. I look around for a familiar landmark but can't locate one. A frightening sense of disorientation swamps me, drowning me. I'm lost. I try to read the bus stop's timetable but the numbers blur as tears threaten. This is ridiculous, I scold myself. I'm a grown woman; there's nothing to get upset about. It isn't as though I'm the one who has deliberately betrayed someone; I didn't intend to be the other woman. Besides, this isn't the first time a man has lied to me and deceived me. It crosses my mind that that's exactly why I'm crying. This isn't the first time and it is unlikely even to be the last.

The sky is low and grey. It suits my mood. It's the sort of sky that seems to wipe out possibility. This sky negates the fact that it's actually a new day. Purple-black night-time skies are exciting. Bright blue daytime ones are productive. Grey skies allow neither thought. I pull my jacket tighter around my body. I need to find a tube station. I need to get underground. Then I'll go to my gym. I won't be able to change clothes, but at least I can get a shower. That way I won't run the risk of bumping into any of my family and I won't cause my colleagues to heave.

Although I speed down the escalators and along the platforms and dash to the gym, where I try my very best to shower as quickly as possible, I find that time dances away from me like a ballerina on pointes, performing in *Swan Lake*. My need to be efficient is hampered by the fact that I don't have a coin for the locker and have to negotiate at reception to secure one, which I then drop. It rolls underneath the pine benches; I find two used Elastoplasts and a soggy hairband before I find the pound coin.

It's just that sort of day. Then I have to queue for a spare cubicle and shower. There's another queue at the coffee shop, but I really can't get by without my morning mocha, so ultimately, despite the very early start, I arrive at the office an hour and fifty minutes late.

When I started working at *Loving Bride!*, I believed with every fibre of my body that it was my dream job. I couldn't imagine working anywhere more romantic, exciting or thrilling. The added bonus was that Martin and I got engaged very soon after I started the job, and working on a bridal magazine allowed me to indulge in every aspect of wedding planning – to the max. I could legitimately have conversations about invitation calligraphy, flower girls' ballet shoes and the latest trend in buttonholes without anyone actually calling me insane. As my job meant I was constantly talking to cutting-edge wedding providers – who were all desperate for positive editorial coverage in *Loving Bride!* – I was in a position to blag a Caroline Castigliano wedding dress, four floor-length strapless raspberry bridesmaid dresses and a tiara designed by Lou Lou Belle, as well as cut-price rates from a photographer, a videographer and a chauffeur for my wedding.

Ultimately, because of my zest and interest in all things bridal, I was given my own column, 'Marrying Mr Right', in which I detailed my wedding plans, triumphs and disasters in a humorous manner, guiding other brides every step of the way as they moved towards their big day.

Calling off my wedding was not only a private catastrophe but it had a devastating effect on my career too. My editor, Verity Hooper, insisted that it was out of the question that I announce to our *Loving Bride!* readers that I'd got cold feet. Instead she forced me to write a piece pretending that the wedding had gone ahead as planned, and even insisted that we stage some fake photos; after all, there were a number of sponsors who were expecting product placement.

I forced myself into the Caroline Castigliano dress and smiled for the camera. What choice did I have? My job was on the line. To say that it was a tough day in the office is the biggest understatement I have ever muttered.

However, my devotion to duty did not go unrecognised. The original plan – that I continue to write my column under the new name 'Being Mrs Right' – had to be abandoned, naturally. Even Verity saw that I could not sustain a fake marriage just so I could deliver a monthly column about domestic bliss. Instead I was given a column with the self-explanatory title 'Meeting Mr Right'. Simply put, it is devoted to ways in which a woman can meet someone she might want to marry. I write under a pseudonym; I'm not even a real person.

'But you write for a bridal magazine; surely the readers have already found the man they want to marry,' Lisa pointed out when I told her what I was going to write.

'Verity thinks my pieces might catch the attention of the single bridesmaids who flick enviously through their friends' mags. She hopes that we can expand the readership beyond the affianced to the struggling and desperate.'

'Charming.'

'I'm quoting.'

'And she sees you as the perfect woman for that job?' I'd pretended not to catch the sarcasm in Lisa's tone. I survive a lot of embarrassment by simply pretending I'm a bit hard of hearing. 'Isn't the concept all a little antiquated and rather more suited to Jane Austen's era than the twenty-first century?' my sister had persisted.

'Marriage is still as relevant today as it was when women embroidered, wore bonnets and never discussed menstruation,' I'd replied. Lisa had tutted and pointed out that that was a difficult position to maintain considering I'd just ditched my fiancé, practically at the altar. However, we both accepted that work is work and at least I still had a job.

In the name of research, I've investigated the pros and cons of speed dating, the authenticity and effectiveness of various dating sites and the triumphs, trials and tribulations of blind dating. I've gone on singles camping holidays where you're forced to share a tent with a stranger (that shouldn't be legal!), I've scoured social networking sites and I even faked a smoking habit so I could give smirting a whirl.

'What in God's name is that?' Henry, my brother-in-law, asked when I told him about that column. 'Sounds like an illness.'

'Flirting while smoking,' I explained. 'Outside, away from the noisy din of a bar, I'll be able to chat to people beyond my usual social circle. Smokers always maintain that smoking is an instant conversation starter, and there's something rather intimate about leaning in to light a cigarette.' Lisa and Henry exchanged one of the many looks they gave each other over my head; this one was amused, smug and pitying all at once. However, my asthma started to bother me and I eventually had to admit that I think smoking is a filthy habit that ruins clothes, looks and lungs; besides, I didn't want to kiss anyone who tasted like an ashtray.

Somehow, every month for five years, I've produced one thousand two hundred words detailing different schemes for meeting and netting Mr Right. No one is more aware of the irony that I have failed to do as much. Recently – although I don't want to admit it to anyone, including myself – I've found that I've been running out of ideas. I sometimes struggle to maintain the necessary hopeful, cheery and bright tone that is required at *Loving Bride!*. I've resorted to bulking out the word count with entire paragraphs comparing wedding favours and bows on chair backs. Sometimes I question whether I wasted my time studying journalism at university.

The email detailing a sudden request for a meeting with Verity doesn't come directly from the editor herself, but rather from her PA. Who sends an email is a slight – but distinctly important – statement that isn't lost on me. The tone of the note is carefully designed to make it clear that my presence is expected, almost demanded, rather than requested.

Panicked, I check that I've actually pressed the send key and delivered this month's column (I occasionally forget this detail), but I'm relieved to find my article has been flung across the web. I quickly reread what I sent to check that it's free of typos and any libellous comments. It was a tricky moment when I wrote about Durex rather than Dulux in the article about tasteful colour palettes at singles parties, but I can't see any similar glaring errors. I wonder whether there's anything in the content that might have irritated Verity. There was that time when I wrote an entire article saying that I simply couldn't *ever* have sex with a man with a hairy back and would rather lick the inside of a tube carriage than do so, only to discover at the corporate summer barbecue, that Verity's husband is more hirsute than a Newfoundland dog. Secretly my view is that Mr Hooper should have kept his shirt on; he was the reason there was so much food left over from that event. Anyway, it explained Verity's slightly frosty response to that particular piece, but this time I'm almost certain I haven't said anything that could be deemed offensive.

Relieved, I note that the meeting is scheduled for 12.50, just ten minutes before lunch; it's most likely that Verity wants to ask me to join her at some swish restaurant. A previous engagement has probably fallen through, and rather than let a booked, long-coveted table at the Ivy go to waste, she is going to invite me to make up the numbers. I'm thrilled. A decent lunch will go some way towards cheering me up.

I knock on the glass door to her office. My editor doesn't look up, but says in a particularly clipped tone, 'Come in. Sit down.' I don't manage to quite settle in the chair before she says, 'Jo, I'm sorry, there is no easy way of saying this, but we're letting you go.'

'Go where?' I ask. Look, I'm not an idiot; part of me instantly understands that I'm being fired, but another part chooses to not quite compute what's being said. 'Am I going on a shoot?'

Verity sighs but doesn't dignify my clasping at straws with a direct response. 'As you're aware, you're on a roll-over consultant contract.'

'I am?'

'Yes, you are.'

'Why?'

'Well, if I remember correctly, you decided you didn't want to be tied down to a three-month notice period.'

I do dimly recall a conversation I had in this very office, years ago. I insisted that Verity keep me on a temporary contract as Martin and I had always planned that, after we married, he would try to get a transfer to his Chicago head office, and I wanted to be able to move with him at the drop of a hat. Martin did secure a role in the head office, but by that time I'd already called off the wedding, and there was no need for me to dust off my passport. I suppose I never got round to changing the terms of my contract.

'Since you've failed to respond to the three formal warnings issued regarding your poor performance, I'm afraid I have no alternative other than to—'

'When have you issued formal warnings?' I demand. I haven't received any warnings. What is Verity on about? This is a disgrace, a set-up. Indignation flows through my body.

'HR sent emails.'

'Oh.' The indignation slinks away and is replaced by embarrassment. I have a habit of deleting emails from HR without bothering to read them, as they're usually doctrines about dress code or some tedious document about time sheets. No doubt anticipating as much, Verity has made copies of the emails; she passes them to me. I skim-read the cold warnings. Seeing the charges in black and white is sobering. I'm reprimanded for poor timekeeping, consistently failing to deliver copy on time and inappropriate behaviour with the guy in the mail room.

I realise I need to defend myself. 'Everyone is late from time to time. It's the roadworks on Islington High Street.'

'Jo, you travel to work by tube.'

'I always deliver copy *ultimately*.'

'Yes, riddled with mistakes and often inappropriate.'

'Didn't you like my piece about honeytraps?'

'You mean the piece where a bride-to-be discovered her husband in bed with the florist and then tried to stab him to death with a pair of florist's shears? No, I did not like it. There was more blood than you find in a Tarantino movie. It's not acceptable.'

'OK, I'll redraft.'

'It's too late for that. I've asked Bridget to write something. *She* understands that *Loving Bride!* is all about romance.'

'Yes, it is. Romance! So why am I being reprimanded about the incident with the guy in the mail room?'

'I'm quite certain that photocopying your anatomy with a boy who is barely out of school has little to do with romance.'

'He was twenty-four and it was Christmas!' I realise that I'm shouting. My lack of control contrasts bleakly with Verity's composure.

'I no longer believe your heart is in this role,' she declares smoothly.

'It is. It is!' I lie desperately.

'Jo, I've made an appointment for you with HR; you're to attend an exit interview. It starts in six minutes. Do try not to be late. I'm sorry, but you're finished here.'

9

Dean

Dean had sat down while his father was asleep; now he was awake, all he wanted to do was jump up and run away, but he found he was frozen. It was a similar feeling to the one he had when women he dated said something like 'We need to talk,' or worse still, 'I've taken a test.' He felt trapped, angry, and whilst he might not have consciously registered it – let alone admitted it – he felt afraid.

The years of silence extended across the room and their history. A desolate quiet seemed to compound in a solid mass throughout the ward, engulfing the dying man's bed, dense and too heavy to shift. Dean searched his mind for something to say that might nibble at the endless silence, budge it a little, but there were no words big enough to stretch across twenty-nine speechless years. Small talk – which in most social occasions sufficed, covered up and built bridges – seemed to be exposed for what it was, a polite strategy. Conversations about the weather were irrelevant, and an enquiry as to whether his father had any holiday plans this year was clearly ludicrous. Besides, Dean didn't want to be polite; if anything, he wanted to be vile and hateful, and although he was normally a master of strategy, he felt too raw to play any games right now.

'So you've come,' murmured Eddie. His breath was laboured; it caught in his chest.

'Yeah, well.'

Dean didn't know what Eddie was hoping for. What he expected. If he was hoping for a tearful reunion, a heartfelt declaration of forgiveness, he was going to be sorely disappointed. Frankly, Dean didn't know what he was hoping for either. Why had he come? What was he hoping to get out of this? Could he get to know his father in this short time? Did he even want to?

He should just go. Part of him had wanted to leave the hospital from the moment he'd arrived, but it was difficult because of the drip that fed his father and the catheter tube that drained him; all that they meant held Dean to his chair. The doctor had explained to him that Eddie had already undergone radiotherapy and chemotherapy to try to curb the cancer and a blood transfusion to combat severe anaemia. He'd had months of treatment. He'd endured that alone. The doctor said that there was nothing left to do now but wait. To die. Dean had discovered that however angry he was, he wasn't angry enough to walk away from a dying man. He couldn't decide if his inability to leave proved he was a hero or a coward.

'Can I get you anything?' he asked, not through a genuine desire to help but because that was what people asked patients lying in bed in hospital.

'Like what? A body transplant?' Eddie rasped. He tutted at his son and turned towards the window, leaving Dean to fight a feeling of humiliation.

Dean had been thinking along the lines of a magazine to read or some help reshuffling the pillows, obviously. Eddie had always managed to make him feel inadequate, as though whatever he did or said wasn't quite enough; he wasn't funny enough, clever enough or quick enough. The bottom line was he simply hadn't been enough to make his father stay. Eddie had left and Dean had always – illogically – blamed himself. This belief had developed not because of anything Eddie had ever said to his son, but the opposite; it was Edward Taylor's prolonged silence that had convinced Dean he was inadequate. Many men and some women left their families, Dean knew that, but most sent the odd postcard from time to time at the very least.

He followed his father's gaze and looked out of the window too. They were high up on the sixth floor; there was nothing to see but a grey, disappointing sky. They both stared at it as though it was the most fascinating thing ever.

Oddly, it was the depth and desolation of the silence that clarified for Dean his reasons for coming to England, to the hospital, to this bedside. He had been questioning the sanity of his decision; the one person in the world he hated hurting was Zoe, and he knew he had hurt her by coming here, but weighing against her disapproval and even more compelling than the catheter tubes, Dean was stuck in his seat because there was something he had to know.

Just one thing.

This was his first and last chance to ask it; he could not pass it up. He realised that his burdensome curiosity was why he had allowed Lacey to bully him on to the flight. It was that which had driven him to hop on the tube and then walk through the streets of London this morning to this dreary place.

He wondered whether he had the courage or energy to ask it. He wondered whether his father had either thing in order to answer. This was so mercilessly confusing. Part of Dean felt like an angry teenager again. He knew he had to shun that level of perplexity and uncertainty; he had to cling to the man who prided himself on being in control, being logical. He'd worked so hard to find balance and reason and he couldn't let that slither away. He knew he wasn't perfect; for example, he didn't do 'deep'. So many women had come and gone from his life, moaning that he was distant or shallow and that he wouldn't let them in. The expression always amused him. Did they think he was some sort of boutique shop that they were entitled to browse round? He assured them that what they saw was all there was: a shiny, affluent, sexy man. He was lying, of course. Deep down he knew it was murkier, but he couldn't afford that part of him to bubble up to the surface.

All he had to do was lean close to the old man's ear and whisper, 'Why did you leave? Why did you abandon us?' It was as simple as that, but he just couldn't do it. He'd never once said the words aloud. He'd never asked his mother. He hadn't had to; she'd shouted, screamed and smashed out her thoughts on the matter over and over again. In her opinion Eddie had left because he was a coward, because he'd found some whore to run off with, because he was a bastard. Was that all there was to it? His whole childhood massacred and his belief in the good stuff – like trust, fidelity and love – injured beyond repair just because his father hadn't been able to keep it in his trousers? Was that it?

He hadn't once asked Zoe. As the big brother, it was his job to beat off the gloom, deny it if possible, not probe. 'We don't need him' was the thing he most often said to her.

Of course he'd internally debated, endlessly asking himself why. Why had his dad gone? He'd come up with his own theories on the matter. The one about him not being impressive enough to keep a dad in his right place, at home. And the other one, the fact that you could never trust anyone, not completely, not truly. Dean thought that if a dad could leave, then anyone could. Would. The world was populated by selfish bastards. There was nothing you could do about that, other than protect yourself. Dean didn't get too friendly with colleagues or too close to his mates, so they couldn't hurt him when they stabbed him in the back as he was sure they inevitably would. One thing he was absolutely clear on: he would never fall in love. He wouldn't have children; that way he couldn't screw them up.

Yet here he was, hoping to be contradicted. Could it possibly be the case that, after all these years of hating and festering, the truth was that Dean didn't want to believe something so bleak? Was he here because he hoped his father would offer up something a little more substantial, something healing and comforting? Did he still think Eddie might make it all better? Not exactly kiss his cut knee and apply an Elastoplast – it was too late for all that – but offer an explanation that would make the hurt recede a fraction, allow the trust to bloom a little.

Eddie Taylor's hands trembled, ever so slightly. They were splattered with age spots and covered in swollen blue veins which created the impression that somehow he had dipped his elbow in a tin of paint and then allowed it to drip down his arms and hands. The skin was thin, almost transparent, like crumpled tracing paper. The man was decaying, even before he'd died. Loose skin suggested that until relatively recently he had been packed and fortified with layers of fat; the cancer had leached away that buffering and now his skin hung sloppy and grey. The hollows in his cheeks were cavernous. His eyes were watery; there was a film covering them that somehow seemed to underline the distance between the two men.

One was vital and of this world.

The older man had accepted that he had an imminent exit.

A nurse appeared at the bedside and broke the silence. Dean was grateful. She was a different one from the one he'd spoken with this morning. 'You're awake, Eddie, that's good.'

Dean thought this was probably what was widely accepted to be an understatement; a dying man waking up must be the high point of a nurse's day. He appraised the nurse with the practised eye of a womaniser. She was probably about his age but she looked significantly more worn in. Worn out. Dean worked out four times a week, he ate organic food and he never smoked or drank alcohol. He cared about his physical appearance. He sometimes thought of himself as a brand; a dynamic, attractive, slick, successful brand. The nurse carried a small tyre around her midriff and looked as though she ate takeaways. Surprisingly, Dean quite liked to see that particular bulge, because it represented contentment, and although he didn't do contentment himself, he accepted that others did and that was a good thing. That said, contented women didn't tend to fall in Dean's way. He dated hard-bodied gym bunnies who had allergies to carbs and were often coldly ambitious.

The nurse had reasonably good legs; there were some benefits to being on your feet all day. He studied her face: big brown eyes and a sloppy, smiley mouth. He briefly imagined that mouth – made up with scarlet lipstick – inching its way from his lips to his chin, his chest, across his belly, down lower, the big brown eyes staring at him all the while. No, the fantasy didn't fly. Even though this woman was wearing a uniform and kept flashing him big, careless grins, he couldn't get anything started. He wasn't really in the mood. He watched passively as she whizzed around the bed, tapping tubes and checking readings.

'Keep trying to drink your fluids,' she said to Eddie. For a moment she allowed her hand to rest on his shoulder. It was a tender gesture. Dean saw his father move his head a fraction towards her. He couldn't lay his cheek on her hand as he might once have done – he didn't have the flexibility; besides which, it would have been inappropriate – but there was something in the movement, however slight, that suggested that he hankered after human contact. Dean wished he hadn't noticed.

'When will he be getting some breakfast?' he asked the nurse. He checked his watch. He had little idea what time it was here in England. Despite being a frequent flyer, he always suffered with jet lag; it played havoc with his reality at the best of times, and this clearly wasn't that. 'Or lunch? It's past lunchtime, right? Where has the morning gone?' He wondered whether it was worthwhile trying to adjust to UK time or whether he should stay in the US zone; he'd be going back soon. When this was all over. The thought made him feel grateful and sick at the same time.

The nurse sidestepped the question. 'If you're hungry, there's a shop on the third floor that sells chocolate and crisps and there's a café in the lobby. They do sandwiches and jacket potatoes, that sort of thing. The BLT wrap is decent. I'll be back in a few minutes with the painkillers.'

It took a moment for Dean to understand. Eddie Taylor was no longer taking solids. The two men avoided one another's gaze and stayed silent until the nurse came back with the medication.

'Still happy with the syringe?' she asked brightly.

Eddie nodded, then wheezed, 'If happy is the right word.'

'Content, then? Not too drowsy? Doesn't make you feel sick?'

Eddie nodded again. This time the nod was sharper, curt. Dean thought the gesture was somehow the physical equivalent of saying 'What the fuck do you think?' Eddie was probably just desperate for some relief. How much pain was he in? Dean suddenly felt overwhelmed with emotions that he only sparingly dispensed and had never felt for his father: pity and sympathy. Then he remembered that it was *his father* dying in front of him and he slammed the lid on that swell of emotions. His father didn't deserve his sympathy; he didn't even deserve his pity.

'What is that exactly?' he asked the nurse. Concentrating on the practicalities of the situation was the best thing to do, he assured himself. He could be good in a crisis. If he remained detached, he'd be fine.

'This is a syringe driver. It's the best way to manage your dad's painkillers. We tried fentanyl as a patch but it irritated his skin. This is so easy to set up. A tiny needle is inserted just under the skin of the arm, there.' The nurse rubbed a dab of something on Eddie's arm and inserted a needle. 'Sorry about my cold hands.'

'I could warm them up? Put them under the covers,' chipped in Eddie. His breath came out in puffs.

'Eddie.' The nurse pretended to look shocked, but her voice was full of tolerance and warmth, despite his improper suggestion. It was clear that she knew how to handle men like Eddie.

'Still, they say cold hands, warm heart. Have you?' mumbled Eddie.

'You know it.'

Dean could not believe it. His father was flirting with the nurse. An old, dying man flirting! Life in the old dog yet had never been such an apt phrase. Dean wasn't sure if he was disgusted or impressed.

The nurse turned back to Dean and held up a small portable pump. 'And this holds enough painkillers for twenty-four hours. It gives a continuous dose. Should I put it on the bedside table or tuck it under your pillow, Eddie?'

'On the table. Thanks.'

The words were barely out before Eddie closed his eyes. Relief seemed to flood through his entire body. Dean stood up and followed the nurse as she walked away from the bed. When he thought he was out of Eddie's earshot he asked, 'Did you give him something to make him sleep? Is there a sedative in that?'

'No. Sleep is natural right now, at this stage. The miracle is that he's awake at all.' The nurse paused, allowing Dean a moment to compute what she was saying. 'If you have any other questions, the doctor or the palliative care team will be able to answer them.'

Dean did have one more question, the only one he needed an answer to, but the doctors and the palliative care unit couldn't help him. *Why did he leave us?* The question threw itself around his head like a small orb ricocheting around a pinball machine. *Why did he leave us?* The words raked around his head, scratching up pain and distress. He strode back to Eddie's bedside and burst out, 'Why did you leave us?'

'I was not prepared to take that particular bullet, son.'

Dean jumped back a foot, nearly knocking over the catheter as his father rasped out his reply. He had thought Eddie was asleep.

'What do you mean?'

'This is a shit way to die, but it's better than dying through living an ordinary life. A slow death of just doing nothing, being nothing.'

Dean bristled with resentment. 'You were a husband and a father. That's not nothing.'

Eddie winced and motioned weakly to the water on the bedside table. Dean reached for the beaker and helped him take a sip.

'Are you a husband?' Eddie huffed. His chest was actually rattling; Dean had always thought that was a figure of speech, not a grim reality.

'No,' Dean admitted.

'Or a father?'

'No.'

'Well you're not in a very convincing position to argue from, are you?'

Fury flickered through Dean's body like a flame. He flung himself back into the plastic chair. 'Thing is, I've always avoided becoming a husband or a dad. I'm pretty sure I'd be lousy at it. I didn't have a role model, you see,' he snapped sarcastically. Eddie's eyes met Dean's, just for a moment, but neither of them could stand the pain and they both looked away quickly.

'I just wanted more,' whispered Eddie.

Dean was furious. With Eddie and with himself. Of course Eddie Taylor was not able to offer up anything healing and comforting. How had he allowed himself to be such an idiot to think he might? He was 'not prepared to take that particular bullet'; just a poetic way of saying he'd decided to do what the fuck he liked. His father was a selfish bastard. It was as simple as that. Well, at least there was some comfort in the fact that Dean had been right all these years: people couldn't be trusted. They'd let you down. Over and over again.

So what had he done, this father of his? What had he achieved that was so extraordinary? Something, please God, something that could go some way to justifying all the hurt. Perhaps he'd written a great novel. A piece of literature that had changed the world; its beauty so sorrowfully exquisite that the words would be quoted for generations to come. But Dean knew this was not the case. He'd have heard. Nor did this man look like the type who had built hospitals in far-flung African villages. And it seemed unlikely that he'd made millions through business ventures because he was here, in an NHS hospital, wearing cheap nylon pyjamas. Dean would have read it in a newspaper if his father had become a politician or a leader of industry.

He dared not ask what it was exactly Eddie Taylor had been searching for, and whether he had found it. He did not want to face the fact that he might have been abandoned so that his father could pursue a life of indulgence and womanising, because whilst that was how Dean spent most of his time, hearing his father admit to as much would somehow seem so mediocre. Anything but that.

'There was a woman,' Eddie said.

'Oh fuck.' Dean wanted to howl.

'Actually, there were loads of them. I wasn't designed for fidelity. I had appetites. I was young.'

'Not that young. You were thirty-four when you left. My age. I don't feel young.' He never had. Eddie closed his eyes once more. His breathing slowed a fraction. Dean did not want him to lose consciousness again. Not before he had his answers. 'Who was she?'

'She was posh. Married. Different to the others. I thought we could live better.'

'Because she was wealthy?'

'No, because she was *her*.'

It seemed an oddly romantic thing for the most selfish man on the planet to say, and Dean found himself asking, 'What happened?'

'She didn't want me once I was free. She stayed with her husband.'

Dean froze. He used every iota of self-control to hold his body in place. If he moved, even a fraction, he might start to flay and spin, break and smash. He might upturn the vital medical equipment that was reducing Eddie's pain; he might rip down the curtains that were offering the last shred of privacy and dignity. He might let out the scream that he'd swallowed for so many years. All that agony. All that sorrow. For pussy that didn't even want Eddie Taylor. He'd hated his father for so long and with such intensity, he'd never thought it was possible to hate anyone more, but now he found he did. He hated her, this woman, whoever she was, wherever she was. He hated her more.

10

Jo

I head back to my parents'. I can't think of anywhere else to go, which says it all really. As I sit on the tube, travelling towards Wimbledon, I think that I might as well be carrying a placard declaring 'THIRTY-FIVE-YEAR-OLD SCREW-UP'. I'm sure my failure is obvious to everyone; it pools around my feet like rainwater around an umbrella. How have I become this homeless, jobless, loveless woman? What will my parents think? They're the opposite. They don't have a hint of failure about them. They own *two* beautiful homes: the family home in Wimbledon and a ski lodge in the Alps. My father is an incredibly successful City analyst, and although Mum doesn't have a paid job, she's a faultless home-maker and she's also enthusiastically involved in raising funds for a number of worthy causes. In addition, they are the most loved-up couple you could hope to encounter. Even after all these years they still hold hands in public.

It's sickening, really.

My parents live in a prestigious four-storey detached house close to Wimbledon Common. My father's income and my mother's dedication to home decor has ensured that it's one of the most impressive and stylish homes most people could imagine stepping into, let alone living in. Floor-to-ceiling windows guarantee that light spreads throughout the house, allowing Mum to be bold with the colour scheme; the ground floor is awash with muted taupe and mushroom, but the tones deepen with each floor, culminating in the pewter and purple master bedroom at the top of the house. The entire place is elegantly fitted out. Carefully selected antique bureaus and writing desks nestle against daring Designer Guild wallpapers, while restored high-backed Queen Anne fireside chairs and slouchy retro leather sofas welcome guests. There are a large number of bookshelves that house early-edition classics as well as impressive contemporary literature. Original artwork hangs on the walls and magazines about antiques are placed carefully on occasional tables. It always smells as though the windows have been open and the summer wind has just drifted through, even in the winter.

We moved to Wimbledon when I was a toddler. We initially lived in a pretty two-up, two-down Victorian cottage in the village on top of the hill, which Dad shrewdly sold when the market was buoyant, and then they rented and only bought when the market was flat again. With a cash offer and no chain they were able to move up by driving a hard bargain. This technique was repeated three times in total, and that strategy, combined with a healthy banker's bonus, allowed us to move into the current much bigger and more prestigious home just after I turned fourteen.

I love my parents' house. I think it's the epitome of success, order, elegance and romance. It's the sort of home every woman admires but few dare to aspire to. Every room is thoughtfully compiled and there's rarely a thing out of place. Yet despite the tidiness and sophistication, it's a comfortable home and people love to receive an invite to visit. My family has thrown numerous parties and countless dinners here; they're generous and impeccable hosts.

The only place in the entire house that ever causes me a

moment's discomfort is the master bedroom. The damson-coloured room at the top of the house is pure decadence. It spreads over an entire floor; there's an ornate superking-size bed slapped in the centre and a stunning freestanding rolltop bath in the corner. There's an antique crystal chandelier, an abundance of scented candles and numerous aged mirrors that Mum picked up at Portobello Market. It's the most romantic, sensuous, dreamy, intoxicating room imaginable, which is why it makes me feel uncomfortable. Even as a grown woman, I don't really like to associate my parents too closely with any of those adjectives. It's all a bit embarrassing.

I ring the bell, but there's no answer. Mum's car is on the drive but it's possible that she has ambled into town on foot; possible but unlikely. Mum's a creature of habit and she likes to walk to the shops on a Monday. Tuesday is art class, Wednesday is yoga, Thursday Pilates, but that finishes by 11.15, and Friday is a visit to her hairdresser's in Covent Garden. She should be at home. My parents' house also boasts a long garden full of mature trees. They make the most of it and often enjoy a morning coffee, lunch or an early evening cocktail out there. There's a chance that she's doing a spot of weeding, or simply admiring the majestic trees; they have endured a cold winter, but now their tight buds are unfurling and will soon develop into fleshy leaves. I check; she's not there. The house and garden are both serene and peaceful. Normally I take on their dignity and idealism by osmosis, but today, when I find the back garden empty, I return to the front, hammer impatiently on the door and yell through the letter box, 'Let me in!'

A couple of moments later, the door swings wide.

'Hello, darling.' My mother holds the door open but keeps one hand on the handle and the other stretched to the door frame, effectively creating a barrier.

'Aren't you going to invite me in?' I ask frantically.

'Well, actually, this isn't a good time. I was just—' I push past and stride into the hallway. 'It's so lovely of you to pop by and say happy anniversary, but Joanna, darling, it would have been better if you'd called. This is not a great time, because—'

'It's your anniversary?' I stop and turn to my mother. She nods. I shrug an embarrassed apology. 'Oh, happy anniversary. I'd forgotten.'

'So that isn't why you are here, then?'

'No.'

My mum clocks my clothes (crumpled black dress, no tights, unsuitable, dangerously high evening shoes) and my face (bleached white, evidence of crying, no make-up). 'I'll put the kettle on,' she says.

I follow her into the kitchen.

'Wow, you've redecorated, *again*,' I say, trying to take a polite interest, since I'd forgotten about their anniversary.

'Yes, we've just finished it.' Mum glances impassively around the blue-gloss, high-tech, minimalist kitchen. It isn't clear from her expression whether she prefers this experiment with modernity to the four-year-old ribbed-wood country kitchen that it has replaced. I think the change is a mistake but don't say so. Sometimes Mum's passion for interior decorating gets out of hand; she regularly guts a seemingly perfect room and redecorates. But then, what's the harm? Dad earns enough to indulge her hobby; indeed, he's also interested and they often spend an evening together happily poring over interior decorating magazines. I've read enough dating self-help books to know that all couples need a shared interest.

I take the white mug Mum's proffering and hoist myself up on to a high black leather bar stool, then immediately begin to tell my mother about the disastrous twenty-four hours I've just endured. I confess to getting 'close' to Jeff. Mum is astute enough to not only comprehend exactly what that means but also to refrain from commenting on either the idiocy or the repetitive nature of this particular sort of bad judgement call. Instead she offers up a large plate of home-made chocolate biscuits and makes reasonably sympathetic clucking sounds whenever I pause in my recounting.

I admit that I've been fired, which gets her attention.

'Oh Joanna! No.'

'In many offices, worldwide, there's a phenomenon whereby the golden girl – or boy – slowly but surely transforms into something much more lacklustre in the eyes of their employers.'

'I suppose.'

'And sometimes it is not their fault; they're victims of their circumstances. A change of personnel or a change of policy might bring about someone's downfall.'

'Right.'

I sigh and realise there's no point in lying to her. Or myself. I come clean. 'But in my case, I think I'm at least partially responsible. The truth is, my dream job has silently yet insidiously transformed into a bit of a nightmare. Month after month of documenting my disappointment as I've failed to meet Mr Right has taken its toll.'

'Well, yes. That's understandable, although you must have known that the column was finite,' she adds. 'You were no longer in a position to write with any authority.'

'Why?'

'You were writing a young woman's advice column about the opportunities and pitfalls of being single.'

'Well, I'm perfectly placed. I *am* single.'

'Yes, but darling, you're no longer actually . . .' Mum pauses, then clearly decides I need to hear it and adds, 'You're no longer *young*. It was becoming silly. Some of the women who read your early columns are not only wives themselves now but possibly mothers. What were you planning to do? Rebrand and keep writing it as a cougar column? "Snaring Mr Right"? Would you still be writing it as an OAP? A column on geriatric sex?'

'Mother!'

'I'm sorry, Joanna. I don't want to sound cruel, but working for this bridal magazine was never supposed to be *it*. It was supposed to be a spring board. That's what you always said.'

'Did I?'

'Yes.'

I can't remember ever saying any such thing. What could I have meant? 'I probably meant until I went to Chicago with Martin.'

'Well, until you found something else you were passionate about, other than planning weddings, at least,' says Mum. She pushes the plate of biscuits an inch closer to me. I've already eaten four. Mum never eats biscuits, or any snacks between meals, come to that. She's horribly disciplined.

I keep my eyes on the plate. Hot tears slip down my face, but by keeping my head down I hope my mother won't notice. It's humiliating. I'm too old to be weeping in my parents' kitchen. I try to sniff silently and will the tears to stop. It's confusing that whilst I feel pure fury towards Mum for speaking out like that, all I want is to be tightly wrapped in her arms. I want her to make it all better, make it all go away. Isn't that what mothers are for?

Truthfully, I know that my mum has never quite provided that unconditional succour that's supposed to flow from a mother to her daughter, not even when I was seven and lost my favourite teddy, so she's unlikely to do as much now that I'm thirty-five and have lost my only means of income. I don't associate Mum with overly indulgent comfort or cuddly warmth. I adore her, but when I think of my mum, I think of a graceful, sorted, practical woman. She would lend me her last pound (although she'd never be down to her last pound, as she sets great store by efficient financial planning) and could teach me to bake faultless filo pastry without getting into a flap, but she's unlikely to ever hold the tissue while I blow. She's the sort of woman I aspire to be but not the sort of woman who understands what I am. I don't want to be a snotty, sore mess, gulping regretfully into my tea. I'm sure that if *I'd* met and married and had the support of a faithful, loving and romantic man for countless years – as my mother has – I too would be chic, in control and, if the occasion needed it, aloof. It's a matter of confidence. It's a matter of luck.

'You know Martin gets married on Saturday,' I venture.

'Does he?'

'In Chicago.'

'How exciting.' I glare at her, because she's missing the point, but my glare falls flat as she has turned her back to me; she's chopping fresh mint to make more tea.

'I'm invited.'

'Lovely.'

'So I've got this hairbrained idea of flying out to Chicago to stop the wedding.' I try to sound as though I'm entirely joking, but I don't think I am.

'I always liked Martin,' Mum murmurs.

'I know you did.' I drop my head into my hands.

'I said you'd regret it,' she points out accurately, but unhelpfully.

'Yes, you did.'

'But I'm not one to gloat.'

'Hmmm.' Actually, she *is* a bit inclined towards feeling smug and frequently repeats the phrase 'I told you so', but I decide not to point out as much. I don't have it in me to fight with her. It seems the whole world hates me as it is and I can't afford to make any more enemies. Besides, I need somewhere to stay tonight. I really can't face going back to Lisa and Henry's sofa this evening; I need a room where I can close the door on the world.

Out of the corner of my eye I spot my mother's purple Carlton hard-shell spinner suitcase. Like all my mum's possessions it is impeccably stylish, modern and boasting the latest convenient additions (an extendable handle, pass-code zip lock and four wheels so that she can swish through airports and hotel foyers with effortless chic). I know that the case will be full of carefully selected and co-ordinated outfits and accessories. My mum is the sort of woman who always looks impeccable. Envy slithers through my body. Obviously my parents are going on a romantic weekend to celebrate their anniversary. They've been married for an eternity and yet they still have a more romantic relationship than any I've ever had. It's a big suitcase; maybe they're going away for a week, or even a fortnight. It simply isn't fair.

'You have no idea how lucky you are,' I say, not able to drag my eyes away from the suitcase.

'Why do you say that?'

'Dad loves you so much.'

'Well, we've been together for so long.'

'Yes, but it's not just about how long you've been together, is it? I know other couples that have been married a long time but they aren't as romantic as you and Dad are. You two are like some sort of fairy tale. I mean, Dad brings you flowers *every* Friday night.'

'Yes.'

'Always has.'

'Yes.' Mum shrugs. 'He says flowers are a way to celebrate the fact that the weekend has begun.'

'And he's always booking you little treats. Weekends away, spa days with your girlfriends, trips to the theatre and shows.'

'He's a very thoughtful man.'

'And he does everything with such style and consideration. You never go to the theatre without him ordering a bottle of champagne in the interval and buying a box of posh chocs. You have the perfect marriage.'

Mum finally stops chopping the mint and turns to me. 'All marriages require some—'

I don't let her finish. 'Do you know, I sometimes think it's the one thing that keeps me going.'

'Our marriage?'

'Yes.'

'Joanna, you're thirty-five.'

'And?'

Mum sighs. She might have wanted to say, 'And your parents' marriage shouldn't be the most important thing in your life.' But after some moments' consideration she says, 'Do you know what I think you should do, darling?'

'What?'

'You should go to Martin's wedding.'

I gawp at her. 'You think so?'

'Yes. A break will do you good and you might find some closure. What have you got to lose? It will be an adventure.'

'I'm not the adventurous type.'

'Well, maybe you should be.'

'But really, I can't remember when I did anything more adventurous than watching a scary movie.'

'Well there you go.'

My head hurts. I need more sleep before I make a decision on this scale. I bury my nose into a tissue and blow loudly, which means I only catch some of what my mother is saying. 'I mean, who is to say . . . what if you had married him . . . happier than you are now.'

Unbelievable. My mum has just agreed that I should try to stop Martin's wedding as I suggested. Well, I did not expect *that*, not in a month of Sundays. But why shouldn't I? He loved me once, didn't he? Yes, he did. And I loved him. Well, at least, I wanted to marry him, which is practically the same thing. I tune back into what Mum is saying. Something about it not being a good weekend to be here. No, it probably isn't, not if my parents are going away on a romantic break. The last thing I want is to be on my own in this enormous house, pottering around like a lost soul. My mother is saying that a trip away will clear my mind; allow me to get some perspective.

'Right? Isn't it worth a try?' she concludes.

'I suppose,' I mutter. I'm surprised. As a rule, my mother doesn't encourage confidences and moochy, ethereal, 'what if' conversations. Oddly, despite enjoying years of happy marriage, she is not known for her endorsement of big romantic gestures. She always seems faintly embarrassed whenever Dad does anything flamboyant. I remember the time he bought her a custom-painted soft-top Mini Cooper in fuchsia pink for her fiftieth birthday. He had it delivered, wrapped in the most enormous silver ribbon; I was practically weeping with joy, but she made him have it resprayed to a more subtle silver-grey. A colour he could probably have purchased for a lot less cash and bother in the first place. I guess that's what happens when you are faced with an embarrassment of riches. Mum's practical, not idealistic, considered rather than impulsive, and yet here she is suggesting that I travel four thousand miles to stop Martin's wedding taking place. She must think it will work. I feel a spike of elation. 'Don't marry her, marry me' is the pinnacle in romantic declarations. This is the sort of moment I live for.

11

Dean

'Zoe said it was a mistake me coming here.'

'Zoe?' For a moment Eddie looked blank.

'Your daughter,' Dean clarified, letting out a short, impatient sigh.

'Of course.' Eddie nodded his head a fraction.

'Well?'

'Well what?'

'Oh, forget it,' Dean snapped; this time his sigh was despairing. He turned and looked at the wall. He read the health and safety notices which told visitors what to do in the event of a fire and warned them against adjusting the beds or touching medical equipment. He wondered whether he was the only relative who had ever sat there and fantasised about pulling the plug. The thought didn't make him feel ashamed; it made him angry. His father's actions had meant he'd grown up livid, but sadly he was not livid enough to be blind and impervious as to what a pity that was. Both men settled back into another silence. Dean was resentful, Eddie was exhausted. Dean breathed deeply. The important thing was that he must not lose it. He could not let Eddie destroy him again. It had taken too long to build himself up to what he was.

Eddie grimaced and gestured to the syringe driver on the bedside table. Dean wanted to ignore him but he couldn't. He put it in Eddie's hands and the man pumped pain relief through his body again. He let out a low groan and then seemed to decide to give his son what he wanted. 'How is Zoe? Doing all right?'

'Good enough.' Dean forced himself to look at his father and was surprised to see that Eddie had arranged his features into an expression of interest. The effort elicited more information. 'She's an accountant. She's married.' The fact that his sister was married was a great source of surprise to Dean as well as a great source of comfort and pleasure. Zoe had managed to trust. She'd found someone to love, who loved her back. A case of what Dean believed to be hope triumphing over experience, but he was glad. Her husband was a good man; solid and dependable. 'She married young, over six years ago now, to a bloke twelve years her senior.'

'Figures.'

'Yes.'

'Father replacement,' Eddie rasped.

'Yes.' Dean was stupefied by the man's perception, combined with his indifference.

'My other two did the same,' added Eddie casually.

'Other two?' Dean felt his blood slow in his veins.

'My other two daughters by my second marriage.'

'You're married?'

Eddie coughed. 'Not any more.'

'I have sisters?' Dean's blood suddenly speeded up again, lurching around his body. He was dizzy. Of course he'd considered it, from time to time, when he was a child. It had seemed the most reasonable explanation for the fact that his father had never once contacted them, in all those years. It was clear that he'd written off his first family in their entirety. They'd been replaced. There was another family.

It had always been a possibility, so why did the actuality still come as such a shock? He had two more sisters. What were they like? Were they anything like Zoe?

'I have sisters?' He repeated the phrase to see if it seemed any more real.

'Yes. Well, half-sisters, technically, I suppose. One is shacked up with a bloke who has two teenage lads. She's like a mother to them.' Eddie struggled for breath. 'Although she's only twenty-three herself. The other is still at uni, I think, but the last I heard she was dating her tutor.'

Where were these sisters? What were their names? Why weren't they here? Dean did not ask these questions aloud, but Eddie must have read his mind, or at least followed his thought pattern.

'Ellie, the student, lives in France with their mother. And Hannah, she lives down south, near the coast. Plymouth or somewhere. I can't remember. We're not in touch often.'

Of course not. More broken hearts. More disappointed children. This man was hopeless, useless. Dean seethed. It was clear that the more he got to know his father, the less there would be to like about him. Not that he had expected anything else.

Dean listened to the sounds of the hospital. He could hear a nurse's feet clip-clopping along the corridor; she was talking to a patient who must be sitting in a wheelchair; he could hear the chair squeaking. He recognised the sound of the elevator clunking to a standstill on this floor and a door slamming somewhere further in the distance. It was time to go. There was nothing for him here.

He was about to pull himself up off the seat when Eddie asked quietly, 'Is Zoe happy?'

The question stunned Dean. He coughed. 'On the whole.'

'The marriage. The marriage specifically. Is it a happy marriage?'

'Yes.'

'Good.'

Dean was exasperated and confused. What did it mean that his father still thought being married was a good thing? Did he regret the breakdown of his own marriage? Either of them? Both of them? Dean wasn't sure. However, he was aware that something had shifted slightly. Deep, deep, as far down as it was possible to go in his stomach – which had been forever clenched with stress – something loosened a fraction of a fraction.

Because his father cared whether Zoe's marriage was a happy one.

It wasn't much. It wasn't enough. It was very late in the day, but Dean recognised that it was something. He wouldn't leave yet. Still, he hesitated. Did his father deserve to know? Was it his news to share? What would Zoe say? Her voice was as clear as a bell in his head. *I don't want to know anything about him. I don't want details. Don't talk to me about him again. Not until you call to tell me he's dead.* She didn't want details, but she hadn't said Dean mustn't *give* any details.

'She has two kids,' blurted Dean.

'I'm a grandfather?'

'Oh yes, it's all about you.'

Eddie seemed to choose to ignore Dean's sarcasm, or maybe he really was so selfish that he didn't pick up on it at all. Dean wasn't sure.

'So what are these kids like, then? Boys? Girls?'

'One of each. Archie is three and Hattie is nearly a year old.'

'Do you have a photo?' The raspy tone didn't entirely mask the fact that there was some level of excitement.

Dean pulled out his phone; it was loaded with dozens and dozens of pictures of his niece and nephew. He held it in front of Eddie and began to flick through the images. The infants' gappy grins flooded into the room. Dean smiled back at them as they splashed in swimming pools, made sandcastles and licked ice creams. He didn't think he was imagining it; he was pretty sure that Eddie's breathing quickened a little. Of course, who could resist Archie's unapologetic beam and Hattie's guileless grin? No one with a beating heart. All the women that Dean showed these photos to oohed and aahed and swore the kids were the cutest they'd ever seen.

Dean felt emboldened by the digital presence of his niece and nephew; they always made him feel better. They made everything seem OK. 'I can get you one printed off, if you like,' he offered, plunging.

'No. It's OK.' Eddie turned away from the phone and looked out of the window again, snuffing out Dean's embryonic compassion and hope.

A deluge of fury streamed through Dean's body and erupted like boiling lava. He couldn't stand the kids being rejected. 'Fuck you, I'm going.' He leapt to his feet.

'Why?' Eddie was genuinely puzzled.

'Because you, you . . .' He didn't know how to finish the sentence. 'Because you don't care about Zoe's kids,' he exploded. It was only part of what he wanted to say.

Eddie appeared surprised. Perhaps he thought he'd shown due interest. 'The lad looks like a bright enough boy. The girl's too young to tell. What can I say? Chubby?'

'She's a baby! She's supposed to be chubby.'

'I didn't say otherwise. They look like strong little nippers.'

The two men glared at one another. The tension sizzled in the air.

'What do you want from me?' Eddie asked eventually.

Dean shook his head. He was the one who had been summoned. What did Eddie want from him?

'I think we both know it's a bit late to be trying for Grandpa of the Year award,' Eddie snapped as sharply as his weak chest would allow; he glanced towards the drip that hung above him.

'Yes it is, isn't it? It's all a bit late. For me, for Zoe.'

'So this isn't about the kids at all. It's about you.'

'Yes, maybe it is.' Dean turned away from the bed. He was jet-lagged, this situation was surreal and the lack of sleep was adding to the overwhelmingly emotional scenario. He couldn't think clearly. He collapsed back into the bedside chair. It wasn't so much that he'd decided to stay; he simply didn't have it in him to leave.

Eddie said nothing for a moment, allowing his son to settle. They both needed to get their breath back. Just when Dean thought they might get stuck in the quagmire of silence once again, Eddie asked, 'How is your mother?'

Dean was blindsided by the question. He never thought of his father in relation to his mother. They were too separate to comprehend any sort of connection. He only ever thought of them in relation to himself and Zoe, or more specifically, their lack of relationship with either him or Zoe. He didn't know how to answer the question.

At last he said, 'She took your desertion very hard.'

'Desertion.' Eddie snorted. He almost sounded amused. Dean wanted to hit the button that made the bed rise or lower. He had a brief flash of the comedic moment that so frequently appeared in cartoons where it folded in on itself, crushing the patient. He knew *desertion* was dramatic; it dragged with it connotations of terrified soldiers shot at dawn during the First World War, but it was a fitting word. The wilful abandonment of a post of duty. What his father had done was dramatic. It was life-defining.

'She started drinking,' he added, peeved that he needed to introduce the subject but determined that his father should know the extent of the repercussions of his actions.

'She was a party girl when I met her.' Eddie smiled, missing the point entirely. No doubt he was enjoying flashbacks to their headier days together.

'She stopped being a party girl; she became more of a solitary drinker. At least that's how I remember her,' muttered Dean. 'An alcoholic.'

The fact was still desolate, stark, unpalatable. No matter how often he had had to confess this over the years – to himself and to carers – he never got used to it.

'Everyone likes a drop.' Eddie's eyes crept to the floor. 'I suppose there was always the chance she might turn to drink. Fewer calories in a gin than a meal. Plus, she had that side to her. An extreme, addictive nature.'

'You knew that, yet still you left us with her?'

Chastised, Eddie moved his shoulders a fraction. He didn't dare shrug boldly.

'Anyway, look at you.' Eddie's glance took in Dean's expensive suit. 'You're a success. It all worked out.' Dean wasn't sure who Eddie was comforting.

'You took away the normality when you left.'

'I didn't.'

'You did. Or at least any chance we had at it.'

'It doesn't exist, son. I don't know what being normal is. I couldn't have helped you there.'

'She was in and out of recovery for years. And we, Zoe and I, we were in and out of care and emergency foster homes.'

'Care homes? Why were you ever put in care homes?'

'So somebody could take care of us. At least, that was the theory. Initially she drank to forget her disappointment. Then she forgot everything. They kept taking us off her. Or . . . or she'd just drop us off at the social services when she'd had enough or fancied a binge.'

Eddie did not allow his face to move. Dean appreciated this

restraint because Eddie had no right to be horrified; it was his fault, he was responsible and that meant he didn't get to be outraged.

'We've been in four care homes. Four. Those places aren't like Butlins holiday camps, you know.'

'I wasn't aware. Why didn't anyone tell me?'

'No one knew where to find you.'

'I went abroad for a while. France.'

Dean imagined his father sitting at a table outside a café, in a cobbled street streaked with sunlight; he was drinking red wine and tucking into a delicious bloody steak and a crisp green salad. There was a beautiful French woman in the picture too; she had dark, intelligent eyes and very white teeth. Perhaps his second wife, perhaps another mistress. This image contrasted starkly with the thought of his and Zoe's Hansel and Gretel existence. They'd huddled together, no one to protect them, no one to take care of them.

'I don't give a toss that you were in France. You left us, you rotten sod. You left us,' Dean spat furiously. He was surprised that he'd been so honest. Normally he avoided saying anything he really meant. Zoe said that was why he worked in advertising.

'It's not my fault your mother drank.'

'Isn't it?' Dean hissed, trying to regain some control. He crossed his hands over his body, to keep them far away from his father; it was an idiotic protest. What did he think might happen? That his father might suddenly lurch for his hand and hold it tight? It seemed unlikely. It seemed impossible.

'Still, like I said, it's turned out OK, hasn't it? You said yourself your sister is doing well. Married, a mother, an accountant. And you, you're . . .' Eddie broke off. He hadn't asked Dean what he did for a living. In fact he hadn't asked him anything about himself at all. Dean filled him in.

'I'm a board account director for a successful international advertising agency.' Dean hated himself for sounding like a kid coming home with a grade A in maths, waiting for his dad to pat him on his head.

'You sell ad space. It's all worked out.'

'Yes, we're fine,' snapped Dean. Another silence cloaked the room.

12

Clara

After Jo had left, Clara felt the need for fresh air. She didn't like walking aimlessly so she decided she'd go out and buy some flowers. True, Tim usually bought them on a Friday, which was very kind, but now and again Clara wished she could put her own arrangement together; that *she* could choose the flowers. It was a small thing to wish to control. Now she had seized the opportunity, she'd gone a bit over the top.

'Special occasion?' the young man serving in the shop had asked.

'Yes, my wedding anniversary.'

'Lovely.'

She'd selected dramatic heliconia, protea and anthuriums in bright scarlet and vibrant orange. She'd bought so many that the young man had had to deliver them; she couldn't possibly stagger home under their weight. She'd filled every vase in the house with blooms. There were flowers in the hallway, above the fireplace, on the dining-room table and three occasional tables; she didn't bother taking any up to the bedroom. They'd smell horribly this time next week – there really wasn't anything worse than the stench of rotting foliage – but that wasn't her concern. She opened the windows in the sitting room and plumped the cushions into more pristine shapes. Then she turned her attention to carefully selecting her outfit; what she wore was so very important tonight.

Clara was fifty-six years old. Was she now officially an old woman? she wondered. Or could she still squeeze into the middle-aged category? Who lived to one hundred and twelve? Who would want to? When did one admit to oneself that one was old? She clearly remembered the first time a shop assistant had called her madam rather than miss. It was a long time after she'd become a wife and even a mother; it shouldn't have been a shock, but it was. Then there was the first time someone stood up to offer her their seat on the tube. It was a handsome European boy. Maybe Spanish or Italian. She'd told herself he was flirting, it was a courtesy, anything rather than the fact that he thought she was old enough to be entitled to the privilege of a seat on crowded public transport. The thing was, she didn't feel her age, so it was always such a shock to register it.

She knew she was a good-looking fifty-six; her high cheekbones still jutted out at a spectacular angle, and the rest of her flowed elegantly from that point. She wished she didn't care what she looked like. She wished she was the sort of woman who just *was*. They were rare but wonderful. But she had always been the sort of woman who was described as 'looking the part'; indeed, that was how she had become the part. It would be a relief to shrug that off. Ageing had its compensations, though no one ever talked about them. By the time you were old enough to appreciate them, you were generally past the age of having to brag about anything at all, so dignified beauty rarely got a mention. But it was real. She knew what she wanted now. After all this time. She'd worked herself out, and that was a marvellous thing. Her eyes sparkled more tonight than they had for many years.

Some changes were to be expected, of course, and however many Pilates classes she attended or however expensive and regular her facials were, she could not alter that. The skin round her eyes was baggier than it used to be, she was more wrinkled, and yes, the flesh below her chin and her upper arms tended to flop about more than she'd ideally like, but she was always careful to hold her head up high and she avoided sleeveless dresses. Her best years, in terms of beauty, were undoubtedly behind her; she'd be insane to kid herself that anything other was the case. Her décolletage and cheeks used to be plumper and smoother when she was in her early twenties, but she'd been a little awkward in those days, unsure. Until she met him, that was. Of course, nothing was the same after that. Everything changed. Clara used to spend a lot of time wondering whether things had changed for the better or the worse, but it had been impossible to decide. She'd stopped thinking about it in those terms and just accepted it for what it was. A shameful mistake or a sweet memory: either way it was part of her history. She hadn't thought about him for so long, but since the letter it was almost impossible to think about anything else.

Her prime time had been her thirties. Then she'd combined a youthful vigour with a new-found confidence. That had dulled a little since, over the years, inevitable given her situation with Tim. It was hard to continue to feel desirable, impossible to kid oneself one was still youthful. Yet undeniably there was something rather gorgeous about her this evening. She'd reignited.

She showered and then moisturised practically every inch of her body. Her skin gratefully drank in the luxurious creams. She chose her underwear carefully. Big, helpful pants, the kind that held everything exactly where it ought to be; even though she didn't have too much spare flesh that might threaten to move around, she didn't want to take any chances. She picked out an extremely pretty bra, a structured one that created a cleavage where there wasn't much of one. She'd had a blow-dry today, even though it wasn't her regular day, and she'd treated herself to a mini mani-pedi. Finally she selected her Chanel skirt suit, in blush. It was cotton tweed, with a cream leather collar and pearl button details. It made her gasp when she put it on, even now, even though she'd worn it on half a dozen occasions. It was so beautiful. It would shield her. She glanced in the mirror. It was a bittersweet reflection. She was an elegant woman, beautiful for her age. She was simply older than she wanted to be. Why had it taken her so long?

Tim arrived home at eight. He'd made an effort, as she'd asked him to. Often he wasn't home until much later; sometimes he didn't come home at all on a Thursday. She smiled appreciatively as she handed him a glass of decent chilled Sauvignon Blanc.

'I thought it might be champagne,' he commented.

'I considered it, but it seemed a little too . . .'

'Bubbly?'

'Yes.'

They clinked glasses out of habit, and wandered into the sunroom. After a disappointing day, the sun was finally trying to make an appearance. Streams of light filtered through the window, making the room feel airy, and the view of the garden, now dotted with daffodils and crocuses, was impressive; Clara hoped it would be enough to keep them buoyant. Tim threw himself back into the couch; Clara perched on the edge.

'So you are still sure you want to do this?' he asked. Straight to the point; there was no other thought in their minds.

'Yes.' Clara was surprised that tears instantly pricked her eyes. Damn them. She'd wanted to remain calm; she normally found it easy to do so. After years of masking what she was actually thinking and feeling, why would she cry now, now when she was telling the truth? She blinked furiously, willing them to go away. 'I have to.'

'Well, that's simply not true, Clara. You don't *have* to. We've managed very well as we are for almost forty years. There's no reason at all to upset the apple cart at this stage. There's the children to consider.'

'They are hardly children any more. Two of them are married. Lisa is a mother three times over.'

'But Joanna?'

'Yes.' Clara sighed. Joanna was a worry. She was still a child, in a way. Today, Clara had come so close to telling her daughter that she simply had to grow up, get on with it. Sweet and whimsical was just a birthday away from silly and inefficient. Haphazard and chaotic. 'She visited today,' Clara said as she took a sip of her wine. It was crisp and refreshing; the citrus notes played on her tongue, separating themselves out from the mineral tones. Clara knew her wines; she'd taken a masters course a few years ago. She'd taken lots of courses over the years: philosophical appreciation of art, interior design, A level Spanish, Buddhist meditation . . .

'Did she?'

'Yes. For one awful moment, I thought she knew. She kept staring at my suitcase.'

'Has she guessed?'

'No, of course not. She came round to talk about her own problems.' Clara bit her tongue to avoid adding, *as usual*. Instead she said, 'She's feeling twitchy because Martin is getting married.'

'Martin?'

'The one she was going to marry.'

'Oh yes, of course. How could I have forgotten? That fiasco cost us an arm and a leg.'

'He's marrying someone else.'

Tim couldn't see the problem. 'Well, she didn't want him.'

'No.'

'But now she does?'

'She wants someone. She's been invited to the wedding. I told her to go. I said that watching the wedding might offer some sort of closure. Help her move on. Besides, I didn't want her around here this weekend.'

'That's my point. She's vulnerable. She's going to take this very badly.'

'Tim, I can't stay for the children. Most people do that for eighteen years, not thirty-eight.'

Tim sighed and looked directly at his wife. 'If not the children, then for me.'

'It's different now. You don't need a wife.'

'I like having you around.' He smiled, perhaps embarrassed by the scanty nature of the compliment. She knew he always said less than he thought. He wasn't one to lavish declarations. Stiff upper lip and all that. He belonged in another world.

'Yes, and I like being around you, too,' she admitted.

'Then stay. I've always been discreet. We've managed it well. I've looked after you. Clothes, cars, the house, the holidays.' Tim glanced around the room, but the perfection sneered back at him.

'I know, but it's not enough. I'm surprised I ever thought it might be.' She handed him the letter.

FRIDAY 22 APRIL 2005

13

Jo

The familiar dial of a phone connecting me to Martin, thousands of miles away, causes my stomach to lurch in a way that reminds me of being a teenager.

'Martin? Martin, it's Jo.' There's a slight pause, which is the worst. 'Jo Russell,' I gabble, squashing down the embarrassment that's threatening to ambush. The pause between us swells.

'Of course. Jo. Well, hi.' Martin sounds jovial enough; at least he manages to be so the split second after he places my name. His not recognising my voice, possibly not remembering me at all, hurts, obviously. A sudden, searing hot pain, like a sharp knife, slices its way through my body. Quickly I remind myself that it's sometimes the case, when cut by a sharp knife, that you don't actually feel anything until the moment you see the blood and your brain acknowledges the damage. If I choose to ignore the blood and refuse to concede an injury, I might just avoid feeling the pain. To be fair, he hasn't heard my voice in nearly five years; not unsurprisingly, he never forwarded me his American telephone number. I've had to call three mutual friends to track it down; no one seemed keen to pass it on.

'How *are* you?' I ask in what, even for me, is an exaggeratedly upbeat tone.

'Great, just great.' He pauses, and then remembers his manners. 'And you?'

'Great.' I realise I sound like a parrot, so quickly add, 'Wonderful.'

I should have rehearsed this call. I don't want him to think I'm wonderful. Not exactly. I need to explain that I'm wonderful aside from the fact that he's no longer in my life. Almost wonderful. Definitely doing well, practically thriving, certainly still a very interesting and desirable person, but just one who is lacking Martin Kenwood in her life. 'Well, you know,' I add, hoping that covers it. 'You?' I ask again, taking the conversation in a rather bland and pointless full circle.

'Great, great, yes.'

'The wedding?' I prompt.

'Great,' he adds again. His tone of voice definitely alters, but I can't quite work out if he sounds more or less enthusiastic about his wedding versus his general well-being. 'Sorry, I'm not exactly with it right now.' Is there a crisis? A problem with the wedding? My heart lifts a little. 'It's late here, well, early. The middle of the night, actually.'

Oh no. Why didn't I think of that? My heart plummets. Why hadn't I thought of that? I decide that all I can do is bluff it out. I push on. 'You must be busy.'

'Not me so much as my fiancée. She's doing all the hard work and rushing around.'

I try to listen out for a hint of impatience or frustration. Arranging a wedding is notoriously stressful. Many previously blissful couples fight like warlords on the run up to the nuptials. Is he being overwhelmed by a bossy and controlling Bridezilla (let's face it, like last time)? And if so, is it annoying him? That would be something. Or is he indifferent to the wedding preparations because, ultimately, he's not that committed to getting married? That would be ideal. I can't tell. Of course there's the chance he's relieved that she's doing all the work and intends to be eternally grateful. That thought is uncomfortable. I also wonder whether it means anything that he called her his fiancée rather than using her actual name? It sounds a bit forced and contrived. Shouldn't they be more relaxed with one another? On the other hand, maybe he just likes saying fiancée and is going to be one of those men who, rather than using their wife's actual name, forever refers to 'her indoors', 'the missus' or 'my better half', just so everyone in the vicinity is clear that he's attached. I already know I'll say 'hubby'.

'So are you . . . erm . . . looking forward to the big day?' I am unsure why I am falling back on clichés and the safety of small talk. That isn't the direction I want to take this conversation, but I'm out of the habit of talking to Martin, especially about important things, if I ever mastered that habit in the first place.

'Absolutely. Of course.' Martin coughs. However excited he may or may not be about the big day, he can't be oblivious to how weird this situation is. After all, *we* were once going to get married. We were going to share a big day, and now here we are talking about his impending wedding to someone else.

'Nervous?' I ask, trying to probe as to his true feelings.

'A bit,' he replies. 'Everyone keeps reassuring us that it will all run like clockwork. You know the sort of thing: that the caterers will nail the timing of the soufflé. I'm not concerned about that level of detail. I just hope she shows up.' He starts to laugh. It's a slightly manic laugh. I join in nervously; obviously I realise he's referencing our own marriage plans. It's not helpful to me if he dwells on the end bit of our relationship (when is that ever helpful?), but at least he is acknowledging that we have a history. Now all I have to do is guide him back to more exhilarating times. We were once very happy.

'It's good to hear you laugh,' I gush. Not mentioning the hint of mania in the joviality.

'Oh Jo, did you think I stopped laughing for ever?' His

directness floors me, because yes, I suppose I had thought that. Plus, there's something more. I'm not being direct with him, I daren't be, but he feels he can cut to the chase with me. I'm encouraged that such intimacy still flows between us.

'I hoped not.' I lower my voice and try to make it as flirty and seductive as possible. I shove meaning and weight into every word. Like an overfull sausage I add, 'I like your laugh.'

Martin immediately stops laughing. He's clearly unused to a compliment, as he's a bit of an idiot when it comes to receiving them. 'Right,' he says stiffly.

Undeterred, I push on. 'So, I got your invite.'

'You never replied.' This time I am sure I can hear disappointment, but it might be that he's disappointed at my lapse of etiquette rather than the fact that on receiving the invite I didn't call him up and beg him not to go ahead. It's hard to be sure.

'Didn't I? How terrible of me. These things . . . well, this thing in particular is so . . .' I pause, 'delicate.'

'Suppose.'

'I wasn't sure how to reply.'

'It's simple, really. A yes-or-no situation.' We must both be thinking about the last time we were in a particularly profound yes/no situation. When I said yes. Then no. I feel horrible. I giggle nervously; it's better than being sick.

'Well, the funny thing is, I wasn't sure exactly what the invitation meant.'

'In what way?'

'Well . . .' I take a deep breath. 'Do you want me to come?'

'That's usually the accepted understanding behind an invite,' points out Martin.

'I mean, now, do *you* want me to come *now*?' He must understand. If I come *now*, it's not just as any old guest – one who returned the RSVP in the prepaid envelope three months ago; if I come now, it means *something*. It possibly means *everything*. My attendance or non-attendance is charged. 'You see, I could. The funny thing is, I'm at the airport. I'm standing just in front of the ticket sales desk. I could just about get there in time. Before it all takes place. Before it's all over, if that's what you want.' He must understand what I mean.

'Well, because we didn't hear back from you, we haven't counted you in.'

We. It's such a tiny word, but lethal. I don't know what to say to stave off its cruelty. 'Oh gosh, I hadn't thought about that. I don't want to mess up the seating plan.' This is a ridiculous observation, because if I do go to Chicago and explain to Martin that I have made a grave mistake in letting the opportunity of being his wife pass me by, then my hope is that there won't be a reception, and seating plans – flawless or muddled – will be redundant. I think about his sentence and scrutinise it for a layer of coded meaning. Of course, he's duty-bound to say *we*, but if he means *I*, then that innocuous sentence has altogether a different meaning. 'Because I didn't hear back from you, I haven't counted you in' could very well mean that he was gutted that I didn't respond to his emotional SOS.

I'm even more convinced that my decoding is accurate when he adds, 'Well, I'm sure we can sort something out, find room for you.' He's practically begging me.

I don't tell him it doesn't matter, that we won't be getting as far as the wedding breakfast, because that would be putting the cart before the horse. Instead I say, 'Don't put me on the children's table, will you? Do you remember my cousin Harriet's wedding? We had to sit with all the little bridesmaids.' I laugh, pretending that it was a happy or at least amusing memory, although at the time I was furious and it wasn't much fun.

'Erm.' Martin sounds a bit confused. I'm surprised that he is clearly struggling to recall the catastrophe; it was quite a big deal at the time, at least to me.

'You must remember. To add insult to injury, they served us the kids' menu too. Chicken nuggets and chips, while all the other guests had roast lamb with dauphinoise potatoes. Of course it was a genuine mistake. Harriet was mortified, but still.'

'We did go to a lot of weddings,' murmurs Martin. We did. We were in our late twenties; everyone we knew was dashing down the aisle. When I called off our wedding, I explained to my parents that that had been half the problem. There was immense pressure to accept the proposal. It had seemed like the obvious thing to do, the next step. Then it hadn't. Now it does again. This is so confusing. Martin adds, 'There were so many weddings, they were all a blur in the end.'

'This one won't blur,' I say ominously.

'No. Of course not.' Martin can't be expected to understand what I am hinting at. 'So, that's it decided, you're coming?' he asks. I know him well enough to remember the tone of his voice when he's thrilled by something; he's practically giggling like a schoolboy. 'You're sure. This time?'

He couldn't be clearer.

'I'll book a ticket.'

So I gather every ounce of courage and belief I possess and blow a sum that is the equivalent of the deposit for a three-bedroom house in some parts of the UK on an economy ticket to Chicago. I am forced to tie myself down to a return date because that is the slightly cheaper option; even so, I still have to split the cost across two credit cards. An open return is out of the question because I don't think Boots loyalty points are a viable currency. I'm quite concerned: will a return flight on Monday give Martin enough time to pack his bags?

I love airports. They combine – in abundance – three of my favourite things, *ever*. They're full of excitement (people are speeding off on wonderful holidays or to invigorating business meetings) and drama (people call out welcoming greetings or collapse into difficult goodbyes) and shops. Excitement, drama, shops, what's not to love? As I gaze around, I wonder how many momentous events are occurring in this very terminal, at this very second. How many declarations of love, how many hearts snapping?

I haven't taken a long-haul flight since before Martin and I split up. We used to travel together a lot; we visited New York, Thailand and Madrid. We planned to go on honeymoon to the Seychelles. I was so excited about that trip: tropical paradise islands, cobalt seas and endless white sand beaches; of course I was excited. I've often imagined since what that trip might have been like; it's impossible not to wonder. I bought three beautiful new bikinis, a floral beach bag and a huge straw sunhat especially. I spent weeks planning exactly what I'd look like lying under a parasol, the waves licking my toes, the gentle breeze brushing my limbs. After I called off the wedding, Martin came to some arrangement with the travel agent and exchanged our would-have-been-romantic honeymoon for a wild trip to Las Vegas with two of his mates. Word got back to me that for six days in a row he drank, gambled and passed out on dance floors.

I didn't indulge in anything similarly healing or commemorative. Swamped in the shame of knowing I'd hurt Martin severely and cost my parents a fortune, I didn't feel entitled to whiz away anywhere exotic, even though my friends and Lisa advised me that it would be a good idea. I've travelled since the split, but shorter distances. I've had three mini-breaks with three different boyfriends. Liam and I flew to Copenhagen; with Jamie I visited Rome; and it was Paris with Ben. I can't remember much about the airport from any of those trips, as on each occasion, I was consumed with giddy excitement. At least, I was on the outward journey; the returns were all considerably more downbeat. Truthfully, I probably do have a tendency to be a little bit too optimistic about the significance of a guy asking a woman to go on a mini-break; on each occasion I was devastated that a proposal wasn't forthcoming. I'm not saying that I'd have married any one of them, but I am saying I would have liked to be *asked* by one of them.

'Why do they even want to go abroad, if not to propose?' I asked Lisa forlornly after the third disappointment. I tend to think of Lisa – a married woman – as the font of all knowledge when it comes to stuff about men (but only if I like what she says). My sister just rolled her eyes and suggested, 'Great weather, food, architecture, or just to get drunk.'

'I know, I know there's all that stuff. I'd just enjoy it more if I thought it was to be shared on an ongoing basis,' I admitted forlornly. Then Lisa invited me along to a two-week all-inclusive family break in Spain.

'Won't I be in the way?' I asked.

'No, we see you as an on-tap babysitter,' Lisa replied; she wasn't entirely joking. That holiday was fun (noisy, chaotic and exhausting), and the huge beach bag finally came in useful for carrying spare nappies, blow-up beach balls and buckets and spades. But somehow it made me miss my honeymoon more not less.

OK, so. Onwards and upwards. Deep breath. It's essential that I approach this trip with some Zen-like thoughts. I have to put good karma out there, because obviously I am asking quite a lot of the universe in terms of return investment, I realise that. I have to be positive and calm. I need to be focused and determined. Truthfully I feel a dangerous mix between giddy with excitement and sick with nerves. I replay the conversation I had with Martin again and again in my head. If I think about my plan for any length of time I begin to feel a bit faint. The only possible answer is not to think about it for any length of time.

I distract myself by wandering around the duty-free shops,

spraying expensive fragrances and gleefully snaffling up any available freebie samples of tinted moisturiser. I dawdle around the luxury clothes shop, lusting after outfits that I can't afford. It's an odd comfort that I can at least tell myself that even if I *could* afford these gorgeous clothes, I don't have anywhere to wear them now I'm unemployed. Of course, if I wasn't unemployed I'd have had occasion to wear them and I might have been able to afford them too; again I decide not to dwell on this fact for long. Not comfortable. Not helpful.

I spend an age in WH Smith as I want to pick out something to read on the plane. As usual, I naturally gravitate towards the self-help books and I'm gratified to find a new title that I haven't read (I've read most of them). *Hook Him. Have Him. Hold on to Him: a modern woman's guide to maintaining relationships*. I flick through to see if there's a section that offers tips on hijacking someone else's wedding. Not too surprisingly, there isn't. But there is a chapter that claims to address 'The ten grave errors to avoid that most women make with men' and another that promises to reveal 'The differences in how men and women think about dating, sex and relationships'. Frankly I think that section probably needs more than one chapter; have they glossed? Still, I decide to buy the book.

I'm so engrossed in chapter two that I nearly miss the announcement over the loudspeaker that rather stiffly instructs passenger Joanna Russell to make her way to boarding gate number 24, as the plane to Chicago O'Hare International is ready to depart.

Panicked, my promise to have Zen thoughts is pushed aside as I run through the airport, faster than I've ever run before, inwardly cursing my disorganisation. My feet slap down painfully on the tiled floor as I duck and dive to avoid other passengers making their way to their flights, most of whom seem to be walking in the opposite direction to the one I need to go in; I'm a fish swimming upstream. The relief when I spot gate 24 and four airline staff, standing like soldiers, is tremendous. I try to ignore the fact that they're all glaring at me icily.

'Sorry, sorry, sorry,' I yell as I approach. I always think it's best to get in there with the apologies as soon as possible; it disarms people, because we live in a world where no one takes responsibility for anything and so saying sorry has the surprise effect of being at least novel. No one acknowledges my apology but no one actively shouts at me, so I'm relieved. In silence one woman takes my boarding pass and starts to type something into the computer. The other three share looks of irritation. The run through the airport has left me breathless; I try not to show that I am panting but I can feel the beginnings of a stitch in my waist and sweat is trickling down my back. It's not a good look or a good feeling. Welcome to my world.

'I'm sorry, but there's a problem with your seat,' says the chilly airline lady at the computer.

'What problem?' I ask fearfully.

'You were allocated the bulkhead seat but we've given that to a passenger who is travelling with an infant.'

I feel a surge of indignation. It isn't fair. The woman with the infant is in a relationship (or even if she isn't in one right now, she has been; after all, that's how babies are made), and yet she has my comfortable bulkhead seat *too*. Some women have all the luck.

'In fact, I'm afraid we've completely oversold in the economy section of the plane.'

'But I just booked that seat a couple of hours ago; they said they released it last minute. I've got a ticket. It was a really expensive ticket.'

The airline woman holds up one beautifully manicured hand, which effectively silences me. She continues to type something with the other hand. 'And we're also oversold in World Traveller Plus.'

'This is exactly why we advise our passengers to build in plenty of time at the airport,' adds one of the other members of staff stiffly. I glare at him but don't bother to mention that I sneaked out of Lisa's at 5.30 this morning and have been here since 6.45. It took me three hours to gather the courage to call Martin and buy the ticket; I've spent another two hours in the terminal shops. I know he doesn't care.

'I *have* to get on this plane,' I insist. 'I'm going to a wedding. It's vital I get on the plane.'

I slam my book down on the counter. I'm not particularly trying to make a statement or a commotion, that's not my way. I'm simply exasperated. The woman behind the computer fidgets from one foot to the other, anticipating a row. She looks to the counter in an effort to avoid my gaze and then she clocks the title of the book. Suddenly her chilly manner shifts, like a glacier cracking, and her face collapses into a broad beam. Not a mocking grin, but a wide, warm, sympathetic smile. She puts her ringless hand on my arm and I recognise her as a sister; we both know it can be cold out there. She says, 'I don't think we have any alternative; we're going to have to upgrade you to club class.'

14

Dean

Dean had hardly been aware that there was a delay in the scheduled departure, although he had felt the rumblings of low-level dissatisfaction in the passengers surrounding him. They'd shuffled in their seats, glugged back more free champagne than was wise at this time of the morning and rattled their newspapers impatiently. Dean had stayed dead still in his chair, drained beyond an ability to fidget. He was just glad to be back in his comfort zone. This was where he belonged, a plush business-class seat rather than an unyielding hospital visiting chair. When the tardy passenger who'd caused the delay finally stumbled through the aircraft door, there was a furtive chorus of fractious grumbles. Dean didn't contribute. It seemed petty.

Hers was the seat next to his. No sooner had she sat down than she leapt up again and started to bundle her bags into the overhead locker. He'd planned on ignoring her completely, but as she struggled to put her luggage away, she lost her grip on her book and it fell, hitting his shoulder. As he retrieved it, his eyes slipped over the blurb.

What to do if your man has a roving eye . . . How to cheat-proof your relationship . . . The top three things women do that irritate men and kill confidence.

Dean had been drowning under a tide of anguish and trauma, but he came up for air and thanked God that at least he wasn't a woman. He wondered who published this crap. Who read it? As he handed the book back to the person who'd dropped it on him, he was surprised to discover that extremely attractive women – with great tits, cute smiles and straight teeth – read this crap.

'I am so sorry, did I hurt you?' she asked.

'I'll live,' replied Dean. Not unpleasantly, but in a tone that he hoped would end the exchange.

'I'm really nervous,' she gabbled. Oh great, he was sitting next to a nervous flyer; just what he needed. As though reading his mind, she corrected herself. 'Well, not so much nervous, I should probably say excited. I've never flown club class before.'

Then the woman did the most extraordinary thing. She jumped up and down on the spot and clapped her hands together, like a child. Dean looked on, bemused. He doubted he was ever up to this level of excitement, and he knew for certain he wasn't up to it today. 'It's amazing, isn't it?' she went on. 'Look at these magazines and this blanket and these headsets!' With each object listed, she grabbed and caressed it as though the magazine was a lover and the blanket was a dear family member. 'Do you think we get to keep them?' Before Dean could say no, you didn't get to keep them, the woman started to talk again; he thought he was probably going to need the headsets she so admired, to lock her out. 'And it's ridiculously roomy! We can lie flat! And look, I can turn round in the aisle without bumping into anyone!'

The woman then chose to demonstrate just how open the cabin was by doing exactly that. It was indeed spacious, but because she decided to wave her arms while rotating, she immediately bumped into the flight attendant, who was carrying a tray of champagne. Even though the attendant did his best to right the tray, three glasses clattered to the floor. The sly grumbles from the other passengers were replaced by sudden blasts of outright disgust.

'For fuck's sake.'

'Who the hell is she?'

'Is she drunk?' people demanded of no one in particular.

'Oh my gosh. I'm so sorry.'

Just as Dean was wondering who said *gosh* any more, she started to wipe his arm in an attempt to mop up the champagne that had soused him. Dean tightened his bicep a fraction; he couldn't help himself, it was just a reflex under an attractive woman's touch. She pulled her hand away as though she'd been scalded. And blushed.

'It's fine,' Dean muttered. What did he care? In the grand scheme of things, this mishap didn't even register in his disastrous twenty-four hours. He wouldn't give the irritable and spoilt passengers any satisfaction; he knew they were all hoping he would tear a strip off her.

The champagne dripped down his arm and leg and on to the floor. 'Is your suit one of those washable ones? The type that you can just pop in the machine?' she asked hopefully. Her gaze lingered on the quality fabric and the elegant cut; she looked crestfallen. 'No, I don't suppose it is. I don't suppose there are many of those sorts of suit in club.' She paused. 'Can I give you some money for the dry cleaning?' It was clear from the way she chewed on her bottom lip that she was really hoping he'd say no.

'It's fine,' repeated Dean. He hoped his curt response also said, 'Now please sit down, shut up and stay silent for the next nine hours.' It didn't, at least not to this ebullient woman. She did at least finally sit down, but only because the flight assistant insisted on it, so that the spillage on the floor could be dealt with.

'Do you travel club class often?' she asked. Dean stared at her with something between incredulity and a reluctant admiration.

132

Even he wouldn't think to hit on someone after delaying their flight, assaulting them with a book and then drenching them with alcohol, but this woman had just tried the aviation equivalent of *Do you come here often?*

'Yes.' One-syllable answers surely said, 'Shut up, I'm not interested.' Dean wasn't interested in talking, to her or anyone. He just wanted to get home. It had been a mistake to come here. A huge, hideous mistake. The sooner he was back in Chicago, the better. He'd put it all behind him. He'd pretend it had never happened. He didn't want to linger a moment longer; he hadn't even found the energy to visit Zoe or meet with Rogers.

The engines started to rumble, filling the cabin with a sense of purpose and progress. Having checked their phones were turned off, people finally settled into their seats, tightened their belts and then – all but the truly neurotic – steadfastly ignored the flight attendant who was earnestly demonstrating the correct use of oxygen masks and pointing out the emergency exits.

'This is just amazing,' said the woman, looking around in wonder. 'Isn't it?'

As another flight attendant passed through the cabin, checking that people were fastened into their seats, Dean caught her eye and said, 'I've changed my mind. I will take a newspaper, please.'

'Which one, sir?'

'The biggest.'

Dean looked meaningfully at this strange woman as he unfolded the broadsheet and effectively created a barrier between them. He wanted to be alone. Under other circumstances he could imagine himself chatting to her, seducing her, even making her fall in love with him, because that was what he did. He flirted and dated, seduced and left. This woman had pert tits and long legs and she was certainly worth noticing. She wasn't young, but she definitely still had something about her; not the flush of youth, it was more of a wash of experience, but that could be attractive. Yes, he might have, probably would have, under other circumstances. But not today. Today, he just wanted to be alone.

The woman popped her head around his paper and hiss-whispered, 'Do we have to pay for the champagne?'

'No,' he replied firmly.

'Not even the ones I spilt?'

'No.'

'Wow. That's good, isn't it?' Dean shook his newspaper pointedly, but she carried on, 'It's very different from back in cargo, isn't it? As I mentioned, I've never flown club. Even with my parents. On family holidays they used to put us kids in the back and sit up front themselves. I used to worry what would happen if the plane snapped in two, but they gave us a hundred quid spending money each, every hol, which eased any qualms I had. But it's another world, isn't it! Champagne on tap, none of that endless waiting for the drinks trolley to come creeping down the aisle. I promise you, no matter where I sit on a plane, I am *always* the last person to be served a drink. It's like some form of torture listening to the bottles and cans clinking merrily against one another, a siren's call, and having to patiently wait my turn.' She glanced at her full glass of champagne. 'This is heaven.'

Dean remained mute. Finally, thankfully, she stopped talking for a few minutes as the plane slowly lumbered along the runway and then, quite suddenly, picked up speed and height. Their seats were in the centre of the cabin, but the woman strained to see past the aisle and out through a window. Dean didn't look up. He couldn't wait for the ground to disappear, for the plane to push through the clouds and get into the vast blue sky. He was more than ready to leave it all behind him.

The moment the plane levelled out, she started to talk again. 'And the nuts?'

He understood her immediately. 'They're free too.'

Encouraged, she thrust her hand around the newspaper and

held it out for him to shake. 'My name is Joanna Russell, but everyone other than my mum calls me Jo.'

Dean didn't accept her hand but felt he had no alternative but to nod. 'Dean Taylor.'

'Pleased to meet you.' She smiled, but he didn't reciprocate the joy; couldn't she tell? 'It's a long flight, so I thought it would be more fun if we got to know each other a bit,' she added.

Dean sighed. He was going to have to spell it out. 'Actually, the etiquette is no talking. There's a screen here, which will divide us, and now we're in the air I'm going to put it up. No offence. It's been a long couple of days. I just need some rest.' He pressed the button that made the dividing screen rise. The annoyingly gregarious woman instantly hit the button on her side and it dropped down again.

'You don't sound American. Are you? A bit? You have a twang. Do you live in Chicago?'

Dean lowered his newspaper and considered. 'Really, no, not a bit, really and yes,' he replied. He was careful not to season his voice with any intonation as he answered her questions.

She smiled at him, a broad beam that flooded into her eyes, which Dean respected as it was rare and candid, but he just didn't want to be social. Couldn't be, even if he tried. She obviously thought he was hoping to be funny, because she giggled. He honestly wasn't.

'I've never been to Chicago.' She paused, clearly hoping for a murmur of 'Fancy that!' or something. He gave her nothing. She ploughed on regardless. 'I've been to New York once, a long time ago. I liked it. A lot. Are they similar places?'

'A little.'

Silence. Then, 'Really, in what way?'

'They both have shops, clubs and restaurants. They're both full of busy, *private* people.'

This Jo woman had the hide of a rhino. The emphasis Dean

had placed on the word *private* sailed way above her head. 'A bit like London in that respect,' she commented. She paused again, and Dean allowed the hiatus to stretch. He really did hope it was a full stop rather than a breather this time. It wasn't. 'I desperately need to get away. I'm going through what's known as a rough time.' She used her fingers to draw speech marks around the words. 'Wow, I honestly don't know why I've just done that strange inverted-commas-with-my-fingers thing. It isn't a gesture I've ever used before. Promise. And having done it once, I doubt I'll try it again. It isn't as though I'm a children's TV presenter,' she gabbled.

'I'm sorry to hear that,' Dean said dutifully.

'You're sorry I'm not a children's TV presenter?' She looked confused.

Dean was beginning to think she was unhinged. He glanced around to see if there were any spare seats that he might be able to swap into. There weren't. 'I'm sorry you are going through a rough time,' he clarified. He didn't want to get into it. He had his own rough time to deal with, if dealing with problems was what he wanted to do, and he wasn't sure it was. His head hurt. His eyes stung. His belly felt hollow. He'd need some calm and quiet if he was to process all that had passed in the last few days. He wished this woman would just shut up.

'Yesterday I discovered my boyfriend was married.'

Yup, certifiable. Must be. Otherwise why would she be so candid, and why had she chosen to be so candid with *him*? He wasn't the sort of person who invited familiarity. He was a good-time guy. Women told him what they knew he wanted to hear – that they were footloose and carefree (whether they were or not) – and blokes told him about business deals and the football results (but only if they were on winning streaks). Dean didn't do deep and meaningful. He didn't know what to make of this stranger who was prepared to pour out her misery for close inspection. Did it show she had guts, or just a masochistic streak? It was hard to know.

She shrugged. 'Yeah, stuff happens. So, now I'm going to Chicago for my ex-boyfriend's wedding.'

'But didn't you just say your boyfriend is *already* married? You mean yesterday you discovered he was *about* to get married?' Dean honestly didn't want to get involved, but he was confused, so against his better judgement he found he was being drawn into this conversation. She had a pretty mouth. Plump lips.

'No. Yesterday's guy . . . well, he wasn't really a boyfriend,' she admitted. 'Not really. More of a . . .' she paused, 'an encounter.'

'I see.'

'Yeah, you probably do,' she said with a defeated sigh. 'The ex whose wedding I'm going to was my fiancé a while back.'

Dean had been invited to a number of weddings of women he'd previously dated. He knew that these scorned and spurned women invited him to their big days to show him, the world and themselves that they were *absolutely* over him. Sometimes they were. Other times he knew they weren't; they just wanted him to see them looking good in a three-thousand-dollar dress. Either way, he never accepted the invites. He simply didn't do weddings. He didn't like them. He didn't believe in the whole marriage thing, his parents had seen to that. But even if he'd been the biggest romantic on earth, he doubted the sanity of going to an *ex's* wedding. It had to be awkward, didn't it? Dean thought back to the woman's reading matter that had fallen out of the locker and on to his shoulder and felt bad for her. He was pretty sure that she was too fragile for such a social occasion; then again, he was also *absolutely* sure it wasn't something he should worry about. He scrabbled around in his head for something to say that wouldn't be too cold or cutting but would draw the conversation to a polite close. He did pride himself on being polite, even charming – just as his father had suggested (it grated that his father could assess his character so accurately; surely nothing more than a lucky guess) – so he had no desire to be unnecessarily harsh, but he really, really wanted to be left in peace.

'Wow, that's fun.' He meant brave or idiotic. 'Good for you.' He was pretty sure he'd hit the right note. Once again he shook out his newspaper, raised it and pretended to read.

'I'm not actually going to go to the wedding. There isn't going to be a wedding,' she added.

No, no, no, no. Dean fought his own curiosity but lost. He lowered the paper and folded it into neat quarters. 'Now I'm really confused.'

'I'm going to stop it.' The Jo woman strained her neck in an effort to catch the eye of a flight attendant. She waved her empty glass, which she wanted refilled with champagne, and then looked at Dean. 'Will you join me?'

She had huge brown eyes. Despite her cheery chatter, he noticed that they hinted at another story. They looked like the eyes of a baby harp seal, the type you saw on animal rights posters; baby seals that were pleading not to be clubbed to death for their skins. She looked weary. That was something he recognised. What the hell.

'I'll take a juice.'

They were swiftly furnished with their drinks and then Jo started to explain her situation in earnest. She told him about how she had once been very much in love with some guy called Martin; how this Martin guy had done all the things that women expected from a serious relationship: he'd been obsessed with his career, had duly been promoted and then had proposed with an impressive ring (Tiffany copy). She'd accepted. So far, so same. Then she gave details about the jitters that led to her calling off the marriage at the last minute. She told Dean that she now realised that this was 'foolish'. He was amused at her word choice.

It was either an understatement or a self-delusion; he found himself wondering which. She explained that despite focused attempts at dating numerous other men since, she'd never met anyone she liked as much as she'd liked Martin. Then she told Dean that three months ago Martin had sent her an invite to his wedding, which unbelievably she'd seen as a clear plea from her ex to be rescued and a cue for her to rekindle their relationship. So she'd decided to do this 'brave and wonderful thing' of flying to Chicago to stop his wedding.

Dean did not interrupt Jo throughout the telling of her story. She was loquacious as she talked of her determination to win back this guy, and her certainty was enthralling. She was sure that this was the most romantic and idealistic gesture she'd ever made in her life. He thought it must be the champagne talking; there wasn't another reasonable explanation. 'Don't get me wrong, I'm not some starry-eyed virgin; quite the opposite,' she assured him. Her eyes widened a fraction as she confessed this, as did those of the guy sitting behind her. Dean had a sudden image of this woman giving head; it wasn't a conscious fantasy, it was just something that happened to him, fairly often. He found it difficult to think about women without thinking about sex, unless they were particularly unattractive women. 'You see, I've finally realised that I've been getting this whole romance thing topsy-turvy.'

Topsy-turvy? She said gosh *and* topsy-turvy. Dean wondered whether she might also say 'whoops-a-daisy' or 'goodness gracious me'; did she actually live in this century? Maybe it was a spoof, something for TV. Was there an elaborate hoax being played on him? He glanced around for cameras but couldn't spot any. Cameras in a business-class cabin were unlikely – no doubt that would be some sort of infringement of privacy rights – but were they any more unlikely than this woman's story?

'You see, I thought romance was all about the big bang.'

'Are we talking about the prevailing cosmological model that explains the early development of the universe?'

'Er, no, we're talking about chemistry.'

'As I said.'

'Sexual chemistry, not,' she waved her hand dismissively, 'not GCSE horror chemistry.'

'I see.'

'I thought you had to be wildly attracted to one another. I thought there had to be dramatic moments, a quickening of the pulse, then – ultimately – knickers and sense being thrown to the wind. I thought love was like in the poems, songs and films. There was none of that with Martin, and so I panicked.'

'What *was* there with Martin?'

'He's tall, pleasant. We didn't row much.'

'But you no longer consider the quickening of the pulse as vital?'

'Not really. I mean, I've had that with other guys since, quite a few others actually, and it never, ever lasts. Take you, for example.'

'Me?'

'Normally I'd be all flirtatious and ridiculous with you because you're very much my usual type, you know, physically, but it wouldn't work out.'

'Really?' Dean was used to being every woman's type and so was not as interested in the flattery as he was in the fact that she was serving it up with a rebuttal.

'No, it wouldn't. I could write our story now, having known you for just half an hour.'

'You could?'

'Yup. If I hadn't seen the light and realised that Martin is my One, I'd have behaved very differently on meeting you.'

'Is that so?'

'I'd have got drunk and slutty, rather than drunk and chatty.

We'd have had hot, irresponsible sex. You'd think it was fun, I'd think it was love, until I realised the number you'd given me was for the local pet store.'

Dean had never actually given out the pet store's number, but he'd once given his real estate agent's number in an attempt to shake a persistent woman who he'd considered to be a transient lay; he could not fault Jo's account.

'I won't make that mistake now, because I've realised that true love isn't about quickening pulses or even the gorgeous butterflies and that sort of slackening in the bit below my stomach that has no decent name.'

'Are we talking front bottom?' Dean asked with mock seriousness.

'We are,' she whispered back, her seriousness entirely for real.

Dean had only asked for verbal clarification so that he could clock the stunned reactions of the passengers around them, who were quite clearly listening in to their conversation. Jo seemed oblivious to anyone else; she was acting as though they were floating in a bubble. 'What *is* love about then?' he asked, showing more interest than he felt.

Only too happy to wax lyrical about her favourite subject, Jo replied, 'The steady stuff. Duty, loyalty, decency and friendship.' Dean doubted any of that lasted either. It was just as ephemeral as a quickening of the pulse, but he didn't care enough to contradict her. 'Do you know, my parents are celebrating their thirty-eighth wedding anniversary this very weekend. I look up to their relationship as a sort of nirvana.' Jo smiled dreamily. Dean wondered if her parents had had lobotomies, or was there some other dark reason for them making it so far. Perhaps they were swingers, or simply pig-ugly and short of options. He doubted the latter; in fairness, this Jo woman – whilst obviously delusional – was a looker, he could give her that. 'I suppose I do still believe in the dramatic side of romance that books and films do so well. You know, missed opportunities, painful goodbyes and lost chances, but only if finally, obviously, there's the happy ending.' She giggled briefly. 'And I'm now going to have *all* of that with Martin.' Dean thought there was a genuine danger that she'd clap her hands in excitement again. 'Are you following?'

'I'm not sure I am.' He understood her argument but questioned her reason.

'I just think that in the final analysis we all have a right to a happily-ever-after. Martin and I are fated. He's my One. It's quite simple really.' She was flushed with her own rhetoric (that and the fact that during the telling she'd consumed quite a lot more champagne).

'Wow,' said Dean.

'Romantic, huh?' Jo drained her glass and immediately signalled for the flight attendant to bring her yet another. It was clear that following the spurting out of her dramatic confession, she was expecting some sort of seismic shift in Dean's attitude, or maybe even coloured tickertape to be softly floating from the ceiling.

Dean considered. How could a woman grow up in the twenty-first century and believe that her best chance in life was finding some half-decent bloke to marry her, irrespective of the fact that he clearly bored her? Sometimes it was as though the last couple of hundred years had never happened. This woman was so blinkered.

'So, let me get this right. If you're successful, this will be the second time you've stopped this man getting married when he's expecting to?' pointed out Dean.

'Erm, well . . .' Jo hesitated. The imaginary tickertape settled on the floor in embarrassing puddles.

'The second time you've humiliated him in front of all his friends and family?'

'No, I'm—'

Dean didn't let her finish. 'The second time you've ruined what's supposed to be the best day of his life?'

'Put like that—'

'Put like that, you sound like a totally selfish cow,' said Dean flatly. He was fed up with selfish people wrecking other people's lives. He'd had enough of it. With those words he turned on his video screen, plugged in his headphones and then pressed the button that caused the barrier to rise between their two seats.

15

Eddie

I have no idea why my son came here. Funny that I knew him. My vision is going. His face swam before me, yet I knew him. But now he's gone. Where? Why? Things are blurred.

My son. Those are words that I haven't spun around my head for years. I can't work him out. Haven't the energy. Haven't the time. Some might say that's always been the case, and maybe it has, in a more philosophical sense, but the hard fact is, it's the absolute cold truth now. I have days left on earth. Where's he gone? Will he come back? He's a fiery one. Difficult and angry. I was wondering whether this is what I want to do with the last days of my life. Really, what is the point of talking to the angry young man who I gave life to but not much else? But then I thought, it's as good as anything else on offer. It's not as though they are going to wheel in a chorus line of beauties for my entertainment, is it? And even if they did, I can barely raise a hand, let alone much else. What good would they be to me? But he's flounced off. Like a woman.

So who is he, this son of mine? He's a good-looking lad, I'll give him that. He reminds me of myself, which I doubt he wants to hear. The truth hurts. Although I'd have turned up at the deathbed of my estranged father, after nearly thirty years of silence. I'm not the sentimental sort. At least I don't think I would have. I suppose it's difficult to guess how you'd act in circumstances you've never experienced.

My father thought the sun shone out my arse. Would do anything for me. My mother is the same. I couldn't imagine what it would have been like without them. I wasn't at my father's side. He died of a heart attack at work. The messy bit all cleaned up by the time I got there. Never even saw his body; didn't want to. Useless bodies. They let you down. My mother is still going. Well, to an extent. She's in an assisted-living place. What will she make of outliving me? Gutted, she'll be, obviously. I have an itch in my buttock but can't move to do anything about it. I should have asked the lad to scratch it for me. Christ, I can only imagine how he'd have reacted to that. Sense of humour seems to have skipped a generation; that or he's inherited his mother's.

I thought maybe Dean came here because he thinks I have money, wants to cash in on a bob or two. Not unreasonable. But he asked the strangest things. Wanted to know if I followed football. I told him no. Not my sport. No doubt that cut off a line of small talk, but it was hardly the moment to start feigning a common interest. He seemed particularly agitated by my response, so despite the fact that it hurts to talk, I gave it a go, this conversation he so clearly wanted. 'Do you?' I asked. He looked up at me. It was a cold stare. Icy.

'Not really. I used to watch it, on the TV, when I was a kid,' he said.

Waste of a Saturday afternoon that, I told him. You should've been outside in the fresh air, I muttered. He looked like he wanted to punch me. Maybe he thought it was a bit late for me to be offering up parental advice, and he'd be right, it is. I wasn't passing comment on him as such, more on the concept of watching sport on the box instead of getting out there and playing it. I'm not an observer. Not part of the audience. I've always been a doer.

'What is your sport then?' he asked.

'Squash, when I was younger. Golf, up until about a year ago. I became too ill to manage a round.'

'Not a team player, then,' he commented with a sneer. The muscle on his cheek pulsed furiously. Still, I envy his angry vitality. Fury proves you're alive.

'Not as such, no.'

'Not as such,' he repeated bitterly, dropping his head in his hands. I understood what he meant by that, of course.

I wonder if my lad is stable. I was shocked to hear they'd been in care. That, I didn't see coming. It can mess with your head, that can. Horrendous. Dean might be a violent man. I know nothing about him. But then there's no point in worrying about it. What's the worst that could happen? He could hold a pillow over my face and end the suffering three or four days earlier than expected. Bigger shame for him than me if he goes down that route. He'd end up in prison. Hope he doesn't try to kill me, for that reason alone. My God, I feel protective of him. Get me.

I haven't had many visitors since I came in here this time round. I don't blame anyone for that. I was never much of a hospital visitor myself. Depressing bloody places. People came when I first got the diagnosis, when there was still hope. A few old boys I used to work with, way back when at the Beeb; we've kept in touch, sporadically. Only Ron had the sparkling career we all hankered after. The rest of us made do, made ends meet. Wrote comedy scripts for smaller and smaller channels, until reality TV murdered us all. After that, I wrote for radio and trade magazines, kept the challenging scripts hidden in the desk drawer, gathering dust. Still, I earned enough to drink whisky at the Groucho and to occasionally eat dinner at the Arts Club in Dover Street. That sort of thing. Good times. Good times. Can't complain.

A couple of my ex-girlfriends popped by. Not her. Don't expect it. She'll have the letter by now. Not sure why I sent that. Not thinking straight. Some of the blokes from the golf club and their once-pretty wives came in. Well-meaning types. They brought newspapers and fruit. But this thing takes so long. People wanted me to get better. I couldn't oblige. They've lost interest and I don't blame them for that. I've never encouraged the sort of relationships where we held hands through the bad times. My usual response to bad times is a first-class ticket right the hell out of there, as my lad could no doubt testify. That's why I resent that I was caught by something so slow. Like my visitors, I wanted to see a swift recovery, but failing that, I wish it would hurry up and kill me. The rediscovered son at least helped me pass the time. I wonder if he's gone for something to eat?

'Do you need me to arrange your funeral?' he asked.

'I thought you prided yourself on being a charmer,' I rasped back.

'I never said that.'

'You never had to. I recognise it.' I tried to laugh, but Dean bristled.

'Well, *do* you need me to plan the funeral? Do you need money?'

Funny that he should have asked me the very question I'd been thinking about asking him. I assured him it was all done. I've arranged everything, paid for everything. I've kept it simple. Breathlessly, I added, 'What's the point of a big party if I'm not there to get drunk?'

'Thoughtful,' he snarled sarcastically.

I raised my eyebrows at him. Actually, I thought arranging the funeral was thoughtful; who wants the trouble of all that? I didn't tell him that I wasn't sure I could still fill a room. Don't want his pity, can't expect it. Besides, truthfully, he has the measure of me. I am selfish. Always have been. Always will be. No point making a song and dance or trying to deny what's as plain as the nose on a face. 'I spent my money as I made it,' I told him. 'Never borrowed, never lent. Didn't own a house, preferred to rent, but there's some savings. What there is, you can divide between the four of you. I've made a will.'

'I don't want your money.'

'Well, give it away then. Give it to a bloody cats' home.' He didn't seem to register that even before his surprise visit I'd done my bit to look out for him and his sister. Treated them just like the other two, even though I was with the other two until they were almost teenagers. 'Whatever, I don't care. Don't burn it, though. That's criminal.'

Then he lost it. 'I tell you what's criminal. Me being here, right at the end. You wanting me to know you now, after all this time. So when you do . . . go, I'll be left wondering.' He didn't shout; it was the other sort of anger, the barely contained type. More vicious that, because it explodes in the end.

That sort of thing is exactly why I didn't ever fancy one of those surprise family reunions that you see on TV. Full of recriminations and reproaches. I can't be bothered with his incessant chorus of outrage. He sounded like a seagull. Never liked seagulls. Or any birds. Or nature, come to that. I like cities, noise, dirt, industry, vehicles. I pause in that thought process. I'm going off track. What was I thinking before? Oh yes. What was he whingeing about? I didn't ask him to get to know me. I don't want that particularly. I'm just passing time. I could as easily lie here thinking about people I've worked with, money I've wasted, people I've fucked and fucked over, but he turned up, didn't he. It was a bit of company. I tried to lighten the atmosphere. I said to him, 'Hey, lad, haven't you heard the saying better late than never?'

He glared at me. Looked right at me, right through me. I thought he was trying to read my mind. I stared back, trying to fix my face into an expression of openness. Here's the thing. I know Dean sees me as some furtive, guarded villain, but I'm not that. Really I'm not. It's true I've had my share of secrets; what man hasn't? Not every woman I've slept with has necessarily been totally aware of every other woman in my life at the time. It's sometimes been a bit complicated, but I've never hidden anything big. I walked out on Diane, yes, but I left her a forwarding address, in case she wanted to get in touch with me. She never did. So the next time I moved, I might have forgotten to keep her up to date with my new address details. I wasn't trying to hide from her or anyone. I was just on the move a lot. I'm an open book. I'm straightforward. Some people go as far as to say I'm shallow. Lots have, actually. Women in particular have yelled that charge at me on countless occasions over the years. But I say, what's so great about being deep? It's just another word for the self-obsessed, or the depressed, or the academic elite who like to think they are more than the rest of us. I'm easy-going. Easily pleased. I don't worry about things. If that makes me shallow, then shoot me. Honestly, I wish to God someone *would* shoot me. I ache in every single bone in my body. This is hell.

I am in hell.

16

Jo

I am used to being humiliated by men. Far more used than is ideal, actually. Especially men with sparkly blue eyes and dark hair. But still this latest humiliation scorches. I only started to talk to him because, well, I need company, any company – even the company of this cynical, clearly uninterested (yes, yes, delicious-looking) man. Of course it is not the first time I've wanted the company of this sort of man, although this time it's different. This time I'm not looking at the cynical, clearly uninterested (delicious-looking) man and pretending he is delightful so that I can start some sort of fantasy about dating him, falling in love with him and then ultimately (obviously) marrying him. I don't need that fantasy any more. I now know why it hasn't ever worked out in the past: I am supposed to be with Martin. That's the whole point of this trip, as I made quite clear to this Dean Taylor. As I wasn't coming on to him, I really don't think I should have to endure being insulted by him. I was just being friendly.

I shouldn't care what he thinks.

I don't care.

I glare at the barrier between us, giving what I admit is the impression of someone who does care, rather a lot. He has fabulous bone structure. A jawline to die for. I try hard to remember exactly what Martin's jawline is like, but I'm afraid I can't. It has been a while. I imagine it was just fine. *Is* just fine. I have to get back in the habit of thinking about Martin in the present tense again. He's been very past to me for quite some time. To be clear, my commenting on Dean's jawline, or any other part of his all-too-hot physique, is simply a matter of aesthetics. Nothing more than if I was in a gallery, say, and I commented that a work of art was interesting, or – let's face it, a more likely scenario – if I was in Islington High Street and commented on a stunning dress or must-have pair of shoes. I'm not saying I am *interested* in him in the traditional sense. I'm almost indifferent to him, which is proof of my steadfast commitment to Martin and my plans for an adult future, free of butterflies and lovely loosening in the bit below my stomach that has no decent name.

Almost indifferent.

The truth is, I only spoke to Dean because the moment I had nowhere to mooch or roam, no perfumes, samples or crowds to distract me, I started to feel, well, anxious. Not about the plane crashing or my chances with the oxygen mask and the floating devices if that was the case, but about what I'm doing. What *am* I doing? The enormity of my undertaking threatens to overwhelm me. I'm travelling four thousand miles to see my ex – an ex who up until this morning I had not spoken to once in five years – to try to persuade him not to marry his fiancée.

It's impetuous, it's insane.

It's also romantic and thrilling and possible. Isn't it? Either way, it's mostly just very, very scary. I've drunk too much champagne already and I can't quite remember what Martin said on the phone. Was he flirtatious and encouraging? Or was he simply being polite?

So this Dean bloke thinks I'm a selfish cow. Ow. Hurtful. Well, he's wrong. He really is. Miles off. I'm not selfish, but how can I explain? How can I admit to being something far more terrible?

Lonely. I'm a bit lonely. Well, more than a bit.

I'm desolately lonely.

How pathetic is that? Who admits to that? No one. But I am. Fact is, I am fed up of being alone. Of course I am travelling alone, but I feel alone in a much wider and more profound context than that. Not just yesterday when I woke up in a show home with a married man who didn't know my name, or today when I wandered aimlessly around the airport watching other people greet their loved ones. Truthfully, I've felt alone for quite some time now. It's not something I'm going to shout about, is it? How unattractive would that be? How embarrassing? It would be easier to talk about my various lovers hunting for the elusive G spot than admit to being lonely. But I do feel lonely when I babysit for Lisa (and not just on Valentine's night, but on bog-standard weeknights too), and when I wander round the supermarket, scouring the aisles and fridges for ready meals for one. I feel it after reading a gripping page-turner or after watching an impactful movie, when I want to discuss plots with someone. Of course I can join a book club, and my friends often come to the movies with me, but still the loneliness seeps into my being. That's why I am on this plane, I'm trying to build a dam against the loneliness. That's why I confided in Dean Taylor. I just wanted him to distract me on this flight to Chicago. I just want some company for a few hours. Is that too much to ask?

Besides, he's been giving mixed messages. I'm aware that the newspaper wall and, well, the actual partition wall that he put between us indicates that he really doesn't want to talk, but the humorous way he responded to my initial questions implied the opposite. I thought he'd also appreciate some company, that he was probably simply too shy to say so.

And he listened to my story so acutely, with such rapt interest, and that was, frankly, a refreshing change. Whenever I talk about Martin, or any of my boyfriends, come to that, I'm used to my friends and relatives butting in and contradicting me or exasperating me with conflicting theories and viewpoints. Dean's silence lifted me. When I got to the end of my tale, I fully expected him to shake my hand and congratulate me on my single-minded, uber-romantic pursuit.

He called me a selfish cow.

That's damn rude, isn't it? What right does he have to judge me? I didn't ask him to comment.

Only I did, of course, by opening up and sharing my intimate thoughts and history; he was bound to think I was inviting comment. I shouldn't have trusted him just because the way he chews his fingernails is somehow attractive and vulnerable, just because he was decent about me spilling champagne down his shirt and trousers. Those things don't necessarily mean he's a good guy. I ought to have guessed he'd be egotistical, sexist, brutal. That he'd only see the situation from his own privileged point of view. What could this beautiful man possibly understand about loneliness or desperation or disappointment?

Suddenly I'm parched; three (or four? more?) glasses of champagne can do that to a girl. I wave down the flight attendant again, and he looks relieved when I ask for water. I quickly glug back two glasses in a row before asking if I can keep the litre bottle. I'm bitterly regretting talking to Dean Taylor at all now. I should've been having a ball on this flight, a free upgrade on my way to reclaim the love of my life: what's not to enjoy? But he's spoilt it. He called me a selfish cow. I'm not a cow. I'm not selfish. I'm just trying to make a life. I stare at my hands and count to a hundred three or four times; it seems preferable to thinking.

I'm given a champagne refill and a menu; I realise I'm supposed to decide between the impressive choices of pan-roasted pork belly with caramelised apples, roast sea bass fillet with braised fennel and Hereford cattle steak with a cognac peppercorn sauce, but I'm overwhelmed and unable to make a decision. It's probably just because I'm so used to the more mundane choice of chicken or beef. I pick something, and when it arrives it looks delicious; even the wholewheat bread rolls and the chocolate truffles that nestle on my tray are amazing, but somehow I can't manage more than a couple of mouthfuls of the entire meal. I consider watching a film; there's an enormous choice, but I doubt my ability to follow a plot.

I glare at the partition between me and Dean. I hope he can feel my loathing through the plastic.

I *am* right about going to Martin. I'm sure I am. I'm not going to hurt him, or humiliate him. I'm not trying to spoil the best day of his life. I'll give him other happy days. Better days. I will.

Painfully, the memory breaks down the door and barges into my consciousness; I've done my best to lock it out for years, but now the recollection is callous and sharp and insists on being present. That cold, bright March evening when I called off our wedding suddenly feels real and large again. I can smell the leaf buds in the air and feel the breeze wrap around my fingers and cheekbones.

I told Mum and Dad that I wanted to call it off before I told Martin. I blurted it out to them following a dress fitting, while we were all sitting in the sunroom in their home in Wimbledon enjoying a glass of wine. Way to ruin the mood. I'd thought – hoped – that once I told my parents, that would be the worst of it over. I'd expected my mother to be a little bit hysterical about the etiquette of cancelling a wedding, and a little bit regretful that she'd been cheated out of the opportunity of wearing her oyster-coloured dress coat and hat, but I'd also expected under-standing, perhaps even indulgence.

'How did Martin take it?' Dad had asked.

'I haven't told him yet. I hoped you might. I thought it would be better coming from you. Man to man,' I'd explained. I looked up and noted that my parents were wearing identical expressions: disbelief mixed with frustration.

'Where is he now?' Dad had wanted to know.

'Playing football with the guys from work. I'm supposed to meet him at the local.'

'Get your coat, I'll drive you there.'

It was awful. Truly the hardest thing I've ever done in my life. Martin immediately guessed something was up when he saw me emerge from Dad's car. He probably imagined that the florist had said she wouldn't be able to source calla lilies, or some other 'disaster' on a similar scale. I'd got into the habit of relaying 'disasters' to Martin on a regular basis in the run-up to the wedding; the seating arrangement, the photographer's vision and the search for bridesmaids' shoes had all been disastrous.

But then, on that fresh spring night, with the stench of mud and sweat still clinging to his well-exercised body, he learnt what a real disaster was.

A disaster was being told by your fiancée that she didn't love you. At least, not enough. You weren't enough. You weren't the One. He'd cried, pleaded, told me it was nerves; eventually he got angry and told me I was a stupid, pathetic effing bitch who didn't know what she wanted. Then he'd apologised for that and cried again. Dad had driven him back to our flat, a home that I'd relinquished; I caught the tube back to Wimbledon.

'You'll regret this; you've just made a big mistake,' Martin had snarled, mud and anger smeared all over him.

Truthfully, he *had* looked very much like a ruined and humiliated man. How could Dean have known? I've managed to lock out this memory for so long, smothering it below a certainty that I did the right thing, that calling off the wedding – however disappointing for everyone involved – was justified because I didn't love Martin enough to make us both happy. I see now that I placed far too much emphasis on the chemistry, or rather lack of it, but I've come to understand that I was wrong about that, and so calling off his next wedding, to explain as much, is justified too.

Isn't it?

My lungs suddenly feel painfully full. I'm drowning in self-doubt. Shame and confusion begin to rush at me from both sides and I feel perhaps I might be crushed under their weight. I unbuckle my seat belt, stand up shakily and head for the loo, bumping into two passengers as I do so; both collisions elicit irritated looks. I know everyone in the cabin hates me, but I need to stretch my legs and splash water on my face. Repeatedly counting to a hundred isn't enough.

I don't notice that Dean is already in the galley until I am standing outside the toilet door. He has his back to me, half-heartedly rummaging through a basket of goodies that are available for passengers to graze on, poring over the confectionery, biscuits and fruit. He doesn't seem that committed to picking out a snack; he has the air of a man who is more mooching than scavenging. I stare up at the illuminated light that announces that the loo is engaged as though it's a death sentence. It will look strange to turn around and go back to my seat, so instead I pray that the loo will become free before Dean makes a decision between crisps and chocolate and then he won't notice me. But the universe is against me; it often is. Just as I'm praying that he won't turn around, he does exactly that. The only way back to his seat is squeezing past me.

'Excuse me,' he says stiffly.

I move my body an inch, but my reluctance to be accommodating means that as he moves past, his elbow nudges up against my breast. I feel it as clearly as a kiss; a rare illuminated moment that sends a taut shudder through my being. It settles low in my gut, startling and confusing me. I don't like this man. He's insulted me. Hurt me. And yet I'm grown-up enough to know when raw sexual energy has suddenly commandeered the situation.

Boom.

This is exactly what I've just been talking about. What I've just been saying isn't particularly important. And it isn't. It isn't.

It just feels as though it is.

A delicious heat and thrilling tension pulses through my body. I find my gaze is drawn to his lips, his nostrils, his ears. I want to nibble, bite and suck, in no particular order. Get a grip. Get a room.

Which is it to be?

I glance furtively at Dean's face, forcing myself to look him in the eye. I wonder if he felt it too. He looks shocked and embarrassed, suggesting he did. I am abruptly aware that up here, with nothing surrounding us other than immeasurable amounts of sky and space, there is definitely nowhere to go.

Will he go back to his seat? Will he say anything more? Can we pretend that didn't happen? What I've just felt is simply to do with the altitude, right? And the champagne. The two combined. Lethal. I can't be attracted to Dean. Not because he isn't attractive – we've already established that he is, quite especially so – but as I've just worked out that Martin is my One, then other men should not be popping up on my radar, let alone reducing me to a quaking wreck. I hope Dean walks on by. Returns to his seat and says absolutely nothing more to me, *ever*.

Or the opposite.

Whatever.

With a sigh and, frankly, what seems like reluctance, he turns to me. 'Are you enjoying the flight?' His breath is warm and foggy. I feel it land on me and I am oddly eased by the intimacy, rather than revolted by it. Annoyingly, I'm ambushed by an image of waking up beside him in bed after a night of raw passion. I shake my head. This will not do.

'No, not really,' I admit. I'm not sure he's going to ask why, so I tell him anyway. 'You've upset me.'

'I see.'

'I couldn't enjoy my lunch. Free food. Free *delicious* food. And you ruined it for me.'

'Right.'

'You shouldn't judge. You don't know me. You can't possibly understand my situation. I am *not* making a mistake.'

Dean closes his eyes and massages the back of his neck. 'We *should* judge one another. It stops us becoming animals. The pressure of failing in the eyes of society passes for some sort of morality.' He pauses, as though he's weighing up whether it's worth the effort. 'And you *are* making a mistake,' he sighs.

I want to say something cutting, or better yet, something considered, because I am secretly impressed with his argument. Has he been thinking about that, or did it just come to him? However, the loo door swings open and an extremely tall and hefty guy emerges, practically knocking us over with his bulk. Dean and I do a little dance to avoid any further bodily contact. I really can't handle another jolt. I'm still trying to convince myself that the first one was static or something; I don't want to deal with evidence to the contrary. Plus, I'm aware of the hideous smell of an overused communal loo, and illogically, I feel embarrassed to be so close to Dean, who must also be able to smell the staleness. It isn't my pong, but it bothers me. Flustered, I can't think of anything funnier or more challenging than a slightly childish jibe: 'And I bet you've never made a mistake in your life. I bet you are perfect.' With that I turn on my heel.

Standing inside the toilet cubicle, with the shockingly bright light glaring down on me, I wish that I'd brought my make-up bag in here too. I'd like to freshen up. I'm not trying to impress

Dean; it isn't that I want to look my best for *him*, but I don't want to look my worst either, and I am pretty close to that right now. I look shockingly pale, any natural colour washed off by the high altitude and recycled air. My eyes are red and my skin is puffy. I splash water on my face and then roughly rub at the smudged mascara that frames my eyes. I pinch my cheeks as though I am some Edwardian debutante at a coming-out ball, and then I tut at myself for my idiocy. It really doesn't matter how I look now. When I get to Chicago I can have a facial, go to a department store and get someone to do my make-up. I might even treat myself to a blow-dry. By the time I see Martin, I'll look better. That's what counts.

Still, I pull my fingers through my hair.

17

Clara

C lara had simply handed the letter to Tim by way of explanation. They were not in the habit of keeping secrets from one another. There were too many other people to keep secrets from; it was exhausting. So long ago, once they had understood everything about one another, they had decided that honesty was the only policy that could exist between them. Not that they ever divulged anything grubby and explicit, no details; they drew a veil, but they never lied or withheld.

Tim had taken the letter from her. His first thought had been that the paper was flimsy and cheap. Quite unlike anything any of their friends might send. Their friends were stylish and competitive. Even a thank-you note or an invite had to be doused in thought and oozing investment; it wasn't enough to tear out an A4 sheet of lined paper from a pad bought on the high street. He'd sighed and assumed he was being handed a blackmail letter.

Dear Clara,

Here it is: the proverbial blast from the past. Sorry to open a long-dead correspondence with a cliché, but I find my options are limited. Apologies for bothering you at all actually, because who needs that, hey? Few of us. Most of us – myself included – usually prefer the past to stay exactly where we left it, but – all that said – I found I had to write. I wanted to, and as you know, I've always tended to do as I want. There's no pretty way to say this, so I'll just get to it. I'm dying. Sorry, again, for the bluntness. Bloody hell, I've apologised to you three times in one short paragraph. I bet that's more often than I've apologised to any woman cumulatively in my entire life.

This letter isn't going to reveal anything astounding, don't worry. It isn't going to be a crass declaration of undying love (that would be ridiculous under the circumstance of me actually dying – under any circumstances, really). This letter is nothing more than a tip of the hat. A nod, a bow. Just don't call for an encore.

I find myself quite alone when I'm penning this. It's not an altogether surprising outcome, considering how I've lived my life and the choices I've made. I'm not asking for pity or anything mawkish like that. God forbid. I've done all right. I've had my fun. On the whole it's worked out as I might have hoped. It's just that I've been told to wrap things up. I wrote to my solicitor and to the funeral director, but there was extra paper left over. So I thought I'd write to you.

You see, lying here, waiting, I've had time to remember. I remembered that we burnt brightly. We did, didn't we? For that short time. Least, that's how I recall it. You made your choice and I respect that. I'm not trying to rake over old ground. I just wanted you to know that in amongst all this pain (and believe me, Clara, this bastard illness hurts like hell), I've thought of you – from time to time – over the last few months, and that has eased things. A little. I thought you might like to know that it is so.

That's all, over and out. Sorry for the interruption.

Best,

Eddie

Tim hadn't quite known what to think, beyond the fact that receiving a letter was so quaint nowadays; most people emailed. And a letter of this magnitude – a dying man's letter – was off the scale.

'You can't be leaving me for him.' He hadn't known whether he was asking a question or making a statement.

'Of course not.'

'He's dying, Clara. Eddie Taylor is dying.' Tim said the name as he had always said it. Twenty-nine years hadn't altered the tone; the four syllables were still spat out with a mix of frustration, envy, scorn and fear.

'I understand that. I said I'm not leaving you for him. I could have done that a million years ago if I'd wanted to.'

'Then why are you leaving?'

'A million years ago,' Clara had repeated, her vision blurring as a film of tears erupted, embarrassing and taunting her at once.

'Then what's your point?'

'When he thinks of me, I ease his pain,' she'd murmured. That was her point.

'I read that.'

'Isn't that romantic?'

'That's a difficult question for me to answer as your husband. It's a difficult question for you to ask me as a wife.'

'I don't think I've ever eased your pain.'

'In many ways you have. It's different with us.' Tim had coughed. The conversation was impossible to navigate.

'Too different,' Clara had stated baldly. What they had wasn't enough. How had it taken her so long to admit as much to herself? 'I won't do this any more. I can't.'

'You knew what you were agreeing to.'

'No I didn't, not at first, not until we had three children, then what was I supposed to do?'

'But in all fairness, I didn't know for certain when we first married. I thought I could keep it under control. I thought it was a phase, something I might curb.'

'Tim, you are a homosexual, not a drug addict or a gambler. It's not something that should be curbed. You should be free to be who you are,' Clara had snapped. She thought she ought to be free to be who she was as well.

'I work in the City, Clara.'

'Other gay men do too!'

'Not old queers like me; young hotties. It's different for them.'

'No it's not; at least it shouldn't be. Times have changed.' Clara had put down her glass, focusing all her energy on her husband.

'I'm too old for change.' He'd shaken his head forlornly.

'*I'm* not! This is ridiculous. *We* are ridiculous. I'm a woman, not facial hair.'

Tim had been irritated by her weak attempt at humour. This wasn't a moment for fun; it was in no way a laughing matter. He'd looked at his wife, carefully, and was struck (as he always was) by the beauty and symmetry of her features. She had always been a pleasure to look at, quite especially aesthetically pleasing. Neat, slim, not in any way excessive. It had been her trimness (of body and mind) that had attracted him. She had an aura of old-fashioned restraint that he appreciated, needed. He wished he'd been able to love her in the way a man was supposed to love his wife. It would have been so much more orderly. 'My career aside, what will the children say? My parents? Our neighbours?'

'I don't care what they'll say.'

'But you've always cared.'

'Then more fool me.' Clara had held the letter close to her heart and started to gently rock backwards and forwards in her seat, as though she was nursing a child. Tim had had no idea why she was behaving like this.

'Let me get this right. You're leaving me as a consequence of Eddie Taylor being given three sheets of A4 notepaper, rather than two.'

'Oh, Tim.'

'You know he only wrote to you because there was extra paper!' Tim rarely raised his voice, but anguish and humiliation had pushed him into new territory. 'Our thirty-eight-year marriage is over because there was extra paper!'

Clara had stopped rocking, straightened her shoulders and responded to Tim's outburst with her usual composure. 'It's funny how things work out, isn't it?' she'd commented with a tone that approached serenity.

18

Dean

Dean watched her materialise from the aeroplane toilet. The attractiveness of her face was almost cancelled out by the anxious expression she wore. Almost. And he felt mean. An old-fashioned emotion, something he usually only associated with Zoe and their occasional childhood tiffs. On the rare instance he had become exasperated with Zoe's clinginess – and had tried to shake her off so that he could hang out with boys his own age and cause trouble, rather than be troubled with the responsibility of babysitting Zoe – he'd always found that any fun he was trying to have was hampered by the fact that he knew she'd be sat by the window, alone, waiting for his return. He generally felt too mean to really enjoy himself with his new friends and would invariably find himself returning early to keep Zoe company. He'd be greeted by her anxious face, which on spotting him would instantly light up with gratitude. This Jo woman looked similarly dazed and concerned, although for less cause, Dean reminded himself, and she wasn't his sister; he didn't have to try to transform her expression, it wasn't his problem. He tried to swipe away the guilt that hovered irritatingly, like a gnat. Bloody hell, as if he wasn't wrung out enough. He had plenty of his own crap to deal with; the last thing he needed right now was someone else to be concerned about.

Yet he found he *was* concerned about her.

Or interested in her.

One of the two.

He'd nudged her tit with his elbow and his cock had shuddered. How was that even possible under the circumstances? His personal upheaval and her obvious insanity ought to have immunised him to any lusty thoughts. He really didn't want to go there. She had disaster zone written all over her.

Despite how it might appear, and despite what half of Chicago's female population believed, Dean didn't go out of his way to hurt women; he wasn't some psycho misogynist. He did hurt them, of course, but that was because they didn't listen to him. When he said he didn't want to get involved, that he wasn't looking for a relationship and definitely didn't want a girlfriend, that was what he meant. But they rarely listened. Every woman thought she would be the one to change him, fix him, keep him. So inevitably they would try, fail and get hurt. But Dean did endeavour to treat women fairly. Coolly but fairly.

If this Jo had been some hard, gold-digging bitch, he might have been able to ignore her, but she wasn't. She was delusional and misguided, but it was clear she meant no harm (although she was certainly going to do some). When she'd spoken about this Martin bloke, she hadn't gone on about the lifestyle he could offer her, the size of his wage packet or flat; she'd used phrases like 'meant to be' and 'fated'. She'd talked about finding her soulmate and all sorts of other rubbish. Despite himself, Dean was intrigued. Could anyone really believe that stuff? It was mental. He wondered whether he could save her from herself, if he put his mind to it. He liked a challenge. Anyway, he hadn't been able to concentrate on a single word in the newspaper; his thoughts kept wandering; he kept thinking about Eddie Taylor and his grey skin and rasping breath. That was the absolute last thing he wanted. He decided that at the very least, this Jo woman would be a distraction. Once she sat down, he held up a packet of shortbread and a mini Twix finger.

'Thought you might be hungry since I put you off your lunch.' She glared at him, clearly not yet ready to relent. 'You can have first pick,' he encouraged. He was used to women being angry with him, and he was used to them forgiving him pretty quickly too.

He flashed his best grin and on cue she said, 'I'll have the shortbread.' Sometimes he felt sorry for women; they were so predictable, so pliable, so malleable. He gently tossed the biscuits to her, but she muddled up the catch, trapping the treat between her right hand and left boob. The boob he'd nudged outside the loo. It was a good boob. They both were. He decided to pretend not to notice either the poor catch or the shapely tits. He stuffed the Twix bar into his mouth in one go, chewed, and then turned to this strangely frank but hugely imprudent woman. He was feeling oddly invigorated; mischievous to the point of delirious. Shock, probably.

'Look, I'm sorry if I offended you. It's none of my business.'

She glared at him as she nibbled on her shortbread. He held her gaze until she softened. He'd decided it would take to the count of three. Before he got to two, she spoke. 'Oh, it doesn't matter, I was just making conversation,' she said, as she swallowed the biscuit. Her eyes belied her pronouncement. Her confiding in him had been more than a conversation starter. It dawned on him that she needed support. He couldn't approve of her nonsense, but he didn't need to make her feel worse about her desperation. There was no glory in that.

'Should we talk about something else?' he offered. 'Start over?' She nodded eagerly, allowing her cute smile to shine through. 'So tell me a bit about yourself,' Dean said, meeting her smile with one of his own.

'What sort of thing do you want to know?'

'Anything, everything.' She stared at him blankly, so he decided to give her some pointers. 'Where do you live?'

'London.'

'Which part?'

'North. Sort of. At the moment.'

'Do you have a nice place?' Jo shrugged but didn't elaborate. 'Do you flat-share?' She moved her head slightly, but it was unclear whether she was nodding or shaking it. Exasperated, Dean asked, 'Have you a window box you'd like to tell me about?'

'What is this? Twenty questions?'

'Why are you being so cagey all of a sudden?'

'Why are you being so nosy all of a sudden?'

'I'm just trying to make conversation.'

Recognising her own words, Jo relented. 'OK, OK. Well, the truth is, I'm sort of in between flats.' She sighed, and then added, 'I sleep on my sister's sofa.'

'Oh, I see.'

'When Martin and I split, I rented a room off my friend, a lovely two-bedroom flat in Islington. It was great. We were fine for ages, then Charlotte moved her boyfriend in.'

'Two is company, three's a crowd.'

'Exactly. Shortly after he moved in, he said he was going to start working from home. He said he'd have to convert the spare room into an office. When Charlotte first explained the situation to me, it took me a moment to understand. I actually said, "But we don't have a spare room."'

'She meant your room?'

'Yup.' Jo shrugged. Something tightened in Dean's gut; he empathised. There was nothing worse than that feeling of having nowhere to go; it chilled the core. 'I quickly discovered that rents have rocketed since I struck my deal with Charlotte and my wages have somehow managed to remain exactly the same for the last few years. There's a disparity. A disparity between what I earn and the rent landlords ask at the sort of place I'm prepared to live in.'

'I see.'

'My standards aren't ridiculous,' she assured him in a tone laced with panic and indignation. 'Although I don't want to share a bathroom, kitchen and sitting room with strangers, I accept I have to, but I do draw the line at sharing a *bedroom* with a stranger. Bunk beds, for goodness' sake. I'm thirty-five, not five!' She blushed. Dean guessed that she hadn't meant to let her age slip out like that. She rushed on. 'So, Lisa's sofa is more attractive than bunk beds and Lisa's sofa, notably, is free. But it's only a temporary measure.'

'Of course. How long have you been there?'

'About five months.'

'Oh.'

'But it won't be for ever.'

'No.'

Jo sighed, then continued, 'I'm not sure how much longer the arrangement will last, actually. I get the feeling that my brother-in-law, Henry, is finding it a tad irritating. He's got into the habit of making me a cup of tea before I set off for work each morning.'

'That's nice.'

'Yup, I thought he was being sweet too, at first, but last month he started circling ads for rooms to let in the local freebie newspaper and handing the paper over with the cuppa.'

'Sharing can be fraught,' said Dean sympathetically.

'He was so snappy the other day because I'd used his razor to shave my legs, and yes, I realise I ought to try to remember to mention it if I use the last of the milk, but it's not as though I put the empty carton back in the fridge. I just forget that the kids need milk for breakfast. I don't have kids; I've never had to think that way. More's the pity.' She threw the last sentence towards the aisle and away from him so he let it drift.

Dean thought of his own home, a sleek loft apartment, full of what estate agents might call mod cons. More importantly, it boasted an abundance of privacy and space; he felt incredibly grateful. Suddenly, surprisingly, he wondered where his father had lived before he went into hospital. As a kid, he'd given a lot of thought to that sort of thing, but he hadn't allowed himself to imagine anything like that for years. It was pointless, a dead end. Unbidden, an image of his father burst into his head. He was sitting alone and pitiful in a studio flat, towers of washing-up stacked precariously around the sink, an unmade bed in one corner and a small TV droning from another. He knew these types of flats. Intimately acquainted. He could picture the relentless browns and greys easily; he could smell the dust, damp and stale stranger sweat; he could hear the neighbours fighting through the paper-thin walls. He shoved the thought away and scrabbled around for the earlier vision of his father in France, indolent, ignorant, distant, but that image had collapsed, vanished. He tried to focus on this Jo woman instead.

'The thing is, Lisa has this huge career, while Henry has a part-time position with the council; some administration job that fits around the kids. Consequently, Henry and I are seeing rather more of one another than either of us is used to. We've had to get to know each other's quirks. It's simply a period of readjustment.' She was obviously trying to convince herself as much as him.

'What quirks?' Dean wanted to know.

'I like to chat in the mornings, Henry is monosyllabic. I'm happy to eat my supper off a tray in front of the TV, but Henry strongly believes the family ought to sit around the table and make conversation. He's kept supper hot for me on four different occasions when I've returned home later than anticipated.

Although I don't know why he bothers; the warm plate can't do a thing to thaw the frosty atmosphere when I delay a meal.'

'Sounds a bit of a nightmare.'

'It can be. Of course, he's always polite enough. I'm family and he's a decent man, so I know I'm safe from out-and-out eviction, but . . .' Dean fully understood why she broke off. She didn't fit in. It wasn't her home. That was uncomfortable. She rallied, and smiled again. At a glance it was convincing, but if anyone cared to look for longer than a fleeting second, it was obviously not one of her heartfelt smiles. He wondered whether anyone looked beyond; his experience had been that no one ever did. People wanted to accept what was easiest and most convenient, regardless of truth.

'I'm sure they love having you to stay,' he said, mustering cheer.

'You think?' She looked doubtful and grateful at the same time. 'I'm well aware that it is *my* responsibility to fit in with *their* lifestyle and habits, so I haven't once complained about my nephews and niece waking me up at six every morning, or the fact that they never watch anything decent on TV. I've been the third wheel to enough couples to receive the message loud and clear: single women have to adapt, single women have to accommodate.'

'Right.' Dean took a long, deep breath in. He thought she ought to as well. He decided he'd better change the subject; her sleeping arrangements were almost as depressing as her romantic aspirations. He went to the old favourite. 'So, what do you do for a living?'

'I'm a writer.'

'Interesting.' He beamed.

'You?'

'Advertising.' He wouldn't let her turn the conversation. 'What sort of writer? Novelist? Journalist?'

'Journalist.'

'Newspapers?'

'Magazines.'

'Which one?'

Uncharacteristically, Jo hesitated, and then eventually admitted, 'Well, until yesterday, I worked for *Loving Bride!*.'

Dean was glad that he'd mastered the art of never betraying any emotion through his expression; least of all hilarity or derision. 'I don't know that title,' he said evenly.

'No. It's quite specialist.' Jo grinned, showing that she'd somehow read his careful tone perfectly. 'You're not in the market. Truthfully, you are unlikely to *ever* be in the market. I don't think a single copy has once been bought by a man.'

'Who knew such an entrenched sexism still existed?'

'Sexism is alive and kicking, never doubt that,' Jo said. She sounded worn out. Dean considered her comment.

'So, you are a hapless romantic and a feminist too? How does that work?'

'As a romantic, I'm in the perfect position to see all the limitations placed on women. Don't you think I wished things were different?'

Dean could barely process, let alone respond to, such raw honesty. There was more to her than gushing optimism. He wasn't sure if this was good to know or disastrous. He pulled the conversation back to her career. 'So what's your new title called? Will I know that one?' he asked.

'New title?'

'The one that lured you away from *Loving Bride!*.'

'Oh. Erm. I'm flattered that you've made that assumption and embarrassed that I have to put you right. I'm sort of between jobs too.'

'Oh. I see.'

'I was fired.'

There was a silence that settled between them like a film of dust. Dean was not often at a loss for words, but he found he couldn't pull to mind anything trite yet charming with his usual efficiency. He was beginning to understand why this woman might have convinced herself that a dash across the Atlantic to sabotage her ex's wedding was her only hope. Hesitantly, he commented, 'Well, I'm sure you'll find something new before long.' It was the best he could do, the usual platitude people offered, and he expected her to play her part, to politely reassure him that she would do just that.

'No, I don't think I will,' sighed Jo. She looked at her hands, which were resting on her lap. The pose oozed resignation.

'I bet you're very good at what you do.'

'I don't think I am. I was once. But I'm not sure any more.'

Dean rubbed his chin. This woman was unbelievable. She'd have to change her tack at interview. He needed a moment to think if there were any other directions he could steer this conversation. 'But you have hobbies, right?'

'Oh yes. I do a French class and I take salsa lessons.'

'Sounds fun,' said Dean. It sounded deadly. Why did single women go to salsa lessons? Did they think they'd meet men there or something? No way, José.

'You think they are terrible hobbies, don't you?' she asked. It seemed she had an uncanny ability to dig through his bullshit and an uncommon wish to do so.

'Well, I think it would be good if just once I met a woman who did something, you know, different.'

'Different? How so?'

'Perhaps sculpture classes, or had an interest in collecting old rave flyers from the nineties; even attending seminars about antique maps would be cool. Anything.' He glanced at Jo and she blinked back at him. Possibly fighting tears. He'd said too much. Maybe she also thought that her hobbies were a poor show. Dean rummaged around his brain for something else to say. Something that would not reveal more of her failings and idiocy but that seemed friendly. He had no idea why he wanted to be cordial towards her but he knew he did. 'Shall we watch a movie? There's a period drama with Renée Zellweger and Russell Crowe that looks like your sort of thing,' he said.

'How would you know what is my sort of thing?' she snapped. 'I might want to watch something completely *different*.' Dean didn't want to inflame her indignation and so resisted telling her that she was an open book. He offered her the entertainment magazine, which she reluctantly took from him. After reading the blurb, she sighed and admitted unwillingly, 'Actually, that is *exactly* my sort of thing. I am going to watch it.'

'So will I,' said Dean with a grin. 'We can watch it together.'

'You don't have to do that.'

'It will be fun. I like talking about a movie after I've seen it. Don't you?'

She didn't answer his question directly, but she stared at him for an age. 'Oh, go on then,' she agreed with a great show of disinclination, but Dean could see that a smile was dancing around the edge of her lips, and he knew that the disinclination was entirely feigned.

19

Eddie

The nurse is at my side almost the instant I open my eyes. She's making soothing sounds, like women do to crying babies. She's not actually saying 'There there,' but as good as. Someone is crying; well, not so much crying as groaning. Moaning. It takes a moment to realise it's me.

'It's OK, Eddie, here's your syringe driver.' As usual, she jabs something into me and then moves around the bed tapping tubes and checking readings. She works efficiently but with an air that puts me in mind of Mrs Williamson, an old bird I haven't thought of in years. She was the group director's senior secretary, back at the Beeb. She used to be charged with the job of counting the employees' heads after a fire alarm. We were daft buggers. Liked to wind her up. We'd move around the line so she'd count twenty-nine rather than twenty-eight, or a few of us would nip to the pub and she'd get flustered over the unaccounted-for blokes. She carried with her a perpetual tinge of panic. She was always expecting the worst. Preparing for it. The nurse reminded me of her. I imagine that Mrs Williamson, a formidable ancient matron back in the eighties, must be dead now. No longer panicking.

'Keep trying to drink your fluids,' says the nurse.

'Has my son been in?' The question, once vocalised, surprises me. I hadn't realised it was on my mind. It blurted out like a confession.

'Not since yesterday.' She places her hand on my arm. I don't have the energy to shake her off, but her touch stings and her sympathy makes me cringe. I wonder if she was on shift yesterday when he was here. I wonder what she saw or heard. There was a bit of a scene. Nothing compared to some I've witnessed while I've been lying here, though. No melodrama, no hysterics or fists involved. Lower key, but for anyone who is in the slightest bit tuned in to human nature, a notable scene. I'd just been scavenging around for something to talk to him about. He isn't the most communicative bloke, and, well, with our past, or more accurately lack of it, conversational avenues are limited. It was something and nothing. Then again, that's all we've ever been. Something and nothing. It was a spur-of-the-moment sort of thing, an impetuous gesture. That's my style.

I said to him, 'Hey, I have something that you might like.' And I noticed that his expression turned; it became a strange mix, somewhere between wary and hopeful. I wonder if he's one of the deep ones, or is he easy-going like me? 'In the drawer,' I told him. He went over to where I was pointing and opened the bedside drawer; rooted about a bit in amongst the crosswords and the audio books that I'd borrowed from the hospital library. When I say borrowed, in truth the disc was foisted on me by a zealous volunteer visitor; she was a nice enough old thing, and I didn't have the energy to turn her down. 'In the box,' I urged.

Dean pulled out the small tin box. It used to contain toffees. Not my toffees. I don't have a sweet tooth. One of the nurses saw that my bits and pieces were rattling around the bedside drawer and she was worried that something was going to go missing. I bet they get accused of nicking stuff all the time in here, so to cover herself she brought in a toffee tin and said I could have it. He was a bit slow about opening it. Cautious or dim. Not sure which. I had to urge him. 'That's it. Open it.'

Dean prised open the tin. I knew the exact contents. A couple of photos: one of me picking up the Captain's Cup at the golf club a few years back – Vince Langton's wife brought that picture in when she visited – and another of Ellie and Hannah. It's out of date, taken when they were kids and used to ride horses. There's my address book, which has my contacts, including the solicitor's details and such – that will come in useful – some keys, my watch and the ring. Dean paused over Ellie and Hannah's photo; I could see that he wanted to ask me about it, but he didn't. Too much pride. Probably didn't want to give me the satisfaction of knowing he gives a fuck. He picked out the ring, held it between his thumb and forefinger like he was going to catch something from it.

'Do you know what that is?' I asked.

'A ring.'

'Einstein, you are.'

'A wedding ring,' he snapped.

'That's it. Mine, from my marriage to your mother. I didn't wear a ring the second time round.'

'Saves the trouble of slipping it off when you're in a bar,' he said. I thought that was funny, although I don't think he was trying to make a joke.

'You can have it. I want you to have it.'

'Why would I want your wedding ring?' he asked.

Truth is, I'm not sure. It's not likely that he'll wear it himself, is it? It wasn't exactly a fortuitous ring; it doesn't come with a history of good luck, health and happiness. But what else could I do with it? Since he was here, I thought he might as well take it. Otherwise I could give it to a nurse, one who might drop it in to a charity shop for me.

'Well, it's yours,' I said with a shrug.

I thought he was going to sling it back in the tin, but he didn't. He muttered, 'Thanks' and shoved it into his inside jacket pocket. I closed my eyes, oddly relieved. It's exhausting, this fathering business.

I must have fallen asleep again. Then when I woke up, it took me a minute to remember who it was exactly sat by my bed. He nearly smiled at me, caught himself and then sort of turned his smile into a peculiar shrug-cum-wink. It was his refusal to smile that helped me place him. My eldest child.

'How are you feeling?' he asked. I tried to tell him *like shit*, but my voice wouldn't break through. He got me some water and I tried to take a bit, but it scratched to sip. A new sort of pain. More extreme. Then he did this thing that I was startled by. He dripped a few drops of water on my lips, the way the nurses do. Who had taught him that? Why did he think to do it? He pumped the syringe driver and asked if I wanted him to get a nurse. I must have looked bad. I tried to shake my head, but everything was uncomfortable, separate from me. I couldn't seem to hold my body together. I was losing consciousness. I do now. Drift. In. Out. The lad looked shocked. He stood up and called for a nurse. One came over. It wasn't this latest one, the one who's here this morning, come to think of it. Which is a relief. She tapped tubes and checked my charts and my catheter again, nodded and then walked away. Nothing to do. Dean looked scared.

'Why did you ask me here?' he whispered. He looked wrecked, probably not that much better than I do. He's desperate. I know it now. He's not slick and showy, like he wants to appear. He *is* one of the deep ones. Poor sod. I knew what he wanted to hear. He wanted an explanation, an apology, a declaration of love. He wanted me, his father, to hand over a bundle of tatty letters and birthday cards that I'd secretly written to him over all these years but had never posted.

I couldn't.

I've never secretly written anything to him.

I have *thought* of him. I'm not an animal. At the beginning, the very beginning, I didn't think of him much. Frankly, I was just glad to be out of it. Didn't miss him at all, none of them. Smelly, noisy, demanding kids; hysterical, slovenly, demanding wife. But a few years after I'd left, I got to wondering about them a bit. Dean in particular. First born. Not so much the girl. Just a baby when I went. I didn't know her at all. But I'd almost known Dean. It was the almost that did it.

I met Bridget around that time. We got on. We got married. We had the new kids. I forgot him again. I'm not one for looking back over my shoulder. What's the point? But seeing him yesterday, I did fleetingly wonder, what would it have been like to know him? That must be the drugs talking. Chemicals in my body. It's not the sort of thing I usually think. Besides, I know enough. I know what Dean came here for. He wanted an outpouring and a balm. Or at least a bloody good row. He wanted a reason. I haven't got one that's good enough. If I ever had one, then I've forgotten it, but I suspect I never really did have a good enough reason.

'You hurt me.' He whispered this close to my ear so I could hear him but no one else could. His skin is fine, clear. He has a face that looks like it has been carved out of marble: smooth, glossy, somehow beautifully intense. I bet he's always more at home with inhospitable climates than sunny ones. He looks used to raw, stinging environments. What has he been taught over all these years? I wonder. How and by whom? I tried to stay buoyant. I didn't want to hear what he was telling me. What would be the point? There's no room for all that now.

'You didn't even know me. You were a little lad. I thought it was best to get out of there before you grew too attached.' It was a labour to get these words out. I'm not sure he understood me, even though his ear was practically in my mouth.

'I am your son. You are my father. I was born attached,' he replied.

'Don't be melodramatic. You couldn't have missed me; you didn't know me. I left before you got to know me.'

'That's the worst of it.' His breath caught in his throat.

What could I say? Nothing. There was nothing that could restore his mother's health. No words that would wipe away the months that added up to years that he and his sister had spent in homes, so what the hell was the point in trying? None.

'What I don't get is why now?' he said. 'Why leave it so late? Why didn't you get in touch earlier?' I thought that possibly he was about to cry. I couldn't see clearly enough to know if his eyes were tearing up – my vision isn't what it was – but his voice gave him away. Despite working in the arts, I'm not that sort. I don't do tears. Men shouldn't. What was he crying over me for? He doesn't know me. I tried to head it off. Back to some facts.

'Look, son . . . I'm glad you're here. Surprisingly pleased about it. But there's something you should know.' It was such a struggle to speak. Not sure if the problem was lack of breath or lack of words. Sometimes there just aren't words. The right ones. I know that. 'I didn't ask you to come,' I told him, because it's the truth and that seems important. There's not much between us except a brutal reality. I don't want to muddy that now. The only real thing we have.

'But the nurse who called me . . .' he stuttered, confused.

'She took it upon herself. Soft bugger. Agency nurse from the hospice,' I explained. 'She was here with me all last week and we got to talking about kids and things. They're trained to ask if everything is in order. I said it was, but she thought you should know I was here. You kids. Not me. Her,' I explained.

I have nothing to tell him or give him. Nothing to reveal. Nothing.

'You didn't even ask me to come?'

'No.'

'Jesus. Not even that.' He pushed back his chair and walked out.

I suppose there's a good chance he won't be coming back. Some might call that poetic justice.

Me? I'd call it sad.

20

Jo

'It's undoubtedly the high altitude that is making me cry,' I explain to Dean.

'Undoubtedly,' he agrees in a way that makes it absolutely clear he doesn't believe me.

'OK, that and the plot,' I admit. As the credits roll to an end, I put away my screen and stretch my arms above my head. 'Did you see it was based on a true story?' I comment, through my sniffling.

'Probably only loosely,' he replies with a shrug.

I have not managed to exercise any control; the tears ran down my face like a waterfall throughout the film. It had everything: true love, triumph over adversity and a bundle of cute, impoverished kids. Dean offered me a handkerchief at one point and I was strangely touched that he (a man who is so obviously the very epitome of the twenty-first century) possessed such an old-fashioned item, until I unfolded it and saw that it had a picture of a buxom naked woman printed on it; it was an ironic handkerchief. Who'd have thought there was such a thing?

Obviously Dean remained dry-eyed, but I could tell he was moved because he chewed his nails through the bit when the Russell Crowe character went cap in hand to beg for money so the electricity could be turned back on and his kids could continue to live with him.

'Did you enjoy it?' I ask.

'The boxing was stunning.'

'The boxing was hell.'

He grins. 'Paul Giamatti was good. They all were. It was a bit cutesy for my taste, but brilliant cinematography. Ron Howard is always reliable.'

'It wasn't cutesy. You've missed the point. It was about an enduring, genuine love.'

'Was it? I thought it was about the 1935 heavyweight championship.' I know he's teasing me, but I can't help rising to the bait. I don't have political causes the way other people do; the only thing I think is worth defending is true love.

'Besides, they nearly *starved*. There's nothing cutesy about starvation,' I point out.

'No, there isn't,' he agrees grimly, and then he shuffles uncomfortably in his seat, fiddling with the buttons that make the chair tilt or rise. There's a sudden sense of oppression in the air. It's not like he's an aid worker or a humanitarian; he works in advertising, for goodness' sake, an industry that will actively encourage people to starve or binge if they can make a quick buck. However, he's taken my comment *very* seriously. It's unnerving; no one ever takes me seriously, let alone *too* seriously.

'What is your usual taste in movies, then?' I ask, pulling the conversation back on to easier ground. 'No, in fact, let me guess. I bet I can name your five favourite films of all time.'

Dean raises his eyebrows with scepticism. 'Go on then. I like a game.'

'*Fight Club.*'

He lets out an abrupt short laugh and nods. 'The first rule of Fight Club is—'

'You do not talk about Fight Club.'

Dean looks impressed. 'You've seen it?'

'No. I wasn't tempted, not even to see Brad Pitt's half-naked, hot body. I know the rule because every man I've ever dated has quoted it to me as though it's some sort of profound truth.' I grin. Dean nods again; this time his nod communicates understanding, perhaps contentment. Men are an alien species. I was offended when he implied I am predictable, but men are different; Dean is clearly pleased that he's part of the right club.

'OK. Lucky guess. What are my other favourite films?' he challenges.

'Hmmm. Let me think. I wonder, are you a *Pulp Fiction*, *The Godfather*, *Braveheart* and *Apocalypse Now* sort of guy? Someone who thinks of themselves as a bit cool. Or might you prefer *The Terminator*, *Lord of the Rings* and *The Matrix*? A proper lad's lad.'

'That's not fair. You've named about twenty films to cover your options,' objects Dean.

'Am I wrong?' I smile. If there's one thing I know, it is popular boy-culture. I've had lots and lots of conversations like this. Too many.

'No, you're spot on. But a real pro would make me choose between the various renditions.'

'Well, with the interminable *Terminators* . . . Snoring. Boring. Most people pick two, *Judgment Day*, but I think you might prefer the first one, when Arnie is a bad cyborg.'

Dean raises his fine eyebrow but doesn't comment. 'And the *Rocky* movies?'

'All five are the same, so I don't care.'

'No they are not.' He makes a face to indicate mock offence.

'Yes, I'm sure they are, although you should know when I make this pronouncement that I haven't actually seen them. Your favourite *Lord of the Rings* is *The Two Towers* because of the massive battle scene, and as far as you are concerned, nothing ever touched the original *Matrix*.'

Dean laughs out loud; his laugh rings through the cabin. I am suddenly aware that I haven't heard him laugh until now. He throws out charming (not always convincing) smiles and grins often enough, and makes sounds that approximate a laugh, sounds that certainly indicate he's amused, but his out-and-out laugh is something different altogether. It's a wonderful laugh that rings with tones reminiscent of heady nights out dancing and drinking wildly. I'm reminded of the occasions I've received a bouquet of flowers and plunged my face into the blooms to breathe in their scent. This particular laugh of Dean's offers promise; it is earnest and reliable. I feel strangely proud to have been the catalyst. His laugh catches the attention of other passengers too; they throw aggravated or jealous glances our way. I stare them down. I don't care about these other passengers, who yawn and snooze their way across the Atlantic, not bothering to swap a word; I'd almost forgotten they existed. But I do care about Dean Taylor.

I don't mean I care *care* for him. In a romantic or deep way. Although again, obviously, that wouldn't be the weirdest thing ever. After all, he is a very sexy, challenging and hot guy, and there was that *thing* outside the loos, the sexual chemistry thing, but there's more. Beyond the obviously attractive thing, there's a sadness about him that's gripping too. I know exactly what's going on here. I've been here often enough. If it wasn't for Martin and my plan to stop the wedding, I'd be in danger of really falling for Dean. Extreme danger. But there is Martin and a plan, so I'm fine. Just fine.

The point is, the other passengers, with their disapproving looks, can go to hell. We are not doing anything wrong; it isn't as though we've joined the mile-high club under the blanket.

Where did that thought come from? I mean, I wouldn't.

Well, probably not.

No, of course I wouldn't. I'm flying towards Martin. Martin, Martin, Martin. I say his name over and over again in an attempt to remain focused. If I seem confused or flighty, it's worth remembering that I've drunk quite a lot of free champagne on this journey. Besides, I haven't been in the habit of thinking about Martin for five years now, and I have been very much in the habit of considering quickies with hot, available strangers.

'Have you noticed no one ever asks about five favourite books?' comments Dean.

'Not on a date, at least. Not that we're on a date,' I hurriedly add.

'But it doesn't come into conversation in the same way as movies do.'

'Books are so much more personal than films.'

'They are, aren't they? I wonder why that is.'

I have thought about this before. 'I think it's because the relationship you have with a book is like a private dialogue, while watching a movie is more like an open conversation.'

'You're right. Sometimes it's just too hard, too personal to explain why you like a book.'

I pause, then add, 'More personal than the fact that you know I want to stop my ex marrying another woman?'

'Probably not.'

'So?'

'So what?'

'So what are your favourite books?'

Dean considers. The silence sits comfortably between us this time and I don't rush him. 'If I had to pick five, which is hard because I like tons of books, then I'd pick Rudyard Kipling's *Kim*, Dickens's *Great Expectations*, *Harry Potter*—'

'All seven?'

'I'll take the first and the last, and *The Kite Runner*.'

'OK, I'm impressed.'

'You thought I only read graphic novels, didn't you?'

I had thought that. 'Do you want to hear mine?'

'Not really.'

'Oh.'

I'm startled, but before I can take offence, he adds, 'But I would like to hear about the five best moments of your life.'

'Really?'

'Yes.'

'Wow, I've never been asked that before. I've never *thought* about it before.'

I wonder why he's asked this. Is it because he has a longing to crawl inside my soul? Unlikely. He's a man. Is he is simply passing the time of day? Possibly. This might be something he asks everyone he meets, a sort of party piece. I once came across a guy who knew the periodic table musical hall song by heart and he insisted on singing it to everyone he met. I literally came across him, even though this was his party piece; the thought depresses me. I heard him recite his song endlessly. It's surprising how often the words 'There's antimony, arsenic, aluminium, selenium, And hydrogen and oxygen and nitrogen and rhenium' still come to my mind, always bobbing about in a catchy little rhythm. Most likely Dean's question about my memories is simply the equivalent. Still, I give it due thought.

'I know what I am supposed to say.'

'What's that then?'

'Something along the lines of the moment I graduated, the moment I got my first job, when I went skinny-dipping in Lake Garda—'

'You've been skinny-dipping in Lake Garda?' Dean raises his eyebrows.

'Once.' I flush slightly. 'I know that's the sort of thing I'm supposed to say, but memory isn't like that, is it? Well, at least not for me.'

'So how is it for you?'

'My memories of good times are very blurry. They're very

187

old.' I don't like the way that came out; it doesn't sound true enough. I try to be clearer. 'There have been lots of good times, don't worry about that,' I add apologetically. 'It's just hard to be specific, to rank and record. I have impressions and feelings of periods of time rather than exact days. Mostly my best memories are connected with my childhood. My childhood is golden.'

'Really?'

'Yes.'

'You rarely hear that.'

I laugh. He's always joking. Everyone had a golden childhood, right? Adulthood is the bitch. 'I can't remember it raining, or at least hardly ever. I remember it as an endless series of picnics on the common or sometimes further afield.' I close my eyes and sink back into the plush chair. 'I remember the sensations clearly. The feel of the tartan rug we sat on – itchy but warm from the sun. The sound of a bee buzzing past my ear and the taste of biting into a salted tomato salad. The juice squirting round my mouth, the pips and flesh slithering down my throat. I remember visiting castles, energetically yomping up the hills to reach the ruins before my brother or sister did. I can still smell the mud and fresh grass.' I rush on as something else wonderful comes to mind, 'And I remember picking raspberries with my family. We'd drive out of Wimbledon to some Surrey farm or other. We'd fill punnet after punnet with far more than we needed; the ones in the bottom of the punnets would be squashed because of our greed, but then we'd go home and make jam. I remember the punchy ruby and amethyst colours and my mum's yellow gingham apron. I must have been very young when she wore that, because I remember one day needing comfort – although I don't remember why: a fall maybe, or a spat with one of my siblings – and I pushed my head against her body and I only reached her apron-clad belly. I surreptitiously wiped my nose on it.'

I giggle at the memory. I open my eyes to check that Dean is still listening and I haven't lost him. He's staring at me with a deep and obvious intensity, clearly drinking in every word. I am torn between feeling flattered and wondering whether I have something smeared on my face. People rarely find one another this interesting.

'What about you?' I ask. 'What are your happiest childhood memories?' Dean snaps his gaze away from mine immediately. All of a sudden he looks exhausted, ashen and deflated. His eyes are vast chambers but I sense the doors are locked. I once visited a pet rescue centre with a friend. All the dogs looked distant and isolated even when they were sharing a cage, even when they were licking your hand. Dean wears a similar look. I try to pull him back. 'Have you ever given it any thought?'

'Lots.'

'And?'

'I don't have any happy childhood memories,' he says flatly.

'None?' I can't imagine how this can be the case. Surely he's exaggerating. 'There must be one.'

'No. There really isn't.'

21

Clara

Clara had packed her suitcase with a prevailing air of calm and organisation – that bit hadn't been tricky; she was an efficient and practised packer – and then she'd booked into a wonderful just-out-of-town (let's-pretend-it's-the-country) spa, the one that she had visited twice a year for eight years. Normally she spent exactly four days and three nights there, just after Christmas and immediately before their summer break. For those four days she rigidly would follow a low-cal, low-carb diet, have a daily massage, an early morning swim and a pre-lunch walk and attend an evening yoga class. She'd read a lot in the hours in between and have her nails painted. This time she booked a one-week stay. She told the receptionist that she would not be following any of the diets on offer and that she didn't need a manicure. She had no plans after that.

Clara sat on the bed and wondered whether she could possibly summon the energy to join the pre-lunch walk around the beautiful and extensive grounds. She really ought to. Fresh air and deep breaths were what she needed right now, but she found she was frozen to the spot. Her tiny body seemed at once leaden and frail.

What had she done? She had left Tim. After all this time. She was no longer a wife. Well, technically she was, she supposed, but she was separated from her husband and so the world would no longer see her as one. Of course the world was blind; Clara had not been a wife for years.

Clara had sat, ramrod straight, all morning on the bed in her small but smart room. Her back ached, and she wanted to lie down, but when she checked her bedside clock (one of those awful electric things with bright red intrusive digits), it was eleven thirty-five a.m.; after eleven it was too late to pretend it was a lie-in and too early for a nap. Naps were for the afternoon, and only then on holidays. Besides, she feared that if she lay down, she might never get up again, as she had held herself up for such a very long time and always done the proper thing; well, at least up until walking out on her husband. She wondered whether she was capable of holding herself up for even a day longer, even a minute.

What was she going to do next? Money was not her problem. She was certain that Tim would be elegant and generous; he wouldn't want a fuss. But how would she fill her time? She was far too old for a career; that went without saying. Besides, what would she do? She wasn't qualified for anything and she had no experience. Clara had never had a career; she'd barely had a job. She'd left school at eighteen with three A levels; although her father said home economics really didn't count, she had disagreed. The thought of it, the delicious thought of disagreeing with any man, let alone her father, momentarily cheered Clara; it took some effort to remember that she had once been a rebel of sorts. The quiet sort, but even so there had been fight in her, there was dissent. She'd enrolled at college to do a BTEC in catering and business studies, because back then, long ago, she'd harboured dreams of running her own catering company. It hadn't happened, obviously. She'd met Tim on her first bout of Christmas holiday work experience and he'd derailed her.

The firm that she was working for had been supplying canapés for a reception at the bank where Tim was employed. Most of the braying bankers had treated the waitresses as though they were invisible, genderless robots; never making eye contact or saying thank you. Tim had been the exception. He had flirted with Clara all evening, practically following her around as she distributed mushroom and Stilton tarts. By the end of the party, she'd given him her number. They'd had a brief but intense relationship and were married within a year of that meeting; she was pregnant within a couple of months of the wedding bells chiming. They'd both agreed she didn't really need to work. Even a relatively junior salary in the City could keep them comfortably.

Her mother had asked her, 'What's the rush?' Clara couldn't quite remember now, but she had been engulfed by a sense of urgency at the time. Perhaps she was fed up of her father bossing her about; all fathers were imposing, controlling and demanding in those days and it was tiresome. Or perhaps she'd simply been flattered that Tim had pursued her with such force and certainty. It had taken her many years to understand what had motivated his vigour and determination; he'd thought she might be a cure at best, a cover at least. Neither of them had understood what he was; it had taken Eddie Taylor to make it clear.

Eddie Taylor. She soothed his pain. He set her on fire. Even now, as an old woman, his name caused an instant swell of lust to flood through her body. It was pitiful. It was pitiless. After the girls were born, Clara and Tim's sex life had stumbled. To be honest, at the time she'd been quite grateful that he wasn't bothering her; so many of her girlfriends struggled to juggle the demands of tiny babies and husbands who threw tantrums as though they were children themselves if they felt pushed out or neglected. Clara had thought Tim was the perfect gentleman, but then the sexless weeks turned into months, months stretched on for years. He'd barely touched her throughout her twenties; it was a sad, lonely time. Clara didn't tell a soul about their marital problems. Tim was such a good husband in every other way; an attentive father, a good provider. She hadn't understood it. He seemed to like spending time with her and the children, talking to them, playing with them, laughing with them, being with her. Except in that way. She'd been far too embarrassed to tell anyone. People didn't talk about things then. Not the way they did now.

One of her friends had watched her shrink, disintegrate under the neglect, and suggested she brush up on her typing skills, perhaps learn shorthand and get a job. It was the late seventies and women were wearing their skirts short and their hair long; working was seen as fun and fashionable. They didn't need the money – everyone agreed on that – but she did need the company, her closest friends would admit as much. Tim had encouraged her, been as supportive as ever. He'd helped her pick out a new wardrobe: flares and hot pants, tops that tied just under her breasts. They both thought that sexy, hip clothes were required for a junior secretary to the head of comedy at the BBC.

She'd met Eddie Taylor within the first thirty minutes of arriving at the Beeb; she'd known instantly that she was done for. He'd looked at her and in one glance he'd flattened her, razed her semblance of propriety and exposed her as an animal. She'd never experienced anything like it before or since. His glance had detonated a riot of conflicting emotions. Effervescent shards of delight blew away all sense of the decorum she'd previously lived by; the devastating notion that decency was shattered sent a splinter to her heart. Her body betrayed her. She trembled. She wasn't sure if it was anticipation or fear.

His eyes were unreasonable. The Ministry of War ought to have commandeered them as a weapon, because every woman he ever met was left defenceless under his gaze. Blue, sky blue, sparkling with possibility, irresponsibility and lust. No girl had so much as a moderate chance at apathy. He was physically magnificent. He had dark, brooding looks, like a hero in a gothic novel. He was big and brutal. He was raw and rude. Far too attractive for his own good, or anyone else's come to that. He was broad, muscular, athletic. Clara didn't understand at first; she couldn't explain why her body leant towards his when he walked into a room, why she sagged when he walked out of it. She had never experienced sexual attraction before. She had no idea of the benefits. She had no idea how it would feel to be the recipient of his attentions, and then to be bereft.

She resisted him for three months. He told her no woman had ever held out so long. Once they had slept together, it seemed to her that she'd never resist anything ever again. He crawled up under her skin, he consumed her. She was at his mercy.

But he had none.

Clara sighed at the too raw memory and glanced at the clock again. Eleven thirty-nine. The minutes crept by. She watched the gaudy digits for an eternity, until the clock reported that it was eleven forty. She sighed deeply and summoned every scrap of energy she had hidden in the depths of her body to push herself to her feet. She wandered to the window and glanced out; she could see one or two of the keener guests gathering near the lawn for the walk. They had sticks and water bottles, although Clara knew from experience that such aids were unnecessary; it wasn't a hike, just an hour's stroll to enhance appetites. Still, she envied the walkers as they exuded purpose. Clara had her walking shoes with her, but where would she find the energy to change into them and then participate? She wanted to cry. The window was surprisingly grimy, and the dirt seemed to create a barrier between Clara and the energetic, outdoorsy types. She felt she was drowning in a damp mist. She could not focus or concentrate. It was probably shock. She ought to eat something. She should ring for some room service. But she couldn't remember how to do that exactly. She didn't know what words she would use.

Clara regretted coming to the familiar surroundings. She'd thought that the stylish hotel might cheer her up, prop her up; it didn't. Every expensive mosaic tile, each tropical plant and all the lotions and potions were intrinsically linked with her old life, a life she was trying to throw over. Past pleasant memories haunted her. This time round, her visit to the spa was anything other than cosy and indulgent. She wondered what she would do to fill her hours, her days, weeks, months and years. What had she done? Who would she go antique shopping with now? Who would she holiday with? Who would she grow old with? She was so alone.

Then she remembered the letter, and she remembered who else was alone.

22

Dean

Dean had to admit to himself that he was grateful he'd stumbled upon this romantic inactive feminist who was prepared to lay bare her chaotic apology of a life, even though she had not managed to divert him away from thoughts of Eddie Taylor as he'd hoped. Instead, she'd created an atmosphere that was somewhat akin to a late-night lock-in in a grungy but welcoming bar. Like people who met at such places, they could freely share confidences and stumble through reminiscences that might usually be left undisturbed. They could do so safe in the knowledge that when the plane touched down and the doors were switched to manual and heaved open – allowing fresh air to explode into the cabin – they'd go their separate ways and never see one another again.

He had no favourite childhood memories to share with her, but he told her about his ferocious desire to win the confectionery pitch and she commented that it sounded as though he had a good chance.

'You think?'

'Yeah.'

'You like the sound of the ads, then?' The strategy was supposed to be top secret, but Dean in a rare moment of unprofessionalism had told her something about the concepts. As he did so, he was vaguely aware that he was showing off to her, strutting a little. He didn't dwell on why this might be the case.

'Yes, but besides that, the marketing guy won't dare risk you telling anyone about the visit to the strip bar.'

'Plus he'll want to go back.'

'Exactly. It's in the bag.'

He elicited her opinion as to whether she thought men looked attractive in pink shirts. He had a purple one but hadn't risked anything more. Did she think he should?

'Definitely.'

He chatted about his mates and colleagues. He told her that his friend was having an affair with his own sister-in-law and that he was fed up of covering for him. 'But I can't blow the whistle, can I?'

'No, you can't, but you can tell him you are no longer prepared to lie for him.'

In her turn Jo recounted the details of the last three occasions that she'd been a bridesmaid, and all the accompanying horrors: unflattering dresses, frantic brides and patronising groomsmen. She recounted the stories with humour and grace, even though they were both aware that living through the actual events had been devoid of either thing. Dean wondered if one of the biggest motivators for her getting married was so she could avenge herself on her friends by insisting they wore three-tier meringues in pistachio green. She asked him his advice about what she should buy for her parents for their anniversary. 'They are a nightmare to buy for. They have everything.' They flicked through the in-flight shopping catalogue for inspiration. Jo liked the idea of buying a silk scarf for her mother and Dunhill cufflinks for her father. 'But look at the prices,' she gasped.

'You don't want to buy those,' argued Dean, although it was

clear from the look of longing that Jo would very much like to buy the expensive products.

'Don't I?'

'No, far too predictable. I bet your mum has a million scarves and your dad will still be wading through the cufflinks people bought him for his last birthday. But that, that is an original gift.' He pointed to another page.

Jo admitted that they didn't have a teddy bear dressed as a pilot, and although it was very unlikely that they'd want one, Dean insisted on buying it for her to give them. She accepted the toy with a giggle. 'Thanks. I guess you've worked out that I'm a bit strapped for cash right now,' she confessed, with a shy smile.

The flight forged an intimacy which Dean valued all the more because he knew it was tenuous and finite. This woman was not part of his real life, and that was probably the reason why he suddenly blurted, 'Yesterday I left my father dying in a hospital. He has pancreatic cancer. It's spread throughout his body. He's riddled with it.'

She gasped, as he knew she would. 'My God,' she muttered. They both knew that death was big. Bigger than a wedding, even the hijacking of a wedding. 'I'm sorry,' she added; she sounded sincere.

'There's no need for you to be. I could have stayed with him to the end, but I decided not to.'

Did she understand he was offering up a mess? That he had the decency to try to tell her his brain was riddled with thorny 'what if' scenarios too? She'd said she'd bet he'd never made a mistake in his life. She, like practically everyone he met, was labouring under the false impression that he was perfect. Normally he was very happy for people to buy into his carefully constructed veneer of perfection, especially women, but for reasons he didn't entirely understand, he wanted to put her right. It was probably because she'd made no attempt to hide any of her many imperfections; in fact she'd gone to some lengths to detail her catastrophic apology of a life. Things were too uneven. 'My relationship with my father is . . .' He broke off. Having opened Pandora's box, he was almost immediately unsure as to what extent he really wanted to share the experience of the last few days. How could he finish that sentence? *My relationship with my father is non-existent* was truthful but perhaps too bleak for Jo to handle. All he could think of to say, even though it didn't so much as scratch the surface, was 'Well. It's complicated.'

'I suppose you had to get back to Chicago. Obviously you couldn't stay in the UK indefinitely. You know, waiting. You had no choice.' Of course she was bound to think the best. 'How long do they think he has?' Her voice oozed gentle concern, like buttercream icing emerging in generous folds from an icing bag.

'Days.'

'My God, what were you thinking?' The buttercream curdled.

Dean didn't know whether to be offended or amused by her condemnation. He thought it was some sort of consolation that she wasn't feigning anything; she obviously was genuinely shocked that he hadn't found time in his busy schedule to devote to a dying father. He shook his head a fraction and met her honesty with his own. 'I wasn't thinking at all.'

He hadn't thought about the dying man. He'd stormed angrily out of the hospital, concentrating only on his own pain, his own shame and anger and disappointment. Truthfully, that was all he was thinking about still. Why should he think of his father? His father had never thought of him. He looked right at Jo. Seeing her clearly. Wanting her – this odd stranger – to see him just as truly. He suddenly became aware that they were tilting their heads towards one another. It felt like they were cocooned. Alone.

'Well, at least you got to say your goodbyes. That must be some comfort,' whispered Jo.

Dean shook his head as though he was trying to dislodge an annoying buzz. He wasn't going to lie to her. It would be very easy to go along with her imagined sugar-coated version of his past. There would be no harm in allowing her to think that things were better than they were, but he didn't want to mislead her. 'We didn't say our goodbyes. We fought.'

'I'm sorry.'

'Right,' he muttered.

'But he'll know how you really feel about him. All your years together will have built up some confidence. This last spat doesn't have to mean anything, not unless you let it,' she urged.

Dean thought that talking to Jo was a bit like having a sick pet. At what point did you decide to put it out of its misery? 'We didn't have years together. I spent less than twenty-four hours with him after a twenty-nine-year separation. There is no bank of shared experience or memories. Nothing fond was said at the end. He is a shit. Lived his life as one and can now die as one.'

'Oh.'

'If he knows how I feel about him, that's great. But all I feel is hate.'

'I doubt you really hate your father. I just cannot imagine that. People have rows, but hate? Hating is so big.'

'I hate him.' Dean felt like a stupid kid for using such a raw and unsophisticated word. But he considered that he was without choice. He knew he'd upset her. Her face collapsed in on itself. This wasn't the way this woman wanted to see the world. She believed in happily-ever-afters, fairies and magic dust too, prob-ably. They fell silent for a moment. He could almost hear her thoughts; she was scrambling around for platitudes and positive spins, hope and twee comments, the sort you saw written up on posters in people's downstairs loos. *Smile and the whole world smiles back at you.* Like hell they do.

She surprised him. 'You must be exhausted,' she said finally.

The words somehow released him, and he felt the tension slip out of his neck and shoulders, slide down his back and disappear, at least for a while. He was suddenly swamped by a desperate need for sleep. It was as though her articulating the fact that he must be exhausted had given him permission to be so. Then she stretched across the wide plush seat and patted his arm. Her fingertips lingered and the gesture didn't feel intrusive; it offered some level of consolation and understanding. Her touch seared through his sleeve and he had an urge to rip off his shirt or at least roll up his sleeves because he wanted to feel her fingers on his skin. He was beginning to like her. He thought he possibly might be able to forgive her for being an idiot and wanting to spoil her ex's wedding, but then she broke the mood when she added, 'It might have made more sense if you'd stayed in the UK. No sooner will you be home than, well, if everything goes as you expect it to, you'll have to go back for the funeral.'

The exhaustion was immediately spiked with irritation. Hadn't she been listening after all? 'I won't be going to the funeral.'

'Oh. So who will organise it?'

'I don't care. I know he's made a will. He mentioned that. It's probably all taken care of.'

'But who will pick the music and the prayers?'

Dean stared at Jo as though she'd lost her mind. 'Maybe there won't be any.'

'There has to be music and prayers.'

Dean doubted there did actually; still, he found himself in the strange position of wanting to again protect her from harsh truths, even while she was irritating him. It was surreal. 'The undertakers are most likely to do that sort of thing, I imagine, if there are no relatives.'

'But there *are* relatives,' she insisted.

'Yes, that's true. But I can't imagine anyone will be keen to pick out prayers for him and I, for one, have no idea what music he likes. That says it all really. Jo, he hasn't led a good life. He isn't a good man,' Dean stated firmly.

Still she wouldn't let it go. 'Maybe not entirely.'

'Not at all.'

'No one is one hundred per cent evil.'

'I disagree. Think Hitler, Stalin, Pol Pot.'

'But your father hasn't committed genocide.'

'No, but he is a weapon of mass destruction. Everything he touches turns to crap.'

'Not everything. You're lovely and he made you.'

Dean wanted to laugh. He'd only met her a few hours ago, and yet she said things like 'You're lovely'. Who did that? She was wrong, of course. He didn't think of himself as especially lovely. Most of the time it was all he could do to hold down the bile and anger. He sighed, expelling exhaustion, irritation and confusion. He rarely revealed what he was thinking. He'd learnt the importance of not doing so during childhood, so he wondered why he was taking so much effort to explain what he was feeling to this stranger. He shouldn't have bothered. All he could think to say was 'Look, Jo, you didn't know him.' He wanted to bring this discussion to an end. He now deeply regretted mentioning his father at all. He wasn't sure why he had. To shock her? To give her some perspective? The man had been dead to him for years; what did it matter if he was now actually dying?

Other than the drone of the ineffectual air-conditioning, the cabin was reasonably peaceful. From time to time Dean's attention was pulled to the sound of someone glugging water from a plastic bottle or someone else intermittently chuckling at the movie they were watching. There was a persistent but insignificant chorus of bored sighs and shuffles as the passengers began to tire of the long journey. The plane's air was warm and sour with perspiration. Acrid and coarse, it found its way up his nostrils and down the back of his throat; he knew it would cling to his clothes too. He couldn't wait to get home, to shower off the past few days and change into something fresh. He needed to be Chicago Dean again.

He might pop by the agency later this afternoon, even though he wasn't expected in. He loved his huge open-plan office with its great view of the city. There had been a time, a few years ago, after the Towers tragedy, when people had started to get nervous about having an office in a skyscraper but Dean had never been concerned in that way. He liked the view and the open space. It was probably true to say that he felt more at home in his huge, high-in-the-sky office than anywhere else in the world, even more so than in his loft apartment – although that was undoubtedly cool too. In his office, Dean was tall and strong. When he sat at his enormous glass desk he felt calm and composed. Triumphant and significant. Sitting by his father's hospital bed had leached away some of that confidence and self-belief. England did that to him sometimes. It was hard to remember who he had become when everything about him reminded him of who he once was.

Fuck his father! he thought angrily. Dean had been steaming when he'd believed his father had got in touch with him as he lay on his deathbed – he'd thought it was selfish and indulgent, melodramatic and confusing – but to hear that he hadn't even done that much was somehow worse. He felt humiliated that he'd gone running when he hadn't even been called. It was the worst. And now his father was dying. Typical of Eddie Taylor; he'd always been top of the class when it came to bailing. Dean felt intense flares of fury burn inside his chest and head. Fuck the woman he had left them for! He wanted to punch something or someone, or everything and everyone, but instead he silently simmered. It really wouldn't do to alarm the flight attendants.

His eyes fell on Jo. She was asleep now. At rest, her face was free of any desire to impress or apologise (the two states he'd already identified as her default settings). She looked neither young nor old, or strong or vulnerable. She was simply being human; she was sleeping and breathing, her chest rising and falling. Her mouth had become slack and hung open. The straightforward effortlessness of that fact caused Dean to draw a jagged, surprised breath.

They'd talked for a few more hours after he'd told her about his father. About something and nothing. She'd wanted to know more about what he did for a living and how he'd got into advertising in the first place; where he lived, how many children his sister had. He'd been glad that she'd kept away from the subject of his father; that she'd understood enough to let the matter drop. He'd recommended a couple of hotels that she might want to stay at. He couldn't believe she'd set off halfway round the world without giving her accommodation a moment's thought. He wasn't sure how big her budget was, so he'd written down the name of a hotel that his company had a corporate deal with and told her to pretend to be an employee when she booked in; they never asked for proof. He'd also recommended that she visit Buckingham Fountain, Millennium Park and maybe take a boat cruise. She'd murmured that she doubted she'd have time for sightseeing but thanked him for his suggestions.

In the end Jo had provided the distraction he'd hoped for, as she was extremely easy to talk to and listen to. She was quite unlike the women he usually met. So raw and open about her ambition to pursue her ex, she was totally devoid of any artifice or guile. Bonkers, obviously, deluded and mistaken, but at least real. Not that he could blame the women he knew for being cagey. Men could be bastards. *He* was a bastard. Of course, women were unlikely to bother to say what they were really thinking or feeling. Still, it was refreshing to get the truth off someone occasionally, even if that truth was foolish and reprehensible. Jo had a naivety – or was it more accurate to say optimism? – that he found intriguing. In fact he found it almost bewildering, because from where he was sitting her life was a lousy mess, and yet she really seemed to think it might get better.

Dean glanced casually around the cabin, looking for some diversion. They were making good time and would land in about forty minutes. Three p.m. Chicago time, just ahead of schedule. He'd take a cab to his apartment. Then later he could walk to his office and spend the rest of the afternoon there: catch up on emails, mooch around the creative department and see what they'd been working on in his absence. Maybe he'd call some of his friends and see if anyone was up for a night out. Dinner, a movie, anything. When had he last slept? It wasn't worth trying to nap now. He doubted he could anyway. He felt jittery and yet depressed. Wide awake and yet out of step. It had been a smooth flight, with just one or two spots of turbulence. When the plane shuddered, people looked up from their paperbacks but avoided one another's gaze, unwilling to show that they were afraid and irrational. Everyone was, though. In the end, despite the shows of civility that were meant to prove they weren't dumb animals, everyone was afraid and irrational.

Dean became aware that the flight attendants were striding down the aisle collecting used glasses and headsets. Then the fasten seat belt sign came on, and as though it had actually instructed everyone to leap out of their seats, rather than the opposite, people all around him suddenly jerked into action. The middle-aged businessmen bounced in their seats, slipping their shoes back on, putting away laptops, copies of *Time* magazine and Sudoku puzzles. Other passengers rushed to the bathrooms and the captain's voice came over the speaker system, informing them that they were now just twenty minutes from landing, that the temperature in Chicago was a surprising twenty-nine degrees and that the captain was aware that they had a choice of airlines and was gratified that they'd picked his. Dean stretched over to Jo and gently shook her awake.

'We're going to land. You have to put your seat up.' She sat up suddenly, looking alarmed and befuddled. Dean wondered whether the enormity of what she was doing had finally sunk in.

He realised he was mistaken when she said, 'Gosh, I must look a mess. Was I snoring?'

'No.' She had been, very lightly, but he didn't think she needed to know; he figured she had enough to worry about.

'Well, that's good. Did you get any sleep?'

'No.'

She glanced nervously at the illuminated fasten seat belts sign. 'Do you think I have time to go to the bathroom to freshen up? I bet I look a state.'

'Not really. There's a queue. The flight attendants are asking people to return to their seats. Anyway, you look fine. Better than you did when you boarded.'

'Oh, thanks. I think.'

'You've got some colour back in your cheeks.' Without giving it any thought, he leant forward and gently, using his thumb, eased out the sleep that nestled in the corner of her right eye.

'Thank you.' She surprised him by bringing up her hand and rubbing his cheek robustly. 'You have a crease where you've leant against the pillow,' she said by way of explanation. He stared at her, startled but not affronted in any way. She stared back as though they were in a playground contest. But she lost because she blushed and turned away first.

They both watched in silence as the plane pushed through the downy bank of clouds, and suddenly Dean could see the imposing Chicago skyline. Terra nova for Jo, home for him. The elephant-grey tarmac loomed up to meet them. The wheels banged on to the runway with one whack, two, and then a third, before they were pinned firmly and safely to the ground. Dean heard a round of applause being offered up from economy class; one or two passengers in club class joined in, Jo being among them, even though cheering the pilot was largely an American tradition. Dean wasn't a nervous flyer so he hadn't realised he was gripping his seat arm. He only became aware when Jo placed her hand over his and wriggled her fingers to thread in between his. She gave his hand a small squeeze.

'It's going to be OK,' she said over the noise of the rushing wind and whirling engines.

'You think.' It was a statement rather than a question, but Jo nodded enthusiastically anyhow. It was odd; if he'd been a betting man, at the beginning of this flight he'd have bet that he'd be the one comforting her as they approached touchdown, not the other way round. She was a peculiar combination; so positive and therefore powerful, and yet so misguided and naive. Did she know what was making him nervous? Did she, with her blissful childhood, have any real idea? For a moment it seemed as though she did know that he needed reassurance, that by squeezing his hand she was telling him what he needed to hear – that everything would return to normal again now, the interruption could be forgotten and buried. He wouldn't sink.

After travelling at such a high speed for so many hours, it was strangely sobering and very frustrating that the plane crawled to the gate. Dean could see portable steps being wheeled out to meet them, and with an accuracy that surprised him every time, no matter how often he flew, the plane locked on to them like the attracting poles of a magnet. The engine stopped. The fasten seat belt sign went off. Passengers leapt up like athletes off the block competing for an Olympic medal, but Dean and Jo stayed still. Her hand still resting on his. Fingers intertwined. She smiled at him. He smiled back.

'As a resident, I get to file through a slightly shorter customs queue than yours. So we probably won't see each other the other side.'

'Right.'

'So we should say our goodbyes now.' He didn't know why he'd said that. What was he planning to do? Shake her hand? Shake some sense into her? Hug her?

'It's been wonderful flying with you, Dean Taylor.'

'The pleasure was all mine, Jo Russell.' As he said it, he was surprised to realise that he meant it; what he said to women and what he thought about them didn't always tally as neatly, but he had needed her company more than he could have imagined. She was not just a distraction, but a comfort too. He'd been comforted by her optimism. Even though he didn't share it, he found he was gratified to think that such hopefulness was out there in the world somewhere. Actually, he was surprised to find that he had remembered her surname; he often called women 'babe' or 'doll' to avoid the complication of having to remember names. They sat quietly for a moment, allowing all the other passengers to rush and tumble around them. 'Good luck with, you know, everything.' Dean couldn't quite bring himself to wish her luck with her ridiculous plan; it was cruel to offer encouragement.

'I'm sorry about the book dropping and the champagne dropping . . .' She allowed her apologies to fade away.

He shrugged. Glancing down at the stains. He'd forgotten all about her entrance. 'Don't worry about it.'

'And I'm sorry about your dad.'

'As I said, don't worry about it.'

23

Jo

I watch Dean's back as he melts into the crowds that are heading for the residents' queue, then join the significantly longer, more higgledy-piggledy non-residents' line. I am continually jostled and urged forward and so I can't let my eyes linger on the sad and ridiculously handsome man for as long as I might have liked. I mentally shake myself. OK, what I have to do is think in terms of practicalities. I need to make this happen with Martin, to make it work. This is my big chance. This is my last chance. I must formulate a plan.

First I have to check into a hotel. Thank goodness Dean suggested one, or else I wouldn't know where to start. Wasn't that thoughtful of him? How far away will it be? I wonder. I bet it's gorgeous; he is clearly a man who values style. Is the hotel likely to be somewhere near the wedding venue? I hope so. Next I'll need clothes for tomorrow. I haven't packed much at all. Whatever came to hand first, without really thinking it through. So I have sleepwear, toiletries, jeans and clean knickers, but I'll need more than jeans and clean knickers to lure Martin away from his new fiancée. Although, arguably, if that is *all* I wear when I confront him, then I might be at an advantage. He's always been a breast man.

Having had my passport and visa waiver stamped, I wander through to baggage collection. I stand on tiptoes and crane my neck. I tell myself I'm not hoping to spot Dean, but I'm proved wrong when a wave of disappointment washes through me as I register that there's no sign of him. He obviously cleared customs before me, and as he had carry-on luggage, he wouldn't have had to hang around this noisy hall. He's probably halfway home by now.

I'll never see him again.

The thought strikes me like a blow. Suddenly I feel sick and tired and lost. I feel my sanguine confidence begin to drain. Rubbing my eyes with the heels of my hands, I mentally chastise myself. This is idiotic. So I'll never see Dean again. So what? He was an incident. That's all. We shared a few hours and that will be it because Chicago is an enormous city and there's no chance that I'll simply bump into him. I shouldn't even want to. How many people live here? Dean mentioned a figure. Was it two and a half million? So, not a hope in hell of ever seeing him again.

Suddenly the thought of Chicago looming, huge and unknown, is not so much exciting as intimidating. I feel coldly isolated and more solitary than I felt at Heathrow. Heathrow was fun. That side of the Atlantic I had shops and hope, and blind faith. Where has that gone to? It isn't just because this airport is new and strange to me; the truth is, I miss him.

I miss *Dean*. It is ridiculous but true.

I wish I'd asked for his mobile number or an email address. It would have been sensible to have a contact here in this unfamiliar city. Sensible and comforting. And something more. Something I cannot examine, admit to or even consider.

I spot my bag trundling around the conveyor belt and sweep it up. I thrust out my chin, a physical and mental act of defiance that makes me feel an iota stronger and more sure. Enough of this wishing and hoping and dreaming; I have been doing that for years, to no avail. It's time to get real, to get serious. To be practical. I need to focus on getting into the city, on checking into the hotel, on buying clothes and on *Martin*. I have to put one foot in front of the other and do what I've promised myself I am here to do.

Yet I can't quite imagine what is next, not clearly, not any more. I can't quite imagine Martin's face, not clearly.

Not any more.

All I see is Dean. Dean's reluctant smile, Dean's tanned hands. I can hear Dean's funny and clever quips echoing through my head. He has a strange way of looking at the world. Slightly savage, slightly damaged. Is that because he's losing his dad, or is there more? What is the deal with him and his father? I'd have liked to have the time to find out, but it needed coaxing. I'd have liked to make things better. Just a tiny bit. If I could. I remember his laugh. The big one. The real one. It's brave and occasional and brilliant. I can smell his cologne.

I walk through the corridor that leads landside and cross my fingers that there'll be a bus into the city; my hundred and fifty dollars cash won't go far if I have to pay for a cab. I have to stop thinking about Dean. Think about Martin. Yet I keep hearing Dean's voice, repeating my name. *Jo. Jo.* It strains above the noise of airport greetings, clanking trolleys and the endless bustle of countless busy people dashing across the polished tiles.

Jo! The tone is persistent, insistent. In fact so persistent and insistent it doesn't sound as though it's in my head; it sounds real. I turn to where the voice is coming from. And there he is. Like a great big smile. Dean. He waves to me from the glass doors that lead outside to the taxi rank.

'Jo, do you want to share a ride? I can drop you off at the hotel,' he yells.

As my eyes land on him, rest on him, I suddenly feel wrapped in certainty and strength again. I fight down tears of relief. With him by my side I am sure I can do anything, anything at all, including destroying a wedding. I hurry towards him. Towards his smile and the sense that he'll look after things, sort things out. I beam at him and he beams back. I'm surrounded by fresh air, a welcome change after the plane and the endless corridors of air-conditioning, and I tell myself that what I'm feeling is all about relief and friendship and nothing to do with falling in love.

'I thought you'd be long gone.'

'I started to worry that you wouldn't be able to find the hotel. Or that maybe there wouldn't be rooms and you'd need somewhere else.' He shrugs, trying to downplay his thoughtfulness.

'I'd have managed,' I lie. I doubt I would have, but I don't want to appear too pathetic. Dean doesn't look convinced.

'And this wedding you're going to. This non-wedding.' He rakes his fingers through his hair; he looks uncomfortable. Unsure. 'I wondered whether you brought anything with you to wear.'

'No, no, I haven't. I was just thinking about that.'

'And whether you knew where to go to shop.'

'No clue.'

'I could help with that,' offers Dean with another shrug. 'I could show you where my sister likes to shop when she comes to visit me.'

'You'd do that?'

'This doesn't mean I'm endorsing what you are doing.'

'OK.'

'I think what you are doing is suicide.'

'Right.'

'I just want you to look your best as you are going to your death.' He grins.

Without over-thinking it, I rush at him, fling my arms around him and pull him into a tight hug. 'Thank you. Thank you so much.'

More cautiously, he pats my back and mutters, 'No biggie.'

24

Eddie

I recognise her the moment she walks in, which is a miracle, because my vision is letting me down and, well, it's been forever. Some might make something of that. There isn't anything to make of it. I recognise her because she hasn't changed. Inevitably, there are a few more lines around her eyes, the skin underneath her jaw has slackened a fraction and she is perhaps three or four pounds heavier – she carries it all on her stomach. But on the plus side, her clothes are even posher than they were – and they were always refined, a cut above. She's wearing white linen trousers and a thin woollen navy top, probably cashmere, I'd guess. The top wafts gently around her as she walks towards me, caressing her shoulders, hips, breasts. Her hair is a little longer than I remember, softer, feathered. She used to wear it in the Purdey style, inspired by *The New Avengers*; she had the cheekbones and the endless legs to carry it off. There were a lot of Joanna Lumley wannabes back then. Clara was one of the few who was convincing.

Yes, not bad at all. She has that air. The air of a woman who was once something in the seventies; awake and aware, desirable when we really knew how to desire. If you've once had it, you're forever conscious of it. Some wear their past glory with bitter disappointment that they're so far from their triumphant conquests now, others with blithe ignorance that this is the case. She wears hers with a quiet dignity; about her is just a whispered hint that she was once fabulous and is now a woman who is not bad for her age. She has definitely aged better than anyone else I know; certainly better than I have. I'm jabbed by a lawless spike of admiration mixed with miserable anger that this should be the case. The moment I see her, I realise that this is what I wanted. Her here. One last time. What I've secretly hoped for ever since I sent the letter. But in the instant I realise as much, I am infused with another thought: I wish she hadn't come.

It would have been better if she'd remembered me as I was.

I'm not usually one for feeling sorry for myself, but this reunion – this stroll down memory lane, or whatever we're going to do – would be a damn sight easier if that bloody catheter wasn't so prominent. She can see my piss. Who wants that? No one. Not after what we were.

The bloke in the bed opposite hears her shoes clip-clattering through the ward and strains to sit up for a better look. It's obvious he doesn't get enough; he's a shadow of a man. I've seen his wife. She's big, bespectacled and bossy. She comes here with bags of grapes and her cheap magazines, hair perpetually tied back in a greasy ponytail. She gobbles the grapes while reading the gossip and lecturing him about cutting back on cigarettes. I've never seen her offer him the fruit. I think he's going to have another stroke when he clocks Clara. He beams like an idiot. I gave her that. Before me she was pretty. After me she was noticed. She was more.

'Hello, Eddie.'

There's pity in her eyes, shining where longing, lust and hate have been. I try to ignore it because it's embarrassing. The last thing I want to see. 'Well hello, sweetheart.' I try for the old confident swagger in my tone; it's swallowed because I haven't breath to spare. 'It's been a long time.'

She sits down. Back straight, head up. 'Has it? Suddenly it seems like yesterday.' She smiles.

And there it is. Bang. The same smile. Slow; starts on one side of her mouth, the right side. At once provocative, teasing and true.

And I know the facts. I'm a dying old bastard. She's someone else's wife who, despite expensive haircuts and make-up and what-not, has seen better days as well. But her smile hasn't changed. It's all still there in her smile.

And fuck, this woman loves me.

25

Dean

Dean had often shopped with women. It was something he did with flair, as he had plenty of style and plenty of cash. He liked dressing women up, watching them become what they secretly hoped they could be: their best selves. He saw it as a hobby, a little like other people viewed interior decorating. Women, on the whole, appreciated his generosity and were happy enough to be indulged, so he often brought dates shopping. The expeditions were normally missions: a performance, a ritual.

Foreplay.

Dean's shopping party with Jo was a completely different experience. Of course she wasn't his date, so there was no question that he should pick up the tab, but the main difference was that she viewed shopping as an opportunity for fun, not a killer hunt. Despite their time constraints, she gamely tried on the most beautiful and ugly pieces in each shop, 'Just to see.' She had clear opinions of her own and she saw potential in pieces that he might have overlooked. Besides, she looked pretty good in almost everything (with the exception of the green cheesecloth maxi dress, which really was hideous), and so it was simply a pleasure to see her emerge from the changing room, grinning and giggling.

Initially Dean had considered visiting a number of expensive, upmarket shops, the ones he usually frequented, but then he remembered that she'd only travelled club class because she'd got an upgrade, and so he tactfully asked what her budget was.

'Modest,' she'd replied.

'Like five hundred dollars?'

'Closer to two.'

'But you've packed shoes, right?'

'No.'

'So two hundred dollars including shoes?' He hoped he hadn't betrayed his shock; he didn't want her to feel bad about her cash limits. Even after years of being financially comfortable, he still remembered that miserable feeling keenly.

'Actually, one hundred and fifty, and I also need a bag. If I spend more I'll have to slam it on a card, and my cards are just about maxed out with the cost of the plane ticket, and I still have to pay for the hotel,' she'd explained with a shrug and a smile. There it was again, her rare and amazing honesty. 'It wouldn't be fair to Martin to start married life with a load of debt.' And there it was again, her dangerous self-delusion.

Dean had thought they'd wander the 'Magnificent Mile', a stretch of North Michigan Avenue between Oak Street and the Chicago River, an area that was a mix between New York's Fifth Avenue and Beverly Hills's Rodeo Drive. OK, he hadn't expected her to buy Bulgari jewellery, Prada bags, or Salvatore Ferragamo shoes, but he had thought they might pop into one of the indoor high-rise malls, where pretty boutiques aplenty were tucked away. Once he heard her budget limitations, he Googled outlet malls.

'Wow, that's quite a drive,' Jo commented nervously when he showed her the location of the mall on his phone.

'I'm not going to abduct you, if that's what you're thinking. We'll take a cab.'

'I wasn't thinking that.' She paused. 'Although now you've said it, I feel foolish, because maybe I should have been thinking that, but I wasn't because I trust you. I was just concerned that I'd be taking up your whole afternoon.'

'Don't worry about it, I don't have any plans.'

'Well, if you're sure . . .'

He knew she was tempted. 'It's that or a thrift store.'

She lit up. 'A thrift store sounds fun.'

'Yeah, doesn't it? It's not. I don't think an XXL pullover will cut it at the wedding, even if you accessorise it with a two-dollar scarf made by an eight-year-old in an underdeveloped country. Let's go to the outlet. I think you're going to need to wear something designer as armour, even if it's last season's design.'

He hadn't intended to hang around the airport taxi rank. He certainly hadn't intended offering to take her shopping. The problem was, every time he tried to leave her, he found he couldn't. It was the craziest thing. Chicago was a busy and confusing city; at every moment it was sliced like a cake by countless trains rattling across bridges, hurtling people from A to B and back again. She'd never find her way around. It wasn't just her big harp seal eyes and her big come-to-mama breasts; there was something far more elusive and far more intriguing about her that he couldn't quite shake. He was fascinated by her . . . her what? Her romanticism? Her idiocy? Different names, same thing, surely. He'd encountered plenty of women who flashed their eyes and their tits to catch his attention, or played the helpless-female card so that he'd felt duty-bound to pay for dinners and cabs, but he'd always found it easy to simply walk away whenever he chose; as the waiter brought their coats, as the cab door closed, before the sun came up. Rarely later than that. He never got involved. But Jo was different. He *was* involved. Not in the traditional sense, obviously, but in some indefinable, elusive way. She wasn't an archetypal damsel in distress. That would have irritated him. She wasn't asking him to save her. The opposite: she was determined that this Martin bloke was going to do that; she didn't need Dean. Which was great, because he didn't like to be needed. Yet . . . Yet he couldn't walk away from her. He certainly hadn't planned to take her to dinner, but what the hell?

The light had started to fade from the day by the time they agreed to go to the restaurant at Millennium Park. Families with kids in buggies were going home for a night in front of the TV, and packs on the pull were emerging. She'd demurred when he first suggested dinner, but he knew it wasn't because she didn't want to be with him; she was worried whether she could afford it. Aware of her lack of cash, he was concerned that if he didn't feed her, she might resort to eating tissues in the hotel bathroom.

'I insist, my treat. I can't let a fellow Brit come to Chicago and not see some of the sights, let alone fail to taste a Colossal Chicago Char Dog.'

'Sounds good. What is it exactly?'

'An eight-ounce hot dog with sweet relish, tomatoes, onions, pickles and celery salt, served with south-western coleslaw. It's really not your average hot dog, I promise. Come on, you'd be doing me a favour. I need to eat too.'

They decided to take advantage of the pleasantly warm spring evening and chose seats outside. They flopped back in the leather tub chairs, prepared to enjoy the vibrant downtown scene. Together they watched as the sun sank and they waited for the stars to begin to glisten. Dean glanced around him and noticed that they were surrounded by couples eagerly embarking on date nights; he grimly predicted that by the early hours the streets would be rammed with the disappointed casualties: bitter men, weeping women. A normal Friday night. He tried to tune out the hopeful glances, the tentative jokes and the desperate plunging necklines, and instead concentrated on studying the cocktail list and appreciating the jazz band that was sizzling nearby.

Jo glanced from left to right, taking in the animated, dazzling surrounds, and beamed. 'This place is amazing! Have you noticed that it's full of lovers?'

'I was trying not to.'

'You never think of Chicago as a romantic city, do you?'

'No, I don't.'

'You think of Paris or Venice or Rome.'

'No, I don't.'

She grinned at his interruptions, assuming he was joking. 'But Chicago *is* romantic.'

'I wonder whether Martin's fiancée will agree with you tomorrow,' commented Dean. He didn't want to burst her bubble, but he couldn't pretend that what she was doing was right.

Jo looked crestfallen. 'Why do you have to bring that up? It spoils everything. Can't we just enjoy the evening?'

'OK, you know my position. I won't say another word.' He held his hands up in mock surrender. She was right: he should just enjoy the evening. What did he care if she ruined some other woman's big day? It wasn't his business. So what if she gave this Martin bloke a heart attack? Or if she simply made herself look like a damn fool? Why should he worry about that? Not his concern. He should just enjoy the evening, not let her shake his world. He didn't have to think of anyone other than himself. Tonight didn't have to be any different from any other night.

'Let's get a drink,' he suggested.

26

Jo

Dean orders a couple of different cocktails, I don't catch their names, and tells the waitress that we'll take 'Dogs and beer later. Or maybe wine.' He glances at me as he says as much, presumably eliciting an opinion. I shrug and smile, happy to leave the decision with him. After all, he's kindly offered to foot the bill; I feel that gives him call over whether we have grain or grape.

The waitress glances in my direction, just once. She swiftly and enviously appraises me. From her disbelieving and disapproving expression I can read her mind. I can practically see the thought bubble above her head: 'Why is this cute guy with this plain girl? She's not even wearing lipstick.' I just stop myself saying, 'Hey, sister, I too wish I had found time to apply.' I know I look a mess. Who can look good after a transatlantic flight, daytime drinking and insufficient sleep? Other than Kate Moss. By rights I should have collapsed with exhaustion by now, but oddly, I feel animated, even vibrant. However, as a nod to personal grooming, I do hitch up my bra strap, which has fallen off my shoulder. The waitress rolls her eyes and then turns back to Dean to give him the full power of her smile, cleavage and knowledge of the jazz band's playlist. When he treats her to a bright grin, she practically crawls on to his knee. He isn't my date and I have no reason to resent her flirtatious ways.

But I do.

Truth is, I want him to myself for the evening. I need moral support; tomorrow is a big day for me. The biggest. I feel jittery; nerves and excitement clash around my gut, making me feel sick. Before I can actually gag, I decide to think and talk about something else. When the waitress finally wrenches herself away from Dean, I turn to him and ask, 'So tell me, did you always dream of being an advertising executive?'

'I dreamt about a lot of things. Like most boys I wanted to be a superhero, a footballer, a fireman, a cowboy.' He counts off his ambitions on his fingers.

'They didn't work out for you, hey?' I say, fighting an image of Dean dressed as a fireman throwing me over his shoulder and carrying me to safety; Dean as a cowboy galloping over the plains returning to me wearing a Laura Ingalls bonnet and bloomers (I'm the one in the bonnet and bloomers, by the way, not him). I shake my head to clear the not-quite-just-friends visions.

'Mostly I wanted to be rich, and certainly to get away,' adds Dean bluntly.

'So what part of the UK are you from that made you want to get away so badly?'

Before he has a chance to reply, the waitress returns to our table with the cocktails and I have to endure more eyelash batting. When she stops creating a draught and leaves us alone, Dean doesn't give me an answer but instead asks, 'What about you? Did you always want to be a journalist?'

'I always wanted to be married. That's been my enduring ambition.'

Dean is sipping his cocktail and so his laugh explodes into his drink, causing it to spurt over the table.

'Hey, don't waste good alcohol,' I chastise.

Still grinning, he replies, 'Actually, it's a virgin cocktail. I don't drink alcohol.'

'Really?' I'm surprised. This doesn't fit with my image of smooth, tall, dark and handsome Dean the ad man. I assumed he spent his life ordering martinis shaken not stirred, James Bond style, but thinking about it, he only had orange juice on the plane. 'Why don't you—'

Before I can finish my sentence Dean jumps in and asks, 'So how did you end up a journalist?'

It's a good question, yet not one I've ever given that much thought to; I spend most of my time wondering how I've ended up failing to marry. 'Well, I sort of fell into it, I suppose. I was good at English at school. I particularly loved reading novels.'

'Let me guess, romantic ones?'

'Yes. So?' I try to ignore his amused sarcasm and his point. 'I read English at university and then when I graduated I didn't really know what to do with myself. One of my lecturers suggested that I do a postgraduate course in journalism; it seemed as good an idea as any, so I did.' I am aware that I don't sound very impressive. I have a great job – or at least I did have, until yesterday – and yet I've sort of shuffled into it rather than striven for it, and then I let it slip away. I feel a faint flush of embarrassment. I need to deflect. 'Look, we're always talking about me. What about you?'

On the plane, he talked about his work a lot. I managed to establish that he lives in a swanky apartment, adores his sister and is allergic to shellfish. I guessed his favourite films and was surprised by his book choices, but I didn't discover what his five best memories are, and whilst he was indiscreet about his mates' love lives, he gave me no hint about his own. By contrast, he knows practically all there is to know about me, including all the gory details of the last half-dozen guys I've dated, the fact that my favourite childhood toy was a doll called Bridie and that I cheated at my Latin O level by writing declensions on the inside of my pencil case. He has a brilliant way of eliciting confidences and he clearly prefers to talk about other people's lives rather than his own; he's the one that should have been the journalist.

'What do you want to know about me?'

What *do* I want to know about him? Everything? Yes, everything. But mostly I want to know if he has a girlfriend. Not that it's any of my business, but naturally I'm curious. Don't read anything into that; it's just that I like talking about relationships. It's my thing. I hunt around for some subtle way into that conversation. 'What do you do with your free time?'

'I eat, make money and have a laugh with my mates.' No mention of a girlfriend. 'I'm a demon for adrenalin rushes. I snowboard most weekends in the winter and I go mountain biking in the spring and summer, grass sledging, water skiing. You name it, I've probably tried it.'

Something about the way he says that last sentence causes me to feel a bit flustered. I can't help imagining that he might mean he's tried all manner of exciting things in other walks of life, namely the bedroom. Images of him tied up, tying up others, licking ice cream off women's buttocks and then systematically working his way through the Kama Sutra spring to mind. I'm not a prude, far from it, but suddenly I don't know quite how to reply. Is he being flirtatious, or am I imagining it? Do I *want* him to flirt with me? No, surely not. I'm bigger and better than that, aren't I? Why would I want that level of complication? Well, besides the fact that when he accidentally nudged my boob outside the plane loos I nearly exploded with sexual tension. A devastating, blatant attraction that I haven't felt in I don't know how long. Possibly ever.

Besides that.

'It's all deeply impressive. What's the most dangerous thing you've ever done?' I stutter, trying to stay on track.

'I've swum with sharks.'

'Is that a metaphor?'

'No. I literally have swum with real sharks, although thinking about the politics in my office, yeah, it could be a metaphor. And I've been abseiling a few times. I've tried bungee jumping, skydiving and rafting.' I really want him to shut up now. I'm actually intimidated just listening to him. He's making me feel like a great big *gap*. The most adventurous thing I've ever done is limbo under quite a low bar at the Notting Hill Carnival (I also ate finger food there, without a napkin, but still, it's not exactly living dangerously). He's the complete opposite to me. Besides the fact that he is a scary daredevil, he doesn't drink, whereas I'm a wimp who is so athletically challenged I might literally drown in a cocktail one of these days. We'd never make a couple. I always look for at least eighty-five per cent compatibility in online dating tests. Totally mismatched. Just saying.

'Very Boy's Own,' I say with a forced smile. His energy exposes my apathy in a startling, not at all pleasant way. I raise my hand above my head and wave frantically to the waitress; she ignores me. Dean raises an eyebrow a fraction and she is at our table in an instant.

'Can we order some bread?'

'With dogs in rolls coming?' The waitress looks aghast, clearly much more concerned about my carb intake than I am. 'I'd suggest olives.'

'I don't like olives.'

'Have you ever tried them?' asks Dean. I glare at him, much like my nephews glare at my sister at the dining table, then I have to admit that no, I haven't tried olives, at least not since I was about twelve. I know what Dean is going to say next. 'How do you know you don't like them until you've tried them? We'll take the goat's-cheese-stuffed olives,' he adds, turning to the waitress.

'Good choice,' she smarms, and then swooshes away back to the kitchen in a veritable cloud of glossy hair. I stare after her perky buttocks. I think she must be a decade younger than I am.

'You'll love them,' Dean reassures me.

I hold my grin. I hate the thought of having to eat food that looks a lot like greasy slugs, but having heard what Dean does with his spare time, it is impossible to admit that I'm scared of trying an olive. We stay silent until the perky waitress returns with the olives. As she leans to put them on the table, she practically wipes her breasts on Dean's face. Not that he looks as though he minds as much as I do.

'Do you know what? When I was a kid, I was a Queen's Guide,' I say, as I take a gulp of my margarita.

'And what does that entail?' Dean asks politely.

'I could change a plug by the time I was eight. I climbed Snowdon when I was eleven. I put on theatre productions with my friends and we performed them for pensioners in their residential homes. I went on trekking holidays with youth groups in Turkey and Norway. I could build a washing-up stand out of sticks.'

'What?'

'Actually, thinking about that last one, I wonder about its actual usefulness, but it was bold at the time.' I pause. 'What I'm saying is, there was a point in my life when I never said no to an opportunity.' I'm thinking specifically about opportunities that had nothing to do with netting a bloke, but I can't bring myself to admit that aloud. I wonder about my motivation for trying the olives. Am I hoping to impress Dean, or do I want to show myself I'm not afraid? It's almost impossible to decipher which. Dean nods, but doesn't add or ask anything more. I have a vague feeling that he's managing me, waiting for me to draw my own conclusion, a conclusion he has probably reached before me.

I should be doing more.

'Why are you such a thrill-seeker?'

'You only get one life.'

'Yes, but it seems to me that you're behaving in a way that is likely to shorten that one life.'

'I guess I'm making up for lost time. I was a slow starter. Things didn't take off for me until a bit later than most,' he says with a shrug. He's avoiding my gaze, which is unusual for Dean; he's normally so direct.

'Did you flunk out of uni?'

'I never went to uni. Are you going to try these olives?' Dean has already greedily gobbled up a quarter of the bowl.

'You didn't go to uni?' I probably shouldn't be shocked. It shows I'm sort of small-minded, with a limited repertoire of friends, but *everyone* I know went to university. Kids who go to private schools have to work really hard to avoid it, and those inclined to dodge tertiary education just can't be bothered to put in the required effort to fail. Some of my friends studied PPE at Oxford, others messed about with home economics courses at colleges that had academic records equivalent to a 1950s finishing school, but regardless of the quality of the actual education, everyone I know had three years being a student and all that entails. You know, saving up, staying up, throwing up, growing up. 'Why not?' Dean seems startlingly clever to me. I'm certain he could have had his pick of unis.

'The right opportunity didn't come along,' he replies, telling me precisely nothing.

'So that's why you snatch at every opportunity that comes your way now, hey?'

'Suppose.'

'Is that something you got from your father?'

'You could say that.' Dean doesn't look happy about the similarity I've drawn. 'From what I understand, my father certainly likes an adventure, and he taught me to stand on my own two feet.' He picks up his glass and takes a big gulp. I get the feeling that just for once he might have liked there to be alcohol in it.

Maybe I'm emboldened by the cocktail, but I decide to take a chance; I honestly think it will be good for him to talk things through. 'Why did your dad leave?' I probe.

'The usual reason: he met someone else. In fact he was always meeting other someones, but apparently one came along that was a bit special.'

'I see.'

'The thing is, Jo, in the world that you live in, the one that was a bit special should have been my mother, and then that should have been it.'

'Yes.'

'That's why I struggle to believe in your theory of "the One". Isn't there just a new one every so often?'

I can't argue with his logic even though I dearly want to. 'You think relationships are a bit like buses?' I joke.

'Yeah, nothing, and then three come along all at once.' Dean grins, but inexplicably I feel a flash of jealousy.

I try to maintain a jokey tone. 'In your dreams.' The fact is, I'm irritated by the thought of these three women that Dean may or may not be dating. The thought of him kissing other women, stroking their thighs, licking their nipples, jumps into my head. That's not right. I think about the waitress, who has suddenly become a conduit for my irrational irritation. She reappears as though she's a genie.

'Hey, how are you doing here? Would you like to order any more drinks?' I glare at her and want to shoo her away, but she's oblivious to my wishes; it's all about Dean. She actually goes to put his napkin on his lap! He orders another round.

The moment she leaves us alone I blurt, 'That waitress likes you.'

'I know. She slipped her number into my jacket pocket.'

'She did what?' I'm outraged. 'But you're with me.'

'Well, not technically.'

'But don't you think she thinks we are a couple on a date?'

'Probably. I don't think she cares. I think she's the audacious type.'

'Does that happen a lot? People pressing their numbers on you.'

'Often enough.'

I have never slipped my number into a man's jacket pocket, let alone a man who is dining with another woman, but of course women would press their numbers on Dean. Look at him. He's gorgeous. He has the sort of face that movie producers scout for. His skin is clear and fine; it rests on his strong and sculptured bones. He's blemish-free, with no sign of ingrowing stubble, whiteheads or even those tiny red spots that come out to play after a chocolate binge. He's tanned, and his tan suggests good health and a wealth of experience. He says he's hardly slept in days and the slightly darker skin under his eyes testifies as much, but even the purple-hued bags manage to somehow look sexy.

'You see, this world is too competitive for me,' I say with a sigh. 'What does your girlfriend say when women slip you their number?' It's a pathetic and transparent question. I'm pretty sure Dean doesn't have a girlfriend. Pretty sure. But for some reason that's not good enough for me. I want to be certain. I need to be. I can't bring myself to form the words 'Do you have a girlfriend?' I know from bitter experience that that question can't fail to sound anything other than stalkerish, weird, needy or nosy; it's much better if he thinks I'm pathetic.

'I don't have a girlfriend.' We share that look. The look millions share when this sort of fact is revealed; the look that challenges, promises and questions all at once. There's a small but undeniable flicker of something in my belly. I know it is delight.

But.

I can't get carried away. For many, many reasons I mustn't get carried away. 'Oh yes, it's different here in America, isn't it? People date non-exclusively and then they have *The Talk* and then it's fast-track to the wedding department at Bloomingdale's. Right?'

'I wouldn't know.' He shifts on his chair and stares over my right shoulder. I pause, waiting until he drags his gaze back to mine.

'But you date?'

'Yes. Well, sort of.'

'Sort of? You either do or you don't.' I know I should not be pursuing this line of questioning with such vigour, yet I'm helpless to do anything other.

'I'm not sure what I do is date.'

'What is it you do?'

'I fuck.'

'Oh.'

Hearing him say the word causes an intense and overpowering shudder to ricochet throughout my body. It starts in my gut and radiates outwards; lower towards my thighs and upwards too, stopping my breath and quickening my heart. *Martin, Martin, Martin.* I say the name over and over again like a prayer or chant. I have to stay focused, that's all. This attraction I feel for Dean isn't real. Well, it is, but it's fleeting; the result of the cocktail, jet lag and the champagne on the flight. Martin is real and enduring. Suddenly Dean leans forward and for a mad moment I think he is going to kiss me, but instead he pops an olive into my mouth. His thumb lingers on my lip. I can't spit, so I swallow.

'Do you like it?'

'Delicious,' I admit.

Dean looks at me carefully, then lets out a sort of sad groan. He holds my gaze and then says, 'Jo, you should know I'm not a nice guy.'

I cough, find my voice and reply, 'You seem like a nice guy.'

'That's the trick.'

I don't want to accept it. 'You've got to be a nice guy, because not nice guys would never confess to being such. They pretend to be nice guys until . . .' I am talking from experience, and suddenly I realise it is impossible to finish the sentence and retain any dignity.

'Until after?' Dean suggests.

'Well, yes. Until after,' I mumble. After sex.

'Normally I follow that rule too, but . . .'

This time I finish his sentence. 'But we're not in a before position.'

'Exactly.'

I can't hold his gaze any longer. I study the menu, giving the impression that I am seriously interested in the daily specials. I shouldn't care that he doesn't see me as anything other than a friend – friendship is what I want from him – and yet a dull ache throbs through my body, replacing the wonderful shard of lust. The dull ache feels a lot like disappointment. I bluster. 'So, as there isn't going to be an *after* for us, you don't need to lie to me, and that's why you're telling me you're not a nice guy.'

'Correct.'

'But the fact is, you have been nice to me,' I insist. 'Exceptionally nice.'

'Well, I can be nice to you. You're different.'

Before I can get excited about the fact that I'm different (every girl's dream), I understand in what way he thinks of me as different. The disappointment solidifies. 'You can be nice to me because you'd never, ever want to sleep with me,' I state.

Dean shrugs. 'Let's just say we're not in that place.'

'Right. Well, I'm glad we got that cleared up.' I force myself to smile. Dean not wanting me in *that* way shouldn't be a difficult thing for me to accept. It should be a matter of total indifference. Surely it's only my pride that's dented, isn't it? Because Dean should not be on my radar. I ought to be totally focused on Martin. 'So we can be, already are, good friends.'

Dean grins. 'Yes.'

I raise my glass. 'To friendship and you being nice to me.' Dean clinks his glass against mine. I drain my cocktail, not giving a thought to the fact that not only is Dean footing the bill but he is stone-cold sober and planning to stay that way. I look around impatiently for the waitress to appear with the refills.

'To friendship. What else? After all, you're here to break up a wedding and marry the groom, so whether I want to sleep with you or not is irrelevant, surely.' Dean is smirking as he says this. Which hurts.

'You have a way of making my plan sound ridiculous.'

'That's because it is ridiculous, Jo.'

'I have your cocktails.' This time I am thankful for the interruption. I am probably as willing to kiss the hot waitress as Dean is. 'Should I bring your dogs now?'

'Yes,' Dean and I chorus gratefully.

I have to rally. I will not let Dean bring me down. I have a plan and it's a good one. At least it's my only one. I need things to work out with Martin tomorrow. They have to. 'Of course, when this is sorted out, I'll be very busy again. I'm not sure how much time I'll have to keep up with friends.' I look at Dean meaningfully. I want him to know that what we have, whatever it is, will be finite. I'm pretty sure I won't be able to accommodate my relationship with Dean into my new life with Martin. It would all be too complicated. 'I'll have to visit venues, shop for my dress and pick out cars and flowers. I'll have to go to menu tastings.'

'Can't you just use all the stuff you bought for last time? Same venue, et cetera.'

'Don't be crass.'

'Yeah, it's me that's being crass here. You are planning a wedding to a man who is probably on his stag.'

I pretend not to hear him. 'I will not be using the old stuff. Fashions change – besides, most of it was borrowed,' I add reluctantly – I really don't want to get into this – 'and those suppliers think I married him last time.'

'I'm not even going to ask.'

'No, don't. My point is, Dean, I'm not a very good correspondent, so if I don't email often, don't feel bad.'

'You mean you're not planning on inviting me to your wedding?' I can hear the amusement in his voice; he wants me to.

'You're teasing me.'

'I am.'

Suddenly a thought crosses my mind. 'You've done it again.'

'What?'

'You've shifted the focus away from you and on to me.'

'Well, you are the heroine here. You're the one doing the big romantic dash across the Atlantic to stop a wedding. I'm just some guy.'

'Whose estranged father is dying.'

The pesky and perky waitress pops up at the side of our table yet again. I really don't know why she doesn't just pull up a chair. 'I have your dogs.' She means sausages. 'Can I get you anything else?' Her orthodontically enhanced beam is flashed exclusively at Dean obviously.

'Mustard.' Then, as an afterthought – his mind is not on the dogs or even the waitress – he remembers his manners. 'Please.'

I add it to my list of things I know about him. He likes mustard. He has good manners. This time I really hope she hurries back, because we sit brooding and speechless, with nothing to listen to other than the sound of other people's good times: the clink of bottles and cutlery, the buoyant murmur of happy chatting and the odd screech of laughter. When she does return with the mustard, she touches Dean's shoulder twice. Twice!

'Do you think your dad has done everything he wants to with his life?'

'Probably. He has a selfish gene. Can we talk about something else?'

'We could, but I really think you need to talk about your dad, Dean.'

'I really don't. Talking about how I'm feeling isn't my thing.'

'How do you know until you've tried?'

'Hilarious coming from a woman who hadn't even tried an olive until today.'

'But I did try it!' I point out. Dean bites ravenously into his hot dog. Ketchup squirts down his lip. He wipes it away with the back of his hand. It takes every ounce of self-control I possess not to pull off my T-shirt and toss my bra on to his plate. He has appetites for food, life, sex. I shake my head. What am I thinking of? I shouldn't care about this man's sexual appetites. I feel disproportionately agitated, frustrated. I want to help him. Our relationship has been uneven so far, and I owe him. I don't accept that he's as impervious and unaffected by his father's terminal illness as he's trying to suggest. I push on. 'Families are important. Worthwhile. Such a support.'

'Maybe some. Not mine.'

'But you can't deal with losing a member of your family by just blanking it out.'

'I lost him a long time ago.'

'But—'

'Shut up, Jo.' Dean's voice is suddenly loud enough to catch the attention of a number of diners sitting close by. Heads swivel in our direction. Dean looks flushed. He bites his lip and then adds more softly, 'Please, leave it. You don't know what you're talking about. This isn't something you can fix. I wish it was.'

Despite the fact that he is so obviously a fully fledged adult, he somehow transforms under my gaze, following his confession that he wishes to be fixed. That he wishes *I* could fix him. His face softens; it loses its angular adultness. I have a sudden and undeniable longing to kiss him. It isn't the firmness of his words that finally silences me; it's the fact that he reaches across the table and puts his hand on top of mine. His touch scorches. I feel tattooed, and stupidly, insanely, I fight the idea that I'll always feel his touch. Normally, I blunder and clatter on, persistently demanding answers, but for once I clamp my mouth shut, respecting his privacy. His hand stays on mine. One heffalump, two heffalump, three heffalump, four hef . . . He lets go. Under the table I pinch myself sharply. It has no effect; I still want to kiss him. Kiss it all better.

27

Clara

She wouldn't have known him. Was it the cancer or the time that had passed or her memory that made him unrecognisable? A combination, probably. Clara thought that forgetting him seemed the biggest crime; bigger than cancer, which was ridiculous, of course. She'd have walked by him in the street. Very well might have, on a number of occasions. How could that be, considering she'd searched for him, over and over again? For years she'd scoured crowds, people picnicking on the beach or in the park, masses at concerts and in galleries, always hoping for a glimpse, a chance. Many a time she thought she'd seen the back of his head on the tube or in the street, and chased breathlessly down a platform or across a road, feet pounding, sense flying, to tap him on the shoulder. She was always cruelly disappointed when he turned out to be simply someone else. Someone with slightly less lustrous hair, on close inspection, someone without challenge in their eyes. The disappointment would crawl all over her scalp, making her want to scratch and scream.

Now he was a thin sack of skin and bone and cancerous cells. The little hair he had left was whiter than the sheets he lay on, and his pallor was grey, like a pitiless winter sky. She doubted he'd lived well. He probably hadn't looked after himself; she'd never expected that, but she had expected someone to take care of him. Some woman must have wanted the job. She'd often thought, as she made fish pie with responsibly caught cod and a minimum of three organic vegetables for her own clan, that no doubt someone was doing the same for him, somewhere; the thought had always comforted her and tortured her. It was a surprise to find that there hadn't been someone. This man didn't look as though he'd had the benefit of a woman picking out his ties, buying him his favourite cheeses, telling him to make an appointment at the doctor's when he first had pains in the upper abdomen, when he started to inexplicably lose weight as he developed a jaundiced hue. He'd been neglected.

Why? Why hadn't there been someone? Had he driven them all away? Had he perpetually run away?

Clara thought about what she ought to say next. He hadn't taken his eyes off her from the moment she'd walked into the ward. She'd sensed him, before she saw him, as she had always done, and now she couldn't turn her gaze away from him either. His eyes were pleading with her. She knew he wouldn't want her to ask him how he was feeling, if she could get anything, whether he'd like some water. Others could do that. They'd always left the dull chores of functioning to others. They were all about living in a more pure and desperate sense. The most pure and desperate sense. His eyes begged her not to let him down now, this late in the day. Not to fall into the abyss of normality.

'Do you remember?' Clara asked. Her voice rang clearly through the ward. She didn't need to be specific. She meant all of it. Did he remember the intensity, the impossibility, the immeasurable need they had for one another? She thought perhaps he did remember, because why else would he have written? But she could not be sure. Not with Eddie Taylor. The only thing one could count on with Eddie Taylor was how unreliable he was. She reached across his bed and threaded her fingers through his. His skin felt papery. Could she damage him? Still, it felt natural to hold his hand. She'd always been consumed by him. Her skin had always melted into his.

'Oh, the sex we had,' he chuckled; the laugh was raspy and laboured but authentic.

'Yes, the sex.' Clara nodded. Although that was not all. He'd rarely called it lovemaking. He'd had her. Taken her. Done her. They'd had sex furiously and frantically in the afternoons. They skipped out of work, took a hotel or borrowed keys to a colleague's home. They did it in spare beds, strangers' beds, hallways and – if needs be – alleyways. In and out. Out and in. Hands all over. Lips. Legs. Hips and tits. She had never seen a future for them, but nor did she have a past when she was with him. She began and ended in those snatched afternoons. She knew he was married. He knew she was. She knew it but never thought of it. Could not. Would not. She had never allowed herself to picture the wife or the son.

'You were perfect,' Eddie murmured. The compliment settled on her, took effect like the first sip of crisp champagne; it trickled through her, causing her to dance on the inside, as his rare but coveted compliments always had. 'The perfect mistress,' he added, immediately fast-forwarding through the delightful drunken haze and flinging her into a regretful hangover. He had not changed, then. She leant close to him and heard him whisper, 'You never asked awkward questions.' Clearing up his definition of perfection.

No, she had never humiliated herself or embarrassed him by asking questions. She never asked if she was his only current mistress, or whether he was still sleeping with his wife. When she first found out, through gossip in the office, that his wife was pregnant with a second child, she thought she would die. The jealousy ripped at her innards, tore at her mind, lacerated her body. She thought she would not be able to touch him again.

She stormed into his office and threw a hole punch at his head. Before then, she'd never given him any hint at how she felt about him. How she was his. She hadn't ever said she loved him, although he said it to her often enough. She had doubted him; she thought he was the type to be quite loose-lipped when it came to saying as much to women.

He'd been mesmerised by her apparent indifference, but her obvious jealousy captivated him entirely. For the first time in his life he wanted to please a woman more than he wanted to please himself. He'd slammed his office door closed, silenced her angry yells with hot, hard kisses and then he'd had her up against the wall, just yards away from where their colleagues were typing and filing.

'You were awful,' she said with a smile.

'Wasn't I?' he replied with eminent pleasure.

'Not in the least perfect, by anyone's standard.' She made sure she sounded as though she was joking – that was always her way with him – but as she said it, she realised she was still angry. She hadn't thought this was the case; she'd told herself she'd reached a state of indifference years and years ago. Immune. The letter had exposed her as a fraud. She was not immune. To him, or to the consequences.

'We had something for a while there, didn't we?' A dying man could say it as it was.

'Yes, yes, we did.' A liberated woman could admit that much. They'd carried on for another year and a half after she'd found out about him impregnating his wife.

'We could have had more.' Eddie squeezed her fingers with his own, but it wasn't an affectionate squeeze; he was trying to hurt her. His grip nipped spitefully; if he'd had more strength, he might have caused some real pain. Was he angry too? More angry than she was? Or was he simply sulking because he hadn't got his own way? She had never known whether Eddie's longing for her was genuine love or a complex mix of selfishness, desire and convenience.

It was true that he had talked of a life he could imagine for them, but she would not let him leave his wife. She told him time after time that that wasn't what she wanted. But he hadn't listened to her. He hadn't believed her. He'd been sure she must love him. No doubt he'd reasoned, what woman could resist? But it wasn't just about the two of them, was it? Or even about them and their existing partners. When Eddie Taylor had talked about their future, he had a cornucopia of dreams and plans. They might live abroad – America, France or even Australia. They might move to Hollywood and pitch his scripts; they might drive around Europe in a camper van; or they might just rent a flat in W1 and make love every day. In none of his visions did he mention their children.

She would not leave her girls.

It had been horrible. He'd turned up on her doorstep in Wimbledon. The girls weren't even in bed; Lisa had answered the door to him. Clara had sobered up in an instant. It was as though someone had plunged her into an icy sea. Her first thought had been horror, then disgust. His selfishness had astounded her. Why hadn't he listened when she'd told him she was never going to leave her family? How could he have left his own? She'd felt ashamed. Deeply, darkly ashamed. She told herself that she'd never loved him; that it had simply been a case of her weak body commandeering the situation, because how could she have really loved such a wild and selfish man? She begged him to go away, and when that didn't work, she demanded it.

'I'm not sure we could have had more really,' she commented. The expression in Eddie's gaze shifted an infinitesimal degree. The happy reminiscing shifted to something harder and colder, like frost solidifying a tumbling brook. Not everyone would have noticed, but Clara had always picked up on the nuance of his moods; she suspected that part of the reason he had found her so attractive was because she found him so interesting. She'd always feared that ultimately his feelings for her were really all about how he felt about himself. How awful, as she believed this to be true of Tim as well.

'So, what did Clara do next?' Eddie asked. The curiosity was shaded by a hint of sarcasm. Eddie probably still believed Clara ought not to have had a next, at least not one that didn't involve him.

Tim had been very understanding and had accepted her apologies and explanation. Magnanimously, he'd even recognised his part in bringing about the crisis; he admitted that perhaps he hadn't fulfilled his role as a husband on every level.

'I stayed.' Eddie made a *humph* sound. Clara wasn't sure if it was due to the fact that breathing was obviously difficult, or because he was disgusted by her answer. 'As I always said I would,' she added. She and Tim had agreed that breaking up the family was the wrong thing to do. They'd been very adult, very sensible. Tim had started to pay her more attention in the bedroom. It wasn't passionate – he did not consume her, he did not crawl up under her skin – but it was well executed, careful, thoughtful and, most importantly, fruitful. They conceived Mark. 'I had another child, a son.'

'Very nice.'

When Mark was three months old, Tim had told Clara that he was sorry, but he didn't think he was going to be able to have sex with her again. He explained that he was gay, that he'd finally come to terms with it and wanted her to as well. She had heard the doors slam shut. She was trapped. She could not pack up the three children and chase after Eddie Taylor. He did not want her three children. By that time he might not have wanted her either; no doubt he would have moved on. And she did not want anyone else.

She'd been struck with inertia. After an extended bout of exhaustion and confusion and a profound but relatively brief bout of depression, she'd agreed to Tim's suggestion that they just carry on as they were. One big happy family.

And they had been happy. There was a lot of love. Tim was her best friend. Not every wife could say that about her husband. The children had everything: a stable home, devoted and loving parents, private schooling, foreign holidays, sunny picnics, seaside visits, happy memories. She'd had a sense of order, a sense of place. Everything other than the sense that she was desired. But nothing was perfect.

28

Dean

'Tell me some more about Martin,' said Dean. Jo stared at him and blinked twice. 'He wasn't in your favourite moments.'

'Sorry?'

'When you listed your happiest moments on the plane today, you never mentioned him.'

'Can't a girl be independent?' Jo bristled. She was so clearly stalling for time.

'They can, and it's lovely when they are, but you're not. So why didn't he feature?' Dean really wanted to know. He really wanted her to think.

'Oh my God. I don't know why,' she answered with an anguish that could be nothing other than heartfelt. She put down her hot dog; as delicious as it was, it clearly stuck in her throat. 'I mean, we did have great times. Obviously. We used to go to the movies, trendy bars and smart restaurants. We were always having friends around for dinner parties; those evenings were such fun. We went on mini-breaks and compiled a wedding list. Great times, fun times,' she repeated firmly. 'I mean, otherwise I wouldn't be here, right?' She held up her hands, indicating that she was taking in the bright, light city.

'Wouldn't you?' Dean tilted his head a fraction towards her. His fringe flopped in front of his eyes and yet he held her gaze. He knew what effect this particular move had on women. He'd been told before that his gaze ran through them, that his eyes were amazing; one woman had actually described them as 'a constellation of bright blue tones'. No doubt Jo, with her shamefully romantic imagination, would be thinking about diving into sparkling Mediterranean seas or similar. Though he'd actually prefer it if she was thinking about the question he'd just asked.

'No, I wouldn't be here if I didn't believe that he was the One for me. This is *it*. This is my big romantic moment,' she muttered.

He wasn't convinced, and from the way she was nervously fidgeting, he doubted even she was.

'So tell me how you know this Martin guy is the One.'

'You really want to know?'

'I wouldn't have asked otherwise.'

Jo took a deep breath and thought about it. She'd try to be truthful, as far as she was able; Dean could trust her to be that. The issue would be, was she being truthful with herself? 'You see, I felt it so keenly when I was talking to Lisa in the London bar, and again in my mum's kitchen.'

'Right.'

'I was convinced I *had* to stop Martin marrying someone else. That I had to have him for myself.'

'Hmm.'

The intensity and certainty of the decision was clearly eluding her now. As she glanced around, aware of other couples laughing and bickering, chatting and joking, she looked panicked and frightened. Dean almost felt sorry for her.

'Well, he's decent, you know, *kind*, and so many men aren't. You've just said as much yourself. He wasn't *ever* unfaithful. He didn't so much as look at another woman once. That didn't seem such a big deal when we dated, I took it for granted, but five years of single life has taught me that fidelity isn't a given.' She sighed. 'In fact, the opposite is the case. Fidelity is as rare as pixie dust; you can't imagine how often men ask me to be discreet.'

'Meaning?'

'They want me to be their mistress, or not even that; sometimes just a quick lay.'

'And is that tempting?' Dean knew women who were happy to be both or either on occasion, sometimes in the hope that something bigger might blossom, or as a last resort. He got it – it blanked out the loneliness for a while – but he found he didn't want Jo to be one of those women.

'Never,' she replied firmly. 'I tell those guys to take a hike. I've never been the bit on the side.' She paused, and then looked momentarily guilty.

'The encounter you mentioned on the plane, the one you said was married?'

She picked up her cocktail and drank a healthy slug. 'OK, I've never *intentionally* been the bit on the side. Sometimes they don't mention they're married until after they roll off the Durex.'

'Charming.'

'Isn't it.' Jo looked weary.

Dean was confused. He was glad, even relieved, that Jo wasn't the sort of woman who was prepared to share; on the other hand, he was irritated, even revolted, by her faulty reasoning. Wasn't this further proof that the dream she hankered after simply didn't exist? Married men slept around, single women sucked it up. How could that be the recipe for happily ever after? It wasn't even as straightforward as that. His father's mistress – the important one, the one Eddie Taylor had abandoned his family for – had been married too. Immorality and disappointing behaviour wasn't gender specific. Indeed, it was the widespread nature of it that depressed Dean. How could Jo know all this and yet draw the conclusion that somehow she'd buck the trend, somehow she'd fall madly, deeply, truly in love? How could she think that was going to happen with a man who was planning on marrying someone else? She was so blinkered. So self-deluded. So frustrating. So . . .

Hopeful. Dean shook his head. Hope wasn't something he usually admired, and certainly had never harboured. Being hopeful in the face of such overwhelming evidence was simply idiotic. He felt he had to explain as much to her. It was his duty.

'And you think it follows that because this guy wasn't unfaithful to you, he must be the One?'

'That's part of it.'

'How old were you two when you dated?'

'Late twenties.'

'So you were at it all the time.'

'I'm sorry?'

'I'm just saying that most healthy dating couples in their twenties have a lot of sex and so he probably didn't need to mooch about.'

'Lovely. You're saying that the only reason a man would be faithful to me is if I shagged him senseless and he didn't have the energy to look about.' Jo was offended.

'No, I'm not saying that. I'm just saying this Martin guy was untested. Maybe he'd have been different in his mid-forties.'

'No. I think he's the faithful type.'

'Then how are you planning to lure him away from his current fiancée?'

Jo looked shocked. She clearly hadn't given her plan enough thought. Flustered, she began to loudly list her ex's other attributes. 'And he's good-looking. Well, at least good-looking enough. Maybe he isn't the sort of guy who makes girls stop in the street, but he's tall.'

'You mentioned that,' said Dean calmly as he sipped on his

drink. He oozed the confidence of a man who did make women stop and stare; he was the recipient of many double-takes.

'I'd like to have tall kids. And he has a good job. I'm not really too bothered about cash, but I do want to be with someone solvent.' Jo sighed. 'I know I am coming across as shallow, but I'm not. My reasons for wanting to marry Martin are complex.' She reached for her cocktail and took another enormous gulp; Dean doubted she could even taste the drink. The millions of lights from the street lamps and from the windows of the shops and skyscrapers that framed the park no doubt were blurring as she fought back the tears that suddenly, treacherously brimmed. Dean refused to succumb to his feelings of sympathy or even pity. This woman needed to wake up.

'Amplify,' he insisted.

'Must I?'

'Can't you?' Dean waited for her response; prepared to bide his time but not prepared to let her off the hook. There was a breeze building, easing the warm day into a cool evening. Dean welcomed it. He felt that they both needed to calm down, but he wasn't sure why, exactly. He was always aware of the size of the city he lived in. His world was vast. He was small. He understood as much and even took a perverse comfort from it. He didn't kid himself that he was consequential, and therefore he was able to be careless without being irritated by twinges of guilt. Jo was small too. So was this Martin bloke, but she didn't seem to get it. They were all insignificant bit players. There was no such thing as fate or destiny. She and Martin were not meant for one another in some magnificent way. Life was chaotic. How could she put so much faith in one man to have dashed across the globe, chasing a wispy concept? He marvelled at the self-confidence that was required to have such thoughtless hope and blind faith, even as he disdainfully mocked it.

'I guess the truth is, I'm thirty-five years old. And I'm lonely.'

Jo allowed the word to settle on the table between them. It was a humiliating but truthful and clear word. He'd assumed she must have doused any flicker of self-awareness at puberty and was therefore shocked by her response. 'Have you ever thought that the only thing you really want to do is screw up your life into a tight ball, like you might screw up a piece of paper, and chuck it away?' She glanced at him from under her eyelashes. It wasn't a flirtatious move; it was genuine shyness. Even this strangely guileless woman with a penchant for over-sharing was struggling to admit to such gloomy despondency.

He had thought this himself, on many, many occasions, but had never heard anyone divulge as much. He did not dare move in case she thought he was nodding; empathy would expose him. She tried to smile, but he knew it was one of those painful, necessary smiles that was entirely about outward appearances and nothing to do with inward emotions.

'Have you ever thought there's nothing you can do except start again but in the same instant realised that there's no chance of that, as few of us ever get the chance to start again?'

'Except Buddhists,' said Dean with a gentle grin. He would never own up to having had those thoughts, however long ago he had them; he'd never disclose as much, so he hid behind humour. Jo grasped at the straw he'd offered her and tried to jest too.

'Yes, but even then there's a lack of control that bothers me. I don't want to start again as a cockroach, or a goat herder in south-east Alaska for that matter. Plus, they're not supposed to drink.' She reached for her cocktail, sipped it as though to make her point. They fell into another silence, but this one was sharper than those that had gone before; it had an edge to it. She wasn't finished; she had more to say. 'I'm sure you think I just want a big wedding, that I'm hung up on the day itself.'

'Well . . .' He had the decency not to finish the sentence, which would have involved either lying or hurting her feelings.

'Everyone thinks the same. I'm a joke to my friends and sister, probably to my parents. They think I'm some desperate man-hunting Bridezilla, without sense or reason. But it's not about the day.'

'Isn't it?'

'I could take it or leave it truthfully. I mentioned my parents have been married for an eternity.'

'Yes.'

'And I told you I think that families are important, worthwhile. Such a support.'

'Yes.'

'That's what I want.' She paused, relaxing and revelling in the simplicity of her statement and at the same time determinedly fighting the mounting despair that she'd ever accomplish her ambition. 'I want a family of my own. A husband to love, who loves me in return. Who'll love me when I'm tired, or cross, or wrong. When I'm old. And I'll love him unconditionally too. We'll have kids. Two, possibly three. Our house will be noisy, chaotic, but happy. We'd have friends and family around for Sunday lunch, and some days it would just be us snuggled up under the duvet watching a movie on the TV. I'd be good at it. I have a lot of love to give. That's what I yearn for.'

Yearn was such an exposing word that it almost hurt Dean to hear her say it. He didn't take his eyes off her throughout her speech; he couldn't. He was mesmerised by her frankness, her surprising self-awareness and her old-fashioned ambitions. His quiet seriousness encouraged her to carry on.

'My mistakes are overwhelming. I've had chances, and it's not just that I've let them slip away; I've actively shoved them away, flushed them down the loo, run away from them screaming. I hate hindsight. Foresight is the hot one. The must-have.' She tried to smile again, but he still wasn't convinced by its authenticity. 'Martin was a chance. A big six-foot-two chance, with blond hair and brown eyes and a relaxed smile. A maths degree from Bristol and a career as a management consultant. He had good legs too. Genetically he'd have been a winner, and he wanted me. He did. He loved me. He really did.'

'I don't doubt it.' Dean could imagine such a man loving this woman. Suddenly, under the stars on this clear night, he thought that most men would love her if they got to know her. 'You'll meet someone else,' he muttered. It wasn't just a platitude; he believed she would. He still didn't believe in the happily-ever-after true-love thing, but he did think someone might do as well as Martin for her.

She shook her head. 'No, I've tried. There isn't anyone out there. I've looked. I really have.' She waved her hand into the evening; bright lights outlined the buildings, bridges and rail tracks, laughter and music cracked the darkness, but Dean knew she could no longer see or hear variety and possibilities. Confirming his thoughts, she added, 'I don't have it in me any more. I've been battling and fighting for so long. Years. It is exhausting. Being eternally my best self on the off chance I might attract someone for long enough for them to be comfortable with my worst self is *exhausting*. It hurts to be such a big failure, of course, but having had chances hurts more. Is it better to have loved and lost than never to have loved at all? It's a question I've often mulled over, and the answer is no! Categorically, definitively not. It's much better to live in blissful ignorance than to know just how happy you could have been when you're not. Martin and I may have some sort of salvageable history. I say he is the One because, well, he's my best chance.'

She pushed away her plate. She'd hardly touched the hot dog or the mountain of fries that had arrived as a side. Dean knew the dogs were delicious; he could only assume that she couldn't find the energy. It was all too much. She paused and fingered the stem of her cocktail glass.

'Shall we get the bill?' she suggested, defeated.

Dean nodded and swiftly caught the eye of the waitress. As he put the cash on the little silver plate, he turned to Jo. 'You know what? I think you're wrong. Martin isn't your best chance. He's just your best chance so far.' It wasn't much in the way of consolation, but it was all he had. She shrugged and wouldn't meet his eye.

Dean was touched by her honesty. Touched and a bit embarrassed. He had been planning on just seeing her into a cab and sending her on to her hotel. After all, by anyone's standards he'd already shown extreme consideration. He'd taken her shopping for a new outfit, he'd fed her, he'd fixed up the hotel; surely his work here was done. But suddenly he was drenched with a sense of anxiety and foreboding. He wasn't sure if sending her off alone in a cab was still the best plan of action. He couldn't quite decide whether her obviously fragile state was the result of her alcohol intake, her jet lag or her sad heart. Whichever it was, he thought there was a reasonable chance that she'd be refused entry into the hotel unless he accompanied her. He didn't want to think about her wandering the streets of Chicago alone late at night, so he hailed a cab for the two of them.

They didn't say much as they sat side by side in the dark. She shivered, and so Dean handed her his jacket. She didn't hang it carefully around her shoulders, the way women tended to do when they wore a man's jacket; instead she slipped it on properly, preferring to benefit from its warmth rather than caring whether she looked cute. They both stared out of the window, watching the bright and the buoyant, the edgy and the inebriated who littered the streets. It was a bustling, vibrant city; Dean wished Jo could see the opportunities he could see – the people she could make friends with, the career she could pursue, the conversations she could have, the places she could visit – but he thought it was most likely that she was still thinking about hijacking Martin's wedding. Her only thought and ambition.

He waited while she checked into the hotel, and then it was time for them to say goodbye. They lingered in the elegant marble-clad lobby, trying to keep their voices low but aware that the bored and fatigued man on reception was following every word.

'Thanks so much for all your help today. The outlet shopping, dinner, finding this place . . .' Jo trailed off. Perhaps it was a bit much, all added. Dean waved his hand, dismissing her thanks as though his consideration was commonplace; he also pretended not to notice how much effort she was putting into enunciating her words correctly. She was trying not to give away the fact that she was in danger of slurring because she was quite drunk, but her endeavours had the opposite effect.

'Hey, it's been . . .' He paused. 'Lovely,' he concluded, borrowing her word.

'It has, hasn't it?' She beamed back at him. 'Although all day I've had to ask myself, why are you even here?'

'What do you mean?'

'With me. Haven't you got better things to do?'

Dean considered. 'I have no idea. Maybe I'm fatally attracted to lost causes.'

'This is not a lost cause.' She poked him playfully in the belly; she had to have noticed his hard abs.

'This is a cause so deeply and darkly lost that I was thinking of buying you a miner's torch and a canary in a cage,' replied Dean.

'Ha ha, very funny.' Jo paused and then asked what Dean had known she would and hoped she wouldn't. 'Come with me.'

'No, I can't.'

'Yes you can. Why not? It would look so cool if I had you on my arm when I walked in. You'd be a confidence boost because you are so very good-looking.' She bestowed the compliment that Dean had heard a million times before in a slightly shy slur;

her desire to be genuine had forced her to abandon all attempts at appearing sober.

He responded to the compliment in his usual way; he smiled charmingly, not touched. 'Thank you.'

'Wow.' Jo looked startled. 'You're, like, totally overwhelmed.' Her fake American accent dripped with sarcasm, which was not something Dean had found her to be before. The way he accepted the compliment told Jo that he'd heard it too often. Dean was almost ashamed of his good looks, certainly indifferent to them. Yes, of course they had helped him to bed countless women, but he didn't value them. Jo made the leap. 'So, do you look like your dad?'

'I thought we agreed we weren't going to talk about my dad.'

'I never agreed. You suggested it and assumed I'd gone along with your suggestion. You do have a way of being, I don't know, slightly supercilious.'

'Or maybe I assumed you would concede because you have a way of being submissive.'

'Ouch, that's not nice. You shouldn't confuse submissive with polite.' Jo waved her finger like a teacher telling off a pupil. Dean assumed her alcohol consumption was responsible for the fact that the banter had suddenly taken on a somewhat dangerous, volatile, even flirtatious tone. 'It's a good job you're clever too, hey? So you don't have to rely on the good looks that obviously irritate you,' she added.

'Sharp.'

'Yeah, I'm often underestimated.'

'Whose fault is that?'

'Are you always this rude?'

'I'm not rude. I'm probing.'

'Come with me!' she implored. 'It's plus one and they are no doubt going to serve something delicious. Even if it is chicken, it will probably be posh chicken. You know, chicken supreme filled with brie and apple, probably wrapped in bacon in a white wine sauce.'

'But if your plan works, there isn't going to be a wedding, let alone a wedding reception,' Dean pointed out.

'Oh yes, of course. Stupid me.' For an instant Jo looked flattened; the colour drained from her face and she vanished against the marble walls in the reception. Had the weight of the reality of what she was planning to do finally crushed her? Was she really capable of ruining another woman's wedding day? Another woman's marriage. This wasn't just about Martin. Of course not. Dean sighed. She was a conundrum, was Jo. Totally insane. Really quite irritating on many levels, certainly exasperating, and yet he felt for her. Despite being the diametrical opposite of what she was, he could not deny that he felt some sympathy. She was a thirty-something woman desperate to be married and deluded by the whole circus known as romance. He was also thirty-something but he was deeply, darkly cynical about the ongoing propaganda that sold false hope (wrapped up in a bow and labelled 'happily ever after'). It simply did not exist; it was a pity she was wasting her entire life relentlessly pursuing it. If she told people she was hunting down leprechauns or pots of gold at the end of the rainbow, they'd have her committed. She was delusional.

And yet he understood her. She was lonely. She wanted a family. He got it.

'No.' He shook his head with genuine regret that he couldn't help her with this. 'I'm sorry, Jo, but I just can't watch you do this to yourself. It's going to be a train crash.'

Jo nodded, the tiniest fraction of a movement. He knew she was being brave, hiding the fact that disappointment ripped at her guts. 'Of course not, why would you want to get involved in my mess?'

'Why would you even want me to?'

'I shouldn't have asked. I can do this alone.'

'Yes, you can, if you must.'

'I must, if I can.' Jo forced herself to grin broadly and declared, 'Martin will be pleased to see me. Delighted. He wants me to rescue him. That was why he sent the invite.'

'If you say so.'

'And I want to rescue Martin.'

'*That* you have certainly said.'

'It's Martin I want.'

Dean nodded his head. He felt suddenly overwhelmed with weariness. He leant close to her ear to ensure that the receptionist couldn't hear any more of their conversation, 'Jo, you know you are going to get rejected, don't you?' He hoped his warning would convey his regret and his sympathy, but most of all he wanted to convey his certainty.

'I don't know any such thing. He sent me an invite for a reason.'

'Yes, to rub your nose in it. He's happy, you're not.'

'He's not that sort,' she insisted. Dean drew away and shrugged. He was certain that she was wrong. 'Dean, the wedding is at six p.m. at the Luxar, East Walton. Have you heard of it?'

'Yes. It's quite a prestigious hotel.'

Jo shrugged; she didn't look exactly thrilled to hear this. Dean was glad that he hadn't elaborated and explained that it was the sort of hotel that boasted large but elegant rooms and suites, gracious service and stunning interior features, including hospitable fireplaces in the winter and expansive terraces in the summer. He'd had sex there at least twice. 'Well, if you change your mind, you know where to find me,' she added.

'Jo, go to the Museum of Contemporary Art instead.' He leant a fraction closer; it was time to say good night and goodbye. He'd decided against going for the two air kisses that were customary, opting instead for one thoughtful kiss. It rested lightly on her forehead. His lips burnt.

'This is goodbye, right?'

'Yes, Jo. Take care.'

'Will you wish me luck?'

He thought about it. He didn't much believe in luck. But she did. 'Yeah. Be lucky.' Then he walked swiftly out of the lobby, refusing to look back over his shoulder.

SATURDAY 23 APRIL 2005

29

Jo

I hoped that when I woke up the weather would offer me some sort of omen as to how things might pan out, or at the very least a dramatic backdrop while the action was taking place. Back in the UK, the night before my flight, I had plenty of time to think through how I imagined today would be. In my imaginings I saw a blazing hot day, I pictured myself wearing a pretty full-skirted dress (probably in a sherbet colour – pink or lemon) and I saw myself scampering through the streets of Chicago in heels until I found the church. This fantasy didn't budge even when I carefully reread the invite and realised the wedding wasn't actually taking place in a church. The vows were to be exchanged at the hotel, but I couldn't quite adjust my fantasy to accommodate that. Martin would be standing outside, handsome in his morning suit. He'd be flanked by two or three distinguished but slightly less handsome groomsmen; as I approached, they'd all notice me and gape in open awe, impressed by my *joie de vivre*, my self-assurance and my stunning good looks.

In my fantasy I looked a lot like Reese Witherspoon, which was odd because I'm not even blonde.

But I'm not unrealistic. Even in my fantasies I allowed for the fact that this reconciliation was to take place in Chicago, and so, because it's late April, blazing sunshine's not guaranteed. I constructed an alternative fantasy with less clement weather. In the second version of events, I imagined that the sky would be full of powerful bruise-coloured clouds. I'd be wearing a vampy black number, practically spray-on and with a plunging neckline. When I arrived at the church, thunder would clap and lightning would flash. It would be extremely gothic and passionate. Martin would still be flanked by two or three handsome groomsmen, all of whom would be mesmerised by my sultry good looks and sexy determination. Think Angelina Jolie. My best fantasies rarely feature me as me.

Disappointingly, when I pull back the curtains, I am greeted by a mostly grey, overcast sky that holds just the smallest suggestion that it might turn an insipid blue later on in the day, but basically the outlook is flat and bland, bordering on the dreary. I almost feel sorry for Martin's fiancée. This isn't the sort of weather any bride imagines for her wedding day. Not that this is going to be her wedding day, I remind myself.

I was surprised when I woke up to discover that it was already three in the afternoon. Jet-lagged, I didn't know whether to eat breakfast or lunch, and then I decided I was too excited (or nervous) to stomach either. I tried to make myself a coffee, but the coffee-making machine defeated me by having a huge variety of buttons and choices, so I settled for a glass of tap water and seriously wished I'd eaten more yesterday. Perhaps I should have drunk less too. I expected (and deserved!) a massive hangover today, but thankfully the sleep-in soothed the worst of my symptoms away.

I carefully pull my outfit from the stiff cardboard bag. I really ought to have hung it up last night but I was too beat. Still, I'm lucky it isn't the sort of fabric that creases too badly. We selected a poppy-coloured sleeveless classic Calvin Klein dress. Neat. Understated, but somehow all the more sexy for that fact. Dean steered me away from the girlie frocks – 'Too mumsie, too sweetie pie; if you are going to do this, you need to be taken seriously' – and vetoed the more obviously seductive numbers too: 'Jesus, you'll give the vicar a heart attack.' His voice rings around my head. It was determined and manly most of the time, but when I emerged in the poppy-coloured Calvin Klein dress, it turned to treacle and I had to lean close to him to hear him properly: 'Knockout.' I hope he's right, as knocking out the competition is exactly what I have to do today. We bought some suede, killer-heel, nude sandals too. They have a strap around the ankle which gives a hint of the vixen. If ever there was a moment to hint at the inner vixen, this is it.

I shower using the hotel's sensuous shower gels. Then I apply about a dozen moisturisers, it's been five years since I last saw Martin. Not especially kind years. My skin has decided to embrace the inevitability of science and has started to accept gravity; my mind is less willing, which is why I continue to apply moisturisers and hope. Will Martin think I've aged terribly? I stare in the mirror and am surprised not to see the jet-lagged hag I was expecting; instead I find that I'm glowing. I smile at myself and my cheekbones spring out to greet me like the long-lost friends they are. I practise another smile; this one is less playful, more hesitant. My eyes sparkle. I continue to play this game as I put on my make-up; I'm surprised to find that I look, well, good enough. It's easy. Whenever I smile, I think of Dean: Dean's face when I spilt my drink on him, exasperated, firm but not unkind; Dean waiting for me by the taxi rank; Dean biting into his hot dog. I wonder what he's up to today. He mentioned that he usually spends a couple of hours in the gym on Saturdays, or sometimes goes to the park with mates to play a casual game of baseball or shoot some hoops. He's very active. I'm not saying it's not worth it; I mean obviously he looks good – I think some of his muscles have muscles – but he's exhausting to just think about. Exhausting and exciting. I wonder what he is up to at this exact moment. Probably reaching for his phone and whizzing through the names of his various not-too-serious girlfriends. He isn't likely to want to spend a Saturday evening alone. I imagine some redhead or blonde picking up her mobile, seeing his name flash up on her screen and her face splitting with the most enormous grin; any woman would be thrilled to receive his call.

It is a good thing I've learnt that raw sexual attraction is never, *ever* linked to something more meaningful. I've accepted that fancying someone is virtually inversely proportional to being happy with them. Martin is my best chance. That said, when my phone beeps, my first thought is that I hope it is Dean texting. This is stupid on a number of counts, not least the fact that we didn't do anything conventional like swap numbers. I pick up the phone and see from caller ID that it's my sister; the disappointment that it's not Dean is as unaccountable as it is overwhelming. I apathetically let it go through to voicemail.

OK, I'm all ready. One last check in the mirror. Pretty good, even if I say so myself, and I have to say so myself because – as ever – there's no one else here to say it.

30

Eddie

She stayed all afternoon. I didn't expect that. In my experience, lovers expect too much of one another and it's a trap I've always tried to avoid. Only falling into it once. With her, of course. Just the once. Fact is, I thought she was in the bag. Back then. All that time ago. I thought she would leave her husband for me; I never doubted it. Yesterday when I said as much, she asked about the kids.

'But Eddie, what about the children? How could you have expected me to leave my children?'

'I never thought about it, Clara.' I had to be honest. With her, like my son; there was no point in starting to lie to them now. She sighed, disappointed. I find it boring when people try to express their disappointment in me. I see it as their fault, not mine, and I think they are hopeless not to know as much. She wouldn't be disappointed in me if she didn't expect things of me. Expect better. Why would she do that? I never was better. Never pretended to be.

'Shall we do the crossword now?' she asked, as she always had when she wanted to change the subject. She bent forward to reach into her handbag that lay on the floor and unintentionally treated me to a view of her cleavage. The cleavage hasn't weathered as well as her face – she's spent too much time in the sun; plenty of foreign holidays no doubt – and the curve of her tits put me in mind of prunes rather than peaches now. Still, her collar bone made me gasp; it was still as beautiful. For a moment I forgot the pain in my body and I just felt pleasure. It was a treat after the hospital sheets, bed baths, needle pricks, blood transfusions, chemo and stuff to just feel something that men are supposed to feel.

Most of our past was secret moments and snatched minutes, glued together to add up to a something that might have passed as a relationship, but if we ever had time to languish we would smoke a cigarette together and complete the broadsheet crossword. She was very good at the anagrams and fair at the cryptic clues. I was better at both.

Yesterday, I noticed her paper was the freebie given away at tube stations; I loathe that sort of paper. Hold it responsible for the demise of proper journalism and the decline in book reading. Told her so. She said it was chatty and distracting, although she complained that the crossword was facile. Was it? I found it hard. It is getting more and more difficult to stay focused, to concentrate. Practically impossible. Still, she patiently read each clue, two or three times if necessary, and guided me to the answers, pretended I was doing better than I was, then leant over the bed so that I could watch her carefully fill in the letters. I remembered her handwriting. I didn't expect that. Wouldn't have thought I'd ever known it, but I did. I recognised it. Goes to show, you can still be surprised.

I wonder who will come today. The lad? Any of my other kids? It isn't such a remote possibility. This dying business is turning out to be more interesting than I imagined. I should have done it sooner. Ha ha. It's good that I can still make myself laugh. Through it all. They've upped my painkiller dosage. Not enough. It still hurts. My bones ache; it feels like they're being squeezed into too tight places, crushed. My muscles ache. They're being chewed, consumed. My back, head, jaw ache. It all hurts like hell. How much more does the body have to endure?

Will she come back? That's what I'd like most. Her. I suppose it has always been her. If it was anyone. I'm not sure it was, honestly. Anyone other than me. But if it was someone, then that someone was her.

31

Dean

Unlike Jo, Dean had not slept well. He'd lain awake most of the night and considered whether he should call Zoe. She would be pleased to hear he had left Eddie Taylor dying; she'd been furious with him for responding to Eddie's plea in the first place. She'd thought he was a fool and she'd been right. He was a fool. Eddie had never even asked him to rush to his bedside. Even when he was dying, Dean had not mattered to Eddie Taylor. The thought was sickening.

Dean felt a wave of bleakness raging through his body. A dead feeling, a hunger. It surged with a renewed and long-forgotten ferocity. The exhausting craving wasn't at all new; it was always there and he'd become used to it, almost accepted it as part of his being. As an adult, he'd largely been able to manage the hunger; it could be contained to a throb or a pulse, a dreary, austere lacking. As a teenager, the ravenous loss would not be controlled. It pelted its way around his mind and body, eating up his confidence and trust, shredding and destroying conviction, poise and any hope he had at future intimacy. He had never given a name to the anguish. Identifying it would have imbued it with more power than he was ever prepared to allow. Better to leave it as a wordless curse. But Jo had spoken so freely about it. She suffered from a different mutation, perhaps, but still the same root.

He'd been so lonely for so long.

Abandoned by his father, neglected by his mother. He'd made his way, what choice was there? He'd had to. He'd owed as much to Zoe. He didn't like to dwell. What was the point of regurgitating all the old crap, all the old pain? He'd done OK. Better than OK. He and Zoe. He'd held them together and they'd risen above it all. He was fine. Just fine.

His only mistake was going back. Peeking behind the curtain. Looking at where the dust mites crawled in their millions. Now, when he thought of his father, he didn't think of the raven-haired bastard who had walked out on them for some bit of skirt. He thought of the rasping chest, the cracked lips, the filmy eyes. He still thought he was a bastard, though. His father had managed to humiliate him, reject him, day after day. Year after year. And then right at the end. It was almost too much to comprehend. He'd nearly cried in front of the fucker. The thought made him leap up from his chair and punch the sitting-room wall.

Shit, shit, shit, that hurt! Jesus. Jesus. He rushed through to the dark grey clinically trendy kitchen, flung open the door of his (empty) oversized fridge-freezer and plunged his hand in the ice box. He used to punch things and people all the time. When he was a kid. When it was needed. To protect Zoe, to take away the pain, to let some of it out. But it had been a while. He'd become civilised. He'd forgotten how much it fucking hurt to punch a wall.

His father had said he was 'surprisingly pleased' that Dean had pitched up. But what was that? What did that mean? Whatever it meant, it wasn't enough. Eddie Taylor hadn't called. It was some agency nurse. Some stranger. Some do-gooder. Some fuckwit who had taken it upon herself. She'd got involved and made the call; made Dean think he was wanted. The agony being that the call, on some level – a deep and well-buried level, admittedly, but on some level – had made Dean think that he was wanted, that he was loved.

But he wasn't.

Eddie still hadn't wanted him. Never had. Never would. The thought pierced. It actually stabbed Dean. A thought caused physical pain; how was that possible? How was he going to get through the weekend? Through the next week? The rest of his life? For a moment he was blind with fury and literally couldn't see a way. Blackness engulfed him; his heartbeat quickened, his chest tightened. Was it panic? My God, he couldn't breathe. His chest stung, compressed and deflated. He could not find the air he needed. Suddenly Jo's face slipped into his consciousness. She was grinning. She had a slight gap between her teeth. People said that was lucky. It was certainly attractive. She had this funny way of crumpling up her face when she was concentrating. It wasn't cute or sexy but it was memorable. It was endearing. And a bit cute, a bit sexy; he supposed he could admit that to himself. His chest began to expand again, just a fraction. He found the oxygen in the air.

He scraped the ice from the box into a tea towel and then, in a ham-fisted manner, wrapped the towel around his injured hand. It was times like this that he understood why people drank. Instead he hunted around the back of the cupboards and found a Hershey bar. He bit into it, not allowing the chocolate to melt on his tongue but chewing swiftly and swallowing hard. It was OK, but nothing topped UK chocolate. He should have loaded up before he left the airport, then at least some tiny good would have come from his trip, but the thought hadn't crossed his mind when he'd been boarding. He hardly understood why he was thinking about chocolate now. It was ludicrous. He wasn't thinking straight. He was trying not to think at all.

He glanced at the clock. What would Jo be doing? Getting

dressed probably. She'd be slipping on her red dress and those sexy shoes they'd picked out together. She might be hailing a cab, unless she had come to her senses, which seemed unlikely. It would be a bloodbath. That was the problem with people. They fucked each other up. Loving hurt.

But what could he do about it? It was what it was.

32

Jo

The polite and eager concierge informs me that the Luxar is within walking distance, but when I tell him that it is my ex's wedding and show him the height of my heels, he suggests that I take a cab.

'They might drive you round the block a couple of times to get something worthwhile on the clock, though,' he warns.

'Is that legal?'

'No, ma'am, but it's reasonable. Everyone has to make a living.' I don't want to admit that I can't afford to be exploited; I am pleased that he thinks I can. It means that I look the part, at least.

The cab driver sails past numerous hip bars and restaurants and I feel a surge of pleasure that I recognise some of the high-end shopping malls on the Magnificent Mile, even though Dean and I didn't linger there yesterday. I nervously finger the hem of my dress as the cab passes by the Museum of Contemporary Art and I remember Dean's advice that I should spend my time there, instead of going to the wedding. Crazy; for one thing, it is already closed.

We venture past well-preserved nineteenth-century town-houses and other grand buildings that line the tree-shaded sidewalks of this affluent neighbourhood, and then the taxi pulls up in front of a magnificent French-inspired hotel. My parents' passion for architecture and design has given me a clear sense of what is in good taste and what isn't. There is no doubt that the mansard roofs, buff-coloured limestone walls and enormous slate-grey window frames are the epitome of good taste. Stepping out of the cab feels just like stepping on to the boulevard in Paris. I admit with a heavy heart that Martin's fiancée has chosen well; I'd rather hoped that she'd have terrible taste and that she'd have plumped for something tacky and obvious; a vampire-themed wedding or one officiated by an Elvis impersonator would somehow be easier to stop than a thoughtful, elegant ceremony. But I have no reason to assume Martin's fiancée has poor taste; after all, she's chosen Martin.

Martin and his groomsmen are not languishing by the hotel entrance as I imagined, which is a spanner in the works as far as my plan goes. I pictured myself drawing him aside and having a quick chat; the idea of hunting him down in a hotel is more daunting. I walk through the elegant foyer, hoping to spot him attending to some last-minute wedding stuff, but he is nowhere to be seen. I suppose, thinking about it, this shouldn't be a big surprise; last-minute wedding adjustments tend to be the domain of the bride or the mother of the bride. Martin is more likely to be hanging out in a bar with his groomsmen, soaking up the attention and final moments of singledom. I begin to feel mildly panicked. What if he is late and I don't have time to talk to him before the ceremony begins? I won't have the courage to actually stop the wedding once it is under way. Irrationally, I start to panic that I am in the wrong place or it's the wrong day. I frantically dig into my handbag and retrieve the invite to check; a passing bellboy notices me and stops.

'You here for the Kenwood–Paige wedding?'

'Sort of.'

'You're a little early, but that just means you'll get a good seat, right? It's that way. They have two rooms. The stateroom, where the ceremony will take place, is past the stairs and through the arch, and the reception is going to be in the ballroom. On the right.'

Because I am planning on the wedding not getting as far as the ballroom, I think I'll stop by, just out of curiosity, and see how the reception room is dressed. I've worked on a wedding magazine for years; of course I need to know whether she's picked white table linen or a colour.

The ballroom is exquisitely glamorous, breathtaking. Martin's fiancée has opted for an elegant and traditional theme of gleaming white and silver. There is nothing to take exception to, only things to admire. Tasteful vases of fat roses sit on each of the countless round tables, the name plates are small white (no doubt hand-carved) wooden doves, the candles (in their gleaming candelabra) aren't lit yet, but when they are, the light will be reflected and refracted around the room because of the generous handfuls of crystals that are scattered on the tables. The chair backs are covered in swathes of organza that coat the room with a general sense of fairy tale and romance. The walls are covered in silk, the ceilings are coffered and the crystal chandeliers are obviously hand-blown glass rather than the cheap plastic sort. They look like they are inspired by vintage jewellery, or at least they look as though that's the story the interior designer's publicist will spin. The floor-to-ceiling windows are framed with pale, rich drapes that only just hint that there is an intimate terrace available beyond, somewhere the bride and groom can steal a moment alone during the reception. It is simple, impactful, thoughtful. The perfect setting for the perfect day.

For no reason I can think of, or at least no reason I want to think of, tears start to well in my eyes. Of course I always cry at weddings. Girls who have been bridesmaids nine times tend to, but usually I wait until the bride is saying her vows or at least the organ is playing before I blub. I blink furiously. I do not need smudged mascara, I really don't. I look around. I am alone other than three or four waiters who are polishing glasses and lining up the layers of cutlery. I wonder where the wedding party is. Are the bridesmaids upstairs with the bride, sipping on champagne and choking in a fog of hairspray? I wonder whether Martin's fiancée held her bridal shower here too. In preparation for her big day, did she retreat to the sanctuary of the spa and health club? I don't doubt she'll have had a skincare analysis and customised make-up session; perhaps Martin has enjoyed a hot lather shave and eucalyptus steam. I know from the invite that there are plans for a bon voyage brunch for the guests tomorrow. This event has been planned with consideration, precision and generosity.

I pick up a menu; it is adorned with Martin and his fiancée's names. Gloria. She is called Gloria. Of course I've known this from the moment that I received the invite. I've simply chosen not to acknowledge that this woman has a name. A face. A body. A heart. Their names are linked by a trail of symbolic intertwined silver hearts. Both names are embossed; Martin's is in matt, Gloria's name shines. I trace my finger across the letters and allow myself to wonder, for the first time, about the girl behind the name. Gloria. Such a big and bright and hopeful name her parents have saddled her with. She has parents and hope; the idea makes my legs shake. What does she look like? I've never thought it through properly. I've thought about Dean's girlfriends, imagined them in high definition, but I've never had the same curiosity about Martin's fiancée. Whenever I think of Martin I think of him alone. On the football pitch. Muddy, angry and desperate. Desperate for me.

'Jo? Jo, is that you?' As though I've conjured him, Martin is suddenly standing in front of me, but he isn't the Martin of my imaginings. He isn't in tails as I thought he might be – as I planned him to be at our wedding – nor is he in a muddy football strip as I last saw him; he isn't even wearing black tie as I thought possible, because they do that at American weddings. Instead he is wearing a dark grey suit, a white shirt and a pale grey tie. He looks stylish and expensive. A tiny bit more sophisticated than I've ever seen him look before. He's had his hair cut and yes, he probably has benefited from a professional shave. He looks confident, happy and every inch of his impressive height. More confident, happier and taller than I've ever seen him before. I think I hear my heart crack. 'Wow. So you made it after all,' he says as he approaches me with a broad grin.

'I said I would.' I lean in and give him a double kiss. The left side doesn't touch him at all; as I move towards his right, he seems to remember what he is supposed to do and his lips briefly land on my cheek. Dry. I wait for the spark. The jolt. The justification and authentication. Nothing.

'You're looking well,' I comment.

'Thank you. You too.'

I beam back at him, and sway from side to side, girlishly holding my dress. It must be nerves that force me into performing this ridiculous parody of flirtation, and I hate myself for it. It's some relief to clock that Martin isn't actually looking at me; he's staring at something over my shoulder (a flower arrangement, I think) and hasn't noticed me making a fool of myself.

'Those flowers are quite something, aren't they?' He slaps his hands together excitedly and then rubs them as though he is warming them up. It is a gesture I remember. He occasionally uses it when he is ridiculously excited about something; when his team won the championship, for example, and when he got promoted at work.

This is harder than I imagined. Now I'm in front of Martin my plan starts to seem hazy, like a mirage. Unreal. I need a way into what I've come to say. This is undoubtedly going to be the most difficult conversation I've ever had to have, probably even harder than calling off our wedding; I am here to ask him to call off someone else's.

'Do you have time for a drink?'

'Well, I don't know.' Martin glances at his watch. 'Gloria asked me not to drink before the ceremony. Her parents have pledged, and whilst Gee and I obviously still enjoy a glass . . .'

'Obviously.'

'. . . we don't want to appear disrespectful to her parents.'

It is suddenly very important to me that I get him to have a drink. If I can make him go back on his word to Gee about something small, I reason that I have a chance of getting him to go back on his word about, well, the whole day.

Lifetime.

It doesn't sound very honourable put like that, but time is of the essence.

'Just a small one. It's traditional, isn't it? The groom and his best man have a quick one before the ceremony?'

'But you're not my best man.'

'No, but we could still have a quick one before the ceremony.'

Martin looks at me oddly, and I can feel a blush spreading up my neck. The double entendre was not intentional.

'Where is Harry, anyhow?' I ask to change the subject. Harry has been Martin's best friend since secondary school. He was going to be our best man; I doubt a slight detail like a different bride will have had any effect on that fact.

'Harry isn't my best man. Gee's brother is.' Ah ha! Am I about to sniff out a bossy bride with overpowering demands who has vetoed her groom's choices? 'Harry emigrated to Australia two years ago. We hoped he'd get over for the wedding but then last week he broke his leg and he can't fly.'

'Oh. I see.' No demanding bride, then.

'Gee's brother was one of my ushers, but he stepped up. I'm so grateful.'

'I bet Gee was pleased that her brother got a promotion in the wedding party.'

'Actually she was gutted. She's been looking forward to meeting Harry for ages.'

'Oh.'

'You know what, she even offered to postpone the wedding until he was fit to travel.'

Cold feet? I wonder. I mean, what bride would offer to postpone her wedding if she was crazy in love with her groom? 'Really?' I murmur.

'Wasn't that considerate? But in the end we decided it would simply inconvenience too many people. Besides, after last time, I didn't want anyone . . .' He trails off, looks around him, a bit embarrassed, then somehow he finds his feet again. 'I didn't want anyone thinking my bride had cold feet. Not a second bride.'

'I'm sure no one would have thought that,' I mutter guiltily. I hate myself. I hate myself for putting him through such hell the first time and imagining (however fleetingly) that it might happen a second time. I don't want Gloria to ditch Martin. I want to tell him I've made a mistake. That he was right after all, that we were meant for one another. I hunt around for a starting place. The words stubbornly elude me.

Martin looks uncomfortable; obviously thinking back to our non-wedding is difficult for him. 'Maybe a drink would be a good idea,' he admits.

The two of us settle at the hotel bar. We order sherries, laughingly agreeing that neither of us are really sherry drinkers but it just seems like the sort of drink a couple of Brits ought to drink before a wedding. Martin says, 'Bottoms up' and then necks his drink. Is he avoiding the potential difficulty of discussing what we should toast? Fair enough. I am not about to suggest we toast the bride and groom's health and happiness, but anything else seems rude, because that's what is expected today. That and nothing else. I'm not used to being rude. I normally strive to be as considerate as possible; a model of good manners and thought-fulness. Thinking about just how discourteous and impolite hijacking a wedding is causes a wave of nausea to flood through my body. I down the strange thimbleful of liquid, but before it even hits my stomach I know it won't be enough. Martin must have the same thought, because he signals to the bartender that we need two more. This time we both sip the liquor more cautiously.

There isn't a hope in hell that we can hide in small talk. It would waste time, and besides that, it's demeaning to both of us. Martin must know that I'm not here to ask about his health or chat about the weather.

I pick up a peanut from the small silver bowl on the bar, and then remember some terrible statistic about how many germs those shared nut bowls harbour so drop it again.

'So you're really happy?' It seems an obvious place to start. If he chooses to, Martin can pretend I've just made a simple obser-vation appropriate to his wedding day; instead he dignifies our shared history and accepts I am asking a question. Still, I don't get much from his reply.

'Extremely.'

'Never happier?' This is perhaps unfair of me. I am basically asking him to compare how he feels now with how he used to feel about me. Clumsy, but isn't that why I'm here? It has to get bloody before things can get better. He used to say I made him happy, that he'd never been happier than when he was with me, and more than that, he used to say he couldn't imagine being happier. I have to find out if he was right about himself. He stares at me across his sherry glass.

'It's a different happy, Jo.'

What does that mean? I'd have been on surer ground if he'd simply given me a 'Yes, never happier' in response, although gutted, obviously, but he didn't say that. Nor did he say he is unhappy. He's chosen to be more considered than that, more truthful. I stare at him as I ponder my next words. He's changed. Besides the smart suit and decent haircut, he is different on a deeper and more profound level. He's grown up. It is attractive, deeply so, but also alienating. I am suddenly unsure that I really know this Martin. Martin the man. I was engaged to Martin the boy.

Gently, carefully, I pull out the old tricks. I look at him from underneath my eyelashes and ask, 'Martin, don't you ever wonder, what if?'

He has the good grace not to pretend he doesn't understand me. I knew he wouldn't. He's never been the sort to play games. Isn't that why I am here? I'm sick of the game-playing. I'm looking for someone trustworthy. I'm looking for a keeper. It's just a terrible inconvenience that I didn't recognise him as such before.

'Well, no, not any more,' he says flatly.

'But you did?' I probe.

'Of course, for a while.' He dips into the nut bowl and scoops up a huge handful. He tips them down his throat; clearly he doesn't have any qualms about germs. It's such a small gesture, but it strikes me as bold. I'm encouraged by his boldness. If I'm honest with myself, it's not an attribute I'd have traditionally bestowed on him; I've always thought of him as kind, honourable and straightforward, but not bold. 'You broke my heart, Jo. Of course I gave our doomed, non-existent future more than a cursory passing thought. I spent quite a bit of time thinking about what might have been.'

'You did?' I can't keep the pleasure out of my voice.

'Yes, but not as much time as I spent on thinking what the hell happened.'

'Oh.'

'Largely I was dealing with the sudden finality of our

arrangement. The shock of how it ended.' So he's bold now and he's never played games, and this is the result. Straight talking. Of course, what did I expect? I shift uncomfortably on my bar stool. It's hard thinking about him upset, confused and anguished. This isn't the particular route down memory lane that I wanted to take. I'd do much better if I reminded him of the good times, but before I can, Martin says, 'Hey, why are we talking about this? Where's this going? This isn't appropriate for my wedding day.' He points this out with a reasonableness that causes my throat to tighten and the skin under my hair to prickle. It feels a lot like shame.

'Well, I think we have to talk about it today. It's now or never,' I mutter.

'Never works fine for me. Jo, it's been five years. We could have had this conversation any time. Why now?'

I'm not ready to answer that question yet, so I throw out one of my own that I hope will edge the conversation in the direction I need it to go. 'Why did you invite me to your wedding?'

'Gee thought it was a good idea.'

'Sorry?' This is not what I was expecting. 'Why would Gee want me here?'

Martin sighs. 'She thought it would stop people talking, you know, about the wedding that never was. Sometimes her friends, or my friends, tease me about it.'

'They do? Even now?'

'Even now.' All the skin on my body is crawling. Of course people tease him. If I'd ever thought about it, I'd have guessed he'd be the butt of jokes. 'Yes, Jo, they do. Not often. Sometimes. Gloria is sensitive to it. Mostly on my behalf. She wanted to see the girl who let me go. In her words, to be exact, "the lunatic that allowed you to slip through her fingers". I guess she's curious. Human. She wanted to send you an invite, so I thought I'd let her. I don't like to deny her anything.'

'I see.'

'Truthfully, I didn't think you'd come.'

'But I have.'

'Well yes. And now you are here, I really hope you have a nice day, but there's a favour I need to ask you.' I suppose he's entitled to ask me a favour. I owe him big time, and besides, it's his wedding day, the one day when people are meant to get their own way, unequivocally. I don't suppose he thinks I'll deny him anything. He's right, I won't. There's something about the combination of his new-found confidence and his more recognisable straightforward way of dealing with me that means I want to oblige him. 'Jo, we can't make today about us. We can't let it be about us in any way. Today is Gee's day. Mine and Gee's.'

The words pitter-patter around me. They land softly, causing me less distress or offence than I might have anticipated they would. Had I been expecting this, on some level? Is that what I thought he'd say? A declaration of undying love is what I was hoping to elicit, but have I ever really expected it? Have I ever thought that I, Joanna Russell, would finally find a happily-ever-after? That I'd find it here at another bride's wedding? No, probably not. I take a deep breath and say, 'I know what you are asking, but the thing is, Martin, there's something I have to say. There's something I just have to tell you—'

'She's brought a date.'

'What?'

'A date, brilliant,' says Martin as he turns in the direction of the interruption. I do too. Dean is standing right next to us, glorious, gorgeous in a dark navy suit, clean-shaven and spruced up.

'Yes, she's brought a date; me, in fact,' he says pleasantly. He holds out his hand to Martin, who accepts it. They shake heartily, and then Dean swoops down and kisses me on the cheek. He slaps the kiss down. His manner is not particularly sexy, the kiss is not loaded or meaningful; it is all about play-acting. From the hearty handshake, the broad beam, the chaste but deeply affectionate kiss, I understand which particular scenario he's picked. He's decided we're a happy, confident, probably quite steady couple who are past the first stabs of lust, and yet . . . the kiss sears. I touch my skin and it's tingling.

'A date. Wow. Well, that's really good news.' Martin looks delighted. Delighted and (I have to admit this to myself) relieved. 'Do you know, this is going to sound crazy,' he continues.

'What is?' Dean asks. I think he knows that his interruption has left me stunned and I'm struggling to scavenge around for words, so he blithely fills in.

'Oh, it's nothing,' says Martin, shaking his head and chuckling.

'What? No, go on,' urges Dean.

'For a moment there I thought she was here to . . . No, I can't say it.'

Dean interrupts again. 'Did you think it was going to be a "Don't marry her, marry me" moment?' he asks, guffawing loudly.

Martin laughs too but doesn't deny it. 'Mental, huh?'

Dean puts his arm around my shoulder and kisses the top of my head. 'Absolutely mental. No worries on that front, this baby is mine.'

I pull away from him, which is harder than it should be. The second kiss, the one he planted on my scalp, felt comforting and pleasant. It acts like a balm to my crawling skin, and for a moment I feel soothed. But that feeling is shoved aside by my confusion. He isn't supposed to be here! I know I asked him, but he said no! Besides, he was supposed to be moral support, not a fake date. He isn't helping. I am in the middle of something. He's not the one who is supposed to be pulling the surprises today.

Both men turn and stare at me. Martin is full of bonhomie and radiates pure happiness. Now he's sure I'm not here to wreck his wedding, he can relax. He's probably already thinking of a way to work me into his wedding speech. People love to brag that their guests have travelled miles and miles to be at the occasion; it's a way of showing how popular and valued they are. Dean looks significantly more apprehensive. His eyes are full of warning and caution. I scowl at him. What the hell is he doing here? Everything was going to plan – well, almost. No, not at all.

What was I about to say to Martin? How do I really feel about him? Seeing him standing next to Dean, I'm suddenly not certain. Martin's blond openness is in direct contrast to Dean's moody dark looks and manner. Dean is a self-confessed womaniser. He represents everything I'm trying to run away from. Cheats and commitment-phobics. Not that I have reason to believe Dean cheats on the women he dates, but I'm pretty sure he hurts them. I know that countless women who have ended up in his bed will have been distraught when he asked them to flick out the light as they left. He's just the sort of man women fall for hard and fast; he is beautiful and damaged, and by anyone's account that makes him irresistible. Martin stands in front of me – this decent, handsome, worthy man – and I know, absolutely *know* that I'm right. He is perfect marrying material. He will make a wonderful husband. He will be faithful and steadfast, which can't be underestimated and should never be undervalued.

And I know, absolutely know, he won't be my husband. He's Gloria's man.

I clear my throat. 'So as I was saying before we were interrupted, there's something I just have to tell you . . .' I cast a quick glance at Dean, who looks totally panicked. He starts babbling on about getting drinks in and asking about the music at the service. If he dared, I'm pretty sure he'd actually gag me right now. I cut through him. 'I came here to say that Gloria is right: I was a lunatic to allow you to slip through my fingers, but hey, my loss is her gain. Right?' I beam, making it clear I'm simply sprinkling the sort of appropriate compliment that a pally but balanced ex might make on a wedding day. Martin's face becomes gymnastic; it springs between bemusement and vindication. 'I'm very sorry that I messed things up, you know, before. But I'm so glad you've found happiness now. I just wanted to be here on your big day.'

'This time. She wanted to be here this time,' Dean can't resist adding. He's clearly cast himself as a bit of a joker. Maybe he thinks he has to be in order to fake being my date.

I lean towards Martin and pull him into a hug. It's a generous hug between friends. I don't try and inappropriately push my breasts into his chest, I don't whisper anything into his ear. I don't make it any harder than I already have. And when I let him go, I try not to think of Gloria's words. I try not to think that this is my last chance of happiness and it's slipping through my fingers.

33

Dean

'So we're staying?' Dean asked Jo, the moment Martin had excused himself, something about having to check on the whereabouts of the ushers. She nodded mournfully. 'Good choice. If we leave now, it's going to look weird.'

He led her to a seat in the room where the service was to take place. Some of the guests had arrived now and were quietly chatting or listening to the 1950s love ballads that played gently in the background. Dean wondered whether the dulcet honeyed tones of the likes of Ella Fitzgerald, the Platters and Dean Martin singing about love affairs taking place when the world seemed shinier and easier would help soothe Jo or inflame her further. They settled on seats, two thirds of the way back, on the groom's side. Jo immediately picked up the order of service and pretended to be interested in the details. Dean could tell she wasn't. She was deflated. Lost.

'Thanks for coming,' she muttered, clearly embarrassed at how close she'd got to the edge, how close she'd been to jumping.

'I didn't want to miss the drama,' Dean replied with a shrug.

'It seems to me that you came here to ensure there wasn't any drama.'

Dean wasn't absolutely certain why he was at the wedding. He just hadn't been able to stay away. 'You did the right thing.'

'Then why does it hurt so much?' Jo bent forward and let her head drop into her hands; her hair fell across her face, effectively stopping Dean from reading her expression. 'I am such a monumental screw-up. No job, no home, no future,' she moaned woefully as a thought struck her. 'Oh God, what will I tell my parents?'

'Your parents?' One thing Dean had never experienced was a sense of obligation to his parents. Until this moment he'd never seen an upside to their neglect, but now he accepted that, since they crawled around in a pungent dung of failure and inadequacy, at least he wasn't ever plagued by a sense that *he* could let *them* down; it would be impossible.

'My parents are so complete. So happy and perfect. They can't understand how I've gone so badly wrong.' Dean wasn't convinced. He didn't believe that happiness and perfection existed, but if it did and they were so happy, why would they be down on their daughter? Surely they'd just feel bad for her. Jo continued, 'I should have just married him five years ago. Why didn't I?' She looked around the room, full of the scent of lilies and the lyrics of love songs. This wedding was certainly set to be as beautiful as Gloria could have hoped and Jo could have feared. It was hard letting it all go.

Dean reached out instinctively and tucked a strand of her hair behind her ear so he could see her face more clearly. She looked startled. 'He isn't the One, Jo.'

'You don't even believe in the One.'

He didn't, never had, but she needed cheering up. He didn't like to see her this way. He paused and then offered, 'I'm proud of you.'

'Of me? How can you possibly be proud of me?' Jo asked with obvious incredulity.

'Two things. First calling off your wedding five years ago.'

'But that was just *stupid*,' Jo wailed.

'I think it was brave. Most people would have gone ahead, but you didn't because you believed in the One and you didn't think it was him. Whether you are prepared to admit it now or not, at the time you wanted more.'

'But I was wrong.'

'Not necessarily. Maybe there *is* more. Maybe you're right and I am wrong.'

Jo moved her head a fraction, trying to bring that idea into focus. She had never considered the fact that calling off her wedding was brave. She thought of it as shameful, embarrassing and stupid, and other than that fraction of time – the moment before she did actually call it off – she'd never even thought her decision was justified. It was almost impossible to do so, considering the fallout: the expense to her parents, Martin's pain and her own subsequent, endless disappointments.

But looking around now, she saw a room full of jubilant guests ready to celebrate a marriage between two people who quite possibly (oh let's face it, quite *probably*) were much better suited than she and Martin ever were. Maybe, just maybe she'd been right. She brightened a fraction and straightened her back a millimetre or two. 'You said two things.' She fished for another affirmation.

'You didn't screw up their wedding today. You came to your senses. Well done. You probably didn't need me here to help you do the right thing.'

'Maybe, but I am so glad you *are* here,' replied Jo with her signature honesty that made him smile. Then she took hold of his hand, laced her fingers through his and squeezed. 'What happened to your hand?'

'I punched a wall.'

'I see.' Next, she gently brought his swollen and tender hand up to her mouth and kissed it. Her lips were hot and soft. They lingered. The gesture was one of infinite gratitude, and (although Dean couldn't swear on this) maybe it was a gesture that hinted at a deeper fervour. She saw the surprise on his face. 'I'm just staying in character,' she explained.

For the first time since they'd met, Dean was unsure whether she was telling the truth, but he didn't get the chance to probe, because her phone beeped. She looked at it and sighed.

'That's my sister. It's the fourth time she's called today.'

'Aren't you going to pick up?'

'What's the point? I know what she's going to say.'

'I take it she's against the whole hijack-the-wedding thing?'

'Probably. I didn't actually tell her what I was doing, although I suppose Mum's filled her in by now, but no, I can't imagine her thinking this is a good idea.'

'Well, call her. Put her out of her misery. Tell her everything is OK. She's just worried about you.'

'I can't make a call in here.'

Dean glanced at his watch. 'We have fifteen minutes before the wedding starts. Come on. Let's go outside. You can call from there.'

Outside the hotel there was a small gaggle of smokers, desperate for their last nicotine hit before the wedding service began. A tall, leggy blonde beamed at Dean, and threw an icy glance Jo's way. Dean smiled back, and Jo rolled her eyes as she peeled away to make her call. The blonde was cute. Clearly she hadn't so much as sniffed a carb for years; she had sharp cheekbones, and notably high tits pushing out of a slight frame, and Dean vaguely wondered whether that was a really good bra or surgery. Normally he'd be able to tell, but he didn't stare for long enough today; his eyes were trained upon Jo. She was chattering into the phone. At first her face looked relieved, almost animated as she spoke, but then she suddenly stopped talking and her jaw fell limp, hung open. Her colour drained. Dean looked to the pavement, fully expecting her vibrancy to be pooled on the floor at her feet. She'd begun to shake.

34

Jo

'Where the hell have you been, Jo? I've been trying to reach you for twenty-four hours.' Lisa's accusatory tone runs down the line and spits out on to the Chicago streets. I look up to the sky. The clouds are clearing and there's the smallest patch of blue sky appearing. I take a deep breath and flirt with the idea that maybe it's going to turn out beautiful after all, despite my sister's furious tone.

'I'm in Chicago,' I reveal.

'At Martin's wedding?' She's incredulous.

'Yes.'

'Oh God, Mum said you'd mentioned going over there, but I never thought you'd go through with it.'

'Mum encouraged me to come here.'

'Mum did?'

'Yes.'

'She probably wanted you out of the way.'

I'm unsure as to what Lisa can possibly mean. I know I'm not always considered a veritable addition to family gatherings, but I don't think my parents ever actively want me out of the way. I decide not to tackle Lisa but instead reassure her that I haven't done anything crazy. 'Anyway, look, it's all been a bit

291

of a storm in a teacup in the end. There's nothing to worry about.'

'Jo, I'm calling because—'

'Don't panic. There's no need for everyone to get worked up. I can guess exactly why you are calling, but I'm not going to try to stop the wedding.'

'No, actually, Jo—'

'I think I got a bit carried away. You know? Sometimes, Lisa – and please don't take this the wrong way – it's hard for me. You're so happy. Mark and Katie are so happy. Mum and Dad are celebrating yet another wedding anniversary this weekend. You guys all float around in a cloud of marital bliss and I'm left out. I haven't pulled it off.' I look up and glance around for Dean. I'm fully expecting him to be flirting with the buxom blonde who was eyeing him up as we came outside, but he's staring right at me as though I'm interesting. I smile. He smiles. For a moment I lose sight of what I'm saying to Lisa. What was it? Something about being lonely, left out. I don't feel quite so forlorn or isolated as his smile settles in my head and soul. I force myself back to the conversation with Lisa. 'It's not about the big day like people think it is. Because I worked on a bridal magazine, OK, maybe I did get a bit obsessed. They think that's all I'm interested in, but it's not.'

'Jo—'

'It's more than that. I think I just panicked. I felt sad, a bit lonely.'

'Jo—'

'Simply put, I want what you guys have.'

'Jo, *shut up*! Let me get a word in. Mum's left Dad.'

'What?' I have to have misheard. Or misunderstood.

'Mum has left Dad.'

The world slows around me. It's as though gravity has just been switched off. I float out of myself, but not in a happy, dreamlike state; rather, I feel I've lost any sense of order or control, my stomach is churning and my head is foggy. It simply doesn't make sense. I cannot compute what she's saying. I hear the words but they don't fit together, I can't understand them. 'That's impossible.'

'She had an affair.'

'What?'

'Years ago. But the guy wrote to her from his deathbed and all hell has broken loose.'

'She had an affair?'

'Get past that. What I'm telling you is that the guy she had an affair with wrote to her saying that simply remembering her broke through the pain of his cancer. Apparently she had this moment of awakening where she admitted to herself that Dad's love has never been like that and that Dad's love isn't enough.'

'Why not? What does she mean? Dad's love is just fine,' I stutter.

'Well, apparently not. Jo, there's something else . . .' What more could there be? Lisa takes a deep breath; I can hear it all these miles away. My big sister is finding this difficult to articulate. She too thinks the world has tilted. 'Dad is gay.'

35

Clara

Clara returned to the hospital. It horrified her and fascinated her, in equal measures, that he still held the same dreadful power over her, but she could not keep away. This morning she had dressed in a hurry and taken a cab to the station to dash to London to be by his bedside. She was drinking him up. A thirsty woman after a drought. He was not the vital, vivacious man who had seduced her unequivocally, unreservedly, unconditionally. He had lost his looks, his health and any vague hope that they had a future together, however slight that chance might have been. They were all about pasts now, but still she could not do anything other than return to him. It used to be about her body. Back then. She used to ache for his touch; she'd felt actual pain if days went by and they could not find a way to be together. Her breasts ached, her groin ached. He'd soothe her; the relentless licking and kissing and having soothed whether it was in the back of a car, in a stranger's office or on a bed in a discreet hotel. Now it was about her soul. She needed to understand this man who had shaped her life, because she still ached. The pain was no longer in her breasts or groin. The pain he caused her was in her head and her heart.

Tim had called her on her mobile several times since Thursday night. Of course she had taken his calls. They weren't silly lovestruck kids who sulked with one another and played attention-grabbing games; they never had been. That was the point. He'd called to ask whether she was settled into the spa. It was a peculiar sort of break-up when the wife left details of her future accommodation with her ex, but Clara had felt it was the most polite thing to do; after all, Tim would be paying for the room. 'It's very nice, I'm quite comfortable. Thank you for asking,' she'd assured him politely, and then, because there was an awkward silence, she added, 'Much the same as all my other visits.'

'Well, hardly.' He'd sounded irritated.

Clara had regretted her tactlessness. 'No, I suppose you're right, it's not the same. Just the rooms are the same.'

He'd suggested she eat a good supper and get some rest. He clearly thought she was suffering from some sort of mental instability, a breakdown. Like the other time. She wasn't. She was very cool, calm and collected. When she tried to tell him as much, Tim became more panicked, not less, so she gave up and instead let him think she was out of her mind. He'd called again on Friday morning. He'd enquired as to whether she'd had a good night's sleep. They talked about the scrambled eggs she'd had for breakfast; she'd commented that they were a little sloppy for her, more to his liking.

'Perhaps next time you visit the spa, I'll come with you,' he'd suggested. 'If you think it's to my taste. We should probably be doing more together. Maybe that's what's at the root of this problem.'

Clara did think that a husband and wife ought to do plenty of things as a couple – shared hobbies did have their merits – but indulging in mini manicures and pedicures together would only exacerbate this particular situation, surely.

Tim had called again when she was at Eddie's hospital bedside. She'd taken the call and lied. She'd considered saying she was shopping but thought the hospital sounds might expose her, so she told him she was seeing her own doctor about the possibility of finding a counsellor. He'd believed her and supported her wholeheartedly. 'I can come too, darling, if that's what it takes.'

'Maybe.' She'd remained non-committal, quickly made her excuses and promised to call him back later.

'Just like old times.' Eddie rasped out his comment but still managed a sly grin.

'How so?' asked Clara as she switched off her phone and buried it deep in her handbag, out of sight, out of mind.

'Me lying in bed, you lying to your husband.'

Clara remembered the guilt and shame and her inability to fight it. 'Not quite. For one, we weren't plagued by mobile phones,' she pointed out brightly.

'True, it was easier to be bad then.'

'Now it's all tracked and traceable. I don't know how anyone manages to have an affair nowadays.' Clara jokingly pretended to sound outraged on behalf of the adulterers, but it was not what she believed. She liked to think of herself as a sort of accidental adulterer. Not someone who sought out trouble or got a kick out of the subterfuge and drama of an illicit affair. It had almost killed her.

'I managed,' Eddie informed her. So there were women after her. Before her. Probably running alongside her. Women other than his wife. Why did it still hurt? Not as much as it had, of course. Then it was agony, a ripping out of guts; now it was more of a sharp twinge akin to banging your funny bone. Not so funny.

'You didn't go back to your wife, then?' Clara had often wondered.

'No.'

'Or the children?'

'Married again, had more children. Two girls.'

'Oh, well that's OK then.' Clara could not quell her sarcasm; didn't even want to.

They fell into a miserable silence. There was nothing to do but listen to the sounds of the hospital: other visitors chatting, talking about the weather or who they might vote for on Saturday night's latest talent show; the hum of the various machines that monitored and maintained; and his heavy breathing. Eddie broke the silence.

'Don't be like that, Clara. I know it's not ideal, but it is what it is.'

'So where is your second wife?' Clara looked around the hospital ward as though she imagined the second wife might suddenly materialise from behind a plastic curtain or from under one of the beds.

'Divorced me.'

'Because? Same old same old?' Clara hated herself for being part of this long list of women. She could see them in her head, all too clearly. They were trailing through the room in nothing other than tiny panties, the way they had trailed through Eddie Taylor's life: plump women, thin women, young women, mature women, sane women, insane women, black, white and golden-hued women. She felt undignified. She was sure she ought to be too old to be jealous.

'No. Not another woman, as it happens. Money. Difference of opinion.' Eddie pointed towards the water jug. Clara jumped up and poured; she tried to hand him the plastic beaker the moment before she realised he wasn't able to take it from her. Helpless. She sat on the bed, carefully cradled his head in her left hand and guided the cup to his lips. His skin was hot. Her fingers tingled. She eased him back down, put the cup back on the bedside cabinet but did not move off the bed. Refreshed, Eddie was able to finish his sentence. 'I had none. She wanted some. She worked out

I was never going to be a big Hollywood screenplay writer. I used up my ambition quite early on.'

'Oh, I'm sorry.' Clara wasn't sorry. This divorce seemed less grubby in comparison to the first one and she was irrationally relieved that the list of women she imagined he'd entranced was not, after all, infinite. 'Are you on good terms with your children?'

'No.'

'None of them?'

'No.'

'Oh.'

'Well, the boy . . .' Eddie looked momentarily confused. Clara wondered whether he might have forgotten his son's name. Was that the result of his illness or his carelessness?

'Dean,' she prompted helpfully, because she remembered all the details.

'He came here.'

'Well, that's good.'

'Not really. He came to tell me how angry he is. He came because he's fucked up.' Eddie's breath was so laboured that Clara wasn't sure he'd said that Dean had fucked up or that Eddie had fucked up. It hardly mattered; the two things were one and the same in Clara's mind. 'Angry, cynical. More cynical than I ever was. Alone. What about you? How are your kids?'

Clara felt her nose prickle; it took her a moment to realise she was fighting tears. She didn't want to indulge in outward shows of emotion; she always preferred to resist them. Usually she was refined to the point of restrained, but this was the first time Eddie Taylor had ever mentioned her children or asked after their well-being.

'Oh, they are fine. Wonderful.'

'Grown-up?'

'Yes. All grown.'

'University and such?' He waved his hand to suggest his enquiry was to encompass all possible accolades children could achieve.

'Yes. My eldest went to Cambridge, middle one went to Leeds and my son went to Bristol.'

'Impressive.'

'Two of them are married. Happily so.'

'And the other?'

'Oh no, she's a romantic.' Clara and Eddie shared a conspiratorial glance; he raised an eyebrow at her joke. They used to tell one another that marriage was no harbour for passion or romance; they'd believed it was only available outside the sanctified union. It was a bit of a sad joke if you thought about it. 'Seriously, I think I ruined her. Overprotected her. She isn't very realistic when it comes to relationships.' Clara could not stop herself confiding her fear to Eddie. Jo was on her mind.

'Who is?' He shot her another look, saying more. Yes, thought Clara, Eddie Taylor was not very realistic when it came to relationships either. His cynicism and aloof detachment hadn't immunised him; he'd simply suffered from another strain of the unreality that her daughter suffered from. Jo was too romantic, too hopeful; she believed entirely in total perfection and expected to find it in everyone she met. For this reason she gave herself fully and was often exposed or hurt. Eddie did not expect to find a glimmer of the good stuff in anyone; he did not expect to have to offer it up. Clara thought that, by contrast, she was realistic. She was the queen of compromise and make-do. 'Glad it worked out for you,' said Eddie. He probably meant it, too.

'Oh yes, they're all fine. It's worked out for them. My husband's gay, though,' she added.

'What? When?'

'Well, always, I suppose. But he told me just after I had Mark.'

'Bloody hell.'

'Quite.'

'I'm sorry.'

'Yes.'

'But you stayed with him?'

'I did.'

Clara almost wanted to laugh. The Eddie she remembered had burst through from the ghostly body of this old man. He looked shocked, animated and almost amused again at last. 'Clara?'

'Yes?'

'Why didn't you come and find me?'

'Eddie, you never wanted the children you sired. How could I possibly hope you'd bring up mine?'

'I might have. If you'd asked.'

36

Dean

'I need a drink,' said Jo.

Whilst he was not a drinker himself, Dean could recognise the need in others; a Hershey bar wasn't going to cut it. There was no question that they could go back in to the ceremony now. Before the phone call, the wedding had represented all Jo believed in but didn't have. Now the bubble had burst. She believed in nothing at all, which Dean knew, through experience, was a considerably harder position to be in.

He took her to the first diner he spotted. It was a grungy basement that had never had the benefit of a makeover. The seats were tatty and the lino was sticky, but Dean was prepared to overlook this providing the milkshakes were delicious. Somehow he instinctively knew what she needed, and it wasn't a glitzy restaurant. Jo needed to hibernate. To hide from the daylight and eat lots of comfort food.

She gave him the facts. An adulterous mother. A gay father. Not quite the fairy tale she'd thought, then, after all. She had probably needed to move out of la la land, but he feared that this was too sharp and sudden a wake-up call; it might rip at the very fabric of this woman's existence. She asked for a glass of red wine, which he ordered, but he insisted that she drink a banana milkshake first. He figured she needed the sugar; she was in shock. She obediently drank the creamy drink as he instructed. She was never the sort of woman to throw out unnecessary objections, and right now she was too beaten to be anything other than entirely compliant. She needed taking care of. She trusted he would do it, and as they sat shoulder to shoulder in silence, he accepted that he would indeed take care of her. He put his good hand over hers and squeezed.

The silence stretched for ten minutes, twenty, thirty. Dean was generally OK with silences, but Jo being so quiet for so long was unnerving him. She'd struggled to hush up for thirty seconds all day yesterday. He was worried. He'd ordered poached salmon, fries and a tomato salad because on the flight she'd told him it was her all-time favourite meal. When it arrived, she automatically thanked him and the waitress but didn't pick up her fork.

'Come on, Jo, you need to eat something.' Her gaze dropped to the plate in front of her and she seemed genuinely surprised to see the food. He wondered where she was, where her thoughts had taken her. He wanted her to come back to him. He forked up some fish and held it to her mouth. Silently she parted her lips and allowed him to feed her. After half a dozen mouthfuls she said, 'I hate my parents.'

'No you don't.'

She took the fork off him, picked up her knife and started to reluctantly feed herself. Dean turned to his own meal, a burger, but was surprised to discover he wasn't as hungry as usual either. Jo's upset was catching.

'How could they?'

'How could they what?' How could her mother have left her gay husband? That didn't seem a tricky one to Dean. He was struggling with the question of how they could have lived a lie for all those years. Why would they? But he wasn't sure what Jo was thinking, so he trod carefully.

'How could they be so different from what I thought they were?' she said with an enormous sigh.

'Oh, that's easy. They're human.'

'They held hands when walking down the street. Do you think that was an act?'

'No, not necessarily.'

'And their bedroom.' She looked confused. 'The enormous bed. I thought it was a faintly embarrassing embodiment of their uber-romantic existence, but in fact they probably have such an enormous bed so they don't have to touch one another. I am such an idiot. I have nothing now. Absolutely nothing. No job, no home, no plan as to who I should marry, and *now*, apparently, no history. At least not a real and dependable history. I've based everything I am, everything I wanted to be on what I thought they were, and they never were that.' Jo looked horrified, terrified. 'You're right, Dean, there's no such thing as true love. There are no happily-ever-afters, no soulmates, no chances.' Two big fat tears slipped down her face. They splashed on to her salmon.

'Shush, don't say that, Jo.'

'What? I'm wrong now because I'm agreeing with you?' She turned to him and for the first time he saw a flash of genuine anger swipe across her face. This was old news to him: disappointment led to anger, finally to bitterness; he knew as much, had always known. Hadn't he tried to tell her, to warn her? But even he had not banked upon her disillusionment coming in this particular and sudden form. He'd fully expected her to be rejected by the tall, dull guy she used to date; he'd expected that to sting. Wasn't that why he'd turned up here today – to mop up, as necessary? He had thought that she'd find out the tall guy wasn't for her and that she'd be sad about it for a while but eventually pick herself up, brush herself down and fall in love all over again. He'd sort of depended on it.

The strange thing was that while he had not expected this

complete and utter disintegration brought on by her parents disappointing her in such a raw and fundamental way, he had expected, predicted, foretold that this strange woman, who lived in a dream world, would wake up in a nightmare, and yet now he was stunned to find this was the last thing he wanted to witness. The erosion of Jo's faith was disastrous. Suddenly he realised, with a sickening certainty, that he'd wanted to be wrong.

Deep down, buried below any and all of the pain and disappointment he'd endured, he'd wanted to be proved wrong. That was why he was so happy his sister was married. Publicly he'd always appeared a little sceptical, a little satirical. He joked that her marriage was a matter of hope over experience, but secretly – so secretly, he hadn't known it himself – it thrilled him that Zoe had nurtured a little dot of hope that had blossomed into a fully functioning relationship.

Jo was an extreme. She believed in a better world that was so glossy and golden that it had hurt Dean's eyes to look at it. He'd laughed it off, dismissed it as a fantasy, and yet he'd been seduced by the idea. It was heartbreaking to watch her glossy golden world rust, then disintegrate. But disintegrate it must if Jo no longer believed in it, because only she could keep it alive. Dean thought it was a little like the Peter Pan story: every time a child said they didn't believe in fairies, one died. It seemed that if Jo didn't believe in the happily-ever-after, then no one could.

He couldn't be expected to pick up the mantle here. This particular responsibility could only be cultivated by those who cherished belief. He had no access. He couldn't help.

Jo's tears were flowing quite swiftly now; they slipped down her face and splashed on to the plate, making a puddle in among the discarded bones and silver fish skin. Her mascara, which had helped her to look so glamorous and appealing earlier, now served to make her look foolish and vulnerable as it ran in black tributaries down her face. She didn't seem aware, or if she was aware, she didn't care.

All at once Dean felt desolate. Her pain, unbelievably, was his pain. He *did* care. He cared about this woman who he had initially dismissed as whimsical and misguided, who he'd thought of as a novelty. Last night he'd admitted she was interesting, but perhaps only in the way an exotic zoo creature was interesting; he'd wanted to watch her to see what she'd do next. But now, *now* he wanted to rescue her, revive her. He didn't want her to be permanently ensconced in la la land – that would never do – but he wanted her to retain some belief in the good stuff, even if he had none. In fact, he needed her to. He didn't understand why it mattered quite so much, but he knew that it did. Mentally he stooped down, grasped the mantle and then with enormous effort held it aloft.

'Do you wish that they had continued to live a lie?'

'I wish they hadn't had to lie,' snapped Jo.

'Your dad is gay, Jo, I don't think he has much choice in the matter. Things are what they are. Do you wish they hadn't told you? That they'd continued to treat you like a kid? Is that what you are saying?'

Jo glared at him, furious, because in truth, she was unsure what she wished for the most. Living a lie hadn't been too bad. Not too shabby at all. At least not for her and her siblings. Even thinking about it for a moment, she had to see that it must have been hard for her parents. Difficult.

The diner was practically deserted. Other than them, there was only one other customer: a skinny, heavily tattooed woman, who sat hunched over her coffee. She stood up to feed coins into the jukebox and a tune Dean didn't recognise sauntered into the room. It was a hopeless love song, not his cup of tea at the best of times. He glared at the tattooed lady but she was oblivious, no doubt drowning in her own personal drama. It shouldn't be this way, he thought. It was all unbearable. He wanted things to be better. Not just better for him, not the sort of better that could be achieved by regularly attending the gym, working hard at the office or filling your apartment with expensive gadgets, but a bigger better than that. He wanted the sort of better Jo had believed in. Feeling frustrated, he tried to soothe her.

'I just mean if you'd never been told about your mother's ancient indiscretion or your dad's sexual preferences, would you still love them as much today as you did last week?'

'Well, yes, of course, but I *do* know about them. That's the point.'

'Jo, the thing to focus on is that they are no less as parents just because you know a bit more about them as people. She's still the same woman who held your hand when you cried, picked you up when you fell over, changed your sheets, cooked your food, mopped your brow, fought with other mums at the school gate on your behalf. All that mum stuff.' Dean paused and waited for Jo to respond; she didn't. 'You can't be angry with her,' he pleaded. 'And your dad, he's still the guy who has worked his arse off so you could have a private education and tennis lessons. The guy who read to you every night, who ferried you to and from parties and loathed spotty boyfriends because they let you down. All that stuff you told me about your childhood, the jewel-coloured fruit, the itchy picnic rug, it all still happened.'

'And I'm just supposed to forgive them.'

'There's nothing to forgive. They haven't done this to *you*.'

'You hate your dad.' Jo spat out the accusation, like venom. 'And you never even talk about your mum. Why do you get to hate, if I'm not allowed?'

'It's different for me.' Dean turned away from Jo; he picked up the laminated menu with faded, dated pictures of knicker-bocker glories and waffles laden with whirls of artificial cream.

'Is it. How so?' Jo demanded, irrational and angry. Unexpectedly, she was sick of being the one who shared all her secrets and thoughts without getting anything in return. She had thought she'd enjoyed being listened to, but now she felt as though she was in a hot seat and she resented the one-way interrogation.

'I don't like talking about it,' replied Dean evenly.

'I got that,' Jo snarled. She reached for her red wine and took an enormous glug.

Dean suddenly snatched the glass off her and slammed it down on the table. Some of the wine splashed out over the rim and landed on his hand. He sucked it clean, then rooted urgently in his pocket, pulled out his wallet and threw a bunch of notes on the table. Even in Jo's distressed state, she could see he'd overpaid by about a hundred per cent.

'Come on. Let's get out of here. Enough wallowing underground. We're going for a walk.'

37

Jo

Dean grabs hold of my arm and yanks me out of the booth. He was holding my hand, which was comforting and even a bit erotic – well, more than a bit, if the truth be known. Despite my trauma, I couldn't help but notice how good it felt when he squeezed my hand, gently caressing me with his thumb. I'm not getting the same vibe now as he strides across the road, his grasp firm to the point of painful. I totter after him in my high heels, the tight skirt of my dress not allowing me to match his long, determined strides.

He marches down the crowded streets, oblivious to the colourful graffiti and the other rushing pedestrians. He dashes across the hectic roads, not noticing that cars have to honk and swerve to avoid hitting us. He is resolutely unaware that he's causing any commotion; he's a man on a mission who obviously has a destination in mind. I follow, too stuffed with self-pity to really care if we do get mowed down. He races through Millennium Park, seemingly insensible of the couples lolling on the lawns, kissing and laughing in the evening sunshine. He does not notice frenetic bladers and skaters who narrowly miss colliding with us on at least half a dozen occasions as we charge along the promenades, and he's blind to the exhausted-looking young parents who are battling with wilful toddlers who seem to continually run into our path like out-of-control missiles. He does not slacken his pace until we reach a part of the park that is signposted the Lurie Garden.

Unlike the rest of the park – which is kept cropped and clean, oozes modernity and throws up surprising urban art sculptures that please and puzzle in equal proportions – the Lurie Garden is a wilderness. I'm stunned by the oasis of colour, which offers instant respite from the surrounding hurly-burly. Purple lovegrass and coral bells teem with the flutter of butterflies and birds, the scent of mountain mint and giant hyssop drifts on the air and instantly soothes. It is living art; a moving, breathing palette of texture and colour. I feel a smidgen better. I turn to Dean. He looks worse. Agitated. Torn. Distressed.

'OK, so you want to know my story?'

I settle on a park bench, but Dean continues to pace backwards and forwards in front of me.

'Yes.'

'OK, princess, you asked for it.' It is the first time he has called me anything other than Jo. I get the distinct feeling that princess isn't a cosy little pet name, indicating we've reached a new level of intimacy – it's not meant as a compliment. 'Where shall I start?' For a moment he looks genuinely at a loss. He's been so eternally in control since the moment we met that I'm unsure how to respond. I realise that he needs me to give him something. A launch pad.

'Well, tell me where you're from. When we were talking about ambitions, you said you wanted to be footballer, a fireman, a cowboy. But you said your overriding ambition was to be rich and certainly to get away. Away from where?'

'Away from wherever they put me.'

'Who put you?' I ask carefully.

'The social workers. I spent a lot of time in care. Don't pin too much on the name. There wasn't anything careful about my childhood.' Dean snaps out his reply. He's stopped pacing but he keeps his back to me.

'I'm sorry.' I am. I'm so utterly, utterly sorry and I don't know what else to say. Words are always pitiless and inadequate in the face of a real calamity. Sorry has been used by too many bad-assed footballers talking to their wives and fans after some tawdry sex scandal, or by politicians after a couple of billion has been cut from a health-care programme; as a word, it has lost its potency. I wish I could think of something bigger to say.

'So my dad left. You got that much, right?'

'Yes, when you were very young.'

'I was five. He left and then vanished. We heard nothing from him ever again. Nothing.' The word has never sounded so bleak or so powerful to me. 'At first we managed. We didn't thrive, but you know, we managed.' Dean comes to sit next to me on the bench but he still doesn't look at me; he stares straight ahead, avoiding my gaze. 'Sometimes my mother held it together. There were weeks in a row when she washed and ironed our clothes, remembered to buy and even cook food, and we were OK. Never happy. We were never relaxed enough to just be happy because things never stayed the same for long, but we were OK. Like I said, we . . . managed.' He rolls the word around his mouth before he is able to spit it out. I begin to get a sense of how hard it is for him to tell me his story. This is not a matter of pride or a penchant for secrecy; this is a personal hell. He carries on. 'However, inevitably something would happen. A friend of hers would get married or have another baby, her latest boyfriend would ditch her or she'd hit a birthday, and it would trigger a crisis. She'd remember that there was a great yawning gap between what she'd hoped her life would be and what it was. So she'd hit the bottle.'

He shrugs. A tiny, defeated gesture that hints he has accepted the facts and at the same time has been defined by them.

'What she forgot to do we mopped up. We learnt how to put clothes in the washing machine and to hang them on the line. And on Tuesdays we'd walk her to the post office to cash the Child Allowance cheque, no matter if she was hungover or smelt of booze. Often she bought a bottle or two and then we'd head home. On Tuesday nights, when she was getting drunk, I'd sneak into her bag and take back what was left of the Child Allowance. It wasn't stealing from her. It was ours.' He sounds defensive and I want to tell him it's OK, but I daren't interrupt. I fear that if I do, he might never be able to finish what he's trying to tell me. 'The first time Zoe and I went shopping alone, we bought crap. Four cans of Tab, Cherry Lips, Kola Kubes and countless packets of Space Dust and Doritos, if I remember correctly.'

Dean counts off the shopping list on his fingers. He clearly does remember correctly. He smiles gently, the memory of the illicit feast somehow breaking through the terrible anguish. 'Obviously we made ourselves sick, so the next week we bought fish fingers, Findus pancakes and Arctic roll. Not exactly the most nutritious meal ever, but an improvement. Over time, the guy in the corner shop started to pick things out for us to try, good value, reasonably healthy stuff. He gave us discounts on food that was nearing its sell-by date. People saw what was going on but they didn't get too involved. People didn't in those days. Thank God. That was how we wanted it.'

I want to reach out and hold his hand as he held mine in the diner, but as I inch towards him, he senses what I'm going to do and he folds his arms across his chest. I freeze. Locked out. 'Going to school in clothes that hadn't been ironed wasn't the end of the world. Of course she missed stuff, school plays, sports day, even parents' evenings, but no one cared about that much. Well, no one other than me and Zoe. Sometimes a teacher with a leaning towards efficiency might grumble that our parent consent forms weren't signed for a school trip, but after a particularly officious cow made Zoe miss out on going to a City Petting Zoo trip, we quickly learnt the value of forging Mum's signature if she was too blind drunk or had passed out and was incapable of doing it herself.' Dean sighs. I'm not sure if it's at the memory he's just relayed or in anticipation of something he has yet to reveal. 'But it became more difficult when it was no longer just about the neglect; when that pushed over to what they call abuse.'

'She hit you?' There's a lump in my throat, the size of a continent. I fight the tears. I have no right to cry. He isn't.

'No, not us, but she did smash things up. Dad's stuff at first. The books he'd left behind she tore and wrenched. She shredded his clothes with a kitchen knife. It was a futile gesture. He'd taken everything he really cared about. The clothes he left behind were the ones he no longer deemed fashionable enough to be seen in.' Dean shrugs and lets out a cold, sharp sound that is, I think, supposed to be a laugh. 'Like his family, no longer needed. She ripped up his photos, and then when there was nothing more of his to break, she broke our stuff, her own stuff, herself. She'd scream and yell and rant and rave. We'd creep down the stairs after a tempestuous night and not know what to expect. She might have passed out in amongst the shards of plastic, glass and crockery; sometimes she was cut because she'd lain heavily on the broken bits. Other times she might have made it back to her bed or to the bathroom to be ill. Not that she always got there in time. I had to clean her vomit from the side of the bathtub, from sheets and the stairs. When she shat in her pants, I refused to touch her. I wouldn't let Zoe do it either. I left her stinking, went to school, told my teacher and they took us away that night.'

I think of the young boy, too small to be a man – let alone a hero – struggling to protect and support his sister. Dealing with the fact that he could no longer shield his mother from the world, forced to betray her to the authorities.

Dean is so still, a yellow butterfly lands on his shoulder. I can't take my eyes off it as the world seems to shrink to just the three of us on this bench, Dean, me and the tiger swallowtail. I think of my ham-fisted attempts as a child to catch butterflies in nets. With my parents, my siblings and I would run through the fields, making too much noise and commotion to have a hope of a successful hunt; I don't think my parents ever really wanted to go for the kill. Sunlight drips through my memories. It glistens on the paddling pool that we splashed in, it shines on the icing of our home-baked birthday cakes, and another light flickers there too: the candles, six, seven, eight, nine, ten, thirty-five, because yes, even last year my mum baked me a cake and my dad lit the candles. My childhood is all about songs and light, laughter and love. I hardly dare breathe.

'The care homes were a disaster. I didn't help myself, I suppose.' Dean nibbled his thumbnail. I waited. 'I'd learnt about breaking things too, by then. I smashed, burnt, wrote obscenities on the doors of the girls' bedrooms. Anything to release a bit of . . .'

'Pain?'

Dean shrugs. 'Anger.'

He's trusting me with so much here, but he can't quite trust me with a hint of weakness, not even weakness he might have felt when he was a child. 'Did you ever run away?' I ask.

'No. I might have, but there was always Zoe. She was of the mindset that we should just sit it out; that it would get better. Hey, and it did. Right?'

He turns to me, and for the first time since he started talking he looks into my eyes. He's changed during the conversation. I can no longer see the cocky seducer who can only promise a woman one thing – that he won't call. Now, I see the boy who has endured neglect beyond my imagination, one who has had to become resilient and self-sufficient to the point of being chilly and closed. But besides that, I can also see the guy who wants to help me to hold on to my dreams; the guy who has risked exposing his shameful, painful past so that I will value my illustrious, indulgent one.

'Right. Zoe knew what she was talking about,' I agree, because I know that's what he needs me to do. Obviously things are better, but I wonder, can it ever be good enough after what they've been through? Will Dean ever stop feeling the lack of what he's missed as a child? His hands are still folded across his chest, but I force him to unclasp and I place his arm over my shoulder and slip my hand around his waist. Thirty minutes ago I thought my world was falling apart. I thought I'd never recover. I felt hideously sorry for myself. Now I see that I will recover. I might even become a better person, the way Dean has. Whatever. None of that matters right now; all that matters is Dean. And in this moment, like Alice biting the Eat Me cake, I become bigger. I grow up.

'OK, my friend. It's been a rough day. There's only one thing we can do now.'

'What's that?' Dean looks at me as though I have all the answers, and for a moment in time, I do.

'Take me dancing.'

38

Jo

Dean glances at his watch. It's just past seven p.m., a little early for dancing on Saturday night, but I know he'll pull something out of the bag. He won't let either of us down. This is a man who scrabbled his way out of his deprived childhood so that he could bungee-jump from the Altavilla Tower in Brazil; he's up to the challenge of finding us a club to strut our funky stuff.

As I predicted, he suddenly looks as though someone has lit a match behind his eyes. 'Hey, I know, let's put your salsa lessons to good use. Let's go to a Latin club.'

'What?'

'A hot and heavy Latin club.'

This is not the moment for me to lose confidence. I grin and nod manically.

The downtown salsa club is everything I could have imagined. The polished parquet floor is scratched, tattooed with good times, and the room is dim, heavy red velvet drapes with generous gold tassels blocking out the daylight. However, the ambience is bright because of the frequent flashes of toned and tanned legs, balanced on spiky high heels. Glamorous women with big bottoms twirl impressively around the room with passion and finesse. Unpromising-looking guys in black T-shirts and jeans turn into gods in front of my eyes as they stamp, pout, throw, turn and rumble with their floral-clad partners. The place is throbbing, pulsing. It's alive.

'It's sweaty out there on the dance floor.'

'It is,' Dean agrees. He looks happier with the situation than I am.

'Look at the way they move.' There is nothing discreet. The men are broad and big, the women sultry. The club is rammed with the type of people who live a full and out-there life.

I wonder what I should do, who I should be. Who am I now? Am I Jo the hopeless romantic? I know that Dean needed me to keep the faith back in the park. Having spent the last twenty-four hours claiming he thinks my ideas on relationships are ridiculous, it was clear he suddenly, desperately needed to believe in a world that was slightly better than the one he imagines we are in, or at least he needed me to continue to believe. And following his shocking but heartfelt confidence, I knew I had to appear to be OK. I rose to the challenge. But do I still believe? It seems unlikely, impossible even, in the light of the revelations about my mum and dad and the fact that Martin (aka my last chance) will now be legally married. However . . .

I look up. Unsurprisingly, Dean is already on the floor; he is not one to lose a moment. He's taken off his tie and jacket; no doubt he's carelessly flung them under a table or on the back of a seat. He's undone his top button and he's now already having the balsero explained to him by a gaggle of willing (exclusively female) volunteers. He looks magnificent. The lump the size of a continent that was stuck in my throat has not gone away; it swells. But it's no longer anything to do with sadness or pity; it's fed by admiration and – I might as well admit it to myself – a very deep longing. My stomach lurches. It's a good feeling. I ride the tide of emotion as it souses my entire body with feelings of anticipation and excitement. Suddenly, possibly for the first time, I know who I am.

I *am* Jo the romantic.

It's weird, but somehow a gay dad and an adulterous mum has confirmed rather than denied that for me. When I return to England, I'll hear more from both of them. I'll try to understand the choices they made, and I'll try to support them both, because however bizarre and misguided the situation seems, I am sure they thought they were doing the right thing. They thought they were doing the best for us kids, for each other. That's love. Messy, unpredictable love. Even hearing about Dean's brutal childhood hasn't taken away my belief in the happily-ever-after, because look at him. He's amazing. He's the most determined, positive, spirited, beautiful man I have ever met. And even if he doesn't believe in his happily-ever-after, I do. More than ever.

I eye the dance floor. It looks inviting. It looks overwhelming. Despite taking salsa lessons, I have never actually been to a salsa club. Ridiculous, I know. No one ever invited me and it has never crossed my mind to go alone. I rarely dance nowadays except at other people's weddings, but then I am, most often, very badly drunk and so I dance forlornly with two or three other single girls, not actually around our handbags but around our trampled self-esteem. I decide that I won't drink any more tonight. It seems insensitive after Dean's story. Besides, when I drink, details smudge and blur, and I already have a feeling that I want to remember every single second of this evening. Dean catches my eye, and without any more hesitation I run to him.

And so we dance. I twirl and turn, shake and shimmy. I dance hard and well. I allow the music to flow through me, take hold of me. I don't block it with concerns about whether I've mastered a step or how silly or sweaty I might look. I just dance. I let it all go. The club is hot and stuffy, which makes me feel younger than I normally feel, younger than I've felt before. I dance until my body is clammy, until my damp hair sticks to my neck, my make-up melts down my face. I feel a blister pop up on my toe, but still I don't stop; I just throw off my shoes. I want to be exhausted; I want my limbs to ache with satisfying exercise fatigue.

Dean is a complete natural at salsa, and whilst he doesn't technically know all the steps, he shakes his hips in an extremely effective way and moves his feet with enough style that before long there's a crowd of women vying for his attention, all desperately trying to bag a dance. He doesn't dance with any of them. He seems oblivious to their luscious dark locks flowing down their backs, their muscular legs that slide and glide and go on forever. He doesn't appear to notice their plunging necklines, heaving bosoms or brilliant smiles. All he notices is me. He doesn't take his eyes off me. I try to look away, but fail. I am conscious of him in the clearest, most absolute sense of the word. I am aware of every muscle in his body, as it stretches and contracts. I can see every pore on his skin, every hair that trembles. I feel him breathe. I feel him be. And under his gaze, I become my best self. Unselfconscious, I pulse to the tunes, thoughtless, careless. I find a place I rarely hit except when I am dreaming. I flick my hair and move my shoulders like a fun, happy person; someone with hopes and possibilities and a future. Confident, I am taller, thinner and my hair is possibly glossier. Other people dance around us. I am part of it, not an onlooker.

The night wears on. I remain at the epicentre of the dance floor and his focus. We occasionally pause in our dancing to drink some water, but once refreshed, we immediately return to the floor. We don't talk to one another much; we limit ourselves to swapping the odd silly comment or joke. There've been enough serious words exchanged for now.

'Sit on that rhythm,' cries Dean. I laugh. The phrase is bonkers and almost other-worldly, but from his lips it is simply funny, as he intended.

'I feel spaced out, drunk on the dancing,' I yell above the music.

'Careful, you might lose control,' teases Dean. From his grin, I know he'd like me to.

'Worse still, I might take it!' I laugh.

Dean laughs too. 'Go hard or go home, Jo,' he encourages.

Instinctively I reach up and cradle his face in between my hands. I draw him to me and, without thinking about it, I kiss him full on the lips. It isn't a long and lingering kiss. It isn't necessarily a sexual kiss. It might just be a kiss between friends. It might. Good, very happy friends. It is a firm, warm and full kiss. I let him go before he drops me. Just in case. And then I start to twirl and turn and dance again.

'That's so cool,' yells some guy who is dancing next to us. Dean has been chatting to this guy over the music from time to time tonight. I've seen them laughing together; I think Dean bought him a drink. He's huge and handsome. His ebony skin shines and his muscles bulge. He grabs my hand and whirls me around as though I'm a doll.

'You sure have some moves,' he comments. 'You're a great dancer.'

'I think I love you,' I laugh. He takes it in the spirit I intended. Playful, not loaded. Tonight I don't have a whiff of cougar about me.

My new friend nods towards Dean. 'He's sick, your man.' The phrase clearly means that he respects Dean rather than thinking Dean needs any medical attention. 'Awesome guy. Lots of fun.'

'He *is* fun. But he's not my man. He's just a friend,' I explain.

'Oh come on, lady. Don't try lying to Rudie. I know these things. He's your man.' I stare at Rudie, amazed, and afraid that he's articulated what I've known but not wanted to admit. Dean *is* my man. Or at least he should be. Could be? The truth is, that all the while I was plotting to bring down Martin's wedding, I've been fighting fantasies of getting down with Dean. But he's dangerous, a path I've trodden so often before. He's too hand-some to have learned to care or to stay; it shouldn't be that way but it so often is.

Suddenly Dean is at my side again. I'm aware of this even before I turn towards him, because tonight – despite dancing my heart out in the crowd – I've always known where he is. I've known if he is sitting, standing, dancing. I've known when he is drinking, or laughing, or still. Or looking at me. He's done that a lot.

'Jo, I'm going to make a move.'

'You are?' Momentarily I misunderstand and my first reaction is delight, then I realise that he means he's leaving. He has his jacket flung over his shoulder; his tie, shoved in his trouser pocket, trails down his leg. 'I think my jet lag is finally kicking in.' My heart sinks. It's a good job the music is so loud or else people might hear it crashing to the floor.

'I should go too. I need to see if there is a room at the hotel for tonight. I only booked one night. I thought . . . Well, you know what I thought. I left my bags with the concierge.'

Dean looks at me quizzically. 'We'll swing by the hotel and pick them up on the way back to mine,' he says firmly.

My heart leaps again. Jumps right up into my mouth. I feel deliriously irresponsible, infatuated and irrational. I adore him.

39

Dean

Dean wished he had some groceries in. Jo had obviously taken the pledge since he had told her about his mother being an alcoholic, which was sweet of her, but now they were back at his place he'd have liked her to accept a drink. Not because he was trying to get her drunk but because he had no other form of hospitality to offer. They hadn't finished their food in the diner; in fact they'd left a trail of half-eaten meals behind them ever since they'd met. He dimmed the lights and turned on the trendy hole-in-the-wall gas fire, which immediately roared into action. The room looked as he'd designed it to look – a lair for seduction – but suddenly he was unsure whether that was the right vibe for tonight.

'We could order in,' he suggested.

'I'm not actually all that hungry.' Jo shrugged and collapsed on to his enormous grey corner sofa. She kicked off her high shoes with evident relief, instantly transforming from minx to kitten. Dean was a bit staggered to note he found her equally as beguiling when she started to inspect the emerging blisters as he had when her high heels had showcased her calves.

'I have milk and maybe some biscuits,' he proposed.

'Perfect,' she beamed back.

He went into the kitchen and rummaged. Normally, if he was entertaining a woman, he'd maintain constant flirtatious banter – he prided himself on witty, loaded one-liners – but tonight he didn't have the energy or the need. He remained mute until he settled down next to her with the tray of goodies. How close should he sit? Were they going to have sex? Normally it would be a no-brainer, but Jo? With Jo it would not be a one-night stand. Was he ready for more? Was he able? She had one stray hair in her otherwise immaculately plucked eyebrow. It was grey and wiry and stood out against the darker hairs. The rogue hair seemed to represent all that was quirky and vulnerable about Jo; she wasn't as young as she wanted to be, or as polished. He liked it. As he liked the small mole on her earlobe. He'd managed to unearth a large packet of peanut M&Ms as well as some Oreos. She beamed as though his hospitality was worthy of five Michelin stars.

'So you are not sad, then?' he asked carefully. Jo turned to him and looked confused. 'About Martin's wedding going ahead,' he clarified.

'Oh God, no.' She waved her hand dismissively, as though they were talking about ancient history, which in a way they were, even though the wedding had only taken place a matter of hours ago. 'No, Gloria is welcome to her wedding.' Jo glanced at her wristwatch. 'Do you know what, I'd never really thought about the actual wedding night.'

'Sorry?'

'The sex.' She leant towards him and whispered the word in a giggly manner, nudging him as though she'd just read a cheeky postcard or watched a *Carry On* movie. 'I mean, right now they are probably rolling around on a king-sized bed, draped in two-zillion-thread-count linens, getting all tangled and hot and sweaty.'

'Or they might be opening their wedding gifts.'

'True. Either way, I don't mind.' Jo paused. 'I guess I should have thought about that before I spent my last ten quid on the flight over here. I'm not jealous of her. I'm not into him in that way. I think I should have been.'

Dean nodded. She should have been. However, right now he did not regret the fact that Joanna Russell had spent her last ten quid on the flight where they'd met one another. 'Ah, so once again you believe that it is all about the chemistry, the tightening in the front bottom.' She elbowed him in the ribs because she knew he was gently mocking her. 'The eyes meeting across a crowded room.'

Dean noticed that Jo suddenly couldn't get her eyes to meet his across this empty room, even though they were sitting right next to one another and her gaze would only have to travel the length of a ruler.

'You need the chemistry, but you need other things too,' she muttered.

'You have a moustache.'

Jo looked horrified. 'Oh God, no. I wax.' Her hand instantly sprang to her face.

'A milk moustache,' Dean rushed to clarify before she revealed any more of her beauty regime.

'Oh.' She rubbed her face clean. That exchange hadn't done anything to help her meet his gaze.

They silently watched the flames flicker in the fireplace. Dean wondered whether he should put on the TV, but he thought it would alter the mood too dramatically. It would be like inviting other people in to party and it would break the intimacy of the evening; he found he didn't want to do that. He considered putting on some music, but he knew that would up the ante; love ballads or even slow ambient music would inevitably place them in a position where they could no longer pretend this was all about just being friends, and he wasn't sure he wanted to do that either. He was stranded somewhere he'd never been before.

'We have chemistry,' Jo suddenly blurted. She turned to him and stared at him with a clear and undisturbed honesty. 'Don't we? You felt it too. On the aeroplane, and last night at the restaurant whenever we touched. Today when you kissed me in front of Martin. When I kissed you at the club.'

'Yes, we do. I did.' Whispering, he added, 'Look, Jo, I want you to know that normally I would try and have sex with you right now.'

Jo smiled. 'Normally you wouldn't have to try too hard.'

'But we're friends, right? So we can't go there.'

'Yes. Friends,' she confirmed.

'Just friends.'

'Well, friends who tell each other everything and help each other through very difficult times and—'

Dean had no idea what she was going to say next, but he didn't give her a chance. He pushed his mouth on top of hers, and this time there was no question about it: the kiss was not a kiss between friends. Her lips felt warm and plump under his; they yielded and fitted exactly. She gently touched his cheek, and whilst the touch was feather light, he felt pinioned, strapped to her. He put his hand on the back of her neck and drew her in, tighter. He kissed her and, with equal enthusiasm and expertise, she kissed back, untamed and ferocious. Dean had done a lot of kissing in his time. A lot. So, as he kissed her, he fought the thought that somehow these were particular and special kisses, more significant and consequential than he'd ever experienced before; he left that sort of sentimental claptrap to women, to the likes of Jo. Yet he had to admit that her kisses felt as startling and interesting as his very first kiss, but as erotic and assured as any he had ever enjoyed.

Swiftly, he moved his hands over her. He put them everywhere he could; speedily, expertly, naturally. He knew how to touch women, how to hold and please them, and this time he pulled out all the stops. He enjoyed the feel of her under his fingers; her neck, shoulder blades, ribs and tits. He swept over her, under her and through her. They were exposed and left with nothing other than their desire and requirement of each other. He could not remember it ever being this defined and unambiguous before. He wanted her. He wanted to please her, to take her, to have her. He sensed that she was on the same page when she stood up and demanded, 'Where's your bedroom?'

Dean briefly wondered whether this romantic woman needed clean sheets or candlelight. His bed was scrambled, sheets crumpled by his own restlessness last night, but as the blind was not pulled, the lights of Chicago's buildings and streets lit up the room like sparkling stars on a black sky, and it was enough. He practically threw her on the bed; the skirt of her dress rode up as he did so, and hastily she pulled down her lacy knickers. He grappled with his flies and then, directly, disappeared into her. Her body received him as though she had been expecting him for ever. And maybe she had. He stared at her and she gazed back, aware of what they were doing and who they were doing it with. It felt amazing. It felt imperative and vital.

It felt truthful.

She groaned and trembled and he roared and quaked. It was tumultuous and rapid and staggering. Dean's body meshed with Jo's and they fitted so profoundly he lost sense of who was who. Whose pleasure he was experiencing, whose pleasure he was creating, whose pain he was blocking.

The cavernous sense of being alone eased.

SUNDAY 24 APRIL 2005

40

Clara

Clara arrived at the hospital at nine o'clock. A young nurse with plump pink flesh informed her that visiting hours didn't start until eleven. Clara locked her eyes on to the skinny band of the cheap engagement ring that the nurse wore; a small cluster of tiny sapphires, it was almost lost within the copious folds of her flesh, but Clara sensed that it was a dearly loved ring.

'I'm his wife,' she lied.

'Oh, we didn't realise.' The nurse's cheeks turned a shade rosier; the embarrassment dripped down on to her neck too. 'We haven't seen you until this weekend and there's no mention of you on his records.'

'We're estranged, but . . .' Clara paused, hoping to give the impression that it was all too difficult to talk about. She didn't consider whether what she was saying was immoral or even illegal. 'There's so little time left,' she added. Whilst Clara was always perfectly polite, she had the sort of beautifully crisp voice that intimidated most people, and so she found that her requests on trains, in theatres, shops and the dry cleaner's were usually met with agreeable acquiescence; it was the same in the hospital. The nurse could not imagine that anyone so well-spoken would cause a problem, let alone tell a blatant lie, because she hadn't ever paid much attention during her history lessons, and so Clara was allowed to go to Eddie's bedside.

It didn't matter to him anyway. He was not conscious and did not wake up even when she repeated his name, gently shook his arm or, finally, hesitantly kissed his forehead. She decided to stay. If he woke up, she didn't want him to be alone. She thought she owed him this much. She wasn't sure why she might believe this, but people did tend to think they were responsible to and for Eddie Taylor; he elicited more loyalty than he deserved. She was not able to stay away and yet her visits did not make her content. He had disappointed her, again. In a profound and unforgivable way. Physically he had changed beyond all recognition, but emotionally he was unaltered.

Eddie Taylor was still the man she should not choose.

He was still the man who did not deserve her, the one who would not make her happy or look after her. It was devastating. Rationally, it might have been worse if he had metamorphosed; then she would have had to deal with the fact that if she had chosen him all those years ago, he might, just might, have been what she needed. They might have been blissful together. But he was still as selfish, brutal and unaware as ever. What she had to accept was that her entire life had been shaped by this man who did not deserve her, who would never make her blissful, who wouldn't even try. She'd got it all wrong.

Yesterday he had told her a little more about his children. The youngest two didn't bother with him beyond Christmas cards and a more often than not late birthday card; he showed a similar level of commitment, although he did speak fondly about when they were little girls taking horse-riding lessons and mastering the ability to tie shoelaces and plaits. He had been involved to an extent and for a time; he felt a level of possession, but it did not stretch to a full-blown sense of responsibility. There were always limits with Eddie Taylor. According to his account, the younger two were cheerful and well enough. They had a mother who'd had the sense to move on with her life when her disappointment with Eddie Taylor could not be suppressed. She'd remarried. Eddie said her husband was 'A decent enough bloke. The girls like him. Lousy handshake, though; probably not much in the sack.'

But the other two, Dean and Zoe.

Clara had shivered when she listened to Eddie's story about the son visiting. Eddie said he was an angry and unforgiving man. 'Narrow-minded,' he surmised. Clara recognised that he was a bruised and wounded child. 'Extremely hurt,' she'd suggested.

'Well, yes. But so long ago.' Eddie did seem embarrassed to admit that the children had ended up in care. 'You'd have thought someone would have told me.' He'd blinked twice and then closed his eyes.

Clara felt a terrible guilt about and pity for these two children. It ran through her being and settled like a concrete mass in her stomach. She had not been able to eat breakfast this morning. She did not know them, she'd never met them, she hadn't even seen a photo – Eddie had never been the sort to proudly or even deceitfully display a family portrait on his desk – but she felt responsible. Clara was the sort of woman who had enough time to be ostentatiously charitable; she now worried whether she'd only ever been ostensibly charitable. She organised an annual ball in Mayfair, one for which her friends spent a fortune on dresses and haircuts and donated a little more to a cause – children starving in Africa; and she arranged regular cake bake-off challenges where her competitive time-and-cash-rich pals paid an astronomical fee to bake in front of one another and display their skills for public acclamation. The monies raised bought underwear for children in war-torn countries, whose own pants had been blown away with their houses because an adult had detonated a bomb. She was energetic and persistent in her fund-raising and had twice been invited to the House of Lords, where she and other well-intentioned do-gooders were thanked for doing their bit to put right some of the world's injustices. She thought that perhaps her next fund-raiser ought to be for a British charity; perhaps a shelter for homeless children or an awareness campaign about the number of children in care who were in need of foster parents. She sighed, aware that she couldn't help Dean or Zoe personally. It was too late for that.

41

Jo

'Right, I am starving. We *are* going to have to send out for something now,' said Dean.

'I'm still OK with the biscuits and sweets, if there are any left. I think I can indulge, we must have burnt loads of calories!' I giggle. Flashbacks to last night sear my memory and I inwardly blush with total delight and unembarrassed excitement.

'You mean all that dancing?' Dean snuggles into my neck and gently nibbles my ear. As he tugs, something low in my belly responds.

'I really enjoyed the dancing,' I laugh, although that wasn't what I meant and I think Dean knows as much. We've made love three times now. Three! After the first frenzied and fabulous time, we did it again, carefully and gently; the third was slower still, but I suspect that was biology rather than anything else. Dean kissed and caressed me with real tenderness. His touch restored me and reassured me, lit me up and excited me with a passion I didn't know I was capable of. The sheets smell of our hot bodies and I can feel his breath on my forehead as I am curled up under his arm; it's raw and intimate and blissful. It's different. I know, *I know* I've made mistakes in the past. I'm famed for my misjudgements, my hasty judgements and my downright lack of

333

judgement, but all that said, I can't help but believe that this *is* different. Not just because of how he makes me feel, but because of the effect *I'm* having on *him*. I'm pretty certain that for once, this exciting, sexy, unobtainable, damaged man is taking notice of me.

'How did last night's salsa club compare to those you usually go to in London?'

'I've never been to a club in London,' I confess.

'But you said you took lessons.'

'I do, but I've never danced Latin anywhere except inside the dusty town hall where the lessons are held.'

Dean pulls away a little, to stare at me with disbelief. I force myself to meet his gaze. Without having to spell it out, I know he understands why I haven't had the confidence and opportunity to take my dancing out of the town hall. Gently he murmurs, 'Jo, you have to stop living a half-life.'

By which we both know he means a life where I only take up hobbies if I think they will lead to finding a boyfriend, a life where I only travel if I'm travelling with some guy, ditto going to hot and sweaty nightclubs and visiting interesting and improving galleries or even fun shops and shows.

'I know, I see that. I'm trying. I've started.' Dean doesn't look reassured, but I *have* started to live a whole life. I got on the plane to Chicago, which was a brave and impetuous thing to do. OK, so my motivation may not have been one hundred per cent admirable, but the outcome has been thrilling and wonderful. I know I've spent a disproportionate amount of my time looking for love, but right now, snuggled under Dean's heavy, muscular arm, it's hard to think that it has been a bad plan.

'Because you really can't pin your happiness on someone else,' he adds.

I inwardly pause. Falter. My nerves contract an infinitesimal amount, because that sounds a little bit like a warning to me.

I've heard enough warnings in my time to recognise them in whatever form they come. The morning-after distancing is something I'm far too familiar with. 'I'm a bit too tied up this week to make any firm plans', 'I'm working towards a promotion and I'm not sure I can do a relationship justice right now', or the worst one of all, the one where he doesn't hand over his phone number but takes mine and says, 'I'll call you.' He doesn't.

I don't have Dean's number.

He hasn't even asked for mine. I freeze. It's interesting that I've listened to dozens of morning-after excuses in my time, but this is the first time I've actually *heard* one. Perhaps, since I discovered that my parents' marriage hasn't been exactly a bed of roses, I've woken up a little and become a touch more realistic.

I glance at Dean; he's smiling at me. It's a broad, open beam that envelops his face and makes it all the way to his eyes, the ultimate test. The momentary panic, fear and doubt recede once again. Yes, I can hear his caution and reserve, but I can also understand it. This man has lived his entire life keeping his distance because no one can stab, slash or cut you from afar. He's not creating morning-after distance because he's a prick; he's creating morning-after distance because he's conditioned to protect himself, because he's afraid. Yet despite the audible caution and possible distancing, I also recognise and value that he has opened up to me, trusted and confided in me. That *has* to count for something, that *has* to mean something.

I can take control. I can draw him in and teach him to trust. I know I can. I have enough optimism for the two of us. I don't mean that I want to chase, conquer and have him through some misguided blindness or due to a faulty stubbornness, as I might have done in the past, but I want to draw him closer with an acceptance that this man has reason to be doubtful and cautious; he's never expected much from love, but I can change that.

'I guess your mum's biggest mistake was pinning her happiness on your dad, right?'

'You could say that.' I pause, and don't rush to fill the silence that sits in the room. I'm rewarded when Dean adds, 'She let this void develop, a void between the life she led and the life she once thought she'd lead, and it grew to such an enormous cavern that it destroyed her . . .' He broke off. 'Look, I'm just saying that I think we should all be responsible for our own happiness, and it doesn't make sense to me that you take salsa lessons but won't go to a club unless someone asks you to. Sorry about the lecture. But I care.'

I kiss him. Leisurely. Gently (but taking care to push my naked nipples up against him, so it's not too chastely). He cares! He's scared. Cautious. But he cares. It's enough. For now. I'm more realistic, he's more trusting; perhaps we can meet in the middle somewhere and make this work. I sense that he needs me to change the subject for a while. Slowly, slowly catch the monkey, as my dad says. I mustn't rush in at this like a bull in a china shop.

'Thanks,' I say when I eventually pull away. I suppose I can see why Dean might be preaching to me about the importance of taking responsibility for my own happiness. My parents have separated, my dad's just been shoved out of the closet, I'm homeless, jobless, one step away from a soup kitchen and I have a collection of invites to other people's weddings that is so hefty my postman might sue me for his chiropractic fees. I probably should be worried. However, this morning I can't help thinking that maybe what I have in front of me is not a great big fat turd of a life but an opportunity for change. There's something about Dean that makes me believe that things can get better. That they will do. He's proof positive that we are in charge of our own destinies. 'OK, let's make a list,' I say brightly.

'A shopping list? Well, we need pretty much everything. Eggs, juice, bacon . . .'

'No, a bucket list. Things I have to do before I die.'

Dean looks surprised, but grins. 'Good idea.' He reaches over me (briefly kissing me en route) and delves around in the bedside cabinet. In among the loose coins, odd cufflink and the Durex box, he eventually finds a pen. 'I need something we can scribble on.' It's obvious that he doesn't want to get out of bed to find paper. I'm glad; I like to feel him folded around me and I like it that he wants it too. 'I'll write on the Durex instruction leaflet,' he suggests.

'Is there room?'

'I'll write small, there's a border.' We lie on our sides facing each other, the instruction leaflet between us. Dean holds the pen poised. Our feet are still entwined. 'OK, fire.' He stares at me with eager expectancy.

I don't want to disappoint him, although I probably will as my mind is blank. What do I enjoy? What do I want to do with myself for the next forty-odd years? I look at Dean, hoping he'll help. 'Any ideas?'

'Would you like to learn to ski?' I shake my head. 'Or go wakeboarding or zorbing? Now that's hysterical,' he suggests.

'Do they *have* to be so active?' I surprise myself by not wasting time pretending to like his hobbies.

'No, no, I suppose not. Not if you don't want them to be,' says Dean.

I rack my brains and then almost yell, 'I know, I'd like to stay in bed all day and eat junk food. An entire day.'

Dean looks sceptical. 'That's not exactly a to-do, is it? It's more of an avoid-doing.' However, he writes *Jo's To-Do List* in the margin of the leaflet, alongside the warning to check the expiry date on the condom wrapper before you use it, and adds: *1. Lie in bed all day and eat junk food.*

'I'd like to try jellied eels. Well, I wouldn't actually *like* to, but I sort of think I should,' I offer. 'People are always saying they're an East End delicacy, aren't they? And I'm a Londoner, so I feel almost obliged . . .'

'Go on, then, you can have that.'

'I'd like to drink cherry milkshake.'

'Are all your ambitions going to be about food?'

'Possibly.'

'Then you should be specific. How about you go to the award-laden Fosselman's, in the LA suburb of Alhambra? They serve amazing milkshakes.'

'How do you even know that?'

'I know stuff. I make it my business to know stuff. The double-chocolate malt is one of my favourite treats ever, up there with eating macaroons at Ladurée in Paris.'

'What? Where?'

'This guy, Monsieur Ladurée, opened his bakery on the rue Royale in 1862; later his grandson invented the double-decker macaroon. Two shells of meringue-like pastry held together by creamy ganache filling. Superb.' Dean smacks his lips together to suggest how delicious these cakes are.

'I'd like to try those. Add that to my list.'

'Nope.'

'What?'

'No. You have to think of your own, Jo. You're just saying what you think I want you to say.' I scowl but accept he has a point. I must have my own ambitions, my own desires. Ones that are not to do with food. I just must have.

After what seems to be about two and a half years I excitedly pronounce, 'I know. I'd like to be an extra in a film. A proper film. Something directed by Scorsese or Spielberg or someone.'

'Good one.' Dean scribbles it down.

'I'd like to plant a tree.'

'What sort?'

'Cherry blossom.'

'Where?'

'In my garden.'

'So you'd like a garden?'

'Yes, yes, I would. I'd like a home of my own.'

More scribbling. 'Now you are getting it,' encourages Dean. I take his comment to mean that he thinks I'm getting the hang of writing a bucket list, rather than that I'm getting more sex, although that would be lovely. 'Where?'

'Where what?'

'Where would you like your home to be?' Dean keeps his eyes on the leaflet, and although I'm really trying not to be too like my old self, the self that projects as far as the birth of our second child even before we've shared a packet of cereal, I can't help thinking that his question is a little loaded.

'I'm not sure. In a city. I like London, but I could go further afield, I suppose. Sydney, New York, maybe here,' I add, elated at the thought of the trains that criss-cross the city, endlessly taking busy and useful people to exciting and important places. Thinking about the stunning skyline that I can see – even now – from Dean's bed because his room benefits from an enormous window, I can imagine making Chicago my home. So far my experience has been that this city is awash with sparkly lights and dazzling smiles.

'What do you like about Chicago particularly?' asks Dean with a cough.

Him. And, 'It strikes me as an energetic, electrifying and am-bitious city. I like the look of Lake Michigan; it must be great to be somewhere urban that also benefits from miles of beach. Besides, everyone speaks English. Hey, don't worry, I'm not suggesting I move in. Well not straight away. Joke. I'm just talking about what might work for me. It's a coincidence that it works for you too.' I glance shyly at Dean to see if he looks totally and utterly horrified. He doesn't. He doesn't even look fazed. 'I'd like to milk a cow,' I add. Dean nods and jots that down too. 'I'd like to stay in the Ice Hotel in Sweden. It's made entirely of ice, can you believe that? The walls, the beds, the plates, the loos! Have you heard of it?' Dean nods. 'Have you stayed there?' Dean hesitates but decides not to lie to me; he nods again. I can see he's worried that he's stealing my thunder, but he's not. I'm impressed. 'Wow, you really have packed a lot in.'

'I told you, I had a slow start, but I've been catching up ever since.'

'I'd like to gallop a horse along a beach. That's a stretch, because I can't ride a horse and I'm not that confident around water.'

Dean laughs. 'In which case, that one is perfect.'

'Maybe I should think about travel journalism. I need a break from tiered cakes and posies.'

It takes nearly two hours but the list has forty-one entries by the time we are scribbling around the small print that explains how each batch of latex is tested and certified at the plantation. Dean says he'd have liked a neat fifty points because he likes round numbers, and he really doubts whether peel an apple keeping the skin in one long string is worthy of the list, but all in all he seems satisfied with my ambitions and I'm thrilled by them. Just the process of writing them down is exciting. I can't wait to get cracking. Although one of the reasons why compiling the list might have seemed such fun was that Dean kept kissing me and playing with my breasts as he wrote.

'What about you?' I ask. 'Do you have a list?'

'I don't need one.' He folds the paper and hands it to me.

'Well, you can't have done everything,' I protest, although I do remember him saying he liked snowboarding, mountain biking, grass sledging, water skiing, sky-diving, bungee jumping, rafting and swimming with sharks, which does sound pretty comprehensive.

'No, of course I haven't done *everything*. There are one or two things that I might put on a list, but when opportunities come along I never hesitate in taking them; in fact I actively hunt them out on a regular basis, so I don't need a physical list. Right now, you see, I have the opportunity of having more amazing sex with a very beautiful woman and I think we should stop talking and seize that opportunity.' He grins, pulls the duvet over his head and starts to make his way down my body, leaving a trail of searing kisses as he goes. I find it impossible to disagree with him, and that has nothing to do with the fact that I'm in the habit of fitting around other people's plans and falling in line with their suggestions; it's just that it is a genuinely brilliant idea.

42

Dean

Dean was staggered to comprehend how he had spent the day in a montage from a romantic chick flick, a genre he was very familiar with because those sorts of movies were often the preferred choice of various women he passed time with.

They'd agreed to start working through Jo's list immediately. Jo had expressed an interest in 'doing something with boats'. Dean had imagined her gaining her RYA Coastal Skipper qualification, chartering a boat and eventually sailing around the Indian Ocean, but it turned out that all she wanted to do was stand on the bow of a ship, spread her arms wide and be held from behind while she sang 'My Heart Will Go On', so they'd set off to Navy Pier. There, they spent an hour on the Tall Ship *Windy*, a 148-foot schooner modelled after a traditional trading ship. The tour guide was obliging and let her sing as many verses as she could remember, as well as encouraging the other passengers to join in the chorus. They also enjoyed the spectacular views of the Chicago skyline from the water, helped raise sail and relayed traditional sailing commands, although Dean wasn't sure how much of the boating history and tales of courage from the golden age of sail Jo actually absorbed; it seemed that she was most intent on running back through their brief relationship, minute by minute, and piecing him together.

'At first I was puzzled as to how and why you reconciled being an obvious womaniser and a strong belief in fidelity. It's because of your father, isn't it? You might have a rotating bedroom door, but it's always one at a time. Right? Fidelity isn't the issue, commitment is,' she said, just as the long-suffering tour guide was trying to scare the tourists with ludicrous stories about spirit ships and haunted harbours. Dean was pretty sure most of the other passengers were more interested in Jo's conversation too.

'I guess.' If she'd wanted him to update his thoughts on the rotating bedroom door, she didn't say so, and therefore it didn't occur to him to elaborate, which was probably a good thing, because he wasn't yet sure what he could say. Twenty-nine years of distrust don't dissolve overnight; Dean was uncertain as to whether he could be a different man. He pushed the difficult thoughts away and stayed in the moment.

As they rode the Ferris wheel, dangling their legs and nibbling candy floss, Jo gasped, 'The movie. On the plane. You were touched by the begging scene not because you were thinking about the lengths fathers should go to for their kids but—'

'Having the electricity turned off. Yes.' She had candy floss in her hair; he picked it out, careful not to pull.

When he did a victory dance after securing five consecutive holes-in-one on the crazy golf course, she smiled indulgently. He knew she understood why he needed to win. At everything. He was a survivor, a fighter, a victor. He had feared that after confiding in Jo she would harp on about his childhood in a pitying way, but during the day, it became clear that was not going to be the case. It was obvious that she was rapt, but what she felt for him was far from pity. Her eyes shone in admiration; she understood his strength and determination, she accepted, perhaps even forgave, his cynicism. Her intense interest in him was not at all irritating; it made him feel fascinating, wanted. Of course women had tried to work him out before; they had scratched and scratched at his impenetrable exterior and broken their nails and hearts in the process, but none had ever got close. He hadn't allowed them the chance to do so; he hadn't given anyone else the key to the puzzle. The miserable childhood had been a secret between him and Zoe – until yesterday. He'd let Jo get past the shiny, affluent, sexy man and closer to the murkier depths, and she didn't seem put off.

The surprise for Dean was that not only had he found himself in the romantic montage cliché of sailing boats, Ferris wheels, candy floss and crazy golf, but he also discovered that he liked it there. There with Jo.

She was fun; her naivety had melted and they were left with a less irritating childlike enthusiasm, which he had to admit he found appealing. She saw the world in such a sparkly light, it was impossible not to be dazzled and brightened in her presence. He was forced to question his long-held belief that the world was *entirely* populated by selfish bastards, that it was foolhardy to trust *anyone*. She was scrupulously and refreshingly honest; when they inevitably talked about their sexual histories, she frankly relayed endless stories that made her appear desperate and deluded, but she did so in a way that was hilariously self-deprecating and comedic. Almost adorable. Besides, she was clever; much cleverer than she allowed people to believe. She had clearly benefited from a broad and classical education and so was not only well read but also curious. He'd always thought that polished and effervescent privately educated girls were, frankly, silly; capable of a strong serve in a game of mixed doubles and identifying several soft cheeses but not much else. Jo, however, knew a lot of stuff about the American War of Independence, and when she talked of Tissot, she meant the nineteenth-century artist, not a brand of watches. Dean thought that she was the sort of woman who might make gallery visiting interesting, and gallery visiting was not normally his thing. The bit he liked most was that she did not waste time and energy on games. She seemed physically incapable of playing hard to get; she could not keep her hands off him and she made it clear. He had feared in the IMAX theatre that she might actually follow him into the loo; instead she had to be satisfied with hovering outside and she practically leapt into his arms when he emerged.

'Let's go home and have more sex,' she suggested. How was it that this woman had been single so long? mused Dean.

'You know, we really should do some of the ordinary stuff at some point.'

'Like?'

'Like I need to unpack, put on the laundry, buy groceries.'

'Really?'

'No, not really. I like your idea better.' He was only flesh and blood.

Dean thought sex with Jo was great. Really particularly good. True, maybe he'd had more athletic sex in the past, enjoyed better-toned bodies and done dirtier stuff with various other women, but then he'd also had less energetic sex, bedded women with flabbier bodies and had very straightforward, not too exciting sex as well. The point being, he had had lots of sex with lots of women and he had been pretty confident that he knew the range of experiences available, but the sex he had with Jo was surprising. It was (and it killed him to admit this, even to himself) different. It was *more*. More than sex. It was possible, he wasn't certain, but there was a chance that for the first time ever, Dean had allowed himself to make love. He'd always thought the expression was, ultimately, a euphemism – the preserve of married couples who wanted to believe that what they had was special, or middle-aged spinsters who were too prudish to call a shag a shag – but now he understood. What he and Jo had created was affectionate. It was loving.

Dean was not saying that he was in love. No, he would not say that, because whilst he was unconcerned about leaping out of small aircraft from a height of five thousand feet with only a thin circular sheet of nylon for security, or diving over a waterfall with rapids gushing beneath him and only an elastic rope tied around his feet to save him from certain death, those leaps and falls were child's play in comparison to making the leap from loner to partner, a piece of cake in comparison to falling in love.

And yet.

He was finding it impossible to think of anything other than Jo's lips. Until she slipped out of her clothes; then he thought about her body. She had a good body: full, inviting tits, as he'd imagined back on the aeroplane, slightly rounded stomach and thighs, but he'd known that about her before she'd taken her clothes off. He liked her shape; it was extremely feminine. She also had just a bit of cellulite. He knew the moment he spotted it that he would never admit as much to her. Even if she asked him, he would say she was as smooth as a peach. Who would have known that ribs and elbows could be so attractive?

After the lovemaking, he found himself telling her even more. Now he'd taken his finger out of the dam, he couldn't stop the flood; he didn't even want to try. For the first time he understood, rather than simply remotely admiring, Zoe's intimacy with her husband. It was a relief for someone who had not experienced the heartache to hear about it. He had spent a lifetime denying the horrors; now he wanted to let the monsters climb out from the shadows. He took a perverse but definite pleasure in seeing her shocked face. He felt vindicated. It *had* been awful and wrong. Jo agreed. He hadn't exaggerated or indulged. He also liked listening to her stories, her glittering ones, and even though it was obvious that with her retellings she was now questioning her memories, re-examining everything in light of her parents' revelations, she still valued her golden childhood and, most importantly, recognised it as such, no matter how confusing things were right now. He knew he'd helped her preserve that and he was proud to have done so.

'So tell me about visiting your father. How did it go?' she asked. She was lying on her side, curled towards him. Dean could practically hear the cogs in her mind whirring. He sighed and turned towards her.

'Badly. I thought the reason he'd got in touch was that he might be able to explain things, even – and I know this is mental – justify them, but he couldn't. In fact it turned out he hadn't actually wanted me there, not even at the end.' His hand slipped below the duvet again and homed in on her bum cheek. It was soft and warm; he was addicted to stroking it. He found confessing to his father's unrelenting indifference tough, even confessing it to Jo. It was still shaming, incredibly painful, relentlessly damning. He sighed so deeply he wondered whether there was any air left in his body. 'The angry spiky man was not how I'd imagined a dying man should be. I'd expected more calm, more resignation. Some answers. I wanted to yell at him, "I'm the one entitled to be angry." You know, I offered to get a photo printed off of Zoe's kids, for his bedside. His grandchildren. He said no.' Dean turned to Jo, outrage plastered across his face.

Jo considered. 'How long would that have taken?'

'What?'

'It might have just been an issue of time rather than indifference. You'd have had to leave the hospital to get a print. Maybe he didn't want to waste any more time by letting you out of his sight.'

Dean thought about her suggestion. It was possible but not probable. Still, it was possible. He smiled at her. 'Do you think you can teach me that trick of yours?'

'What trick?'

'The one where you insist on seeing the best in people?'

'I could try.'

Dean let the possibility seep into his brain. He'd previously been impervious to any suggestion that he might be able to think better thoughts or believe in more advantageous, pleasing scenarios. Was it achievable? 'Hey, there was one big thing.'

'What was that?'

'I found out I have two more sisters.'

'Really?' Dean knew that Jo was stuck for words. He appreciated the fact that she didn't assume he'd see this as delightful news, especially as she probably did think a bigger family was a bonus. She had the sensitivity to understand that he might be a little more cautious. 'Will you get in touch with them?'

'Maybe. But I'm not sure how much we'll have in common.' Dean didn't want to get his hopes up. 'They're kids really. One is still a student, the other is in her early twenties.'

'How old is your father?'

'I don't know exactly. Less than sixty.'

'Youngish, then. I don't imagine he is ready to go.'

'No, I don't imagine he is. For once he must want to stay. How ironic.' Dean tried to gather the determination not to be dragged down by the facts. Mentally he had to shrug this off, he had to. 'I'm beginning to wonder whether it even matters any more. Whatever he said, it couldn't have changed anything. An explanation as to why he left wouldn't give me back a normal and stable home. An explanation wouldn't allow me to be a different man.'

Jo gasped. 'Thank God. I wouldn't want you to be any other man.'

Well that was good, then. 'It was a fool's errand, a wasted journey.'

'No it wasn't, it had a purpose.'

Dean read her urgent and insistent gaze. 'We met.'

'Exactly. It was fate, and don't say you don't believe in fate.'

'I wasn't going to,' said Dean, kissing her. He didn't believe in fate, but he'd always valued opportunities. He was relieved that she hadn't tried to pacify him with ill-informed consolations. She did not suggest that his father must love him deep down; she did not presume to know more about the situation than he did. She simply listened, quietly and carefully. He put an end to the discussion, but for no better reason than he wanted to kiss her, more and more and more.

As Dean ran his hands over her waist, her hip bones, her thighs, he began to wonder. Could he make the leap? He was self-aware enough to know that if he were ever to draw up his own to-do list, a list requiring him to move outside his comfort zone, to confront his fears and add a new dimension to his already successful, action-packed, adventurous – although somewhat insular – life, there would be just two things written on it:

1. *Tell someone about my mother*
2. *Fall in love*

The only two things he'd never tried.

Dean watched as Jo reluctantly climbed out of bed, searched around for something to wear and then went to the kitchen to forage for a drink. She settled on his scruffy sweat pants and a saggy T-shirt, her sexy red dress long since discarded, a crumpled heap by the bed. Other than the light from the hall and the skyline, the room was dark. Dean was losing sense of time, but a glance at the bedside clock informed him that it was nearly midnight. The day had scurried away on a breeze of endless smiles, laughter and conversation. He spent a few minutes enjoying it for a second time, then Jo returned to the bedroom carrying two mugs.

'I unearthed some tea bags from the back of your cupboard, but we've used up all the milk so we'll have to drink it black.' She handed him a mug. 'Careful, it's boiling and I don't want you blistering your tongue.' Her smile was at once concerned and wanton. It was an irresistible combination; they both were aware of what she wanted from his tongue. She tentatively perched on the edge of the bed. Dean was already familiar enough with her to know when she wanted to say something but was struggling to find the right words. 'So, my flight home is tomorrow evening.'

'Right.'

'Then you'll finally have time to food-shop.'

Dean didn't know how to reply. He hadn't really given much thought to tomorrow, or the day after, or the one after that; it wasn't his habit. However, it now started to dawn on him that he might need to make it his habit. If he was hoping to have a relationship with Jo then planning would be required as she lived a continent away. He was pretty sure he was hoping to have a relationship with her. It was clear *she* was hoping to have a relationship with *him*; he wasn't being especially vain, but women invariably wanted a relationship with him, and Jo had done nothing to hide her enthusiasm about relationships in general, him in particular. There would be complications, of course. He'd need to look into that Skyping business he'd recently read about, and his phone bills would no doubt go through the roof. He wondered whether he had any more European business trips planned. It didn't really matter; he could afford a couple of flights anyway, and he had a mountain of air miles that he could use. It would be a start.

He had a vague sense that they ought to talk about the logistics, about the future.

'I was wondering whether . . .' He coughed, surprisingly unsure of exactly how to phrase it. 'Whether we should swap phone numbers,' he concluded. It was woefully inadequate and he was aware of as much. He looked at Jo, concerned that she might find him lacking. It was strange to suddenly be so unsure around a woman.

'Definitely. Actually, I've just updated the contacts in your phone. I've already plugged in my phone number, but mine is a company phone and I guess they'll soon realise I have it and insist I give it back. I'll need to set up a new email account too. And because people are always losing their phones, I've jotted down my sister's numbers on that notepad by the fridge. And, erm, her address, you know, in case you wanted to write the traditional way, or send flowers.' She smiled sheepishly. 'I left my parents' number and address as well, although God knows who lives there now. I want you to be able to reach me, and losing touch is so easily done when there's no fixed abode.'

Dean burst out laughing. His laugh hit the wall and ricocheted around the room. He loved this woman's honesty. Who else would expose themselves in such a way? She'd left herself open, emotionally naked, so much more daring than physical nudity. She'd put herself at his mercy; she'd done so because she trusted him. Jo grinned back at him. Her grin pushed through her blush; she was blushing as she too was considering who would expose themselves in such a way. Dean shook his head in wonder. Even if keeping in touch was going to be a logistical nightmare, he was sure she was worth it. He kissed her again, a long and lingering kiss.

'So what shall we do tomorrow?' he asked.

'Don't you have to work? It's Monday.'

'I'll bunk off, say I'm ill.'

'Won't you get into trouble? What if someone finds out?'

'Well, I'll take holiday, then.'

'You'd use up your leave to go souvenir shopping with your new girlfriend?'

'So, you're my girlfriend, are you?'

Jo hesitated. 'Well, love interest, then.'

'Love interest,' Dean mocked gently. 'Where do you find these phrases?'

'Do you know, you can be objectionable? What would you like to call me?'

'Actually, I'm OK with girlfriend *or* love interest,' he admitted. 'Although I am a bit worried about souvenir shopping.' Jo grinned back; it was a face-splitting smile. She yanked off the T-shirt and wriggled out of his sweat pants and clambered back under the covers. Dean realised that she'd needed to be fortified by tea and clothes to have that conversation; now she relaxed and smudged back into him. They lay silently for minutes, and he brushed his hand over her silky hair; it felt good.

'You know what I was just thinking about?' she said.

'What?'

'Your mum.'

'Oh.'

'I mean, OK, you are at a dead end in your relationship with your dad—'

'Literally.'

'Oh yes, sorry.' Jo looked as though she didn't know whether to laugh or cry over her lack of tact. She rushed on. 'But what about your mum?'

'It's too late for a relationship with my mother.'

'Don't say that. Tell me more about her.'

Jo turned her sun-kissed – or, more likely considering their location, wind-kissed – face towards Dean. She looked vivid and healthy. She possessed a luminosity that he hadn't seen in her before. She had an air of excitement around her, the sort of excitement that comes with experimentation. She was experimenting with life and there was nothing finer. Dean knew this from his very many adrenalin rushes. He decided he too needed to take the plunge. The dim, warm room that smelt of sex cocooned him, her brilliance lit his way.

'She was once a very beautiful woman, certainly on the outside. She had to have been to have hooked Eddie Taylor, who from all accounts – even my mother's reluctant one – was quite a catch. I can't remember far enough back to know with any conviction whether she ever glowed on the inside. I suppose that it's quite possible that she did, once upon a time. I don't know. If so, he snuffed out any lightness or beauty that she may have possessed. When he slammed the door closed, we all fell into darkness. I suppose it's equally possible that they were both always irredeemably bad, and like had simply drawn to like. I hardly know which would be worse.'

'I don't understand why there was no support, why nobody else stepped in. Weren't there any other relatives? Someone who could have taken you in or at least helped out before things got so dire?'

'My mother was an only child and she lost her parents not long after she married Eddie. I suppose I have to recognise how hard it must have been for her when Eddie left. She was isolated. Drinking was a comfort and a substitute for company. There was a great-aunt at one point. I don't know what happened there. Maybe she died, or maybe my mother drove her away. She did that to a lot of people.'

'What about your paternal grandparents?'

'They bailed on us too. I don't know why. I don't know whether they were ashamed of their son's behaviour or whether they backed him; maybe they loathed my mother. Or perhaps two young kids were simply too much work. Our relationship had degenerated into two parcels each a year, Christmas and birthdays, by the time we were taken into care. They visited the children's home that first night, of course. They had to – the social services called them – but I can't remember them visiting again.'

'It doesn't sound like your mother had much help.'

'No, she didn't. Eddie must have known that when he left us for the rich bitch. A woman who ultimately was so in love with her husband, so bound up with her own family ties, that she didn't even want my father.' Dean could not hide the bitterness.

'When did you last see your mum?'

'Years ago, Jo.'

'When?'

'I was fourteen.'

'Oh, Dean, I think you should call her.' Jo looked animated. She was awash with the radiance of the newly in love. She didn't believe any hurdle was insurmountable; she didn't believe there was a hurt that could not be forgiven, a wound that could not be patched.

'I can't,' said Dean flatly.

'Of course you can. Don't be stubborn. I bet she's dying to hear from you.'

'No.'

'Just pick up the phone.' Jo grabbed the handset of his landline and was holding it out towards him. It was unlikely that he knew his mother's number off by heart, but she was too excited and animated to consider such practicalities. 'Things are always salvageable. Think back to the last time you visited her; really, was it that bad?'

'I remember it very clearly.'

With horrible clarity he remembered the interior of the little red Toyota that the social worker drove. It was an old car but she kept it clean; it smelt of pine air freshener and there were always imperial mints in the glove compartment. The social worker invariably offered them; Zoe would accept, Dean would refuse. He didn't want anything from the social services, not even a sodding mint, and he wasn't going to co-operate by allowing her to think she could make him feel even a tiny bit better, as if a mint could do that anyway. On the infrequent and chaperoned visits to their mother's, he'd keep his hand on the door handle for the entire journey. The moment the car started to slow, as it pulled up outside his mother's tiny council flat, he'd hastily fling open the door and jump out. He remembered doing exactly the same thing that last time they'd visited.

His mother had moved to Epping by then, into a scruffy, insignificant place. She'd drunk away their house in Clapham and everything in it. She was lucky: at least this new flat had a minute, neglected outside area, although the reality was no one felt comfortable describing the scruffy patch as a garden. She got this perk on account of her having children; the idea was for their time there to be made as pleasant as possible. Dean remembered thinking that they'd need more than a few shrubs and a thin covering of scorched grass to make the visits bearable. That last time he'd noticed that the outside space had been cemented over, suggesting that even the council had given up on the fairy tale that he and Zoe would ever benefit from the fresh air. He'd noticed that weeds had already sprung up through cracks in the cement and he'd almost admired their tenacity. There was a lean-to shelter bolted on to the outside of his mother's ground-floor flat, a dubious home improvement that was the legacy of a previous tenant; the roof was made of corrugated plastic, which had yellowed with age. Dean could see piles of junk stacked inside, waist-high towers of cardboard boxes and cheap weekly magazines. He also remembered that there was a cracked plastic sledge propped up against the back wall – he'd wondered who it belonged to; he knew it had never belonged to him – and there was the inevitable upturned supermarket shopping trolley. He'd thought, well, at least she's eating, but in the next moment he realised that the trolley was just as likely to have been used to bring home booze. In the garden there was a skeletal Christmas tree. It was May. It had probably belonged to one of the neighbours. His mother hadn't celebrated Christmas for years.

He'd run down the path before Zoe had even unfastened her seat belt. The social worker thought it was keenness to see his mother. It wasn't; he just wanted to check the state of his mother and the flat before Zoe was confronted with either. Just a fraction of a minute was usually enough to work out if Diane was drunk or sober, if the flat was just a pigsty or a distinct health hazard. He always hated pushing open the back door. His mother was not the sort of woman who got much company. That much was betrayed by her eternally grubby cardigan, her lack of make-up and her self-conscious stance. The air in the rooms was always stale, smeared with sweat and cigarette smoke.

'She's dead, Jo.'

Silence. There were no words.

'She killed herself. A cocktail of sleeping pills, vodka and her own vomit. There's some question whether it was intentional or not. It doesn't matter, does it? I was the one who found her, on that last visit.'

She often forgot to lock the back door, too drunk to care, too poor for anyone to want to steal anything from her. He'd pushed open the door with the vigour and force of a fourteen-year-old boy. It had cracked against her head as she lay sprawled on the floor. He'd smelt her vomit and her death instantly.

'No.' Jo reached out for Dean's hand and brought it to her lips. She gently kissed his fingers as he fought the memory of trying to use his too thin, too young body to block Zoe's view. His shoulders simply hadn't been broad enough.

'I almost missed her at first, as weak and pathetic as she'd been. Almost.' Dean looked embarrassed to admit as much. 'Then there was more ferocious and extreme anger, but eventually I got past blaming her and hating her. I recognised that she was simply helpless and hopeless. I blamed my father more. Loathed him. But he's dying now too.'

'So it's all over,' suggested Jo. Was Dean free to love now he could stop hating?

'It might have been until he told me that there was a particular bitch he left us for, and she's become the villain of the story. Now I find that even as a grown man, I'm still angry. Ever since my father mentioned this woman, I've been consumed with such hatred. I hate someone I've never met; someone I didn't know existed until this week. It's not civilised. It's—'

He broke off, unable to say the words 'It's unfair' without sounding like a child. He allowed Jo to slowly kiss his shoulder, his neck and his jaw while he tried to barricade the memory of Zoe's hysterical screams as he scooped her up and carried her away from the back door; she'd kicked and sobbed, punched out, not at him but at the unreasonable cruelty. He let Jo gently, tenderly kiss his chest, his belly and his cock. He let her climb on top of him and make love to him as he tried to block out the vision of a fly settled on his mother's cold blue vomit-smeared lips.

And he let her see him cry.

Afterwards, when they were spent, they lay on their backs, staring at the ceiling, holding hands; they were too clammy with exertion to spoon. Dean's eyelids felt like lead as he started to drift into what promised to be a deep sleep. He was exhausted by his own memories and emotions, but in some ways he felt lighter, safer; more free than he had ever been before.

Jo wasn't as close to sleep. Her mind was racing. The more details she heard about Dean's childhood, the more respect and admiration she felt for him and the more grateful she felt for her own easy start in life. Of course she was still shocked and confused about her parents' revelations, but she'd put that part of her life on hold for now; their fairy tale falling apart didn't compare to the nightmare Dean had endured or, more importantly still, to the relationship she and Dean were forging. She was beginning to realise that the past wasn't what mattered; what was important was what would happen next.

She thought about his choice of favourite books. 'The books you like, they're all about orphan boys who make good,' she murmured into the darkness. 'Rudyard Kipling's *Kim*, Pip in *Great Expectations*, *Harry Potter*.'

'That's right.'

She could hear the drowsiness in his voice. 'Dean, you know I think I was right after all.'

'Hmm.' He was on the very edge of consciousness.

'I think it is all about dramatic moments, a quickening of the pulse, then knickers and sense being thrown to the wind. I thought love was like in the poems, songs and films, and it is. It's that and more.' She whispered into the blackness, 'Dean, I think I am falling in love with you. In fact, I know I am. I love you, Dean Taylor.'

She waited to see what he'd make of that, but the only response was a solid silence. Minutes later, he started to snore. Jo couldn't be certain whether he'd heard her and chosen not to reply, or whether he'd already fallen asleep when she said it. It didn't matter; she'd have plenty of other opportunities to tell him, because what they had was good and honest and decent. What they had was a future.

43

Eddie

Dying has turned out to be more interesting than I anticipated. The pain has been crap, obviously. Every time they
stop one thing aching, another starts up. But not now. It's gone
now. These latest drugs they are giving me are the big guns. It's
all drifting. It's fine. I'm nearly there.

At least there's been entertainment. I've had my memories to
keep me company. And the real people too. The lad. Not all bad.
Clara. Patient. Remembered me. It became clear that I was still
something to her. Had always been. That's a comfort. A pleasure
to think about. She has been coming here for days now, I think.
Quiet. Elegant. Talking to me in her low voice. Even though I
can no longer talk back. Asked if I remembered that weekend in
Manchester. The one stopover that we ever managed to steal.

I do. I remember it all. The train on Friday afternoon. Full of
loud northerners, who worked in London during the week,
returning to their families, keen to get drunk before they had to
hand over their wages. We shared a drink with them, bottles
hidden in paper bags, fooling no one. Quaint. The station was
bustling. We walked to the hotel. Sunlight bounced on the pavement. Shone up the back of her legs. I carried her bag. Then
later we had pre-dinner cocktails; potent and unfamiliar. Not to

her. She knew her cocktails, her wines, her French menus and the names of all those cold meats they served up at breakfast. Posh bird, I used to tease her. She had *it*. Class, and I liked it. Wanted it. I was going up to Manchester for work, researching a documentary I was penning; she told her husband that she was going away for a shopping spree with girlfriends. Documentary about the crisis in mass manufacturing affecting the north-west of England. Very bad. The inner city was haemorrhaging inhabitants. Unemployment was rife. Run-down houses everywhere. An industrial wasteland. Factories abandoned like frigid wives. Crawling with out-of-work residents. We didn't talk about it but I think she'd have preferred Paris.

She'd said she wanted the works, not just the bedroom. So I'd booked us into the Palace. Took a suite. On expenses. Dinner reservations at the, oh, I forget its name. An Italian. Authentic. Decent. We were quickly drunk, couldn't finish our food. Giddy with the excitement of just *being* with each other without having to look over our shoulders all the time, without having to check the time. Couldn't wait to get back to the hotel. Didn't wait. Had her in an alleyway. There weren't cameras everywhere in those days. Ruin a man's fun, CCTV can. I'm glad I was young then.

Wasn't a weekend, though, not in the end. Just one night. She missed her kids too much. Felt too guilty. Turned moody and funny on the Saturday morning. We shared breakfast. She said the coffee was too weak. She insisted we got an earlier train back to London. I should have known then.

Still, it was good of her to come here. To throw me back in amongst the tangled sheets rather than let me wilt in these hospital ones.

MONDAY 25 APRIL 2005

44

Clara

Clara knew that she had to ring Joanna. She'd spoken to her other children and their reactions to her leaving their father were largely as she'd expected: they were both horrified and hurt. It was obvious that Lisa agreed with Tim; she'd suggested that Clara must be suffering from some sort of nervous breakdown. She'd muttered about the power of stress but then added that she couldn't imagine what Clara might have to be stressed about. Lisa had barely acknowledged the fact that Tim was gay. Clara could not decide whether her daughter had long ago guessed as much and had been quite comfortable with the in-closet situation, or whether she was blanking the uncomfortable truth. Clara couldn't blame her if this was the case; after all, wasn't that exactly what she herself had done for years? Lisa repeatedly asked, 'But how will you manage?' then explained that with three children, a demanding career and her sister sleeping on her sofa, she really couldn't be expected to do much to help. Clara accepted this as being at once very true and a little selfish. Lisa was the type to assess a situation from an entirely practical point of view.

Mark had been still less sympathetic; he obviously found the whole situation extremely embarrassing and made it clear that he just wanted the status quo re-established as swiftly as possible.

He'd comforted himself by continually repeating to Clara that she would no doubt change her mind soon and go home, thus saving his father and the entire family from 'a huge amount of unnecessary difficulty'. Clara disagreed with him – it had been such an enormous effort to leave, she couldn't imagine summoning up the energy to return – but she didn't contradict him. Despite their lack of sympathy, she understood Lisa and Mark's reactions; they were frustrated and fearful. They each loved both of their parents and naturally wanted them to be happy, but they had not been brought up to expect that their own happiness might in any way be compromised by their parents' pursuit of contentment or cheer. Hadn't that been what she'd hoped to achieve all these years? She'd wanted to give her children a sense of entitlement to bliss. She knew her bid for happiness, or at least independence, was a great inconvenience to them. It crossed her mind that when they were children she should perhaps have focused more on them taking turns.

But how much worse would Joanna's reaction be? Lisa had called her and given a succinct update, even though Clara had begged her not to. She would have much preferred it if Joanna had been left to enjoy her little break in Chicago, and then on her return Clara could have explained things face to face. Joanna wasn't a clear thinker at the best of times, far too idealistic and romantic, and Clara hated the idea of her dealing with this extraordinary situation all alone in a strange city. Lisa had reported that Joanna was devastated. The word had ripped at Clara's heart and conscience, just as Lisa had intended it to. Clara knew her eldest daughter well enough to know that it hadn't been spite that had motivated Lisa to call Joanna in Chicago; it was Lisa's belief that her sister had a *right* to know what was going on, that she *ought* to know what was going on. Lisa had never agreed with Clara's policy of protecting Joanna from the harsh realities of the world.

So now Clara had to call Joanna. She left Eddie's bedside and went to the day room, which was open to visitors as well as those patients who were well enough to move around. The room was painted in a beige colour that Clara thought had been wiped from the face of the earth at least a decade ago. The pine chairs were scuffed and covered with thin school-uniform-green cushions; they didn't look comfortable. Not that Clara would sit in them, as she felt squeamish about how many sick people must have done so before her; could chairs carry diseases? Whilst it was impossible to believe that anyone could have smoked inside a hospital for at least twenty years, the room was haunted with the smell of ancient cigarettes; specifically cigarettes hungrily smoked in desperation, boredom or fear. The TV was permanently on, the volume turned up quite high for the benefit of the elderly, hard-of-hearing patients. Clara hated the room and so went outside and made the call from the busy London street.

She pressed the number on her mobile phone and after just three rings Joanna picked up. Clara was relieved; she'd feared her daughter might have refused to speak to her.

'Hello, darling, how are you?' asked Clara in a rush.

'Fine,' replied Joanna, and although she was whispering, Clara could hear a distinct smile in her voice. It was the last response she was expecting. 'Hang on, I have to take this in the kitchen.'

Clara waited and puzzled as to where her daughter could be. Whose kitchen? She'd assumed Joanna would be staying in a hotel. She didn't have any friends in Chicago, other than Martin, and no matter how accommodating and welcoming Martin's new bride was, Clara couldn't imagine her opening her home to an ex-girlfriend while they went on their honeymoon. 'Where are you?' she asked with a mix of anxiety and curiosity. Even though her daughter was a fully fledged adult, and Clara had called to talk through her own emotional situation, she sensed that Joanna might have embarked on some sort of dalliance as she invariably did, and so she braced herself for another complication and yet more problems.

'I'm in a friend's kitchen.'

'Friend? What sort of friend? A man friend?'

'Yes, I'm in a man's kitchen,' laughed Joanna, acknowledging her mother's shock and indignation. 'But there's nothing to worry about, he's very clean. It's a very clean kitchen.'

'Are there knives, guns? Who is he, Joanna?' Clara's anxiety rose. 'You can't just latch on to some stranger. Some American stranger.'

'He's British, actually, not that I see what his nationality has to do with anything.'

'Did you read *American Psycho*?'

'No, I didn't. Did you?'

'Yes. It was extremely frightening. Hideous. It's about a wealthy New York investment banker who hides his alternative psychopathic ego from his colleagues and friends. All I need tell you is that there are a lot of dead women by the end.'

'Well, my guy is a lovely man, and we're in Chicago not New York and he's an advertising executive not an investment banker and I don't think he's hiding anything from me.' Again Clara could hear a definite smile in her daughter's voice. 'Besides, you're talking about fiction; what I'm talking about is real.'

Real? Joanna didn't normally place much emphasis on what was real.

'Be careful, darling.' Clara lived in terror of one of Joanna's casual dalliances ending up in something far more fatal than a broken heart.

'You know, Mum, it's OK. I met him on the plane coming over here. He's been a big help. He stopped me doing anything stupid at Martin's wedding.'

'For the record, I never intended you to stop their wedding. I don't think you were listening to me. I just wanted you to have a break. Find closure.'

'Well, I have, thanks to my new friend.'

'Oh Joanna, are you in love again?' Clara could not keep the fretful apprehension out of her voice.

'I'm having a really wonderful time. He's the most interesting, courageous man I've ever met. We're having a lot of fun.'

Clara was stunned. She had expected Joanna to be a vulnerable, weeping wreck (at best) or a furious, resentful accuser (at worst), but she seemed to be brimming with confidence and oozing satisfaction. Clara wondered whether she was doing drugs; it was a possibility. She was certainly behaving out of character. Clara had never heard Joanna describe any man solely in terms of his mental attributes before. She could only think of one reason why her daughter might be sounding so sanguine. 'Joanna, darling, don't tell me you've done something ridiculous, like eloping. You're not in Vegas, are you?'

'No, I'm not in Vegas,' laughed Joanna. 'I hadn't thought of that.'

Joanna not having thought of marriage within the first forty-eight hours of meeting a new man prompted Clara to ask, 'Does he look like Quasimodo?'

'No, he's really . . .' Clara could not see her daughter glancing at a photo of Dean that was pinned to his fridge. He was on a boat and had his arms round the necks of a couple of other guys, all beaming like crazies. The reason for their jubilation was apparent: one of the guys was holding up a fish the size of a sack of spuds. Clara had no way of knowing how Jo felt as she caressed Dean's cheek on the image. 'He's really handsome.'

Clara thought the choice of adjective was suspicious. 'Very old, then?'

'No, in fact he's younger than me.'

'Is he legal?' Shots of fear ricocheted through Clara's body.

'Mum, he's just a year younger than me.'

'Married?'

'Mum! He's beautiful, legal, single. He's perfect, OK. Just perfect.'

Having spent three days at Eddie Taylor's bedside, Clara doubted the authenticity of a perfect man. Her mind whirled and she quickly rationalised that there were three other explanations as to why Joanna might not be hysterically gabbling on about wedding dresses. One, she might have decided this man was out of her league, and might be simply enjoying wild, hedonistic sex for a weekend. Two, he might be gay, hardly an explanation either woman could ignore right now. Or three, she might be reeling from the shock of her parents' split after all, and have been jolted completely out of character. None of these were comfortable lines of conversation to pursue, so Clara simply said, 'Well, just perfect sounds wonderful.'

Joanna laughed. 'It is.' Clara heard her take a deep breath. 'Anyway, I can't imagine you've called to discuss *my* love life.'

'Well, no, I haven't.' Clara hesitated. 'I know Lisa has filled you in.'

'Yes.' A silence descended down the phone line. Clara instantly missed the intimacy and camaraderie that she had been enjoying with her daughter just a moment ago. She longed to talk about the perfect man again, or Martin, or even the in-flight entertainment, but she knew she couldn't.

'I'm so sorry, darling. I know this must be very hard on you.'

'I don't imagine it's been easy for you either, has it?' Clara nearly choked on surprise and relief. Joanna's words were the first she'd heard that in any way acknowledged Clara's own relentless pain and sacrifice – sacrifice that had occurred over many years – and the enormous difficulty of making the choice to finally leave.

'I thought you'd be very angry.'

'More sad.'

'I'm sad too,' Clara confessed. She breathed the words down the line, hardly daring to give them any volume; they were powerful enough as they were. She wondered if Joanna would actually be able to hear her as the traffic roared past.

It seemed that Joanna not only heard but understood. 'Are you sure?'

'That your father is gay? Quite sure.'

'I more meant, are you sure you'll be happier alone?'

'God, I don't know, Joanna,' Clara admitted frankly. 'I think so, maybe, eventually.' She knew she didn't sound convincing. She wasn't certain. 'I'm staying at Bluecolt Spa, although I haven't actually spent much time there. I've been in London mostly.' Joanna didn't ask her what she was doing in London and Clara found she couldn't confess to sitting by the bedside of her old lover, no matter how surprisingly sympathetic Joanna was being. 'It is surreal being there without my pals or a calorie-controlled menu. I'm booked in for a week, but I'm not even sure I'll manage that. It's not much of a plan. I haven't really thought about the long term. I need time to work things out.'

'What does Dad think? Are you speaking to one another?'

'Yes, by telephone, all the time. Last night he said that he thinks I should move back home. He thinks we're good friends. We *are* good friends. He says that's enough, especially at our age.'

'But you don't agree?'

'It was enough. Or at least, for a long time I thought it was enough; after all, so few marriages are ideal. But then I received this letter.'

'From your old lover?' If Jo found it difficult to say that word to her mother, Clara certainly found it difficult to hear. She squeezed her mobile so tightly that her knuckles turned white and she squeezed closed her eyes at the same time. After all this time, she was still trying to block out the shame and the pain, but besides that, she was still trying to hold in the tremendous, unparalleled, exquisite beauty of her affair. It was confusing. Was she making a fuss? Was it too much, too late? 'Were you in love with him?' Joanna prompted.

Clara still didn't know how to answer this question; she never had. 'I couldn't leave you and Lisa,' she replied. It was the most honest explanation she could give.

'Are you hoping to strike something up with this man, after all these years?' Clara could hear the incredulity in her daughter's voice. It was a bizarre exchange of roles; Joanna clearly thought Clara was being unrealistic about her romantic expectations and that she needed some sense talked into her. Under less dramatic circumstances, Clara might have been amused. 'Lisa said he's ill. Dying. I mean, Mum, it's an impractical, improbable plan.'

Clara thought of the old, grey man, who probably only had days, hours, left. 'No, I'm not hoping for anything with him. It's not about him so much as the effect I had on him. In his letter he said I eased the pain of his cancer. He said that thinking of me eased his pain. Can you imagine that, Joanna?'

'Yes.'

'It was so wonderful to hear that I'd ever made such an impact on anyone.'

'But you have made an impact, Mum. On me, Lisa and Mark.' Clara thought it was kind of her daughter to try to rally her.

'It's not the same thing. You understand. Suddenly, I feel resentful that my life has flown by and I've never experienced such superb intensity since then.' Clara was confused as to how she'd been plunged into this world that seemed to be wholly about feeling; she'd always been exclusively concerned with what she ought to do, what was being done. She felt disorientated.

'Dad loves you.'

'Yes, I know he does. But not in that way. However, in answer to your question, I don't have any intention of starting anything with Eddie Taylor, but I don't want to spend the rest of my life lying to myself either.'

'What did you say his name was? Did you just say Eddie Taylor?' Joanna interrupted.

'Yes, darling.'

'Was he married?' Joanna demanded.

'What?'

'Was the man that you had your stupid little affair with married?' Clara didn't understand the sudden change in her daughter's tone. Joanna had been so understanding, so sympathetic and rational, but now, in a split second, she sounded half-crazed and ferociously angry.

'Well, yes.' It never sounded good.

'Did he leave his wife for you?'

'There was some silly madness, an offer . . .'

'And his children?'

'There were children.' Clara was embarrassed and reluctant to say as much, even now, especially now.

'Oh fuck, oh fuck, fuck, fuck, fuck.' Joanna, normally so mild-mannered, well-spoken and such a people-pleaser, cut her mother off in a torrent of expletives. The line went dead and Clara was left stewing in complete bewilderment.

45

Dean

Dean woke up and automatically stretched his arm out towards Jo. His first instinct was to pull her into a hug. His hand floundered on an ocean of cold sheets. He rubbed his eyes and then stretched his hands above his head. He felt relaxed. A glance at the bedside clock told him that it was after eleven; clearly his body had required a marathon sleep after such an emotionally and physically demanding day, but he was irritated with himself. He sat bolt upright. He hadn't meant to sleep in; he wanted to soak up every moment of the day with Jo. He flung back the duvet and leapt out of bed, calling her name as he did so. He didn't waste time hunting around for a robe, but strode naked and confident around the apartment. She wasn't in the kitchen or the living room; there was no sign of her in the shower. He banged on the loo door.

'Jo?'

Silence. He was not unduly worried. He assumed she'd nipped out to buy them some breakfast. Right then she'd be deciding between coconut and passion fruit yogurt or traditional straw-berry flavour; she wouldn't be able to choose between chocolate or plain croissant, she'd probably bring both. That would be just like her. Caring, thoughtful. He wished she'd hurry back, though;

he was hungry, but mostly for her body to be next to his again, rather than for pastries. He sniffed under his arm and pulled back from the stench of his own sweat. He really had exerted himself last night. He decided he'd have a quick shower so that he'd be fresh and appealing on her return.

He spent a long time in the shower. He hadn't planned to, but the hot streams of water hammered down on his shoulders and it felt good. He found himself singing, a tuneless rendition of the latest pop song that was getting far too much airplay at the moment. He took time to shave because he thought Jo would like it, then cleaned his teeth, flossed and even clipped his toenails. When he emerged from the bathroom and padded into the bedroom, barefoot and damp, looking for clean underwear, he glanced again at the bedside clock and noticed that it was nearly midday. It was only then he started to feel uneasy. Just how long did it take to buy a croissant and a paper? Could she have got lost? He called her phone but it immediately went through to voicemail. He didn't want to sound flustered, so he left a cheery, jokey message telling her to get her beautiful arse home. He hung up and waited another ten minutes, but the cold fingers of panic that prodded him began to tighten their grip. Had she been knocked over or mugged? Was she lying injured on a hospital trolley in some corridor somewhere, while an administrator tried to check who she was and whether she had health-care insurance? He doubted she would have. Did she know to take her passport with her when she roamed around a strange city so that in the event of an accident she could be identified? He should have told her to do that. Dean felt ferociously protective of Jo. Oh God, maybe she wasn't awaiting treatment; maybe she was already cold in a morgue. It was a bleak, hideous thought and Dean quickly shook his head to dislodge it. He tried not to be so negative and pessimistic, but the horrendous idea persistently battered his brain. He'd only had Jo in his life for a matter of days, but as he looked around the empty flat, he was already pretty sure he couldn't imagine her out of it.

He started to search the rooms. He wasn't sure what he was looking for. A note? Her bag? Where had she put her bags? Time was ticking on. She had an evening flight; she'd have to leave for the airport in a couple of hours. She couldn't have gone shopping on her own and simply lost track of the time, could she? It was possible, but she'd seemed so excited about their plans to shop together; she'd seemed as keen to spend every moment with him as he was to spend every one with her. Why hadn't she woken him up? Besides, she didn't have much money with her, so it seemed improbable that she'd gone on a wild spending spree without him. Last night she'd asked if she could borrow some cash off him to buy gifts and souvenirs. She'd said she'd leave him a post-dated cheque; they'd joked about what date she should put on it. She'd suggested 25/12/2050, a sort of long-term Christmas gift, something to look forward to. She'd said she hoped that by then her cheques wouldn't bounce. Dean dashed to find his wallet; he knew it was in his jacket pocket, and his jacket was hanging over the stool in the kitchen. The moment he walked into the room, he spotted the open wallet on the breakfast bar. He wasn't sure why he hadn't noticed it before; probably because he hadn't been expecting to see it. It was empty. Next to the wallet there was a cheque for one hundred and forty dollars, the exact amount the wallet had contained. It was not post-dated to a future Christmas; rather, it had next week's date on. Jo was obviously hoping to replenish her bank account with sufficient funds to cover the loan by then. What did this mean? Had she gone shopping on her own? If so, why had she left the cheque now, rather than just giving it to him on his return? The post-dated cheque had a miserable finality about it. It felt like a full stop.

It was only after he'd carefully studied her signature, for quite a few moments, that he noticed the third object on the breakfast bar – his father's wedding ring.

Oh no. No. No. He slapped his hand against his forehead in a dramatic (and slightly painful) way. No, no, nooooo. He instantly pieced together what had happened. He could see it with awful clarity. Jo had been hunting around for his wallet, no doubt intending to go out and buy them a delicious breakfast, as he'd first surmised. As she'd rooted through his pockets she'd come across his father's wedding ring. She'd jumped to the incorrect conclusion that he was yet another rat who had slipped off his ring just before he'd slipped between the sheets. It was horrifying. Dean felt his usually taut and powerful body turn to liquid. It poured away from him and he felt like a melting candle; formless, powerless. He felt his skeleton collapse – he was sure he had no backbone without her – and his organs swoosh away in a gory mess; another abandonment would break his heart and gut him completely. For a moment, this usually resourceful man floundered. A desolate, vicious understanding of the situation caught him in a vice-like grip. She had not trusted him. She had not kept the faith. She was not all she seemed. His bloody father had ruined things again.

He called her number again and left a second message. This one was not cheerful or playful; he simply asked her to call him.

Then he called Zoe.

Dean didn't know where to start with Zoe. He had yet to tell her that he'd left their father dying, that he hadn't been there at the end because she was right, there was no comfort or consolation to be gained from Edward Taylor. Should he tell her that they had two sisters they hadn't previously known about? He had no clue as to how Zoe would greet that news. Anyway, he found that what he wanted to talk to her about was the woman he'd met on the plane. The woman he'd trusted enough to share their terrible past with, the woman who had just left his apartment in an unfair hurry, leaving a huge gap.

He couldn't trust himself with any of those subjects, so he passed a few moments asking after the children, pretending to take his usual interest in their small but wonderful achievements with footballs and crayons; he asked after Zoe's health, her husband and her dog, but she knew him too well. 'OK so why have you really called? Is he dead?'

'Maybe. Don't know,' he replied, somewhat abashed by her bluntness but not really surprised by it.

'You didn't stay with him?'

'No.'

'I'm not going to the funeral when he does die, if that's why you're ringing.'

'It isn't. I feel the same. You were right, there is no happy ending for us there. Our relationship with our father is what it is.'

'Not much.'

'Exactly.'

'I'm sorry.'

He wanted to hug her. 'I'm sorry too.' They both knew that they were sorry that they'd had a spat, and more, they were both sorry there had been no resolution.

'That's not why I called, though.'

'So, why did you call?'

'It's a long story. Do you have time?'

'For you? Always.'

Dean held nothing back. He told Zoe about meeting Jo on the aeroplane. He explained that she'd irritated him with her naivety and her ridiculous, ill-considered plan to stop her ex-boyfriend's wedding because she thought he was her last chance at happiness. He told her about the fun, impromptu shopping spree, the hot dog meal at Millennium Park, the jazz band playing in the background, and about the surprisingly warm evening that had oozed through his bones and seemed to exist especially for them. He then admitted that he had not been able to allow Jo to embarrass herself by stopping the wedding.

'I mean, it would have been an enormous mistake.'

'I see.'

'So I turned up at the hotel and pretended I was her date. But it didn't matter, because she'd worked it out herself. She'd decided it wasn't the right thing. She knows all about doing the right thing. She's very moral. Very sweet.'

'I see,' Zoe repeated.

Then he told her about the adulterous mother, the gay father and the salsa dancing.

'I never had you down as a salsa dancer.' Zoe did little to hide the amusement in her voice.

'You know me, sis, I'm prepared to try anything once. So then we . . .' He paused. How was he to explain it?

'Had sex?'

'Several times.'

'There's more?'

'There's Ferris wheels, candy-floss sharing and mini-golf playing.'

'You *like* her.' Zoe pronounced the word in a way that was as laden as the hand luggage of a passenger on an easyJet plane. She sounded in equal parts incredulous and delighted.

'Don't rush ahead.' Dean told his sister how he had revealed the details of his mother's death to Jo. Zoe was breathless with delight and exhilaration. 'Wow, Dean, you don't just like her, you've fallen in love with her.'

He didn't deny it; he just stated flatly, 'She's gone.'

'Sorry?'

He brought Zoe bang up to date with the morning's events. Zoe was astounded.

'You don't think you've just been served, do you?'

377

Dean thought of all the times he'd made quick exits from various women's apartments, not waiting for breakfast or a debrief because he simply wasn't that into them. He felt momentarily guilty, the sands shifting beneath his feet, but despite his discomfort about his past form, he did not think he was being served a cold dish of karma. 'No, I don't think so. At the risk of sounding arrogant, I'm pretty sure she was really into me.'

'Maybe it was because you told her about our mother. People get freaked out about alcoholism and suicide and things,' said Zoe matter-of-factly. They did, she knew it.

'She wasn't freaked out. She was really sympathetic. But not in a do-gooder way.' Both siblings hated do-gooders and knew there was no greater condemnation. 'In an extremely sincere way.'

'But there was no note?'

'No. There was only . . .' Dean hesitated. 'Eddie Taylor gave me his wedding ring.' He didn't know how to call Eddie Taylor anything other than Eddie Taylor to Zoe.

'His wedding ring?'

'From his marriage to our mother. He'd kept it all this time. It was in my jacket pocket and she found it.'

'She was going through your pockets?'

'For cash.'

'For cash? Are you sure she wasn't just some con artist?'

'No. I told you, she's sweet. And sincere.' Dean could clearly imagine Jo's slim fingers flicking through his wallet. He liked her fingernails. She wore them short, with clear varnish. 'Very moral. I told you, she's truly romantic. In a good sense. You know, she really believes in that entire knight-in-shining-armour, true-love-conquers-all stuff. She was a little bit lost. I thought I'd found her. She wasn't stealing from me, she was probably going to buy breakfast, but then she found the ring and now she thinks I'm married. Can you believe Eddie Taylor has fucked this up for me as well? He's still ruining my life.'

'I'm the last person likely to defend him, but I honestly don't think this is his fault. Not this one,' said Zoe. 'Why didn't she wake you up to ask you about the ring? It's sort of her fault for jumping to the wrong conclusions.'

'Yes, but she's a thirty-five-year-old single woman living in London; she's programmed to think men will be cheating.'

'I suppose. I don't know, Dean, something about this doesn't add up,' mused Zoe.

'There was one other thing.'

'What?'

'Last night, she told me she loved me.'

'And what did you say?'

'I pretended to be asleep.'

'Oh, big brother, I am so proud of you.' Dean knew his sister was rolling her eyes in exasperation, as she often did when they talked about his romantic life.

'It was all moving so fast.'

'Not any more.'

'I'm hurt that she could think so badly of me.'

'Look at it from her point of view, Dean. A self-confessed commitment-phobe shags her senseless, ignores declaration of love and secretes a wedding ring.'

'Put like that, it doesn't look good. What should I do?'

'You know what to do. You have to find her. Explain you're not married, if that's what she thinks. You have to sort it out,' stated Zoe, applying her signature no-nonsense view of the world to this problem. It was this approach that allowed her to be a successful accountant, a faithful, loving wife and a devoted and reliable mother.

'But if I fly across the Atlantic for her, aren't I sort of showing my hand? I mean, it's hard to come back from that position. I'm kind of all-in committing then, aren't I?'

'I thought from everything you've just told me that you have committed to her.' Dean fell silent. Zoe sighed. It was a big sigh. It seemed to fill the thousands of miles that separated her noisy, cramped kitchen in Winchester, populated by her children's clothes, creative endeavours and noise, from his chic, neat but empty loft apartment in Chicago. 'You just have to decide: do you love her or not?' Dean remained silent, although he was pretty sure his sister was hoping for a definitive answer. 'You know, I hated the fact that you went to Eddie Taylor's bedside, but I thought it meant that you had learnt something.'

'What was I supposed to learn?'

'That you are capable of love, and that you deserve it too.'

46

Jo

The flight back to Britain from Chicago could not be more dissimilar to the outward-bound flight. Returning, I do not benefit from a lucky upgrade or, more poignantly, fascinating company, and there is no hint of misplaced hope or any sense of anticipation. Instead I am steeped in a solid feeling of utter devastation. How can it be possible that in the very weekend I finally understand what love is, and meet someone I believe might love me too, I also have the opportunity blasted right out of the sky? The unfairness and impossibility of the situation hits me with such a weight that I feel it physically; my lungs struggle to breathe. I'm crushed. I understand the true meaning of the flip expression. I'm trampled. Flattened. Compressed. Because I am certain I'm less without Dean. I'm smaller.

I do believe Dean was beginning to feel something for me. Something major and true. This is not another case of self-delusion, otherwise why would he have confided in me all the terrible details of his childhood and the loss of his mother? There was a flicker of a chance; more than that, there was hope for us. Not that any of it matters now. How he did feel, how he might have felt, is irrelevant, because the woman he hates most in the world – the woman who is indirectly but quite definitely responsible for his mother's death and all his childhood deprivation and devastation – is my own mother.

He would never be able to recover from that.

Walking away from Dean is the hardest thing I have ever had to do in my life. I feel I am paying for every single moment of my sunny childhood in this one terrible action. When I first realised that my mother was Eddie's lover, I tried to imagine a way we could get through this. I stood over Dean's bed and feasted my eyes on his beautiful body and wished, wished with every fibre of my being that things were different. That Eddie Taylor and my mother had never met. That Eddie hadn't decided to leave his wife. That Dean's mother wasn't an alcoholic. Any one of those things would have saved Dean from the terrible trauma of feeling eternally alone. And if none of that could be the case, then I simply wished that I'd never pieced it all together. Yes, I'm that shallow and selfish that I would have had Dean and my mother rub shoulders for an eternity, if only they could have done it in ignorance.

I briefly considered whether I could simply hide the fact from Dean. I'm certain my mother won't be in a hurry to tell everyone this latest gory twist to her grubby story, and my father, well, he's clearly very able to keep secrets. But I'm not. I could not betray Dean in that way. I respect him too much for that. He has been honest with me from the moment we met, and he expects truth in return. If I didn't reveal what I know, I can see what would happen. Inevitably, further along the line, when we were even closer, even more committed, there would be a moment of disclosure and he'd guess I'd known all along. I can't betray him in that way.

I considered waking him up and telling him who she is, who I am, but I didn't have the courage. I couldn't watch his vision of me disintegrate. Over these past few days I've seen real love shine out of his eyes. I know, the way I've never known before – even after spending four years with Martin – that this is *it*. This is what they all talk about. The elusive otherness. When someone makes you feel better and you make them feel better, when you trust one another and lust after one another. When the hairs on their arms are precious to you, fascinating to you, almost as fascinating as their stories and hopes and fears. I love Dean Taylor and he loves me. I was quite prepared to watch the exciting spikes of lust and new love settle into something more prosaic and comfortable in time, old love; I was looking forward to as much. But I could not watch the love in his eyes turn to loathing. He would despise me.

How could we sustain a future when every story I told him about my past would torture him? Every time I talked about picnics on tartan rugs, with bumble bees buzzing past my ear, he'd have to be thinking of the fly that settled on his dead mother's cold lips. If I talked about family days out visiting castles, energetically yomping up the hills in a playful competition to reach the ruins before my brother or sister, he'd have to be thinking about Zoe, who is so scared of the world that she wet her bed until she was a teen and still sleeps with the light on. And as for the stories about smudging my face against my mother's gingham apron, wiping off the jewel-coloured fruit stains, well, he'd be thinking about the day he chose to no longer clean up his own mother; the day they were first taken into care.

It's too uneven.

It's unforgivable. I can't be a constant reminder to him, not after he's worked so damned relentlessly and spectacularly to put it all behind him. I won't be the one who dredges it all up.

So I left the beautiful man sleeping. Accepting that this is true love after all. It turns out I was right all along. Oh yeah, they laughed at me, but I was right. With Dean I had the quickening pulse, the gorgeous butterflies and slackening in my body, and I had the steady stuff too: a sense of duty, loyalty, decency and friendship. The bit I wasn't aware of was the sacrifice. And so now I know and my chest has been ripped open.

As soon as I land, I call my sister and she tells me that Mum has given up on the spa; she was lonely among the pampered and preened even though she has often been comfortably counted among their number, so she is now staying at Lisa's.

'On my couch?' I ask.

'Actually it's my couch,' replies Lisa with a hint of exasperation. 'But no, in fact we've given her one of the kids' beds. Charlie is sleeping in with us. Not that any of us are getting much sleep,' she adds wearily. 'This whole business is so disruptive.'

'Tell me about it,' I sigh.

'How are you, anyway?'

'Fine,' I lie. I don't give her any details. In the past, I've been far too garrulous about my problems, especially those of a romantic nature, but this time I can't find the words that will cover it. It's too big. It's too raw.

Lisa must hear despondency in my voice, because she makes an effort to almost hide her reluctance as she adds, 'So the couch is still here; if you want it, it's yours.'

The thought of living in such close proximity to my mother right now is too much for me. I don't want to have to explain. 'I think I'll go and stay with Dad. He's probably lonely. I'll go straight there from here.'

'Good idea,' agrees Lisa, with a little too much enthusiasm. 'There are plenty of spare beds at the parental home.'

I can't wait to get out of the airport. I decide I hate airports. I resent other people's excitement as they speed off to wonderful holidays or to invigorating business meetings, and now that I am at the centre of my own very real drama, I can't see the allure of other people calling out welcomes or phrasing difficult goodbyes. The shops are beneath my notice as I gaze around the terminal, no longer curious as to how many momentous events are occurring at this very second. The sound of my own heart breaking drowns out all the other declarations of love.

47

Eddie

I'm going to close my eyes now. Enough.

TUESDAY 26 APRIL 2005

48

Dean

Dean decided to hire a car. It was quite a journey to Islington and it would no doubt have been quicker and certainly cheaper if he'd caught the tube, but he didn't feel he could dredge up the effort required to negotiate the tube and then find Jo's sister's home on foot. He wasn't familiar with that part of London and he was shattered; three transatlantic flights in six days was insane. He'd told work that he had to deal with urgent family business; it wasn't quite a lie. He did not know what time zone he was functioning in, nor was he sure if the uncomfortable ache in his body was the result of tiredness, hunger or loss. He feared it was loss.

It was a loss tinged with anger, as so many of Dean's losses were. He was nipped by bouts of irritation and disappointment with Jo for being such an idiot. She should have had more faith, or at least sense. If only she'd woken him up. How could she have thought he was married? After all they'd talked about, after all they'd done. A flashback as to exactly what they had done seared his brain. Thoughts of her perfect smile and her fingernails, her peachy arse and her optimism mingled and clashed about his head. Hot images of him kissing and licking her, stroking and entering her cut through his anger. She should have trusted him, but he'd sort it out. He'd explain and reassure, and eventually they'd laugh about this, wouldn't they? Dean was buoyed up by an inner confidence; despite the vanishing act, he did not think it was likely that Jo had simply fallen out of love with him. Women didn't do that to him; Jo wouldn't do that to anyone.

The house was, as Dean might have imagined it to be if he'd taken the time to imagine, a three-storey early Victorian family home in Islington. It was built in an attractive grey stone; imposing in its day, but now shabby enough to appear comfortable and inviting. He climbed up three steps and rapped on the door with the enormous silver knocker; it thudded against the shiny navy paint.

He'd expected Jo to be home alone. He'd thought that her sister and brother-in-law would be at work and the kids would be at school or nursery. So he was surprised when a woman in her late fifties flung open the door. Her face was initially hopeful, then momentarily disappointed; finally she efficiently rearranged her expression into a picture of polite serenity. It was the show face that allowed Dean to guess that this woman must be Jo's mother. He knew enough about her life to deduce that she was used to and capable of putting on a best face when needed. He grinned, and for the first time in his life his grin did not have the effect he was hoping for. Rather than succumb to his evident charm, Mrs Russell suddenly turned pale; she looked bewildered and nervous.

'Hello, can I help you?' she asked cautiously.

'I'm looking for Jo Russell.'

'Joanna Russell doesn't live here,' Mrs Russell stuttered.

'Yes, I know that. I realise this is her sister's home. It's Lisa, isn't it? But I thought she was staying here.' Jo's mother remained rigid and wary. Dean got it; people who lived in big cities generally gave little away to surprise visitors. He took on the responsibility of putting them both at their ease, pulling out his best

Sunday manners. 'You must be Mrs Russell. How do you do?'
He stretched out his hand. 'I'm Jo's friend from Chicago.' He
smiled, and this time he took care to flash his most appealing
and winning one. 'I'm Dean Taylor.'

Mrs Russell's hand had been reaching forwards to shake the
one Dean proffered, but on hearing his name she pulled her hand
to her heart as though she'd been shot. Dean thought that Jo
must have told her mother all about him and that she too thought
he was a married scumbag.

'I'm not married, Mrs Russell, please let me explain.'

'Did you just say your name is Dean Taylor?'

'Yes. But I can explain about the ring.' Dean put his foot on
the threshold so that she couldn't close the door on him and lock
him out; she looked as though she wanted to. 'It's not my ring,
it's my father's.' Mrs Russell looked more confused, not less. 'I
know Jo thinks I'm married, which is why she left in a hurry, but
I'm not. Please let me explain. I've come all the way from America
to explain.'

Mrs Russell had now turned so pale she was almost transparent.
He was sure that she was going to slam the door in his face, but
she didn't; she held it wide open and with a sigh muttered, 'You'd
better come in.'

49

Clara

Clara made tea. She was British and clearly slap bang in the middle of a crisis, and so, of course, she made tea. She needed time to think, to process and understand, so she left the handsome man alone in Lisa's sitting room. He perched keenly on the edge of a chair, desperate to offer his explanation. Clara knew that she'd be the one delivering explanations, and she was considerably less keen to offer up hers.

She hovered in the kitchen while the kettle boiled, occasionally sneaking into the hallway to peek through the open sitting-room door and steal a look at him. Dean Taylor was so especially beautiful. She saw more of her Eddie in him than she had seen in the dying grey man whom she had visited for these past few days. He had the same eyes; eyes that could raze and expose a woman's soul in an instant. Deep, endlessly deep eyes that sparkled with possibility. He had the same dark, brooding looks that Eddie had once possessed. He was big, broad, muscular and athletic. Yet he was not exactly like Eddie. Dean Taylor exuded a confidence but not an arrogance; he had a fragility and wariness about him, the like of which had never touched the older Taylor. She didn't see any irresponsibility or lust in Dean's gaze; he was more about hope and nervous excitement. She hadn't thought it possible, but here was a man who was more attractive than Eddie Taylor. She fully understood why her daughter had fallen in love with him.

Clara wished that Lisa had cups and saucers rather than just mugs; mugs were more intimate than Clara felt ready to be with this young man. She did her best to bring some protective formality to the situation, although she feared it would only be a matter of minutes before the whole thing collapsed into a swamp of emotions and retributions: she made the tea in a pot, with leaves, rather than in the mugs using mathematically shaped tea bags, and she put a jug of milk and a bowl of sugar on the tray, along with spare spoons (people seemed to forget that one spoon was required for tipping, another for stirring). She hunted around and unearthed a packet of chocolate chip biscuits; she put half a dozen on a plate, wondered if that looked stingy and then added another two. She wished she'd baked this morning. Lisa never baked, but Clara didn't like offering shop-bought produce.

As she carried the tea tray into the sitting room, she was aware that she was shaking, because the tray rattled tellingly. Dean Taylor must have assumed she was struggling under the weight; he jumped to his feet and offered to take it from her. 'I'm quite all right, I can manage,' she said firmly, her tone harsher than she'd intended; it was her nerves making her sound officious when really she simply didn't want to trouble him.

They sat opposite one another but not looking at one another.

'Tea?'

'That would be lovely.'

'Milk?'

'Yes please.'

'Sugar?'

'No thank you.' Neither one felt it was the moment to throw

out the usual quip that he was sweet enough. Clara glanced at him from under her lashes. He was, though, there was no doubt about it.

'Biscuit?'

'No thank you.' Then, 'Actually, yes please. Thinking about it, I am hungry.'

He took a biscuit but Clara noticed he didn't bite into it. She wondered whether he'd accepted it to be polite or because he was tense too and having a biscuit in his hand meant he'd have something to play with. Clara never snacked between meals, but she found herself taking one as well.

She didn't know where to start. 'So you're the young man my daughter met in Chicago?' It seemed as good a place as any.

'Yes, we met on her flight over there.'

'And became lovers?'

Dean was at that moment sipping his hot tea and so spluttered it over his knee, a little spraying on to the carpet. Clara's directness clearly shocked him. She hadn't been aiming to shock; she simply wanted the facts.

Dean obviously wasn't ready for that level of confidence, and would only confirm, 'We became close. Very close. But on Monday morning she found a wedding ring in my pocket.' He reached into his pocket and dug out the fat gold band. He held it between his thumb and forefinger, briefly examining it as though it was an object from out of space before throwing it on to the coffee table between them. Clara gasped at the sight of it. The ring spun for a moment, and then clattered to a standstill. The sunlight caught it and winked. Neither of them could tear their eyes away from the damned thing. Clara had always found Eddie's wedding ring horribly compelling. Dean continued. 'She thought it was mine, but it isn't. It's my father's. He left it to me. He's dying and he left me his wedding ring.'

Clara closed her eyes, but it was too late. She could not shut out what she knew to be unequivocally true. His looks, the familiar-looking ring, his father dying; there was no room for doubt. She'd wanted it all to be a coincidence, even his name, but it wasn't; it was evidence. She could feel tears under her lids. She remembered her call with Jo on Monday, the abrupt way the conversation had ended. Jo had showered the line with expletives just after Clara had mentioned the name of her lover. These tears were for Jo and Dean. What had she done to them? She sniffed robustly, in a manner that was quite unlike her usual ladylike one.

'I'm so sorry to hear about your father,' she said carefully.

'Thank you, but we weren't close.' Dean jutted his chin out a fraction. He evidently did not want to labour under the weight of unasked-for sympathy. He put down his mug and thoughtlessly picked up a tiny toy car that had been left on the floor. He played absent-mindedly with the wheels. 'In fact I hated him until very recently,' he blurted.

'I see.' The chocolate chips in Clara's cookie had melted as she'd gripped the treat throughout the conversation; she put it down on the tray untouched and carefully, bravely asked, 'You no longer hate him?'

'I'm not sure. I think it's impossible to hate someone who is dying. I'm closer to indifference.'

'Well, that's better.' Clara meant it was better for Dean. She didn't want him to be ripped apart by hate, not on top of everything else. She hoped he didn't think she was simply a priggish old woman morally judging him.

It was clear he had understood her when he admitted mournfully, 'Not really. I think I've just transferred my hate to another subject.'

Clara hazarded a guess. 'His mistress?' Dean's head shot up and he stared at her with surprised admiration; he clearly thought she was psychic, or at least especially insightful. How else could she have waded through this quagmire and reached the correct conclusion? 'I am his mistress,' she declared bluntly.

Dean's look of admiration instantly changed to one of fear and mystification. 'What?'

'I'm the woman your father left you for. At least I think I am. Your father was Eddie Taylor, correct?'

'Yes.'

'And he left you twenty-nine years ago?' This time Dean could not find words; he simply nodded. All doubt extinguished. Hope with it. 'I'm so sorry,' finished Clara.

Of course it was not enough; how could it be? Clara hadn't expected it to be. No longer fearful and mystified, Dean looked as though he wanted to slap her, but a man like the one he'd forced himself to become would never do such an uncivilised, ungallant thing. He simply glared at her. Blind fury and – so much harder to bear – undiluted agony flooded out of his eyes and bored into her. His cheek muscles quivered. 'My guess is that Jo worked out as much and I think that's why she left you. She doesn't believe you're married. I think she simply believed that the two of you could never have a future. So she left.'

'Because of you.'

'I suppose.' Clara shrugged. Her gesture wasn't motivated by carelessness or apathy; it was the result of a profound despair. How could it have come to this? She'd spent her entire life trying not to hurt her children, and now there was this. She thought she'd probably made the right assumptions. Oh, her poor daughter. This poor man. What a state they had been left in. Clara was engulfed in a new wave of shame and despair. When would it stop? When would the consequences of her actions cease to have an impact? The ripples seemed to spread endlessly, widening rather than depleting. She'd dropped a pebble, but the tsunami waves still crashed around them, threatening to drown them all.

'Because of you, my mother drank herself to death, my sister and I were brought up in children's homes,' Dean muttered coldly.

'I know. Well, at least I knew about you being in a home.'

'How? How could you know that?' yelled Dean furiously.

'I've been to see your father. We talked about you.' Fat silent tears slipped down Clara's face.

'Why? Why couldn't you have left him alone?' Clara was unsure whether Dean meant now, or years ago when the affair began. It didn't matter; either way she had no answer. She'd asked the question of herself, many times.

She bravely met Dean's eyes. 'I am so deeply and completely sorry for all the hurt I have caused you.' She enunciated every word carefully. She'd been rehearsing them all her life; still, she doubted they were adequate. Dean clearly could not trust himself to reply. He nodded sharply. Clara didn't think it was absolution; she assumed he was simply acknowledging her. She watched as he pieced together the sequence of events, just as she had. 'You look a lot like your father.' Dean threw her a look that was the equivalent to flicking the finger. She stuttered, 'I simply mean, when I saw you on the step, I immediately started to make the connection, but I thought I was imagining things. Then when you said your name, I knew there was no doubt.'

'Well this was a wasted bloody journey,' spat Dean. 'Because Jo was right about one thing: we can never, ever have a future.'

Clara looked aghast. Desperate. Any beauty she had preserved flooded away in an instant and was replaced by ugly self-hatred. 'Why? Because of my past?'

'Exactly.'

'But that's insane, Dean. It doesn't have to be that way,' she protested.

'It does. It just does. I could never look at you without thinking about him. How would we gather round the table for Sunday lunch or at Christmas or Easter? How would I be able to marry the girl whose mother had ruined my life so that she could self-ishly keep her own life cushy?' Dean spat out the words in a blur of confusion and anger.

Clara was taken aback that he had mentioned marriage, even if he had done so in the context of saying it could never happen. It was obvious that this man was serious about her daughter. Clara had had just one conversation with Jo since she'd arrived back from Chicago. They'd spoken on the phone last night. Jo had been very quiet and thoughtful, almost pensive, not her usual self at all. It was as though she had left a girl and returned a woman; the only problem being that she had left as a hopeful girl and returned as a heartbroken woman. Clara had realised this instantly. She had thought that Jo's seriousness and silence was to do with the fact that Martin was married and another avenue had closed. True, Jo had described the new man she'd met as 'perfect', but she had given this slick endorsement to many unsuitable men before; she'd described debtors, philan-derers and cross-dressers as perfect in the past before their true natures were revealed. Clara hadn't thought that Jo was grieving for the perfect man she'd left behind, but now she understood, she understood completely. She knew herself how difficult it was to walk away from these Taylor men. Physically magnifi-cent men. Dark, brooding, big and gripping. Men who crawled up under a woman's skin. Then she remembered. Jo had also said that Dean was the most interesting and courageous man she'd ever met. Clara had never heard her endorse anyone else in that way. Something was different. Perhaps this embryonic romance was greater and more advanced than she had imag-ined. Perhaps it could have consequence and significance. After all, Dean had travelled all the way from Chicago for Jo, and Jo had given him up when she thought staying with him would cause him more pain than it would ease. These acts seemed a lot like love.

Clara felt nauseous with the threat of more loss. She scrabbled around her brain, desperately wondering how she might fix this. Was it in her power at all? She stared at the wall, painted a predictable Farrow and Ball red; the colour caroused with the blood pumping around her body and head. She wished Lisa had picked a soothing vert de terre. Clara always thought very carefully about what she was going to say. This time she was particularly vigilant.

'I understand that you are angry that I had an affair with your father. It was very wrong of me, obviously. I'm sorry. But you need to know I never asked him to leave his wife for me. I didn't want that.'

'Exactly, it was just a bit of fun to you, an inconsequential little bit of fun, but for me it was a life-changer.'

'It wasn't inconsequential.' She knew she had no right to justify or offer excuses. 'But I just couldn't leave Tim,' she explained.

'Yet you've left him now.'

'Yes.'

'Why now? If not then?' Dean challenged.

'Because I couldn't leave the girls then.' The words pit-pattered around the room like summer rain. Dean nodded stiffly. That he would understand and respect. Clara sensed she'd caught him. 'We both know that none of this would be any better even if I had left Tim then. There would simply have been more pain, more waste. Dean, does it make any difference if I tell you I wanted to leave? I wanted your father so, so much, but not above everything, not above my girls. And I'm sorry that he left you. I'm not asking to be forgiven for my part in your past, but I want you to know that I've paid. I've paid every day of my life, because I *did* want him.'

Dean remained mute; Clara hoped he was considering what she'd told him. They both listened to the sounds of the house; a wall clock ticked, the fridge hummed. 'You chose to do the right thing,' he stated finally.

'I wanted to keep my family together.'

Throughout the weekend Jo had entertained Dean with countless stories about her glittering and happy childhood, and he'd thought he understood, he'd thought he could imagine the privilege and pleasure. However, it was only now that he was speaking with Clara that he began to get a true sense of what it really was. Jo had truly had it all; besides the music lessons and the tennis camps, the foreign holidays and the home-cooked organic dinners, she'd had this – a parent who put the child's needs first. Something in his face shifted. He looked microscopically less angry.

Clara wondered whether a grain of a thought might have begun to occur to Dean. She hoped that he could see that having Clara in his life didn't have to mean he'd always be full of anger and resentment; perhaps he too could be swept up in her warmth. His in-laws (because possibly one day, why not?) would love him too, protect him and value him. He would finally have the parents he deserved and longed for. And his children, they'd have *doting* grandparents. The thought was a good one. Of course it all depended on whether he could get past the anger. If Jo's love was enough. If his trust in her and in himself was infallible.

'I used to spend a lot of time wondering whether meeting your father was for the better or worse,' ventured Clara.

'What did you decide?'

'I still have no idea. I'm not sure life is ever that neat, Dean.'

She hoped that he could see she was not the devil incarnate; she was an old woman who had made mistakes and then held her hands up, who was trying to put things right. Eddie Taylor had shaped her life too. He was a force, that much was certain.

Dean sighed. He looked so weary. 'What did you talk about when you went to visit him? Did he give you what you wanted?'

'There were no declarations of love, if that's what you mean,' replied Clara carefully.

'*Is* that what you wanted?'

'I don't know. You?'

'No declarations of love.' Dean didn't quite swallow his bitter fury. Clara wished feverishly that she could tell him that whilst visiting Eddie, he'd announced that he was proud of his son, that he deeply regretted leaving him, that every moment apart had been hell, but she respected Dean too much to lie to him. She couldn't heal him that way.

'My father told me that he'd wanted more than staying with my mother could give him.' Dean sighed, threw himself back on his seat and stared at the ceiling. 'He said that you were his more.'

Clara realised Dean was offering her a gift by sharing this knowledge. It was hers to do with as she pleased. Perhaps he thought she might find comfort in it, but she was too aware of the reality of Eddie Taylor to do so. 'It might have been the case that if I had left with him he would have tired of me too, sooner or later.'

'Probably.'

Clara decided to take the plunge. She thought he was following her, that she was taking him with her, but she wasn't certain. She had no idea how much had to be forgiven and forgotten, but her love for Jo and her extreme sympathy for this man gave her the courage to push on. 'Is Jo your more?'

Dean looked wary. 'I'm concerned that this is all moving too quickly. We might not be right for one another. I mean, we only met a few days ago, and only then because she was on a plane going to the US to try to marry another man.'

'But she didn't stop the wedding. She fell in love with you.'

'I know, she told me. I didn't know what to do with her declaration, so I just pretended to be asleep.'

'You can't do that any longer.'

'Her life has been so very different from mine. She's coming
at love from a totally different direction.'

'That's true. But you could end up in the same place. It's your
call, Dean.'

Dean looked panicked. 'How do you know that I won't tire
of her eventually too? Break her heart? How do I know that?
How can you trust me? I don't trust myself. What if I'm just
like him?'

'You're made of better stuff, Dean. You're his son, but you're
your own man.'

Dean let his head fall into his hands, and Clara's mothering
instincts made her dash around the coffee table that separated
them. She sat on the arm of his chair and carefully put her hand
on his shoulder. She wanted to wrap him in an enormous hug,
but she knew she hadn't earned the right. She was suddenly so
certain that she wanted to gain that right to familiarity; she wanted
this man to be in her life, to love her daughter, to visit on a
Sunday for lunch. She wanted the chance to make up, in some
small way. She was grateful that Dean did not shrug off her
touch.

'I set off on this journey to find out why my father left me.'

'Have you found any answers?'

'Not from him.'

'But you do have answers?'

'I realise now that it wasn't anything to do with me. It wasn't
my fault.'

'Quite so.'

Dean paused, and then brought his head out of his hands and
turned to her. 'I don't think it was your fault either. It was,' he
sighed, 'simply a bad call. His bad call.'

Clara thought he was a brave and forgiving man. To reduce his life's experiences to a bad call – so that she could wriggle away from the guilt that plagued her – was beyond generous.

'Before all of this,' she waved her hand in the air, 'the letter, Jo going to Chicago and me leaving Tim, I'd been struggling to work out whether I'm old.' A flicker of shock registered on the polite young man's face; he did his best to hide it almost immediately, but the instant gave it away. Clara smiled wryly. 'Of course you know the answer: I am old. You don't know why I'm struggling with something so obvious.' She wanted to giggle to herself. 'But my point is, I don't always feel old. Sometimes I feel exactly like the young woman I was when I gave birth to the children, or younger still – the girl I was when I met Tim. However, I admit that other times I feel ancient. It goes by so very quickly, Dean. Time. It's possible not to notice it flying past. I recommend that you don't waste it.'

'Are you going to go back to your husband?' Dean had seen what her own children had yet to pick up on. Her fallibility. Her good sense.

'Yes, I think I am.'

'Good.' He smiled, a brief but definite smile. 'I don't want my father buggering up anything else.'

'Yes, it is good. We made one another happy in our own way, and it's too late for me to start again. Dean, I've punished myself every single day. Never forgiving myself, never living the life I wanted. Your father was the opposite extreme; he never considered another living soul. He was the cancel and continue sort. There has to be middle ground. You should start living the life *you* deserve. Today. Now. Trust yourself. If you need me to, I'll stay away. I'll give you both space. I won't hang around to be an eternal reminder, but I won't let you mess this up. You deserve one another in a way your father and I didn't deserve one another, and you can have one another too. You really can. There's nothing to stop you but your own fear.' Clara was unsure whether she'd ever before made such a long and emotional speech; she paused to see if it had had the desired effect.

50

Dean

Dean had stared at Clara Russell for minutes, maintaining an absolute silence as he'd tried to weigh it all up. She'd said there was nothing to stop him but his own fear. He knew she was trying to be inspirational and motivational, but a cold slither of dislike had shimmied up his spine. He wondered, was it permanent? What did she know of his fear? Perhaps she knew and understood more than he was giving her credit for. Maybe she was trying to challenge him because she'd somehow sensed that he was the sort of man who rose to a challenge, the sort of man who conquered and lived another day.

But this was different. He thought he had made the biggest emotional leap he'd ever have to make. He'd started down the path of loving someone. Trusting someone. But look what had happened, almost instantly; through no fault of her own, loving Jo had led to this hideous pain. Loving was a risk. He was terrified that he couldn't love her enough. Love led to love, but he hadn't been trained up in it the way she had. The way Clara Russell seemed to be. There had not been enough love in his life for him to be sure. Clara did not seem to be the hellcat he'd imagined; he was grown up enough to admit as much. She was not totally responsible for all his troubles, of course. But would he be able to forgive her fully? Forget at all?

It was perfectly possible, even understandable, that at some point down the line he'd start to resent Jo's mother, and then that resentment might lead to hate. How long would it be before he hated Jo too? He imagined the moment. He and Jo would be married and they'd have the three kids she dreamt of, that he too would like. They'd be doing fine. Very happy. Then one day, not a remarkable day in any way, Clara would pop by to drop off some small, inconsequential but thoughtful treat for the children – a bag of Cherry Lips or Kola Kubes, perhaps – and she'd push open the back door, cheerfully yelling, 'Yoo hoo.' But Dean wouldn't hear 'Yoo hoo'; he'd hear the clunk of a door bashing against his dead mother's head. The thought made him sick.

But then he thought about Jo – her optimism, her thoughtfulness, her intelligence, her outstanding performance in bed – and he felt less lonely. Less unsure.

Almost comforted. Almost sure.

Could they make it work? Was this one of those sorts of moments? The moment before the leap into the deep choppy water or the dive out of the plane was always the most terrifying, but experience had shown him that it was also the moment ahead of the fabulous rush and the exquisite feeling of triumph.

He'd asked Clara where he'd find Jo. She'd beamed delightedly, assuming he'd made up his mind.

'She's at home. In Wimbledon. Do you have the address?'

'Yes, I do.'

'Are you going to go to her?'

'OK.'

'OK?'

'OK!' Dean suddenly saw the moment for what it was. It was one he had to seize. Without so much as a backward glance, he rushed out of the house.

The traffic was frustratingly slow. He sat nose to tail, crawling along the London streets. He wound down the window and tried to think whether he knew any short cuts. Down through Clerkenwell, Waterloo, Clapham and then on to Wimbledon would take about an hour. He wanted to get to Jo as quickly as he could, while he was this sure and this full. The important thing was not to let any doubts slide into his mind in the next hour. Not to dwell on the contrast between him and Jo but instead to concentrate on the things they had in common. He could just imagine her face when she opened the door to him.

He flicked on the radio for company. He found it interesting that it was a universal truth that rental cars were always tuned in to a local station, the sort that played retrospective music for middle-aged housewives and the retired. Dean hated the sort of tunes they played. He preferred to listen to Radio 1 so he could hear current tunes, or Radio 4 so he might learn what was going on in the world. He started to fiddle with the radio buttons to try and retune, but before he could successfully do so, he heard a blast of 'There Must Be an Angel' by the Eurythmics. For a fraction of a second he smiled at the sunny thought that no one on earth could feel like this. He actually indulged in some pop culture cliché and thought that he, for the first time ever, understood the lyrics. Then he placed the song exactly and it started playing with his heart.

It had been *the* song of the summer of 1985, and just a few short chords brought the summer back to him. It was a typical British summer, in so much as there were cold, wet patches throughout May and June but finally, in July, Londoners enjoyed a few weeks of decent sunshine. It was around about then that the world became aware of Kelly LeBrock. She was the perfect woman as engineered by two geeks in the movie *Weird Science*. If 'There Must Be an Angel' was the song of the summer of 1985, then she was the woman. She was the pin-up who made ice cream melt faster; girls wanted to be her, boys wanted to have her. She starred in all of Dean's pubescent fantasies; he remembered he'd had a poster of her up on his bedroom wall in the home, but some twat stole it, wanked on it then left the sticky mess under his pillow. Fourteen-year-old Dean could never feel the same way about Kelly LeBrock after that; she'd been ruined for him. It was around that time that some blokes started to wear tight trousers, frilly shirts, asymmetric haircuts and eyeliner. That was not a look that Dean experimented with; it wouldn't have been advisable in care. That sort of thing was judged severely. One lad made the mistake of playing a Culture Club cassette in the common room, and besides the fact that he could never again shower in peace, he was forever after known as 'gay fucker'.

July 1985 was the month when Live Aid made a fortune for starving African kids and *Back to the Future* made a fortune for Hollywood executives. It was the month his mother had swallowed a bottle of sleeping pills, swilled down by a couple of bottles of vodka. Making it very hard for Dean to believe in angels.

51

Clara

Clara went upstairs and repacked her case. She'd packed to leave Tim, unpacked at the spa, repacked and then unpacked once again at Lisa's. This time she knew she was packing for the final time. She was going home. Her marriage to Tim was not conventional, it was not what she'd imagined a marriage to be when she was a child, but it was enduring, worthwhile and loving. They had three children and three grandchildren together (she hoped there would be many more if Mark and Katie and Jo and – dare she say it, even to herself – Dean got busy). She and Tim had a history together. She wanted to go home to him. She could not dash there immediately; Jo and Dean needed some time to sort things out. She'd stay at Lisa's, make something nice for tea for her, Henry and the children. They could eat together, and then Clara would announce that her little break was over, that she'd thought it through and was returning to Tim. She'd go home at about nine o'clock. There would be champagne in the fridge – there always was – and she and Tim could at last celebrate their anniversary, while Dean and Jo would celebrate their fresh start.

It took all of Clara's self-control not to telephone Jo. She so wanted to put an end to her daughter's trauma and uncertainty, but she knew that a forewarning call would spoil the impact of Dean arriving on the step in person. Instead she spent the after-noon imagining her daughter's romantic reconciliation and making an organic beef lasagne. She did call Tim to tell him that she planned on coming home.

'Well, that's wonderful news. I am glad.' She appreciated Tim's steely goodwill. Goodwill and manners helped in a marriage.

The dinner was cheerful. Lisa and Henry were able to be generous in their hospitality, knowing that their guest was about to leave. They were also delighted that Jo had finally found her happy ending, and grilled Clara for details about Dean. She told them that he was honourable, sincere and 'wonderful to look at'. She didn't tell them that he was the son of the man she had once had an affair with; she would eventually, but there was a time and a place for everything, and tonight around the family's large wooden dining table was neither that time nor place.

When the taxi pulled up outside her home in Wimbledon, Clara took a deep breath and inhaled the scent of the garden buds and grass; how could she ever have thought of leaving this place? She was not surprised that there weren't any downstairs lights on at home. Tim's home office was at the back of the house, and it was very possible he was there, working, while he waited for her. She guessed that perhaps Jo and Dean had gone out for a bite to eat.

She pushed open the front door and allowed the space to settle around her. Home. She let out a contented sigh, slipped off her shoes and turned on the hall light.

'Good lord, Joanna, you gave me a start.' Jo was sitting on the bottom stair, surrounded by darkness.

'Sorry, Mum. I've been here for hours. I suppose it got dark around me. I didn't really notice.'

Clara was puzzled by the gloom in the hall and the desolation on Jo's face. 'Where's Dean?' she asked.

'Dean?' Jo was bewildered. 'Dean's in America, Mum.'

'No, he was here. Well, at Lisa's.'

'When?'

'This afternoon. He's here in England. He's come for you.' Clara beamed, thrilled to be the bearer of such wonderful news.

'You met him?' Jo's tone did not match her mother's cheery one.

'Yes. He's lovely.'

'You know who he is then, I suppose,' her daughter said glumly.

'Yes.' Clara felt mildly uncomfortable; it would take some getting used to, but she rallied. 'And he knows who I am, but it's OK.' She sat down next to her daughter on the stairs. She considered putting her arm around her and giving her a congratulatory, celebratory squeeze, but she didn't. 'He loves you.'

'Did he say that?'

'Well, not in so many words, but he was coming here to tell you. He did say that.'

'He never came, Mum.' Bemused, Clara looked around the hall as though she was expecting him to suddenly materialise. 'He would never be able to be happy with me, knowing about you and his father.'

'But we talked about everything. He was reconciled to it.'

Jo too looked around the empty hallway. 'Clearly not.'

2013

Epilogue

Jo thought she was imagining it at first, but Dean was not a particularly common name, and it was all the more distinct for that. The woman sitting next to her on the park bench was repeatedly calling to her son.

'Dean, be careful. You're going far too high on that swing.' Jo followed the direction of the woman's gaze and saw a boy, aged about six, swinging dangerously high but squealing with the joy of it.

Smiling at the coincidence, she turned to the anxious mother beside her. 'My son is called Dean too.'

'Really?' The woman's anxious face instantly transformed, and she beamed back. 'Which is yours?' she asked. Jo pointed to her blond, curly-haired two-year-old son playing contentedly in the sandbox. She was aware that the box was probably used by all the neighbourhood's stray cats as a litter tray, but she didn't have the energy to deal with the issue at that moment. She rubbed her taut belly. 'He looks significantly less of a handful than my Dean,' commented the other mum with a wry smile.

'He has his moments,' laughed Jo. 'But on the whole, yes, he is very good.'

'And when are you due?' The woman nodded towards Jo's enormous belly.

'Any minute.' Jo was amused by the return of the slightly anxious expression that this comment provoked. 'Don't worry, I'm not having contractions or anything. When I say any minute, I mean in the next week or so.'

'Have you thought of names for this one?'

'It's a girl, and we're still deciding between Eva and Frances.'

'Both are pretty.'

'Thank you. I think we'll wait to see which she suits.' Jo thought that the conversation would probably come to a close now; it was a pleasant but unremarkable exchange, similar to dozens of conversations she'd had in various parks, cafés and soft play areas since she was first obviously pregnant. Women liked to chat about due dates and baby names. They both sat quietly and listened to children laughing and rowing, teasing and bossing one another as they climbed, swung and ran around the park. The sound of trainers and sandals scurrying across the tarmac and rubber created a pleasant rhythm.

'How did you pick the name Dean? Did you have a choice of two then as well?' asked the mother of the older Dean.

'No. He was always going to be Dean. He's named after an old friend of mine,' replied Jo.

'My son is named after my brother.'

'That's nice.' Jo paused. She wasn't sure what propelled her on. Maybe it was simply the lure of a coincidence – she was interested in the woman who had a child with the same name as hers – or maybe it was because the woman had a gentle, somehow familiar, open face that invited confidences; maybe it was simply Jo's hormones playing havoc with her common sense. Whatever the reason, she suddenly gushed, 'Actually, Dean is named after the love of my life.' She allowed the huge phrase to slip out accompanied by a grin, which she hoped might mitigate some of the gravity of the confession. 'Obviously, I haven't ever told my husband as much,' she laughed.

The woman smiled sympathetically. Most women had an understanding of that sort of thing. 'So what happened to the love of your life?'

'The usual, he dumped me. It was complicated. There was lots of baggage and it wasn't meant to be. It was the briefest of flings, really.' Jo felt she had to pull back from her large statement that Dean was the love of her life. It seemed disloyal to Andy to talk of Dean in that way; after all she'd only known Dean for four days, and she'd been married to Andy for four years now. Still, that was how she thought of him. Even now. The love of her life. 'I've been with my husband for four years, and don't get me wrong, we are very much in love. We're very happy, but sometimes I do think back to Dean. Fondly. He was good for me.' She had not been able to resist calling her son after the man who had taught her to love, for real. The man who had helped her through the most brutal and embarrassing weekend of her life. The man who she had cried over for months and months. The one she had longed for for years.

The woman on the bench shifted; she rummaged in her handbag and pulled out some imperial mints. She offered one to Jo, who took it. At eight and a half months pregnant, Jo would eat anything anyone offered, even a dusty mint dredged up from a stranger's handbag. 'Besides, if I hadn't met Dean, I'd never have met Andy. It's strange how things turn out.'

'Were they friends?'

'No, nothing like that. Dean was this very adventurous type. You know, always skiing, snorkelling or surfing. He thought I lacked interests, so he made me draw up a list of things I'd like to achieve in life. I met Andy on set.'

'On set?'

'Andy is an actor. I was an extra. So indirectly Dean is

417

responsible for us meeting. He gave me a lot of confidence and direction. I've carried the list with me ever since. I've pretty much worked through the lot we drew up together and I've since added more.'

'Mummeeee, look at me.' Both women looked up just in time to see the older Dean let go of the swing chain and fly through the air. Remarkably, he landed on his feet. He laughed hysterically with adrenalin and pride.

'He is just like his uncle.'

'I'm Jo, by the way.'

'Zoe.' The woman did a little wave, even though Jo was sat right next to her. It would have been odd to shake hands in the park. Jo's brain wasn't firing on all cylinders, tired from the pregnancy, and it took her a moment to make the connection. When she did, she didn't think it could possibly be true.

'Your brother didn't used to live in Chicago by any chance, did he?'

Zoe looked startled. 'Actually, yes, yes he did.'

'Oh my goodness. I don't believe it. Dean Taylor?'

'Yes, that's right.'

'Your brother Dean is the love of my life *Dean*.' Jo's delight at the coincidence almost cancelled out the embarrassment she felt saying such an exposing thing so many years after the event. She beamed, thrilled to have found him again, albeit indirectly. 'Well how the hell is he? Is he married? Sorry, that's really cheeky of me,' Jo gushed. 'But I can't tell you how much I loved that man. I thought I'd never get over him. Don't tell him that, will you?' She paused. She'd rushed on because part of her still wasn't ready to hear the inevitable. No doubt he'd married an American model, they'd have four beautiful children by now and he wouldn't even remember her name. Jo? Jo who? he'd say when Zoe relayed this story to him next time they caught up. Or worse still, Zoe might tell her that he hadn't ever married; he was still stewing, consumed with fury at her mother and his father, unable to move on with his own life. That would be worse than anything.

When her mother had come home to Wimbledon all those years ago with the news that she'd met Dean and that he had flown to England to find Jo, Jo had allowed herself to hope. For a week or so she'd imagined that at any minute he might walk up their drive, explain that he'd needed time but was ready now to declare that they could begin again.

He didn't come.

She'd phoned his mobile, dozens and dozens of times, but he'd always allowed her call to go straight through to voicemail. Initially her messages were calm and cheerful; eventually they deteriorated into undignified pleas. It didn't matter, as he never returned any of her calls. It took months for her to accept that he never would. Years for her to stop wishing that wasn't the case.

She had surprised everyone by not falling to bits. She had been determined that she would dignify her encounter with Dean by turning her life around, so she'd applied for countless journalist jobs. After some months, she'd finally secured a position on a trade magazine as a travel journalist. She'd travelled extensively since. She'd visited South Africa, Australia, Canada, India, Bali, Cuba and most European countries. On her trips she'd nursed baby cheetahs, played the didgeridoo, gone ice skating on a frozen lake; she'd had her face painted with henna, slept on a beach in a hammock and visited most of Europe's impressive galleries and major museums. She'd learnt to accept challenges and welcome opportunities. At first she did so imagining that one day she'd tell Dean all about her adventures and prove some point or other to him, but as the years passed, she simply got into the habit of relishing opportunities and new experiences in their own right. She allowed the longing for Dean to fade, but she retained the lessons he'd taught her.

Falling in love with Andy, a non-identical twin with an unreliable income but a great sense of humour, was one such opportunity, and becoming a mother was her most profound and significant experience. Jo loved being a mother and a wife as much as she'd always hoped she would, and she loved the fact that her work was flexible enough to allow her to maintain a career too. Last year she'd planted a cherry tree in her small but well-kept garden, she regularly peeled apples and maintained one continuous strip of peel, she'd visited the Ice Hotel and she'd eaten macaroons at Ladurée in Paris, even though Dean had never allowed that to go on her official list.

Jo owed Dean a great deal. They had not managed to be together for ever, but he was always with her. As she made this mental tally, she prepared herself to hear about his no doubt glittering life. She wondered whether his wife would be a blonde or a brunette.

'So how is he?'

'He's dead, Jo.' Zoe reached out and squeezed her new friend's arm. 'Are you . . .' She paused. 'Do you happen to be Jo Russell?'

Jo could not speak. The world had ground to a slow, painful halt, no longer able to orbit without him. She had stopped breathing, unable to find oxygen in the air now she knew he was no longer doing so. Her heart pounded against her ribs and the beat ricocheted through her entire body. She could feel it thumping behind her eyes, in her ears, in her nostrils. Deep, deep low between her legs, where she'd always felt him and always would. She could taste metal in her mouth. She could not focus.

She'd heard Zoe's words, she'd understood them, but they could not be. They were so very, very wrong. Dean was the most alive person she had ever known. He'd taught her to live. It was impossible that he was dead. He was immortal. Zoe's words just didn't make sense. They circled Jo like flies but she couldn't bat them away, nor could she catch them to try to order them and understand them. They ducked and dodged the part of her brain that should be able to process them, yet at the same moment she knew they were permanently tattooed on to her heart.

'Do you happen to be Jo Russell?' Zoe asked again.

Jo nodded. 'Yes. Well, I was. Jo Doyle now. Married name. I changed, not for work but for everything . . .' She trailed off. She didn't know how her mouth was managing to relay these ordinary facts. How could ordinary facts be, when he no longer was?

'Oh Jo, he was coming to you. He crashed his car. He swerved to miss a kid who was chasing a football into the road . . .'

Zoe broke off. Although she had told this story hundreds of times, she still found it unbearable. Jo wished she'd stop altogether. She didn't want to hear it. Why was she in this park today of all days? Why were they both on this bench? If Zoe had picked a different park, then Jo would not know this awfulness. If Zoe had even sat further away, or if little Dean had not swung so high and she hadn't had to call out his name, then they'd never have started to chat. Jo didn't want to hear; hard as it was for Zoe to say, she had the feeling that it would be much more bloody to listen to. Jo wanted to shush Zoe, put her finger over her ears or, more desperately, gag Zoe. Jo swayed. She was sitting down, so she had nowhere to fall, and yet she felt she was slipping. Down, down, down.

Zoe's lips moved. Jo studied them, but she didn't know that Zoe was asking her if she was all right. Whether she'd like some water. Zoe scrabbled around in her bag for a second time that afternoon and produced a plastic bottle of mineral water. Jo took it from her but couldn't remember how to open bottles. How to drink. The bottle rolled off her lap and on to the dusty ground. Zoe's eyes oozed concern.

'He ended up with the car wrapped around a lamp post. He'd

421

sat in traffic for ages, apparently. Taken some back streets. He was going a little fast; wasn't he always? They told me it was instantaneous.' Zoe sighed and looked doubtful. Jo wondered how many nights this sister must have agonised over that detail. Was it fast, or did he suffer? Please God, not that.

Jo's head imploded. She felt it deflate and then fall down her neck, causing a severe pain in her spine. It was right that she should implode, dissolve, disappear altogether, because he had. Even though she and Dean had not spoken for years, she had always lived bigger because she'd thought he was somewhere on the planet, sharing the sky and the sun and the moon with her. Now she was in danger of splintering, cracking, vanishing.

'I'm so sorry, Jo. We didn't know where to find you.' Zoe's voice was gentle and even. Jo hated her voice because of the things it was revealing, but she also loved it because Dean had listened to it over and over again. By being next to Zoe, she felt somehow closer to Dean, even though this was their final goodbye. 'We called all the contacts in his phone, but it took a few days, and by the time we called you, your number was out of use.'

'It was a company phone.' Jo remembered this detail because when she'd reluctantly handed back the corporate phone to *Loving Bride!* she'd been very aware that they might lose touch. She thought that was the worst thing that could happen. She hadn't known the worst thing had already happened. 'He had the addresses of my family members written on a pad in his kitchen,' pointed out Jo pitifully. This was a fact she'd tortured and comforted herself with, in equal measures, for months after his silence.

'I didn't clean out his apartment, I couldn't face it. Some of his friends did it for me. They probably thought—'

Jo jumped in, understanding perfectly. 'That I was one of a number of women who wanted him to stay in touch, one of a number of women who he had no intention of staying in touch with. Insignificant flings.'

'Except you weren't that.' Zoe squeezed Jo's hand. Jo looked at her hopefully.

'I wasn't?'

'No.'

'What was I?' She thought she knew. She'd always tried to believe it, but she needed to hear it.

'We talked about you once. I knew immediately that you were different for him. You eased the anger in his soul. You were the woman who taught him to trust and to forgive. You taught him that he deserved love and that he'd get it.' Zoe put her arm around the shoulders of the woman swollen with pregnancy, and Jo reciprocated by slipping her arm around Zoe's waist. 'You, Jo, were the love of his life.'

Shhh . . .

We immediately fell in love with this very special book, and
we hope you have too.

We think the ending deserves to stay just as memorable for
everyone who reads it after you, so we'd like to invite you to
join us in keeping it a secret.

We know you'll want to talk about it, and we'd love you to!
But just remember not to reveal any spoilers.

Welcome to the secret . . .

With our thanks,

Headline x

#KeepTheSecret

ACKNOWLEDGEMENTS

A huge thank you goes to my fantastic, supportive, generous editor, Jane Morpeth. I'm grateful to the entire team at Headline; you are – without exception – impressive, dedicated and, well, just lovely! Sorry I made you all cry when reading this one. Special thank yous are due to the hardcore team: the fabulous Georgina Moore, Vicky Palmer, Barbara Ronan and Kate Byrne who all work so tirelessly on my behalf. I also owe a huge thank you to the marvellous Jamie Hodder-Williams.

Thank you, Jonny Geller, for another year of immense brilliance. That says it all really. This thank you extends to all at Curtis Brown for your amazing promotion of my work, home and abroad.

Once again I'd like to thank my readers; I hope I always thrill and entertain you. Thank you to my family and friends, my fellow authors, book sellers, book festival organisers, reviewers, magazine editors, TV producers and presenters, The Reading Agency and librarians who continue to generously support me and my work.

Thank you, Jimmy and Conrad – it's still all about the two of you.

THE STATE WE'RE IN

BONUS MATERIAL

AN INTERVIEW WITH ADELE PARKS

Jo and Dean's relationship makes for an unforgettable and thoroughly emotionally involving love story – what elements do you think are essential for a great love story?

A truly fabulous hero is paramount. I hope all my readers fall a little bit in love with Dean. I certainly did. However, a sympathetic heroine is also vital. They have to be evenly matched, the reader has to want them to get together and to believe they'd be good for each other and deserve one another. A great love story demands honesty and difficulties.

Were you inspired by anything specific to write The State We're In?

I'm increasingly obsessed with how personal histories and childhood experiences shape individuals. I wanted to write about how important our parents and backgrounds are in creating who we become, and what a responsibility that is. Whether we wish to imitate our parents and accept their morals and philosophies or whether we wholeheartedly reject them, they are still the foundation. I think that was my starting point. I also wanted to write a great big fat, proper love story. Do you know, I never have? People assume that commercial women's fiction is only ever about boy meets girl but I've never written a novel about a single man meeting a single woman.

The book very effectively alternates between first- and third-person narration. Was it a conscious decision to write only Jo's part of the story from her point of view, or did this just feel most natural to you?

I think on some levels Jo is quite a tricky character to sympathise with, at least initially, unless you happen to relate to her predicament. She can seem a little bit too idealistic and anyone who has had a tougher upbringing than hers might want to shake her! So, I deliberately allowed her to narrate in the first person to give her the best chance of presenting her story sympathetically. I used the first person for Eddie for the same reason.

Which character did you most enjoy creating?

Possibly Eddie. I always enjoy writing a baddie – always have, always will. I'm generally quite a 'good girl' so writing less sympathetic characters is a fun way to investigate my darker side.

Jo and Dean are complete opposites in so many ways. Do you believe in the concept of 'opposites attract' in relationships?

I don't have many rules about relationships; I've seen enough of the world to know you can never stop being surprised. In some cases, opposites really *do* attract. In others, people are searching for a mirror image of themselves. I have enough in common with my husband to make sure we can agree on the big stuff but we're different enough for us to both continually find excitement and challenges. I'd hate to prescribe.

You absolutely make us want to visit Chicago from the brilliant descriptions of the city. Is Chicago a place you know? Why did you decide to set part of the novel there?

I do know Chicago quite well and I love it! Before I became a novelist I worked for Accenture, a management consultancy. I wasn't a consultant, I worked in the marketing department. Accenture's headquarters, and my boss, were based in Chicago and I was lucky enough to travel there a number of times. However, like most work trips, I saw most of the city from the taxi, hotel and office window. It was such a joy exploring the city in a more leisurely manner for the novel.

What was your favourite scene to write in The State We're In*? And which was your least favourite?*

I really enjoyed writing *The State We're In*. I loved my characters and, because I placed upon myself a time constraint (in so much as the action takes place over a few days), I was constantly challenged and energised by the plot. I always love writing the scenes where there are big emotional dialogue pieces, so the one where Dean and Jo are in the Lurie Garden, and he tells her about his dreadful childhood, is perhaps my favourite. My least favourite scenes to write are always the set-up ones because I know what's going to happen further into the story; I always want to bounce ahead to the action! However, I know it's vitally important to share with my readers details such as environment, history, family tensions and dilemmas. In this case, writing the scenes where Jo gets dumped and then sacked in twenty-four hours were my least favourite. I kept promising her things were going to get better! Then worse, then better . . .

You've often said that you carefully plan when it comes to plotting your books, so did you know from the outset that this book was going to come to a tragic conclusion? Did you ever consider changing your mind about it?

I absolutely knew from writing the first sentence how this story was to end. I wanted it to have shades of all the great epic love stories that we are so familiar with. Classically, in love stories, the lovers are 'star-crossed' and ill-fated; think of Romeo and Juliet, Anna Karenina, Tess of the d'Urbervilles. It couldn't have ended any other way and retained its power and message.

Despite what happens, do you feel that The State We're In *has, in fact, a happy ending?*

No, not a happy ending. The loss and suffering endured means that a traditional 'happy ending' is impossible. However, it's an ending that suggests contentment, growth and possibility. I think it's reflective of some of the harder parts of real life.

READING GROUP QUESTIONS FOR
THE STATE WE'RE IN

- The novel tells the story from several points of view. Which did you enjoy the most? Did the first person narration from Jo's point of view make you feel closer to her than the other characters?

- The novel's main love story hinges on one chance meeting. What role do coincidence and/or fate play in the story?

- Jo and Dean arguably bring out the best in one another. Do you agree? Did your reaction towards each of them change once they'd met?

- Jo and Dean don't immediately realise that they are attracted to one another. How does their relationship differ from other, more traditional love stories? Would you say that their story is a more realistic and less romanticised depiction of falling in love?

- What was your reaction to Eddie? He could be judged the villain of the story but it is difficult not to feel for him in his suffering. Did this make you feel more sympathetic towards him and forgiving of his past actions?

- The theme of being alone is a powerful one in *The State We're In*, as demonstrated by Jo's inner feelings of weary loneliness concealed beneath her outward show of optimism that she'll find 'the one'. How susceptible do you think the characters are to society's expectations?

- In *The State We're In* the people Jo and Dean have become has been influenced by their upbringing. How have they been shaped by their parents' choices?

- There is a dramatic twist to the end of *The State We're In*. What emotional impact did this have on you? Were you expecting it?

- Are Jo and Dean soul mates? Or is their relationship a result of fortuitous timing? Do you think they would have had a happy ever after?

- Would you agree that the novel ends on a note of positivity and happiness for Jo?

Have you read all of Adele's fabulously addictive novels?

WHATEVER IT TAKES

How far would you go for the people you love? For Londoner Eloise Hamilton, there can be no greater sacrifice than uprooting to Dartmouth, leaving *her* perfect world so that her husband Mark can live *his*. Good marriages need compromises, don't they? But when a life-changing family secret emerges, Eloise suddenly finds her world imploding as she struggles to hold everything together for the people she loves. Someone is bound to be overlooked, and the damage might be irreparable . . . What if love's not enough?

ABOUT LAST NIGHT

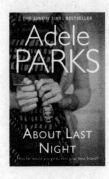

There is nothing best friends Steph and Pip wouldn't do for one another. That is, until Steph begs Pip to lie to the police as she's desperately trying to conceal not one but two scandalous secrets to protect her family. Her perfect life will be torn apart unless Pip agrees to this lie. But lying will jeopardise everything Pip's recently achieved after years of struggle. It's a big ask. How far would you go to save your best friend?

MEN I'VE LOVED BEFORE

Nat doesn't want babies; she accepts this is unusual but not unnatural. She has her reasons; deeply private and personal which she doesn't feel able to share. Luckily her husband Neil has always been in complete agreement, but when he begins to show signs of changing his mind, Nat is faced with a terrible dilemma. She begins to question if the man she has married is really the man she's meant to be with . . .

LOVE LIES

It's a girl's ultimate fantasy – being swept away by Prince Charming and living a life of luxury, wealth and celebrity. But after a whirlwind romance with pop star Scottie Taylor, modern-day Cinderella Fern must ask herself if love is telling the truth. Can she find her Happily Ever After in a world where there isn't much room for fairy tales?

TELL ME SOMETHING

When Elizabeth and her Italian husband Roberto decide to leave London for romantic Italy, Elizabeth hopes the change in lifestyle might help her boost her chances of conceiving their longed for child. Except it's impossible to relax with a mother-in-law bent on destroying her marriage, and Roberto's beautiful, significant ex living next door. Is Elizabeth's ferocious hunger for a baby enough to hold a marriage together or is it ripping it apart? And what about the gorgeous American stranger who's suddenly walked into her life?

YOUNG WIVES' TALES

Lucy stole her friend Rose's 'happily ever after' because she wanted Rose's husband – and Lucy always gets what she wants. Big mistake. Rose was the ideal wife and is the ideal mother; Lucy was the perfect mistress. Now neither can find domestic bliss playing each other's roles. They need more than blind belief to negotiate their way through modern life. And there are more twists in the tale to come . . .

JAMILA GAVIN

From out of the Shadows

EGMONT

'Gone to Earth' is dedicated to my dear friend, Ilsa,

who showed me a magical place.

First published in Great Britain 2002
by Egmont Books Limited
239 Kensington High Street, London W8 6SA

Text copyright © Jamila Gavin 2002
Cover illustration copyright © Kim McGlivary 2002

The author and illustrator have been asserted their moral rights

ISBN 1 4052 0280 7

10 9 8 7 6 5 4 3 2 1

A CIP catalogue record for this title is available from the British Library

Typeset by Avon DataSet Ltd, Bidford on Avon, Warwickshire
Printed and bound in Great Britain by Cox & Wyman Ltd, Reading, Berkshire

Contents

The Desert Singer   1

Forbidden Clothes   25

Just Friends   49

Mona   69

Gone to Earth   91

The Paradise Carpet   121

The Demon Drummer   133

The Bridegroom   169

The Desert Singer

'I met an angel the other day.'

The traveller paused. Faces surrounded him, hollowed out by the flickering firelight. Eyes, like dark mirrors stitched into pale, plastic-coated skins, reflected him over and over.

People didn't talk about angels these days – nor about God. They only wanted to talk about their fears. Whenever travellers happened by their city, they wanted to know how it fared in the Desert World. Were their any signs of regeneration? Was anything growing? How long were other groups surviving? That's what they had come to hear – outside the city walls, in the no-man's land, where strangers were allowed to camp for

3

a while. Before the evening was over, they would ask the dreaded question.

The traveller took up his stringed instrument and began to sing:

> *I met an angel the other day.*
> *He was made of*
> *Water and blood and bone*
> *And skin and sinew and muscle*
> *And iron and tin and zinc*
> *And air and earth and fire*
> *And liquid gold.*
>
> *I met an angel the other day*
> *Whose feet were on the ground.*
> *I was flying*
> *Flying*
> *Flying.*

His voice broke into falsetto, soaring like a hunting bird, making the back of the neck prickle. Then it

dropped down to the depths, gravely low, as if the notes were formed in the hollows of his stomach. His long fingers plucked and fingered the thin strings. When his voice died away, he let the sounds of his instrument wander on awhile, resonating, before expiring into a last chord.

Silence; a held breath; then a gasp, and a sob broke from somewhere. His song reminded them of Orph.

At last, someone asked the inevitable question. 'Never mind angels, did you come across any . . .?'

Above the outline of the canyons, where a desert sky stretched like silk from one horizon to another, *Perdita* passed in orbit as it had done every evening for the past sixty years, barely distinguishable from the evening star which glimmered in the darkening sky.

'They're coming nearer,' said Martin, our father. 'The troubadour saw them in the valley beyond the canyon. If they were determined enough, they could be here by midday tomorrow.'

I looked at our mother, Lara. Her face was ashen

and she pressed her hands across her abdomen as if in pain. Then she rushed from the room and I heard her retching outside.

The 'they' were the Arifi people. We feared them because they wandered the desert, which most of the world had now become; because their skins had yellowed and dried with disease, and ultra violet rays, and lack of vitamins; because they swirled across the sands like the Arifi dust storms of North Africa, sucking up anything in its path. They had no faith in a future, but lived for the day. Dispossessed from a once industrial world, they advanced, stripping everything and leaving nothing behind them.

This is what we had been brought up to believe. I didn't know anyone who had seen an Arifi and sometimes I was curious and wondered about them.

Although our enclave was a secret, it was inevitable, that one day the Arifi would hear about us and track us down – there were always people who stumbled upon us from time to time, like this troubadour. Then we would allow them their legislated twenty-one days of

hospitality outside the city walls, and send them on their way again. We knew, inevitably, word would get out. We lived in dread. And then came this solitary troubadour with his appalling news.

Lara re-appeared. She had bathed and was wearing a white home-spun cotton dress. She stood next to our father, Martin.

Lara and Martin are not our real parents. Hardly anyone over thirteen has birth parents alive. Foster parents are allocated – themselves barely older than the orphans. We are a society of children. Twenty's the average age, thirty is old. Something will get you. I've already got skin cancer – despite my plastic coating. We all get it sooner or later. And if cancer doesn't get you, asthma does, or brain disease, or the immune system collapses.

'Navarth has called a meeting at the Assembly Hall,' Martin told us. 'Everyone over the age of eight can attend.'

'Oh good!' cried my little brother Rhett. 'That means I can go.'

Martin made me change into a white linen tunic like Lara, though Rhett stayed as he was in green.

'Why?' I asked. 'I thought we only wore white tunics for death.'

'It's just ceremonial,' said Martin, then he and Lara wouldn't answer any more questions. They just urged us to hurry and held each other's hands as if for support.

We joined a throng of citizens making their way to the Assembly Hall. Many wore white tunics. I wanted to ask questions, but no one was talking. There was just the footfall of hundreds of people. The silence frightened me.

We reached the Assembly Hall, a strange circular structure created out of a multiplicity of re-cycled and regurgitated materials – paper, wood, metal, wool, hair, glass and stone – all moulded and pressed and shaped and carved and sculpted. It was like a gigantic wasp's nest.

We entered, and found ourselves in a complex structure of chambers and passages, dark and sticky like resin, as if we walked through the labyrinth of a mind.

We plunged into the brightness of the main chamber, vast and circular, rising from earth to sky. Tiers of steps for the citizens to sit, rippled upwards towards the glass domed roof. As in the centre of an eye, sat Navarth on a great carved chair – the Oracle Chair. I had heard of it. It must have been right there that Orph, our founder, had sung.

Navarth looked alone and sad. Something was wrong. Tremors of panic rippled round; the word 'Arifi' whispered fearfully.

A debate began – fitfully – barely under control. Navarth struggled for calm and sanity during the discussion.

Speaker after speaker gave their opinions. Emotions overflowed; some ranted with anger and urged us to face the enemy and fight. Others wrung their hands in defeat and said we should end our existence with dignity in the Chamber of Hades. The Arifi outnumber us by thousands – millions; they were sure to get us in the end.

'We should have killed all travellers,' a voice

declared. 'We shouldn't have listened to those softy liberals. Look where it's got us!' There was a roar of agreement.

'That could be one of them out there now. That troubadour. How do we know he's not a spy?'

There was a moan of support and people looked at each other as if to reinforce their anxiety.

'We should have made a deal with them up there!' Another citizen prodded the air above his head.

Every face tilted up and gazed through the glass dome to the evening sky beyond. In a few minutes, *Perdita* would rise, just a little ahead of the moon and glow as a constant reminder of the safety of a privileged few.

Just days before the Great Devastation, a group of technocrats, politicians and wealthy business tycoons from the old industrial world, had vacated the planet. They had known for at least nine decades that this would happen, and had secretly planned their escape. The so-called Space Programme which began in the 1950s and 60s, was all part of a project to build a huge

artificial planet which could sustain up to a hundred thousand specially picked people. It was never space exploration for its own sake, but a plan which anticipated the end of the world. As the millennium drew to a close, what with pollution and ozone depletion, it became clear that there would be some kind of catastrophe, which could happen at any time and destroy all life.

So a secret agenda had been drawn up to prepare *Perdita*. It would be launched into space to orbit the sun, until it was required as a safe haven for those who could negotiate or buy themselves a place on it.

It was said the experts knew to the very day when the catastrophe would come. A number of shuttle space craft bearing the chosen few, secretly took off from several corners of the earth and rendezvoused with *Perdita*.

It was thirty years before *Perdita* made contact with us. Things weren't working out, despite all their fancy technology. Their population was falling. They had watched our progress from space and now wanted us

to join forces. They suggested a fixed number of us be allocated every decade and shuttled to *Perdita*.

Orph had rejected them contemptuously. He refused to have anything to do with those who had gone there. He felt that the powerful and wealthy had put all those skills and resources into saving their own skins, instead of ensuring the safety of Earth.

No one argued with him. At least, not openly. Orph was a legend – like Moses. His name was synonymous with law, scholarship and purpose. He brought us all up to believe that we must somehow pass on some semblance of what human beings could be – the best of them, not the worst.

Orph said we should trust nature; that if we respected nature enough, it would see us through. Otherwise, he said, we would always be a nation of exiles. We stopped talking about Gods and angels and things like that. It had caused too much trouble, although some thought Orph was a kind of angel. He was a part of our mythology and history.

We were taught how Orph turned up at our camp

when our ancestors were on the brink of extinction. A thin child, not more than seven or eight, he had lost the power of speech. He was more wild animal than human, who had hung about the outer edges of our settlement with a pack of dogs, scavenging alongside them for scraps and leftovers. His only possession was a mouth organ, which he played like a magician. With it, he seemed to control beasts and humans alike. He was taken in out of pity; but in time, in his dumb way, with signs, gestures and his mouth organ, he began to impart a clarity of vision and a depth of wisdom which made everyone take heed of him. An old teacher called him Orpheus, after some ancient Greek God who was a musician.

One day, Orph spoke. He stood on a rock in the middle of a barren, waterless place. My people had come there after a dreadful trek, during which scores had perished and the rest had given up hope and were waiting to die. 'I know where to go,' he said. He began to sing – a strange, wordless, incredible song.

I wish I'd been there. They said his voice was like

the wind in a cave, or a spirit locked in a metal bowl or a ghost howling in the desert. It could be a low, liquid, cavernous sound, gushing fitfully out of his throat, or like the cry of an eagle soaring high on currents of air. It could be like a floodgate burst open as he broke into a torrent of speech and song.

The people fell to their knees as if he were a god. He sang for four hours. Then without warning, the rod jumped in his hands and tugged him from the rock. It tugged so hard, that he had to run. The tribe ran after him. Even those who were sick and dying, somehow struggled after him. He ran for an . hour. Then abruptly, the stick became inanimate. Orph had found an underground river. They must follow it to its source, and there they could build a new Athens.

They made him a chair – the one Navarth was now seated on. From then on, anyone who sat in the chair would be listened to.

'It is my belief that we should no longer fear the Arifi,' Navarth's voice was steady as she addressed the

assembly. 'We have our planet, Earth. It can sustain us all. If we do the right thing, more and more of it will recover. Look at our success. Look how we have extended the fertility of the land. We've replanted forests and meadows and cleaned up rivers. We should consider making links with the Arifi and help them to help themselves. We can't hold them back forever. Sooner or later, they will come. *Perdita* is an illusion. Orph was right to reject it. Our future is here. We should stop being so afraid of outsiders.' Then she added, 'Let us face the Arifi and negotiate.'

Even Orph had never made such a suggestion.

The intake of breath was like the hissing of a serpent. Blasphemy. We have never made deals with any outsiders let alone the Arifi. So no one was surprised when a citizen coldly ignored Navarth and tabled a motion. 'I propose we contact *Perdita* and ask for refugee status.'

Navarth sat pale and motionless as another voice cried, 'I second that!'

'Hear, hear!' The chamber exploded excitedly.

'They'll never take us all,' warned someone, and there was a groan.

Navarth spoke with composure. 'If that is your democratic wish, then you will have to draw lots. The Law Lords will select the healthy ones for the lottery. *Perdita* will only allow on board those who are disease free. The rest can operate the Option if they wish – or stay with me in the city and face the Arifi.'

The groans faded to silence. The Option was to enter Hades, the great marble underground suicide chamber. It had been built for those whose terminal illnesses made life unbearable. But more and more talked of the Option as an alternative to being overrun by the Arifi.

Suddenly I was gripped by panic. So that was why! That was why Martin and Lara had made me put on a white tunic? I knew – I knew it was the garment of death.

Martin and Lara both had terminal illnesses – with not much more than a year or two to live. It was natural that they should opt for Hades. I turned to them terror-stricken. 'Am I to die too?'

'You have cancer. Hades is the best choice for you.'

'But what about Rhett?' I cried. 'He can't be separated from me! He'll need me!'

'Rhett is young,' said Martin, 'and as yet totally free from disease. He is sure to be selected for *Perdita* if he wins in the lottery.

'But I don't feel ready to die,' I cried and looked around to see if others felt like me.

'Better to die than fall into the hands of the Arifi,' came the response of those in white tunics.

Already people were opting for the lottery or Hades. I looked at Navarth. No one was coming to her. No one was prepared to stay.

Martin and Lara embraced Rhett and said they had loved him dearly. Then they tried to make me say goodbye to him, but I refused. 'This feels wrong!' I cried. 'I'm not ready to die – and I'm not ready to leave Rhett. We'll stay with Navarth.'

'Would you deny Rhett the chance to live?' asked Martin softly. I felt his hand on my shoulder. His fingers tightened, and I knew that any moment now, he would

hold me by force. Lara, on the other side, took my hand.

'Rhett!' I cried, shaking myself free and kneeling down to hug my brother. 'Rhett. Goodbye. I love you, little brother. I hope they choose you for *Perdita*,' then suddenly I whirled him round, thrust him into my 'parents' and fled.

I thought I would never get out of the labyrinth. I twisted and turned until, in despair, I flung myself bodily against a wall. It was as thin as a honeycomb. I tumbled into the open air. I was free. I ran and ran, to get as far away as possible from that assembly, away from Martin and Lara and the choices that they wanted us to make. Away from my little brother. 'Goodbye Rhett! I love you!' I screamed without looking back.

I didn't go home. I knew I had no home. No house, no street, no place anywhere in our enclave. I no longer belonged here. Our Athens was doomed. There was only exile.

Suddenly, all I wanted was the desert itself, to be out there – out, out, out in the world – whatever it cost me, whatever my fate. I wanted to be like the birds, like

the hawk, soaring. I wanted freedom – if only for a brief moment.

'Wait for me! Wait for me!'

Rhett. I heard him wailing behind me. I stopped. He panted up the slope, then his hot sweaty hand thrust into mine.

'Where are you going? Why did you leave me?'

I looked down at him. The only living thing on this planet who shared my blood and genes and ancestry. 'Oh Rhett!' I threw my arms round him and held him tightly.

Perdita was gleaming like a white moon above the razor edges of the valley skyline.

'Look! There's *Perdita*. You could enter the lottery and have a chance of winning a place up there. You'd be safe. Safe from the Arifi and safe from the horrible diseases we all get here. You're healthy at the moment. No cancer, no allergies, nothing. Go in for the lottery, Rhett. Save yourself.'

I was crying as I spoke. Crying for the loneliness of the world, the loneliness of living with the unknown, the loneliness of our lost planet. Yet I wasn't without hope. I

wasn't ready to die. I couldn't just give up. I wanted to possess every single last minute that was mine – good or bad, painful or calm. Death was the absolute and final end of everything. It was crazy to rush towards it so long as there was one scrap of air left to breathe.

A piercing note caused a bird to rise flapping fiercely, its wings catching the last rays of a dying sun. It wheeled away, its cry echoing discordantly against a human voice which suddenly vibrated around us.

'I met an angel the other day.'

The troubadour was sitting just a few yards away, holding a stringed instrument close to his body as though it were another limb. I stared at his face; his skin, like the skin of a drum, stretched, taut from neck to shoulder and elbow to wrist and waist to thigh and legs to ankles. His frame was rounded and shaped and moulded as if he had been cast out of sand.

The song ended. We stared into his clear desert eyes.

Rhett left my side and ran to him as naturally as a lamb to its shepherd.

'You live out there?' I called to the troubadour,

waving my hand beyond the plateau to the barren wastes below.

'Yes.'

'And you're going there now, where there might be the Arifi?'

Even as I spoke I heard the whistle of the desert wind, and felt grains of sand scalding my cheeks.

'I am an Arifi.'

Rhett didn't move. Neither did I.

The troubadour rose and held the bow of his instrument before him.

'Are you a dowser?' It was Rhett who spoke first. 'Like Orph?'

'I only go where my bow leads me.' The troubadour held his bow in front of him. It sprang and swivelled in his hands, and seemed to turn him towards a track barely wide enough for a goat.

'Was Orph an Arifi?' I asked.

The troubadour shrugged. 'He came from the desert as you did once. I just sing, that's all, and I follow my bow.' He patted Rhett on the head then set off down the

track which twisted away between high rocks and boulders at the head of the canyon. Below, the darkness gathered. He raised his hand – to say goodbye? Or was it as a guide, to wave us on? He began to sing. I could hear his voice echoing through the caves. Now I knew how Orph must have sounded.

The shadows enveloped him. Rhett returned silently to my side.

'I'm going where he's going,' I said, without looking at my brother.

'Good,' he said simply. 'You lead. I'll follow.'

As I set off, I heard Rhett skipping behind me. He was humming in harmony with the troubadour's song. After a while, his hum burst through his open mouth into a shrill boy's treble.

> *And when he sang, his voice*
> *Like pinprick stars*
> *Pierced the heaven of my heart.*
> *And when he sang, notes*
> *Hollow and dark*

The Desert Singer

From subterranean depths
Shuddered, when he sang.

I met an angel the other day
Whose feet were on the ground.
I was flying
Flying
Flying.

Forbidden Clothes

'They are taking her away from us.'

Mrs Khan articulated her words in a flat, monotone voice but, as she spoke, she leaned forward and stared intensely into the eyes of her volunteer English teacher, Margot Henderson.

Margot stared back, momentarily shocked out of her boredom. This was the first English sentence Mrs Khan had put together herself after nearly six weeks of lessons.

'What do you mean?' asked Margot.

Still leaning forward, Mrs Khan spoke again. She repeated the same sentence, hammering it out with staccato precision.

'They are taking her away from us.'

'Who is taking who away from you?' asked Margot, looking round.

Then she met the large, dark eyes of the fifteen-year-old girl in the school photograph. It sat alone on the mantelpiece, testifying to the reverence and devotion accorded to an only child.

She wasn't beautiful. Her face had been left to fend for itself, framed only by a severe headscarf which swept her hair away out of sight. Her nose was too long and narrow, her cheekbones too angular, her mouth too broad. Yet there was something compelling about the way she looked almost defiantly into the camera, as if she was trying to say, 'Yes, this is me. There's more to me than meets the eye.'

'Nasreen.' Mrs Khan whispered her daughter's name.

'Ah, yes! Nasreen!' repeated Margot, brightly. 'How is she getting on at school?' Margot asked her question loudly and slowly as if the woman were deaf.

Mrs Khan opened her mouth and drew in her breath sharply as she struggled to find the words.

'She . . . she . . . not . . . fine. Fine . . .' She shrugged helplessly and slumped back in her seat, drawing her veil across her face.

Margot felt the irritation rising up in her. Mrs Khan was not her favourite pupil. She was a slow learner, and she resented the sense of dumb depression which seemed to envelop the woman, slowing down her movements and imprinting an expression of wooden despair on her face.

'Don't just say "fine", Mrs Khan. Put it in a sentence,' urged Margot with exaggerated patience. 'Nasreen is fine.'

'No!' exclaimed Mrs Khan sharply. 'Nasreen is . . . no . . . fine . . .' she struggled desperately.

'You mean, Nasreen is *not* fine,' corrected Margot.

'Nasreen is *not* fine,' repeated Mrs Khan obediently.

'Is something wrong at school?' asked Margot. She glanced at her watch and noted with relief that their time was up.

Mrs Khan saw the movement. She stood up, twisting the ends of her veil in her fingers.

'Yes, it is time for me to go,' said Margot, thankfully. She was really not in the mood for trying to extricate sufficient English out of Mrs Khan to find out what was bothering her.

'If you have a problem with Nasreen, the best thing to do is talk to the school,' said Margot. 'Perhaps your husband can. He speaks good English, doesn't he?' Then, giving her a kindly pat on the arm, she gathered up her text book.

'Try and work through the exercises we have covered today, OK? and I'll see you next week.' Then she made her own way to the front door and opened it.

'Goodbye, Mrs Khan.'

Mrs Khan didn't reply, but stood in the semi-darkness at the rear of the hall. She looked as if she were being swallowed up within her satin tunic and pyjamas, as she clutched the veil around herself.

'By-ee!' repeated Margot, giving a cheery wave, and shut the front door behind her.

'Nasreen! Nasreen! Come on, we'll miss the bus!'

Louise Dibben danced impatiently at her friend's elbow, as she stood in front of the long mirror, fluffing out her hair and squirting clouds of hair lacquer into it.

'How do I look?' asked Nasreen, twisting her head to examine her profile.

'You look great, really great! Now come on. If we miss the bus it will all be for nothing.'

'OK, I'm coming.' She gave a last critical glance at herself. The transformation was pretty good. From her demure, sexless school uniform with headscarf and slacks for modesty, she had squeezed herself into a tight elasticated pair of jeans for which she had secretly saved up for weeks to buy. They flattered her figure, she thought, emphasising her long legs and narrow waist.

'Does my bum look too big?' she asked, turning sideways.

'You look great, I tell you,' insisted Louise, 'and I like your top an' all,' she added. 'You got better boobs than me, lucky thing. But hurry up.'

'We're all right for time,' said Nasreen, glancing at

her watch. 'Stop panicking! We've got five minutes yet. I've got to do me eyes.'

Louise sighed and sat on her bed. 'God! If your mum and dad could see you now they'd have a blooming fit.'

'My dad would kill me,' murmured Nasreen, as she brushed the mascara on to her eyelashes.

Nasreen had taken to coming back to Louise's house most days after school. Gradually she had built up a secret wardrobe of leggies and low-cut tops, of miniskirts and T-shirts, sometimes plain and sometimes with slogans blazoned across her chest.

'My forbidden clothes,' she would laugh. She felt like Cinderella transforming herself to go out and have a ball, then rushing back to change into her uniform, headscarf and dull slacks, so that when she went back home she would once more be the demure, innocent little girl her parents thought she was.

Nasreen still shuddered when she remembered the pain of those early days at Merton Close. She had

never been made to feel different before. But now all people seemed to see were her differences: her different coloured skin, her different clothes, her different voice and, most of all, her different religion. She was nothing but a Paki, until Louise decided to be her friend.

Louise was brash, Louise was loud, Louise was a leader. People listened to her. She seemed so grown-up. She was the first to perm her hair and wear tight, short skirts; she was the first to have a boyfriend and sit smoking in the bus shelter with him. She had opinions, and talked back to teachers, so Nasreen was astonished when, one day, Louise marched up to her with a maths book and said, 'Hey, Nasreen! You're good at maths. Help me with this.'

They began going to each other's houses, but Nasreen knew her mother didn't like Louise and thought she was a bad influence so, instead, she only went round to Louise's house.

Nasreen loved the Dibben household. It was so different from her own clean, silent, scrupulously tidy

home. Here it looked as if a tornado had struck it most of the time: always buried under a rubble of toys and washing, of babies' bottles and half-chewed rusks. Yet it was a good-natured chaos, and no one minded if she and Louise slumped across the sofa watching television and munching sandwiches.

'Wanna go with me to the disco?' Louise asked her one day.

'Oh, no! I couldn't!' Nasreen looked shocked at the prospect, then disappointed because she wished she could go. 'I'd never be allowed,' she said, sadly.

'Don't tell 'em then,' snapped Louise, bold as brass.

'Anyway, I've got no clothes,' added Nasreen. 'I couldn't go like this!'

'Borrow mine,' retorted Louise. Then she shrieked excitedly. 'Hey! Let me dress you up! Please, Nasreen! Just for fun!'

So that's how it all started.

'There! OK?' She turned round to show her friend her face with her painted eyelids, stiff, blackened lashes, the

hint of blusher on her cheeks and just the right shade of lipstick to tone in.

'Beautiful!' exclaimed Louise, generously. 'Now let's go!'

The two girls clattered downstairs.

An admiring whistle rang out from the kitchen. Louise's younger brother, Craig, gave a cheeky wave. 'Like your jeans, Nasreen! Sexeee!'

'Oh shut up!' squealed Nasreen, but she was pleased.

Sitting at the back of the bus, Nasreen and Louise admired each other and laughed at the world they had set out to conquer. In ten minutes they had alighted in the centre of town and made their way along to the precinct where they knew all their friends would be congregating.

'Carl's there,' Louise hissed at her friend.

'So?' exclaimed Nasreen, flushing.

'You know you want to get off with him, and he's just split up with Denise.'

'Has he?' cried Nasreen. 'Why didn't you tell me before? Oh God, how do I look?'

'I've told you. You look fabulous. If he doesn't fall for you, he's a blind dope. Oh good, there's Mark,' Louise squealed, and ran over to join her boyfriend.

The telephone rang. 'It's me . . .'

'Where are you?' wailed Mrs Khan. 'Why weren't you on the bus?'

'Mum, I went back to Louise's house. We're doing our homework together. She's miles better at geography than me, and she's helping me,' explained Nasreen, convincingly.

'But what about tea?' asked Mrs Khan. 'I've got yours all ready here.'

'Sorry, Mum,' said Nasreen. 'Louise's mum gave me some, so I'm fine. Must go. We've got tons to get done.'

'When will you be home?' asked Mrs Khan quickly, trying to hang on to her daughter's voice.

'Well . . .' Nasreen answered vaguely. 'I think we've got another hour or two's work, because after geography, I said I'd help Louise with her maths. I'm better at that than her. OK?'

Mrs Khan hesitated, trying desperately to assert her authority.

'Get back before your dad does, won't you?'

'Of course I will, Mum. Must go. Bye!' And the phone went dead.

'OK?' asked Carl as she came out of the phone booth.

'Yeh!' Nasreen smiled sweetly at him, and slipped her arm in his.

'Have we time to go to the Flamingo? Have a quick drink?' asked Carl. 'Louise and Mark have gone on ahead.'

'Of course!' cried Nasreen, happily. 'But I've got to be changed and on that eight o'clock bus home. Me dad gets in at nine, and I've got to make it before he does, or else there'll be hell to pay.'

Mrs Khan stood in the bay window. Although darkness had fallen, she hadn't put on the light, but had drawn aside the net curtains to gaze, invisibly, up and down the empty street outside.

A hard lump of anxiety pressed into her chest so

that it hurt to breathe. She was afraid, but then she realised she had always been afraid. Ever since Nasreen had moved up into secondary school, things had changed.

They used to walk together, side by side, friends; but then Nasreen took to going on ahead or dawdling behind her mother. Even the way she walked changed. Instead of the leisurely, shy walk, she now strode, long-legged, looking more and more like a western girl despite her headscarf and the slacks under her school uniform. On approaching the school gates she would suddenly see her friends and, tossing out the word 'goodbye' as if to no one in particular, she would disappear into the school, arms linked and immersed in the sound of gossip and laughter. She never looked back these days.

That was when the lump of misery took residence in Mrs Khan's heart.

'They are taking her away ... taking her away ...' She hissed the words out in English, as if someone would hear and understand her fears.

She felt a sudden surge of anger as she remembered her English teacher.

'They? Who's they?' Mrs Khan could hear the indifferent voice as Margot Henderson asked the question.

'They? Why the Dibbens of course!' Mrs Khan answered it now to the empty room, spotlessly clean, neat and devoid of any signs of human activity – just as Mr Khan liked to have it when he came home.

The Dibbens. Mrs Khan clasped her arms tightly around her body, straitjacketing herself, as if afraid if she did not she might scream at the world: 'I'm lonely! I'm lonely! And they're taking my child away from me.'

'Nasreen?' The sound of the front door sent her scurrying to the hall. Nasreen tossed her schoolbag inside, and kicked the front door closed.

'Hi, Mum!' she said indifferently, and did not look her in the eye. 'Sorry I'm late, we had tons of homework. I'm going to my room. I'm tired and I just want to flop!'

'Nasreen!' Mrs Khan reached out and touched her

daughter's cheek. She wanted to clasp her, reclaim her. 'Did you have supper?' she asked. 'I made your favourite pakoras. Come to the kitchen and have some.'

'No, Mum!' Nasreen refused impatiently. 'I'm not hungry. I had plenty to eat at Louise's. Just let me go to my room,' and she shook herself free from her mother's grasp and rushed upstairs.

Once in her room, she hastily removed the rest of her forbidden clothes. She carefully folded them into a carrier bag and tucked it right at the back of her wardrobe.

Then she sat in front of her mirror. Had her mother noticed remnants of make-up? She leaned forward to scrutinise herself and looked into her own eyes. They were still shining with excitement.

Carl had seen her home. Carefully, of course, because it wouldn't do for any of the neighbours to see her – especially anyone from her own community. They had hidden in a bus shelter while she took off her jeans and put back her school slacks under her uniform.

'What about the headscarf?' he asked, after she had shaken out her hair and re-plaited it. But she dropped

her head with embarrassment. 'Oh that doesn't matter,' she said.

Of course, it did, and when he said goodbye to her at the corner – he kissed her till she felt she would faint – and hurriedly walked away, she tied on her headscarf when he was out of sight, and went home slowly, giving time for her flushed cheeks to calm down.

Now, as she stared at her reflection, she felt guilty. She didn't like feeling guilty; it made her angry. She didn't want to think about the shock and disappointment her father would feel if he knew what she was doing; she didn't want to think of how she was hurting her mother. At the moment, it was her mother, above all, who made her angry. She was so pliable, so pathetically vulnerable; her whole life was devoted to serving. Serving her husband; serving her daughter. Nothing she did was for her own benefit. She allowed herself to be a victim.

'I won't be like that! I won't, I won't!' Nasreen swore to herself.

Suddenly, Nasreen heard the front door. She heard

her mother's puzzled footsteps hurry into the hall.

'Nasreen! Nasreen!' It was her father's voice, rough with anger.

'Nasreen's up in her room,' she heard her mother say nervously. 'You're back early. Is everything all right?'

He ignored her and called again. 'Nasreen! Get down here! I wish to speak to you.' Fiercely he switched on all the lights.

Nasreen slowly descended the stairs, pausing halfway down, her pale face looming over the bannister.

'Hi, Dad!' She tried to sound unconcerned.

'Get down here.' He prodded his finger into the air space before him.

She continued her descent, meeting her mother's puzzled eyes at the bottom. Then she faced her father.

'Here!' He prodded the air in front of him.

'Nasreen!' Mrs Khan touched her daughter's arm. She had never seen Mr Khan look so angry. Mrs Khan wanted to protect her. She clung to her arm, pulling her back.

'What is it, Rashid? What has she done? Please don't harm her!'

'Let go of her!' His voice was cold and determined. 'Nasreen has shamed me and her family and her community, and she must be made to realise what she has done.'

'How?' cried Mrs Khan. 'What has she done? Nasreen?' She turned pitifully to her daughter. 'What have you done?'

'She has been seen in the town without her veil and slacks, dressed like one of those loose English girls, wearing a tight miniskirt, high heels and made up like a prostitute. How dare you! How dare you do this to us.' He began to remove his leather belt.

'No, Rashid, no!' begged Mrs Khan. 'I'm sure Nasreen won't do this again, will you, Nasreen?'

'And it's not the first time.' Mr Khan's voice choked with emotion. 'I now hear that this has been going on for months. Everyone in the community knows about it. Everyone has been talking about it behind our backs. You have ridiculed me!'

'Nasreen!' She looked at her daughter for some sign of repentance. But to her amazement Nasreen stood

before her father, upright and unflinching as he raised his arm, moved round her, and brought the belt down across her back.

'Why are you doing this, Nasreen?' the head of her school pleaded with her.

'Why do you go on behaving in a way which upsets your mother and father and your whole community. All you get is a beating. Is it really worth it?'

Usually, Nasreen took her beatings and remonstrations sullenly, and without a word, but this time she looked up at her head teacher and said quietly, 'Sir, I'll be sixteen in two months' time. That's all the time I have left to be free. When I'm sixteen, they'll marry me off; I expect it'll be to some bloke from Pakistan who I've never met. I'm clever enough to go to university, aren't I? But I won't be allowed. I'll have to stay at home and have babies and be nothing but a good little housewife, sewing and ironing and having a meal ready in the evening. That's how it'll be when I'm sixteen. That's how it'll be for the rest of my life. Well,

sir, I've got two months left, and I don't care how often I get beaten, I'm going to go into town, and dress as I like, and smoke in shop doorways, and my dad'll have to kill me before he stops me having what freedom is left.'

'Did you ever find out what that Mrs Khan meant when she said, "They are taking her away from me"?' asked the colleague.

She and Margot Henderson had met again in the precinct coffee shop.

'Funny you should ask,' said Margot, putting down her coffee cup. 'After I last saw you, I got a message to say that Mrs Khan wanted to give up the lessons. Can't say I was disappointed. The last I heard was that the daughter, Nasreen, had run away and gone to live with her best friend.'

'What are you doing?' Louise woke and stared into the darkness. 'It's the middle of the night. Are you ill?'

She could just make out Nasreen, standing in the centre of the bedroom.

'Nasreen!' She sat up in bed and switched on her table lamp. 'What are you doing? Where are you going?'

Nasreen was fully dressed, but in her tunic, pyjamas and veil. By her side was a suitcase. She picked it up and moved towards the bedroom door.

'That's it for me now, Louise,' she said quietly. 'It's my birthday tomorrow.'

'Yeh! I know. Me and the gang, we've all got a smashing party organised for you,' cried Louise.

'Well, you'll have to have it without me,' said Nasreen. 'I'm going home. Don't try and stop me. Please –' She put out a resisting hand, as Louise flung her legs out of bed and made to hold her back.

'Just let me go. I know what I'm doing. I've had my fun, but it had to end. I made a pact with myself that when I'm sixteen I return to my community. It's where I really belong. Don't make it hard for me, Louise. Please. Thank you for everything you've done for me. Thank your parents, too. I'll make it up to you one day. Promise. Meantime, just let me go without any fuss.'

Then she slipped out of the door and was gone.

* * *

It wasn't quite dawn, yet Mrs Khan woke to see a rosy glow through the bedroom window. She had barely slept all night long, as she had barely slept since Nasreen left home. Now, with a dull curiosity, she slid out of bed without disturbing her sleeping husband, and went to the window.

'Rashid!' she called out uncontrollably.

He awoke instantly, alerted by the urgency in her voice. He went to her side and looked out of the window.

Nasreen had lit a bonfire. The flames shot upwards into the night sky. They could see her figure silhouetted against the firelight as from time to time she bent down and, taking a garment from the open suitcase, tossed it on to the fire. Sparks flew upwards, scattering like fireflies.

When she had emptied the suitcase, she stood transfixed for a while, staring into the embers, then, pulling her veil over her head and drawing it tightly round her shoulders, she turned towards the house.

'Nasreen! Nasreen!' whispered her mother. 'At last! You have come back to us!'

Just Friends

In the beginning, they were five. Five of them who started primary school together, moved up to the comprehensive together and turned into something of a gang. The word gang is probably too strong. It wasn't exclusive or menacing, they were just five friends growing up together and who, despite the changes, continued to like each other.

There was Emma, Clare, Ben, Nick and Tom. They were the core – although later, at the comprehensive, the circle often widened to include others. Each one at different times might hang out with other, newer friends. For a while, Emma saw no one but Jane; Clare found a mutual passion for riding with Rachel; and Ben

and Nick both began having scenes with girls. Ben fancied Kate and went out with her for absolutely ages, whereas Nick enjoyed getting the reputation for playing the field. He was particularly good-looking – and when he was fourteen, he shot up so tall, that even older girls didn't mind going out with him.

Only Tom made no friends outside the group. He was a quiet lad; fond of music and serious about his work. So he confined himself to seeing which ever of his old friends was freewheeling at the time – and there was usually one of them.

In fact, it was Tom who became the kind of father figure of the group. He was a listener; happy to sit, always a little apart, watching his friends as they struggled with the ways of the world, giving his opinion when asked for it. It was Tom to whom they naturally turned with confidences. Emma wept on his shoulder when she was dropped by Richard – the first boy to ask her out and who she thought she loved. Clare asked his advice about how to deal with her mother's new boyfriend. Even Ben and Nick turned to

Tom to chat things over about girlfriends, parents, teachers or sex.

The five of them looked out for each other. Nearly ten years of friendship – of sharing neighbourhood and school – meant that they were as concerned and devoted to each other's well being as if they were a family. For instance, they were alarmed when Clare began getting a bit wild. She had always been a trail-blazer, the one who had the ideas; the one who would say 'Hey you lot, why don't we . . .?' She was the first to smoke, the first to bring a bottle of vodka round one evening, and the first to try drugs.

The others were excited by the challenges she threw out to them. She set the pace and the others were only too glad to follow – except Tom. In the nicest possible way, Tom would just grin shyly and refuse the cigarette saying, 'You know me, I just can't stand the smell,' or, 'I don't think I want to rot my brains,' when he was offered alcohol, declaring that he preferred a cola. When one day a reefer of cannabis was passed round, it was the same. The shy shrug and the apologetic refusal

– 'You know me! I'm just not into that sort of thing.'

Yet he was never judgemental. It was as though he didn't need to go through these rites of passage. 'You were born grown up, weren't you, Tom?' Clare teased him with a laugh.

One day Emma told the others that she had called round for Clare to find her drunk and hysterical. The group closed round protectively. Sitting in Tom's room in a blue haze of smoke and rave music playing on the tape deck, Clare managed to blurt out, 'Mum's boyfriend . . . well you know . . . he tried something.'

The group discussed her predicament long into the night. They all agreed that if Clare's mother wouldn't do anything and if the boyfriend continued to make advances, Clare would have to move out. 'You're sixteen now, you have the right,' said Tom. It was always Tom who knew the law.

'But where would I go?' wept Clare.

'You can come to me!' they chorused in unison.

It wasn't uncommon. There were often people who would fall out with a parent and land up

spending days or even weeks on the sofa of a friend.

Tom said, 'You can come here. Mum wouldn't mind – and we've tons of room.'

So Clare took to turning up for the odd few days when things got difficult at home.

'You've never really had a girlfriend have you, Tom?' Clare said one evening after she'd been telling Tom about her new boyfriend, Jake. 'Don't you fancy anyone?'

Tom smiled with slight embarrassment. 'I can't be bothered,' he said. 'I just don't want the hassle.'

'Yeah, I see what you mean,' laughed Clare, remembering all the boyfriends she had had. It wasn't all fun by any means. 'Jake's nice, though. Don't you think?' She probed him. It was important to all of them that Tom approved of their various relationships.

'Yeah, he seems OK,' Tom answered lightly, and that was good enough.

'His sister's really pretty – Melissa! I think she fancies you. When I told her that I sometimes stay round your place, she looked really interested. Do you hear, Tom?' Clare nudged him knowingly. 'Lots of boys fancy

Melissa Parsons – but she'd go for you if you wanted.'

'I'll wait till the right girl comes along, thanks, Clare. She may be nice and she may be pretty – but, honestly – I'm not interested.'

They were all sixteen now and struggling with their GCSEs. They met up less as a group during the week – though they broke into twos or threes to help each other with homework. But they felt entitled to their weekends – come hell or high water – to seek out gigs or raves or parties.

However, despite parental misgivings, they all got comfortably through GCSE. Tom predictably got six As and three Bs, and everyone knew he was destined for university.

That summer, they all agreed to go Eurorailing together. They took weekend jobs and evening jobs, mostly waitressing or helping out at the supermarket to raise the money. When their exams were over, they pored over a map of Europe wondering if they could fit in both Amsterdam and Athens, the French Riviera and the Baltic coast.

* * *

They started in Amsterdam and that's when Emma and Tom found they shared a love of culture – or, to use their own terminology – found that they were both square.

'I've always wanted to see *The Night Watch*,' said Tom.

'The what?' cried Nick. 'Is that a group?'

'Dumb idiot,' jeered Emma. 'It's a painting by Rembrandt. I'd like to see it too. I'll go with you, Tom.' And that continued to be the pattern for the next six weeks as they made their way across Europe. Where the others wanted to head for the social scene, find the good clubs or, if they were anywhere near the sea, find the sun-soaked beaches, Emma and Tom found themselves splitting off from the others more and more, to look for the art galleries and museums and old churches.

That holiday set the two of them apart from the rest. It meant that they had different things to talk about. It meant that they built up their own confidences and their own vocabulary, and their names soon became

linked – Tom 'n Em. But both quite cheerfully denied being an item. 'It would be like falling in love with my own brother,' giggled Emma when challenged by Clare.

Back home, Emma finally scotched any speculation, by falling madly in love with a passing New Age traveller called Amos.

They were all fascinated by Amos. He seemed like a mixture between a gypsy and an Old Testament prophet. He was older than all of them – somewhere in his twenties. He had done his A-levels some time ago, it seemed – and even got a place at university; but he declared that all institutions were enemies of the people – and that the only pure life was one spent on the road, being beholden to no one. He claimed that he didn't even draw social security benefit, but mostly made money by busking or helping out on farms in the season. He was a magical musician, playing a guitar and singing heart-rending Irish folk songs. Dark-skinned, with henna-dyed dreadlocks, there was something deeply mysterious and compelling about him. He seemed a kind of Everyman, a man who had

really lived and suffered. He'd been beaten up by police at the Battle of the Beanfields and seen the inside of a prison. It was said he came from a rich family and could have had everything he wanted, but was morally strong enough to give it all up. He believed in simplicity and no one ever saw him in anything other than his hand-knitted rainbow sweater, threadbare corduroys and well-worn boots. He had two lurcher dogs, called Castor and Pollux, who shadowed him off the lead wherever he went, and who obeyed his every command – they added to his image of someone with powers over man and beast.

The group discussed the travellers and their way of life intensively. They wondered whether they would find such a life appealing. Nick said, 'It might be all right for a bit – perhaps a year – but I'd start wanting my little luxuries after that, like a decent bath.'

Clare agreed. 'It's not being able to wash my hair when I want that would really get me down.'

'Always having to move on would bother me,' said Ben. 'They come at three in the morning – the police –

and don't care if there are kids or whether it's raining. They come with their dogs and torches and batons, smashing up the place, looking for drugs. I couldn't stand all that.'

Emma was silent. That's when Tom knew that she was besotted with the man. He had thought it would pass – especially when it was known that the travellers' site had been raided by the police.

'Amos and his lot have been issued with a court order, haven't they, Em?' Tom asked gently.

Emma looked white and strained. 'Yeah! They've got to move on in ten days.'

'Where will they go?' exclaimed Nick.

'I think there's a friendly farmer over in Somerset. They can stay there for a bit,' she answered with bowed head.

'Huh!' said Nick sceptically. 'The police know how to deal with "friendly" farmers all right. They won't last long there!'

'That's what I mean though,' cried Ben. 'I couldn't stand all the uncertainty of where I was going to be next.'

The group hardly saw Emma for the next ten days – except fleetingly, at school. Even then, she kept herself to herself and seemed to be deliberately avoiding them. But they knew – as everyone knew – that Emma was spending every possible moment down on the site with Amos.

'Hey Em!' Tom called out to her one day as they were going home from school. 'Where've you been! I haven't seen you for ages!' Tom caught up with her, even though she seemed reluctant to wait for him.

'Ben, Nick and Clare are coming round tonight – and Clare's boyfriend, Jake. You will come too, won't you?'

Emma looked flustered. 'I . . . I don't think so, Tom. I promised to see Amos.'

'Bring him too,' persisted Tom.

But Emma refused to commit herself – and, at the railway bridge, they parted company; she to go on to the layby and Tom to go home through the town.

That evening, they all discussed Emma and expressed increasing anxiety about her infatuation

with Amos. 'I've tried to warn her about him,' said Clare. 'I mean, he's too old for her and he's not one to be tied down. I've heard them talk about him. He's had loads of girls. But Emma's totally besotted. She doesn't care. She thinks this is different. She wants to live with him. She talks about their plans – how they're going to get hold of an old ambulance and convert it into their home. She says Amos is brilliant at making things.'

Ben snorted with disbelief. 'I find that hard to believe. You should see the state of his van.'

'All these years we've worried about Clare,' said Nick shaking his head. 'I just never dreamt that Emma would get involved with something like that. I mean she's so straight. Now, if she had fallen for Tom . . .' All heads turned to see Tom's reaction. Some of them had speculated among themselves whether Tom secretly fancied Emma.

Tom looked saddened and worried, but not distraught. 'She was going to have to break out of that cosy middle class family one of these days,' he

commented philosophically. 'But she's intelligent. She'll come through.'

Emma's sudden departure though, shook them all to the core. No one dreamed that Em would go with Amos – not so soon. She hadn't even confided in Tom. They had thought she was the last person to opt out and bunk off her A-levels. It had always been Emma who had talked about going to art college, when others were still uncertain what they wanted to do.

Emma's parents were distraught. They came round and talked to the group pleading for information; desperate to learn where she might have gone. Apparently, they drove all over the country talking to groups of travellers. They looked everywhere for her without success. When she finally dropped them a card, it was to tell them she was all right, and they should not try to find her.

So there was nothing for her friends to do but to get on with working for their A-levels. When the exams

were over, instead of hanging around waiting for the results, Tom took off. He took the ferry to Amsterdam. He went alone – and he went in an easy frame of mind. He allowed each day to dictate to him what he wanted. Somehow, he didn't want to make plans or be too systematic. If he felt like an art gallery, he went to an art gallery; if he felt like visiting a squat – he visited a squat. If he wanted to sit in a café by a canal for hours on end, he did. He had a month to wander about, and could have carried on into Germany and Switzerland, but something kept him in Amsterdam.

He remembered Emma and their summer together when they Eurorailed two years ago. What had happened to her? He remembered their companionship; the alleys they had walked; the bridges they had looked over. He remembered all those art galleries and historic buildings and churches, which only she in the group had wanted to explore with him. Funny how you can know someone all your life – think you know them – and then suddenly, a blank; they've gone like a puff of smoke, as if all those years had counted for nothing.

Just Friends

It was on his third visit to *The Night Watch* that he saw her.

At first he didn't recognise her. He saw her from behind, looking like a regular traveller – her hair dyed henna and very frizzed out; a long Indian skirt and tasselled jacket; long woollen tights and boots. But it wasn't the clothes which disguised her, it was her thin, thin body. He could see her shoulder blades from behind, sticking out like wings. He walked up warily, still not recognising her, but nevertheless drawn to her. She had sat down cross-legged in front of the huge canvas, oblivious to the visitors swirling around, and the troupes of tourists being lectured to by their guides.

He came level with her and stood close by, then looked her full in the face. 'Em?'

He had hurried her out of the gallery for, at the sight of him, tears had poured down her face. They walked and talked all day. At nightfall, she took him back to her squat – yes, she lived in a squat along with several others. She managed to earn a bit of money working in

a tulip bulb factory. Amos wasn't there. No, he had gone months ago. He hadn't even told her. She couldn't face going home in this state, feeling so humiliated. She wanted to try and get back on her feet first.

Tom stayed the night in the squat. It was just an abandoned shell of a building choking with rubble and dust. It had no running water or electricity and broken windows rattled in their rotting frames. The smell and the damp and the cold made Tom want to flee, but he didn't have the heart and, after whispered conversations long into the night, they slept fitfully, back to back in sleeping-bags, snuggled together under a duvet.

The brazier of burning charcoal cast long desperate shadows of others who crouched over glowing embers, passing reefers to each other and snorting their substances.

Next morning Tom pleaded with Emma: 'You must come back with me. You'll be OK. It's awful here. Home must be better than this. You could still do your A-levels and go to art college, just as you always planned.'

'Amsterdam is like a huge art college!' laughed Emma. 'The world is my art college. Do you think Van Gogh did A-levels and went to art college? Course not! He just worked and lived and painted and . . .'

'. . . And was poverty stricken and went mad and chopped off his ear and died in an asylum.' Tom finished off for her bitterly.

Later, after they had had a final walk round the city and were leaning over their favourite bridge, Em said shyly, 'Isn't it stupid that you and me aren't – you know – in love with each other? I mean, we're so suited. We like the same things; we never quarrel. You're my best friend, Tom . . .' Her eyes filled with tears.

Tom sighed and squeezed her arm. 'Yeah. I've thought the same sometimes. Love doesn't seem to be about getting along, does it?' He remembered Amos. 'It's about something quite different. Something you know about, Em, and I don't.'

'Do you think you'll ever marry, Tom?' Emma asked.

'Probably, but I don't want to think about it yet. I want to go to university first, and I want to travel.' He

gazed down into the shifting waters of the canal. They both let the silence drift. Then Tom said, 'I tell you what. If you and I are still free in five years time, let's meet here. On this bridge in Amsterdam, and let's see then whether . . .'

'Whether?' Em whispered.

'Well, whether you and me should be together.'

They hugged each other, not with passion, but with all the years of love and friendship that they shared. Then they parted; she walked off the bridge one way, he the other. Before they lost sight of each other, they both instinctively turned. 'See you in five years – here, this date, this time!' Then they were gone.

Mona

'Meet Mona!'

Uncle Cedric stood in the doorway holding a leash. The light from the hallway fell on him, but it trailed away into darkness behind him, so they couldn't quite see what was on the end of the leash.

'Oh great! It's a dog!' cried Duane, who had always wanted a dog.

'Bags I walk him,' shouted Saffron, as usual trying to be the one to stake a claim first.

'Her,' corrected Uncle Cedric.

The children rushed outside excitedly. But when they saw what was on the end of the lead, they stopped short. Duane backed away uncertainly till he reached

his mother's side. Saffron just stood there staring, dumbstruck for once. Molotov their cat, looked electrified and fled.

'Well you'd better come in,' said Mum. She was still feeling half cross because she had let Uncle Cedric twist her arm and agree to look after his pet for a week while he went away. She realised he hadn't told her what kind of pet, but Uncle Cedric had always had dogs, so she assumed it was a dog.

Being a very house proud sort of a mum, she didn't care for dogs. They left hair everywhere and a strong smell – especially after a walk in the rain. She was a cat person. But Uncle Cedric had always been so generous with them in the past, she felt she couldn't refuse.

'I can't stop,' said Uncle Cedric. 'My car's on a yellow line, and in any case, I'm a bit on the late side. Look, here's everything you need.' He thrust a large holdall into the hallway. 'It's got her feeding bowl, pet food, you know biscuits, cereal and things – but, really, she eats anything except meat. She's vegetarian. Otherwise, give her your leftovers. Whatever. Oh – and

I've put in a whole bag of mini Mars bars. She's very partial to those. You can make her do anything with a Mars bar.'

'Uncle,' said Saffron strangely. 'What kind of dog is that?' She peered into the gloom.

Uncle Cedric tugged the lead. Something black moved within the darkness. It came blinking into the light. 'Her name's Mona,' said Uncle Cedric. 'You know – after Mona Lisa. She's beautiful isn't she?'

She had large, flappy ears with pinky grey insides; she had a funny thin straight tail which fluffed out at the end, and four little cloven feet – only little because they supported a great round belly which hung beneath a huge, shining, black, silky body. She gazed up at them with small squidgy eyes and a snuffling snout.

'She's a PIG!' yelled Mum, backing away, with Duane clinging to her skirts. 'I'm not having a pig in this house. You said it was a dog.'

'I never said it was a dog,' protested Uncle Cedric. 'Anyway, she's as good as a dog – better. She's called a Vietnamese pot-bellied pig.'

'I don't care what she's called, she's a PIG!' insisted Mum.

'I didn't know there were black pigs, only pink pigs,' said Duane.

I told you, this one's Vietnamese – from Vietnam. They have black pigs there – they are very intelligent – probably more intelligent than you.

'I thought pigs only lived on farms. We live in the city,' mumbled Saffron.

'Makes no difference,' retorted Uncle Cedric. 'She's a household pet she can live anywhere.'

'She's huge,' Mum's voice rose in hopeless protest.

'Well ... er yes ... I didn't expect that. She was small and cuddly when I bought her. But she's still loveable. Now look, I'm late – I'll miss my flight. I really must get on. There's nothing for you to do but feed her and take her for walks. Just treat her as if she were a dog. She's house-trained and she doesn't leave hairs all over the place. It's only for a week.' Uncle Cedric thrust the lead into Mum's hands. He dashed back to the car and returned carrying a large dog basket with a

blanket. 'She can sleep in this.' He strode past them carrying everything into the kitchen and dumped it in a corner near the fridge. He knelt down in front of his pet, put his arms round her thick body and pressed his nose to her snout. 'Goodbye, Mona my sweetheart,' he drooled. 'See you in a week,' then he fled.

'CEDRIC!' bellowed Mum.

'Don't forget the Mars bars!' His voice yelled above the car engine, as he pulled away with a cheery wave.

They stood in the kitchen staring at Mona. Mona stared back.

'Who's Mona Lisa?' asked Duane.

'She's a painting,' muttered Mum. 'A painting of a beautiful woman with a mysterious smile,'

'Oh.'

They looked again at Mona. 'I can't see a mysterious smile,' said Saffron.

The lead had trailed out of Mum's hands. Mona began to shuffle round the kitchen. Her tail swung relentlessly like a pendulum. She oinked as her snout, like a checkout machine, slid over every object she

could reach. Oink, oink, oink! When she got to the cupboard below the worktop, her tail stopped swinging and stood rigidly on end. Food. Oink oink oink. She oinked faster and faster. Her snout levered up the handle.

'Oh no you don't!' cried Mum, leaping forward and grabbing the lead. 'Let's get her cereal out. She's probably hungry.

They got out the bowls; one for the cereal and the other for water. They placed them side by side near the kitchen door. Mona's oinking got even faster. She stuck her snout into the bowl and with a swoosh, it was gone. Her tail swung furiously back and forth. She looked round for more. 'Oink, oink, oink.' She saw the cat's bowl. Molotov always knew when he'd had enough, and left what he didn't want. The tail went rigid. 'Oink, oink, oink' and swooosh! All gone.

'Oh, she's one of those,' said Mum wearily. 'An eating machine. Well let's get her to bed. She fixed her eye on Mona and pointed to the dog basket. 'Bed,' she commanded.

Mona's tail swung. 'Oink, oink, oink.' She took no notice.

Mum grabbed her collar and tried to pull her over. 'Bed, Mona!' she repeated. But though all three of them heaved against her, Mona didn't budge an inch.

'Uncle Cedric said she'd do anything for a Mars bar,' said Duane digging his hand into the holdall for the Mars bars. He ripped off the wrapper and held it over the basket. 'Here, Mona! Mars bar!'

Mona turned like a guided missile and was in the basket in a flash.

'Good girl, Mona!' cheered Duane, daring to give her a pat.

Mona flopped an ear over an eye and looked coy.

'Where's Molotov?' Everyone looked around for the cat.

'He'll come when he's ready,' Mum reassured the children. 'He can take care of himself.'

'See you in the morning,' Mum gave Mona a reluctant smile. She switched out the kitchen light, firmly shut the door, and they all trooped up to bed.

The next morning. The next morning. The next . . .

From her bed, Mum awoke to a faint sound. Someone was moving around in the kitchen below, perhaps Duane making her a cup of tea. Good boy! She rolled over waiting. A second later she sat bolt upright. She heard Duane in the bathroom. She leapt from her bed and went downstairs.

It was like all hell had broken loose. Mum screamed, one great long terrible scream. Saffron and Duane rushed down expecting murder. Instead, they saw the biggest upset in the kitchen since World War II.

'Oink, oink, oink!' Swing, swing, swing! Everything had been tipped out of the fridge; everything had been tipped out of every single cupboard in the kitchen – even the upper cupboards. In the middle of the mayhem, with butter paper licked clean, and jam slurping out of jam pots, and remains of eggshells, cartons, tins, vegetables and fruit, stood Mona, her tail upright and her snout in a yoghurt pot. She looked up at them and smiled – a mysterious smile.

It's not as though life didn't have to go on; that the

children didn't have to go to school and Mum to her part time job. Mum found wings, flying around between Mona – who she managed to drag outside with the aid of a Mars bar, and tie to the apple tree – rushing back to clear up the mess, make breakfast, yell at the kids to get dressed and look for Molotov, who wouldn't be found.

They ate their breakfast standing up. Mum firmly shut all the cupboards and drawers. She propped a chair in front of the fridge and pushed the kitchen table as a barricade for the kitchen cupboards. Mona was brought in from the garden. Mona oinked and her tail swung.

'Basket!' commanded Mum. Mona looked the other way.

'Mars bar!' yelled the children throwing one into the basket.

'Oink, oink, oink.' Mona's tail went rigid as she plunged into the basket.

'Right, let's go!' cried Mum and slammed shut the door.

* * *

Mum was waiting for Saffron and Duane when school was over. They walked home. 'We'd better take Mona to the park,' said Mum. 'She's been in all day.'

Molotov was sitting on the doorstep when they arrived at the gate. He looked miffed, and didn't come down the path to greet them as usual. 'Poor Molotov. He doesn't like having Mona around.' They went inside.

They stood before the kitchen door. 'It's funny to think there's a huge, black, Vietnamese pot-bellied pig on the other side of that door,' whispered Duane.

'I can't hear her oinking,' muttered Saffron.

Mum opened the door. 'Hello Mona, we're ho . . . AAAaaah'

Havoc. The chair in front of the fridge was tipped over and the fridge door was swinging open; all the cupboard doors were open top and bottom and, strewn across the floor, were the chewed, spewed, crunched, scrunched, ripped, stripped and gnawed remains of any tin, jar, carton or bag which had contained anything which could be eaten.

Where was Mona? They couldn't see her. Then they heard a deep snore. They didn't see her at first. She had gripped the end of the blanket in her teeth and pulled it right up over her head. But there she was in her basket sound asleep, looking as if she had slept through the mayhem rather than caused it.

'How did she do it?' gasped Saffron looking around aghast.

Mona Lisa's head appeared from under the blanket. She opened an eye, showed her teeth and smiled a mysterious smile.

'Get her out of my sight, or there'll be bacon for breakfast,' yelled Mum.

Mum cleared up yet again. Saffron and Duane stuffed their pockets with Mars bars and took Mona to the park. It took two of them to hold her. She was very strong. But she was as good as gold – or as good as Mars bars; so long as one was waved in front of her nose, she stopped at the zebra crossing, she didn't tug and try to chase the little Jack Russell who dashed up yapping and sniffing, and she didn't puncture

the football which rolled up to her snout.

Quite a crowd gathered. Not many people take pigs for walks. 'My he's a grand fellow,' said one.

'She,' corrected Saffron.

'What's her name?' asked another.

'Mona. You know, after Mona Lisa,' announced Duane.

'Oh yeah! The lady with the smile.'

That night Mum said to Mona, 'It's the garden shed for you tonight, madam. Forget about luxury and mod cons, warmth and home comforts.'

'But Mum . . .' pleaded Saffron. 'She was ever so good in the park. Give her another chance. It'll be cold in the shed.'

But Mum was adamant. Firmly, she led an oinking Mona up the garden to the wooden shed. Saffron and Duane followed in procession, carrying her basket and bowls. 'There's no food to be found here, madam,' she said icily. 'You'll just have to make do with what's in your bowl.'

Saffron and Duane moaned, 'Poor Mona.' But

Molotov looked pleased, and slept in the kitchen that night.

Saffron had now decided she loved Mona, so she was the first to wake up the next morning. Her first thought was Mona. 'Fancy sleeping in that cold shed all night.' She ran downstairs and out into the garden. It was early. Only a few birds cheeped sleepily. The curtains were still drawn in all the surrounding houses. She got to the shed. The door was half open. The garden hose trailed out of it and disappeared across the lawn. Had Mum come out to water the garden early before work?

'Mona?' whispered Saffron, peering inside.

As the daylight flooded in, she saw the terrible sight. Mona had had a feast. She had chewed all the gumboots, ripped up the gardening gloves, mangled the straw hats, gnawed at the tool handles, spilled all the trays of seedlings, knocked over every jar, tin, bottle and as for the garden hose . . . what had she done with the garden hose?

'Oink, oink, oink!'

Saffron followed the oinking and the garden hose. It coiled round the apple tree, across the lawn, through a hole in the fence (which, the day before, had just been a crack, but was now a very large hole,) into next door's garden. 'Oink, oink, oink!' Across a flattened flower bed, a tipped over bird table, all the way to the treasured vegetable patch of Mrs. O'Connor. 'Oink, oink, oink!' There lay Mona in a tangle, with the hose wrapped round her neck and legs, looking like a captured battleship. A half-chewed cabbage hung out of her mouth.

'Mona!' gulped Saffron. 'Oh Mona!'

Mona looked up at Saffron innocently and – well – just smiled a mysterious smile.

'This is war,' declared Mum.

She led Mona to the garage. She found a long chain and a padlock. She looped the chain through Mona's dog collar and attached it to a hook on the concrete wall, winding it round and round several times.

Mum took the children to school, and then went on to her job.

At the end of the day, when they all got back, Molotov came purring down the path top greet them. They went to the garage to see Mona.

'Oink, oink, oink!' Mona sniffled all round the garage dragging the chain behind her still attached to the hook on the wall. No mayhem, no mess, everything was as they left it – except, 'I think she likes eating nuts and bolts,' murmured Duane who noticed a glittering store of them in her basket. But Mum grinned with satisfaction. 'I think I'm winning,' she said.

'Good girl, Mona!' shouted Saffron throwing her arms round the pig.

That night, after walking Mona in the park, Mum eased the car into the garage and, left the pig chained again to the wall for the night. 'This is obviously the best place for her,' she said triumphantly.

'Goodnight Mona!' sighed Saffron, giving her a kiss. 'Be good.'

'Here's some Mars bars for you,' soothed Duane, dropping them in the basket.

Mona's tail stood upright.

* * *

It was the first morning it had been peaceful since Mona arrived. The kitchen was clean and immaculate when they all trooped down for breakfast; the garden was calm and, when Mum looked out and saw Molotov prowling lazily through the bushes, she knew all was right with the world. They had made their peace with the neighbours promising to fix the bird table, sort out the vegetable patch and the herbaceous boarder and all the trouble Mona had caused. They had a leisurely breakfast, and then went to the garage to get the car and check on Mona.

The garage door was closed when Mum went over, but – not locked. Odd. Moments later she was rushing back in distress.

'What's up, Mum?' cried Saffron and Duane.

Mum was on the telephone. 'Police? My car! It's been stolen!'

No one knows how, or when – except it was sometime in the night – but the car was gone. So was Mona.

'A PIG as well?' asked the police woman on the other end.

'Yes . . . no . . . I don't know! But she's gone too.'

Mum tried to answer all the questions. 'The car is blue and six years old, registration L666 HRU. The pig? She's a black – yes, BLACK – a Vietnamese pot-bellied pig. She's called Mona, yes M-O-N-A, you know after Mona Lisa . . .'

The thief thought he was so clever. How silently he had broken into the garage. Easy peasy. People hardly ever locked their cars when they were in the garage. Cor! This one hadn't even shut the passenger door at the back. He closed it gently, and kicked in a chain which was hanging from the front. His torch flashed in the darkness as he opened the driver's door and released the handbrake. He would ease the car out into the road before starting it up.

Soon, he was off, speeding away through the empty neighbourhood heading for the country. He left the city streets behind with their harsh orange lights and

roaming police cars. He hit the motorway and sighed with relief. 'Boom, boom, boom!' Someone had left a great cassette in the tape deck. He played it loud.

He slipped his hand into his pocket and pulled out a Mars bar. He tore off the wrapper. It was then he glanced in his rear mirror. A face loomed from the back. A black face, with great floppy ears, a nose more like a snout and two beady little eyes which gleamed like a demon. It smiled – a mysterious smile.

Later that day, the phone rang. It was the police. 'We've found your car, and your pig – and we caught the thief. At least the pig did. It seemed to be something to do with a Mars bar . . . We found the thief blubbing his eyes out with terror, jammed in the car with the horn going, and this great oinking pig sitting in his lap like a ten ton truck. The thief said he only wanted to eat a Mars bar and this thing came over the back like a bat out of hell – or rather a pig out of hell. Clever pig, that one. Could do with him in the force.'

'Her,' muttered Mum weakly.

'You can come and get her and the car any time you like.'

Mum, Saffron and Duane went over to the police station. The car was outside. 'Where's Mona?' asked Mum.

'She's in the cells,' said the policeman. 'Didn't know where else to put her. Took four of us to rugby tackle her to get her in mind you.'

Mum looked at him with pleading eyes. 'You couldn't just keep her there? Could you? Just for three more days?'

'This is a police station not a farm, madam,' replied the policeman sternly.

'Yes. Oh well. It was just a thought,' said Mum wearily. 'I think we're going to need some more Mars bars, I'm down to the last!'

They went down to the cells. The policeman got out his big bunch of keys and opened the cell door.

Mum waved her last Mars bar.

'Come on out, Mona Lisa. You're free to go,' said the policeman.

Mona looked up and smiled.

Gone to Earth

Liam stared into the fox's eyes. They burned like fires.

The fox was on the other side of the boundary wall, standing stone-still, just where the soft tilled land rose and gave way to the wild, stony moor.

'I'm not allowed,' Liam's gaze sent back the message. He looked at the crags rising steep and sharp as giant's teeth. He remembered warnings about caves in which you could be lost forever, underground rivers which hurtled through the guts of the earth, potholes so deep they ended in eternity. 'I'm not allowed,' he repeated.

The fox ambled across the flat, limestone surface heading for the steep escarpment. Liam hesitated. He had often disobeyed and gone on to the Stones – not

badly, he would argue to himself, to calm his guilty conscience. He only went as far as his friend, the Giant's Head, a huge boulder with a rounded dome of a forehead, rested as if waiting for its body to return.

A deep slit smiled across its face like a kindly mouth; two hollows which were his eyes gazed out towards the distant ocean, and a noble nose with flaring stony nostrils, seemed to breathe in the landscape which lay below him, spreading on and on as far as the sea. The whole head was indented with fossils and shells dating back to a time when it, and all the land around, had been under the ocean. From out of the pores and wrinkles and cracks of its hard, grey skin, grew a delicate forest of ferns and flowers, creepers and grasses so that he was fluttering with butterflies and humming with bees. There was something about his ancient pitted face which made Liam feel comfortable and safe.

'Are you my friend?' Liam always whispered into his shell encrusted ears.

'Yes, yes! I will always be your friend.'

The fox turned again and looked at him with its burning eyes. Liam followed, moving over the thin, multi-layered surface, peering down through cracks, down, down into some impenetrable darkness, from which void seedlings, ferns, creepers and clinging twines had straggled upwards towards the miraculous sky.

The fox stopped. Liam stopped too. His conscience troubled him. He ought to go back. He felt afraid. There was such a sense of loneliness; of wilderness, of raw nature. A piercing shriek from the turf at his feet startled him. A kestrel had plummeted to the ground and killed a stoat. Liam watched the death struggle between fur and feathers. Should he intervene? He took a step forward. His movement sent the kestrel hurtling skywards again, with shreds of entrails dangling in its beak. It would return. He shuddered and turned away from the quivering animal and looked for the fox. But she had gone.

That's when he saw the cave.

It was high; sandwiched between two jutting crags,

and shielded by a screen of thin spiky saplings that crowded round the opening.

The entrance to the cave was narrow. He squeezed inside. It was quite wide, with odd rocky shelves jutting out, and a deeper, darker depth that challenged him to explore.

Something gleamed on a ledge, high in the darkness. It was a pelvic bone, white as the moon, sharp, sheared, hollowed, with empty eye holes like spy holes; shaped like a lyre; singing, ringing, with thigh bones to twang. He reached for it and held it to his face.

The socket holes fitted exactly over his eyes; it was like a mask. He peered through. The world changed. His body changed. The bone of the fox welded to the bone of his face: his brow broadened, cheeks bones narrowed, nose lengthened to a muzzle; dark, slanting, crafty, predatory; with pointed ears and gleaming eyes, and rust red tail fanning out behind, he sped from the cave – a fox.

In the distance, the hunting horn blew, its notes carrying in the wind.

* * *

All that day he had been a fox; skulking over the stony ground, sniffing at tracks, nibbling at berries, pouncing at rabbits and voles; had a stand off with a pine marten and, just for fun, he had dashed off to play the hunters' game. He teased the hounds by running with the wind to entice them with his smell. At first he let them chase him. Wheee! How he ran – how they followed, their high-pitched barking causing the hunters to wheel their horses round and set off at full gallop, the hunting horn cutting through the wind with its wailing war cry. Then he doubled back against the wind, his scent disintegrating into the air and, taking cover in the middle of a dense briar patch, he rolled on his back in the dust, snuffling and wheezing with foxy laughter as the dogs broke ranks and milled around whining, disorganised with confusion.

Evening fell. He wanted to be a boy again, but didn't know how. He sped across the milky surface, panic beginning to choke his breast. He heard the thin, distant sound of a fiddle. 'I know that!' he cried with

relief, and ran towards the sad, heart-broken strains from the fiddle played by a flesh and blood man called Charlie Connor.

Everyone knew Charlie Connor. It was his sister, Teresa, who had vanished when she was only eight years old. That was sixty years ago now – but the search never stopped, not in the mind or living memory, or in the story handed down and handed down.

Many a parent tells the story of Teresa. Playing on the Stones one day, she had found a baby cub abandoned in a cave after the hunt had killed its mother. She had wanted to keep it and rear it as a pet, but no one would let her. They said it was unthinkable to rear a creature which would be such a menace to their livestock. She begged and pleaded, wept and screamed, but her father locked it in the shed to dispose of the next day. But when the next day came, they found the shed door open and both Teresa and the fox had gone. Although they searched and searched – searched till her mother and father were grey – she was never found.

Her brother Charlie is old now, and is mostly found propping up the bar in the local pub. He's a brilliant fiddler when he's not drunk. He blames himself for what happened, because he told on her; he told his ma that Teresa had secretly smuggled a baby fox cub into her room. Often, after closing time, Charlie Connor would stagger on to the Stones with his fiddle yelling for Teresa. 'Treeza, Treeza! I'm sorry I told on you! Please forgive me and come back home.' And he would play; draw his bow across the strings, and long heart-breaking melodies would ring through the air, and mothers who heard the music would say to their children, 'See what happens when you do disobey your parents? You see what happens when you wander alone on the Stones?'

Liam slunk round the base of the mound, curious to see Charlie. The old man was hunched over his instrument, pulling the bow over the strings, sculpting the shapes and sounds of the music, and sobbing drunkenly as he played.

'Treeza Reeza!' He called for his lost sister. 'It's me,

Charlie! Come on out and put things right. It's time to go home now. You won't get into trouble – I promise you. It was all my fault for telling on you, but come on out and show you forgive me.' Weeping with sorrow and drink, the old man put down his fiddle. Mumbling and stumbling, he scrabbled about on the ground. He examined one great shining stone after another, until he found the shape and size he wanted. It was a huge thing, embedded in the moss. He heaved and levered until he got both his arms round it, then dragged it over to add to a pile of stones which rose like a wobbly pyramid – sixty-eight of them, for the sixty-eight years that his sister, Teresa Connor had been missing.

'Hey mister!' Liam the fox spoke directly into the brain of the rambling, shambling man. 'Can you help me?'

'I can't, I can't! I'm just an old coward; lily-livered, spineless, yellow, useless . . .' He burst out sobbing again and ran away with his fiddle tucked under his arm, leaping from stone to stone like a goat, dodging

boulders and springing over crevices and gullies, until he disappeared in the white mist that came rolling up from the western sea.

Liam watched him; helpless and hopeless. Sadly he turned and found his vixen standing just above him on a great boulder, patient waiting, as if forever. She loped up the track. 'Wait for me,' Liam's voice cried silently in his head, and he followed her back to the cave where he had found the bone.

There was an animal, furry warmth, and a scuffle of sleepy movement as he entered. This time, the cave was inhabited by four cubs. His fox guide flopped down panting. Liam did too, aware of nuzzling noses and throbbing bodies. Sleep overwhelmed him.

Outside in the wind-singing night, the Giant's head sighed.

Charlie's fiddle tune echoed through his dreams.

Lian was woken next morning, not by the wind, singing in the trees, but by a child's voice:

Where is the flower that once did shine
Up on this desert shore . . .

The sun's rays fell red upon his coiled body. Liam's stirred and sniffed. With instant recognition, he knew that it had rained in the night, that a flock of feral goats had passed on the lower path, that a stoat had looked in and thought the better of it, and that a full set of hare rib bones had been brought back some time in the night, but were now chewed to oblivion by five sets of razor-sharp young teeth – including his own.

He opened his eyes without moving. He had spent the whole night in the cave. Was he here? Or disappeared like Teresa? How would he know if he had disappeared? He twitched a leg and an arm; licked his lips and felt sensations. No – so far as he could tell, he was here.

The vixen came close and gently licked his hands.

A half-chewed carcass of a young goat lay near by. Its stench turned his stomach. But she had brought it to him, knowing that he must be starving. He could

only eat it as fox – though he longed just to be a boy.

He stared into the green wild eyes of the vixen – and then fearfully, beyond her. He began to sob inside like a boy. He curled up on the earth floor with his tail wrapped round himself, and sobbed and slept, too terrified to face the world – any world. Yet hour after hour, when ever he looked up through red-rimmed eyes, there she was, waiting at the mouth of the cave; staying with him, not caring whether he was fox or boy. Then hunger and thirst overwhelmed him. He fell upon the carcass of the kid; and when he had gorged on its flesh and chewed all the bones and sucked its blood, he followed the vixen out of the cave. She led him to the side of the cliff where there was a secret pool of water, which seeped out of the limestone cliff from inner streams – and there he gulped and gulped until life and strength returned to his body.

When the world was created, the eagle asked for eternal light, so that he could always see his prey, but the fox asked for darkness so that he could steal and stalk invisibly. The vixen showed him; and Liam

survived in a fox-like way: sly, spry, cunning, running, sneaking, wreaking havoc among the trembling rabbits, dive bombing into burrows.

One day, he climbed the promontory and gazed across beyond the stones to where the farms clustered among distant green fields dotted with pink, blue, yellow and white cottages and the narrow grey roads which wound away.

He saw Charlie's cottage. At the sight of it, memory surged back, bringing with it homesickness, churning guts, grief; sick to the stomach with longing for human contact, and he went flying across the stones, down down the cliffs to Charlie's cottage.

Old Charlie Connor was lying in a drunken stupor on his living room sofa. The front door was slightly ajar. Liam nuzzled it open and slid his furry body inside. He stared silently at the old man, and his fiddle just lying on the carpet within reach of his gnarled fingers. Liam stepped towards him, sniffing softly. He licked his hand. 'I followed a fox onto the Stones. I went to a cave on the mound and found a mask of bone. I put it on and

became a fox – and then. Charlie, wake up and listen, something happened.'

The old man groaned and smacked his lips but didn't wake up. Liam crouched down on the floor next to him. He would wait. He would wait and wait until the old man woke up.

When he did wake, Liam the fox was still sitting patiently. 'Can I stay with you?' He cocked his head and asked with pleading eyes.

'You and me seem to have a soul understanding,' muttered Charlie. 'But don't you go for my rabbits and chickens.'

Liam the fox never went for Charlie's rabbits and chickens. Instead, he went prowling up on the Stones. There, he chased after wild rabbits and lunged at stoats, he played dead to deceive the voles, and then, when they ventured out of their holes, pounced on them – one paw on the body, a sharp bite on the back of the neck.

Sometimes, Charlie would talk to Liam, as a friend. He told him another boy had disappeared, just like

Teresa. He must have gone on to the Stones, stupid boy. 'Liam Fitzgerald – that's the lad.'

Hearing his name made him sit up with a rush of memory.

'But that's me, Charlie! That's me!' Liam barked, his fur ridged along his back with excitement. 'I am Liam Fitzgerald.'

But Charlie just rambled on and didn't notice. 'Now he's vanished, same as Teresa, same hue and cry. I told them not to waste their time looking. You won't find him, I told them. But they looked; they're still looking. Oh the grief of it. His mammy and daddy – all in pieces. I just hope he's with Teresa. Ah Teresa!' And he would start weeping again. 'Have you seen or heard anything – eh old chap? If you do; then don't forget Teresa. Where he is, she must be.'

'Yes, yes, that's right.' Liam the fox was heartbroken. 'Where I am, she must be too, and my mammy and pappy all in pieces just like Charlie? Tell them, Charlie, tell them will yer? I'm trying to come home, and I'll bring Teresa too if I find her.' And he

thought how good it would be to find Teresa and bring her back to Charlie.

But it was hard to hold on to memory when being a fox meant thinking of other things like hunting and being hunted.

One day, Liam the fox was out ambling and rambling about, when suddenly the hot breath of a hound streamed into his nostrils. Caught by surprise, Liam whirled round and glimpsed brown and white fur, black noses, furious tails. Dogs, dogs. From zero to forty, he broke into a dash, twisting and turning, double-backing and zig-zagging, desperately trying to shake them off. But he was out in the open, and his scent was all the stronger for the fear, which oozed through his glands. Metalled hooves, shining stirrups, black boot and brown shoe; velvet black-capped killers on horses were coming in waves towards him.

He headed for Charlie Connor's cottage. Charlie will save me – Charlie would never let them kill me. He and I have a soul understanding. He could hear the hooves thudding behind; he could hear the haloos and

war cries, and the sound of the hunting horn whooping them on to the kill. He made it to Charlie's walls. He made it over into Charlie's garden. Then a set of burning fiery teeth sank into his rear quarters and brought him down to the ground. Blood rushed into his eyes as the whole braying pack descended on him – scarlet jacket, cream jodhpur and blue jeans flashed around him kicking, trampling, heel to flank, whip in hand, reins clasped, frothing mouth. He smelt sweat and leather as they tugged and reared.

BANG! It was Charlie with his gun. 'Get off my land,' he roared, firing into the air. 'Leave him alone. He's my friend.'

Liam was aware of saddles, reins, stirrups; wheeling horses, pink tongues, slobbering at the bit; saliva foaming as they fell upon him. His ears were roaring, eyes bleeding; pain burned through his body as his bones fractured, fur ripped, sinews torn. Then darkness overwhelmed him and he sank into oblivion.

Liam heard a child singing. He knew the tune, but

couldn't place it. He tried to open his eyes and roll over, but he had no strength. He was lying stretched out, face down; his body burned, as though it roasted on a spit. Yet from time to time, something sweet smelling was waved past his nostrils, and cool broad leaves laid across his buttocks and his back. He saw long white arms dangling on either side. They were his arms. He was a boy again. And he saw the bone. It was on the ground. He stretched out his fingers and touched it.

> *Where is the flower that once did shine*
> *Upon this desert shore?*

'I know those words,' grunted Liam.

He picked up the bone and stared at it. He twanged the prongs. Its sound broke the silence in the dark sky-slitted dome.

Then somewhere far – but not so far – he heard fiddling.

* * *

Where the sweet face with childhood's bloom
And eyes of waters pure?

It came closer. Sounded nearer. It sounded right here. He twanged the bone in rhythm. Something emerged from the light and dust. It hurtled past him into the dome; a creature, or was it a child? With red hair, pale cheeks and eyes the colour of gentian violets; part fox, part flower, part water? And surely human too, the way she looked and listened so thoughtfully.

'Shush,' she whispered, putting her finger to her mouth. 'Listen.'

Liam stopped playing the bone and listened. From outside, inside from above and below, from somewhere far, far away, they heard a faint scratching fiddle, and a voice which sobbed, 'Treeza, Treeza! Won't you come home now.'

'That's Charlie!' whispered Liam.

'Charlie!' The little girl broke into a wail, just like any little lost girl.

Liam took her hand. 'Are you Teresa?' he asked.

A shadow fell across the doorway. It was the vixen. She stood watching them, then turned away. Teresa ran to her side like a cub and followed her.

'Don't leave me!' cried Liam desperately. 'Wait for me.'

Liam followed the vixen and Teresa back to the cave and Liam the boy hunted with the vixen and Teresa. Darkness became as familiar as day. His night vision became sharp, his nose picked up scents and smells, and his ears heard every twitch and rustle and squawk and flutter. He learned where to find bird's eggs and young hares and to creep up unawares on the ducks and geese who flew in to winter on the dew ponds of the Stones.

Liam's hair had grown quite long now, hanging in long dark curls around his shoulders. To keep it out of his eyes, he twisted some fur and skin and gut with the twine of a creeper and tied it round his head as a bandana. Teresa showed him how to skin the furs of the weasels and hares that he caught, and string them together to make footwear and extra layers of

clothing. He hung his fox bone round his neck.

They took him to a secret glade of birch trees and showed him the corpse of great ancient Billy Goat who had lain down and died. Teresa stripped the body of the thick black fur, hung it and dried it and then gave it to Liam to wear. He kept the huge horns; the sharp inner bone for weapons and tools, and the heavy, ringed outer shells as symbols of his strength and power. He carried his weapons tucked into a belt and also made a pouch for carrying smaller stones and loops round his waist, from which he could hang the bodies of smaller mammals after hunting them.

Liam would have forgotten everything about life before he found the bone, but one day he and Teresa climbed the promontory. He didn't recognise anything, for there were none of the gentle fields, and daisy-bright cottages that he knew, no ribbon-like roads winding from village to village; only a deep dense forest, stretching on and on. Then he saw the Giant's Head far in the distance on the other side of the canyon.

He grabbed Teresa's hand and made her run. They

slithered and scrambled down the hill, through the forest and up again to the other side, until they reached his friend.

There was the stone, his stone – the huge Giant's Head. To see the familiar in an alien world was like seeing a friend among strangers. He approached it tenderly, coaxing, as one might approach a stray dog or a runaway horse, with hand outstretched. 'Is it you,' he whispered in awe, 'is it really you?' He touched the stone brow and trailed his fingers down its face, feeling into the sockets of the eyes and into the slit of the mouth, then put his arms round as far as they could go and hugged it.

Teresa stood apart, quietly watching as Liam leaned into the hollow of its neck – as he had done so many times in the past. He sank down to its base, pressing his back into the curve of the stone, remembering.

'If you are here, then where is everything else?' asked Liam, looking around.

'Everything hasn't come yet,' whispered the Giant's Head.

'I heard Charlie,' Liam told his friend. He looked in

the direction of Charlie Connor's cottage. How often he had done so before. This time there was nothing. 'What shall I do?' He pressed his lips to the ear of the stone. 'I've found Teresa. How do we get home?'

'Go.' A deep syllable seemed to breathe out through the slit of its mouth.

Liam held the encrusted, fossilised stone head between his hands. 'Where must I go?'

'Follow the raven.'

Liam looked up into the blank face of the sky. A black speck circled. A raven was waiting to be their guide.

'Shall we go now?' asked Teresa.

Liam hugged his rock pressed his ear to its skin. 'You'll always be here, won't you?'

'Always!' breathed the stone.

Through the thick scrub of hazel bushes and flowering blackthorn, Liam and Teresa followed the raven who flew sometimes above, sometimes alongside, weaving in and out of stunted trunks and moss-covered boulders. They skirted glistening chilled

dew ponds and ancient stone rings and burial cairns. They slept in dug outs by day, and hunted by night, but each dawn, the raven was there waiting to lead them on and on.

They reached a high rocky plateau with barren headlands overlooking the ocean. Here, everything was grey. No trees or grass; nothing soft to ease the eye or the body. Just hard grey rock flattened in sheets, or looming up as cliffs, or glowering as monstrous boulders; open to the grey sky, grey sea – a distant sea, ghost grey in the mists – and the mound.

Liam took Teresa's hand. The raven had vanished. They stared at the mound. It seemed to materialise out of the grey mist, lop-sided as a mother's breast. It enfolded them – so closely, that they could hear a beating heart and pounding of the life's blood.

'Come, come!' The mound was wavering with silvery trees, grasses, flowers, and star-shining stones – all seemed to be whispering to him. 'Come to where there is eternal laughter and love, music, fun and youth . . . Never grow old. Never grow old!' Yet at that

moment, what he heard louder than anything were the shivering strings of Charlie's fiddle.

The music came from inside. They circled the mound looking for an entrance. They had surely gone round once, then twice, finding no way in – then suddenly, there was an opening. They walked inside. Though so huge on the outside, it seemed no bigger than the inside of a beehive. As they entered, the music got louder.

'Charlie!' cried Teresa and ran ahead.

There was no Charlie, just the vixen sitting there – or was it a woman? She was such a mixture of fur and long red hair which coiled around her, and dark unfathomable eyes which gleamed in the darkness.

Liam took off the fox bone from round his neck and held it out. White as the moon, sharp, sheared, hollowed, with empty eye holes like spy holes; shaped like a lyre; singing, ringing; and he twanged the thigh bones with his thumb.

Teresa flung her arms round the woman fox. 'Please forgive me for leaving you. I want to go home now.'

All around them, the stones began murmuring and muttering. 'Go home then, go home and you will grow old . . . old . . . old . . . like Charlie.'

Liam looked at Teresa, shining like a desert flower, with skin like petals and eyes as blue as gentian violets. 'Do you still want to go, even if you become as old as Charlie?' he asked.

She nodded, 'I've been lost for too long. I just want to go home.' The fox woman reached forward and placed one prong of the bone in Teresa's hand, while Liam held the other. The two children stood before the fox woman and wept because they loved her.

Where is the flower that once did shine
Upon this desert shore?

They turned towards the music. Opposite and ahead of them was an exit. A rush of cold air swept over their faces as they walked towards a bent hunched up figure, clearly etched in the moonlight. He drew his bow across the strings.

Where the sweet face with childhood's bloom
And eyes of waters pure?

'Charlie?' The girl ran towards him.

When he looked back, there was no mound. Only the cairn of stones Charlie had been building for sixty-eight years.

Beyond, where the stars hung low in the sky as bright as sunflowers, the Giant's Head waited. Liam glided over the moonstruck Stones to his friend. 'You are always here,' he murmured into its ear, 'just as you said.' Then with a feeling of unbearable weariness, Liam sank to the ground and, pulling his billy goat skin around him, slept.

Once, near dawn, he awoke. An old old lady bent over him. Her skin was as wrinkled as lichen which covered the ancient stones, and her hair was as thin and silvery as cobwebs. But her eyes, oh her eyes, they were the dancing eyes of a child, and how they smiled at him as she whispered, 'Thank you.'

Liam sat up and leaned against the Giant's Head,

twanging his fox bone and humming, as he watched two ancient people, arm in arm, picking their way across the Stones in the dawn light, heading for Charlie's cottage. In a while, he too would go home.

The Paradise Carpet

'One knot blue, two knots yellow, three knots red, four knots green . . .' The young boys chanted the pattern of the carpet they were weaving. Bony little fingers deftly drew the card down the thread; warp and weft . . . wrap and weft . . . top to bottom, right to left . . . warp and weft and knot.

Behind a loom inside a dark mud hut, crouching like caged animals, sat a line of boys. With backs against a wall, their thin arms rose and fell as they drew the threads from top to bottom, right to left, warp and weft and knot. They could have been musicians plucking at strings, but these were carpet weavers whose harmonies were of the eye not the ear as, bit by bit, the

glorious patterns and hues of a rich carpet emerged in the darkness. 'One knot blue, two knots yellow, three knots red, four knots green . . .' The boys wove their thread, prompted and guided by old Rama, the only man among them, who had the pattern pinned to an upright in front of him.

'Ishwar, you're dreaming again!' bellowed a harsh voice. THWACK! The hand of the overseer struck a boy round the head.

The boy, Ishwar, faltered and nearly fell over sideways, but Bharat, crouching next to him, braced his body and managed to keep his friend upright.

'Keep your mind on the job. There'll be no supper for any of you tonight until you've woven another ten inches,' threatened the man. His great shape filled the doorway and blotted out their only source of light. Then he was gone. There was a low groan from the boys. Another ten inches before they would eat! That could take two hours or more, for this was the most complicated carpet they had ever woven – and the whole thing was to be completed within seven months

– when an ordinary carpet took at least twelve.

A wealthy man had come along the rough track to the village in his white Mercedes. When he reached the brick house of Anoup, the carpet manufacturer, he got out like a raja, surrounded by shy jostling children and deferential elders, all of whom noted the gold rings embedded in his chubby fingers, and the chunky foreign watch just glinting beneath the cuffs of his smart suit.

'I want a carpet for my daughter's dowry,' he declared. 'She is to be married next December.' (Everyone did an instant calculation. That was only seven months away.) 'And this is the pattern I want you to weave.'

Anoup took the piece of paper the rich man held out for him. He stared at it long and silently, then gloomily and apologetically shook his head. 'Impossible,' he said. 'I need at least twelve months to do an average carpet – but this … this … and in SEVEN months, you say … No. Impossible.'

The rich man pulled out a fat briefcase from the car.

He opened it up. There was a gasp from the onlookers. No one had ever seen so much money. Great wads of it, all stapled and bound straight from the bank. 'This is what you get now – and the rest when its finished. I'm sure you can do it. Just work a little harder – and a little longer each day, eh?' He tweaked the ear of the nearest little boy.

'I ... er ...' Anoup hesitated.

'Take it, take it ...' voices around him urged.

Anoup's brain spun. Common sense said, don't do it ... you can't do it ... But the money ... 'I'll do it. Your carpet will be ready on time.'

Anoup gave old Rama the pattern. 'You'd better study this,' he said.

Now Rama knew why Anoup had hesitated. The pattern was of a paradise garden; of strutting peacocks with sweeping tails, gold spotted deer leaping through undergrowth, squirrels coiling round tree-trunks and monkeys swinging from bough to bough; all sorts of exotic birds swooped and trilled and pecked at luscious fruit and flowers. Most extraordinary of all, was the

Tree of Life, from its spreading roots at the base, rising up and up through twisting coiling branches, all the way to the top where the rays of rising sun pierced golden shafts through the leaves. It would need threads of every colour in the rainbow. 'There aren't enough hours in the day . . .' Rama protested softly.

'Then we will use the hours of the night too,' Anoup retorted harshly.

Ishwar stared at the bright blue square in the doorway – the blue of the sky outside. He longed to leap up and charge into the daylight and play, play, play. He had almost forgotten what the outside was like. It was two years since his mother had brought him to this village to be bonded to Anoup, for debts incurred in his grandfather's lifetime. Since then he had worked behind a loom in the dark, airless mud hut. It was like that for all of them; bonded and enslaved – even old Rama – and Ishwar knew he too would die in bondage, that the debt would never be paid off in his lifetime either.

Ishwar could hear the voices of the village children

being taught under the neem tree to chorus out their times tables and their alphabet. Ishwar tried to listen and learn – but it was no use. He must chant for ever with the other carpet weavers, the colours of the thread they were weaving . . . one knot yellow, two knots blue, three knots red, four knots green . . .

The paradise garden shimmered on the loom. If he couldn't play outside, then he must roam within its green shade and splash in the stream and chase the deer and climb branch by branch up and up the Tree of Life until he reached the blue sky there on the loom. With a strange eagerness, he took up the thread and moved his card top to bottom, right to left, warp and weft and knot, as if he would weave himself into the carpet.

Exactly when the seven months were over, the white Mercedes came. The villagers watched anxiously as the rich man came before, right up to Anoup's door.

'Is it ready?'

'It is,' answered Anoup, eyeing the bulging briefcase on the back seat.

'Show it to me. You realise that if it is not exactly what I ordered, I will not take it.'

'Sir, it is exactly what you asked for in every detail,' boasted Anoup.

'I'll be the judge of that,' snorted the rich man. 'Bring it out in the daylight where I can examine it properly.'

Anoup clicked his fingers. Rama and three boys ran to the hut.

'Hey, Ishwar!' exclaimed Rama, 'Wake up, boy! Help us with the carpet.'

Ishwar was sitting in his usual place behind the loom, his head leaning against the upright. He didn't respond.

'Hurry up!' bellowed Anoup impatiently. Rama and the boys lugged the carpet outside and with almost holy reverence, unrolled it. Even the villagers gasped in amazement at the beauty and workmanship. It was a miracle. They beamed with pride.

The rich man came forward till his nose nearly touched the pile. Inch by inch he scrutinised the carpet. Suddenly, he roared with fury. 'What's this!' he shouted. 'I didn't ask for this! What kind of idiotic thing

have you done here! I can't take it – not with THIS!' He dragged the carpet out of their hands and trampled it into the dust. Then leaving the villagers appalled and stunned, the rich business man got into his car and sped off at top speed.

Nobody moved. Fearful eyes turned to Anoup. He was standing as if turned to stone. At last he clicked his fingers. In horrified silence they held out the carpet. Anoup's expert eye began at the top and scanned the carpet, as he had done twenty times each day. In his mind's eye, he wove each thread himself. He panned along the twisting branches of the Tree of Life, the glowing colours of humming birds and nightingales, dropping down through ten shades of green leaves and a dozen shades of blossoms of red, pink, purple and violet; he noted the golden fur of a deer darting through the grass, the hundred eyes of a peacock's tail shimmering near a silver fountain . . . and . . .?

Then Anoup's body shuddered. He shuddered so hard, they heard his teeth rattle, and the bones of his fingers clicking as he ground his knuckles into his fist.

'What is it?' murmured the villagers. 'What has he seen?' They surged forward. Speechless with rage, Anoup pointed to a spot deep in the undergrowth. Almost hidden among blossom and foliage, the young face of a boy peered up at the Tree of Life, an arm upstretched, ready to climb.

'Ishwar!' Rama muttered under his breath. 'It's Ishwar!'

'Ishwar!' The name was shrieked in vengeance! The villagers rushed to the hut.

The boy still leaned against the loom as if resting his aching head. Anoup strode over and kicked him. The boy slipped forward, face down, on to the earth floor. When they rolled him over, they saw he was dead.

The Demon Drummer

The link between the Demon Drummer and Mompesson House in Salisbury, Wiltshire, was slight. There was only the name – and reports of people experiencing 'a presence' in the Green Room. What clinched it for me was the discovery of a drummer boy's badge 300 years later . . .

No sword, nor rope, nor witch's fire
Can cause a demon to expire.

Tum tiddly um pom pom . . . Tum tiddly um pom pom . . . Down the moonlit road came the demon; across the great white plain, where many a ghostly legion had marched – following a drum beat on and on

into eternity. 'I want a drum, I want a drum . . .' the demon cried. 'Tum tiddly um tum. Tum tiddly dee . . . When I get my drum, you'll follow me!'

It was the sound of the drum which drew the demon to the drummer boy. How smart the lad looked in his scarlet uniform, with yellow sash and blue stockings and the round, shining brass badge pinned to his floppy hat. But it was not the uniform the demon coveted, it was the drum which was strapped across the boy's chest and rested on his left hip, below his heart.

It's not your soul that I require,
Your drum is all that I desire.

He was new to the regiment, the boy; and so, hour after hour, he practised his drumming, learning to beat the advance, the charge, the retreat, the Roundheads and Cuckolds – and all the points of war.

The drumsticks twirled in his fingers as his beat became sharper and more skilful; volleys of rat tat tat,

as piercing as gunfire, echoed round the barracks and were carried high on the winds, which swept across Salisbury Plain; and soldiers smiled to see the young lad strutting about, anticipating the day when he would lead the troops into battle.

But there were those who sighed too, for they knew that the young drummer boys who marched ahead, rapping out the fearful heartbeat of every soldier, were the ones the enemy liked to cut down first – to silence that pulse and make their foe feel that they were dead already.

The demon hung about watching and waiting. He heard another rhythm hammering through his dreadful being. 'I want that drum . . . I want that drum . . . I want that drum . . .'

The demon didn't have long to wait. It was a time of civil war; of uprisings and skirmishes between Royalist and Roundhead. Small armies were being rallied all the time. The Mompessons of Wiltshire were all for the king. Thomas the Younger and his cousin, John, galloped round the villages and towns, recruiting men

to fight for King Charles I against the Parliamentarians.

The drummer boy practised even harder. A few dozen men, with barely uniform or boots to replace their farming smocks and mud-caked clogs, set forth with a miscellany of rifles and pistols, hayforks and staves. Not much else engendered confidence, except the fierce, heartbeat drumming of the drummer boy. The demon followed.

'Forward, lads!' bellowed Thomas Mompesson from the lofty heights of his battle horse.

'God save the King!' yelled John Mompesson.

'God save the King,' echoed along the lanes as Royalists came out to cheer, though it seemed utter folly. How could such a raggle taggle of men hope to defy the disciplined troops of Cromwell's Round Heads? But they waved and shouted words of encouragement just the same, and the young drummer boy broadened his shoulders with pride and beat a brisk pace, while the demon marched alongside, longing for the moment when it would be he who beat the drum.

They marched across the high plains of Wiltshire

and joined up with the forces of John Penruddock – as much a ragged band as they were. The drums rattled out above the sounds of horses' hooves and clashing swords and the heavy tramp tramp of soldiers' feet.

The battle was a fiasco. Cromwell's Model Army cut them down like ripe corn. Survivors swore they saw the drummer boy fall early on, yet somehow the drum never ceased to beat that day. It beat and beat, even though scores lay dead and wounded. It beat like one demented, when the leaders of the uprising, Penruddock and Grove, were captured and hanged, and when Thomas Mompesson and the others fled into hiding.

Somehow that drum never ceased beating; even though the little drummer boy's soul had gone straight to heaven, even when the war was long over and Charles II was restored to the throne and all those men had long since laid down their arms and gone back to their farms.

Thomas and John Mompesson had returned to live in Tidworth; Thomas, to become a Member of

Parliament and John, a magistrate. John swore he could hear the drum beating even by day, throbbing like blood pumping through veins. It was as if someone marched up and down outside his house practising. Mrs Mompesson worried about her husband. The war had changed him. Sometimes he seemed deranged, the way he would leap to his feet with wild eyes and shout, 'There it is again – that infernal drumming!'

Many a time he sent out a servant to drive the drummer away, but there was never anybody there.

Then one day, it was louder and closer than usual, and John Mompesson rushed out himself and demanded to know who was annoying the neighbourhood hour by hour, day after day, disturbing the peace.

There, in the road outside his house, he saw a strange scarecrow of a boy. Shreds of uniform of the Royalist colours hung about him. The drum, strapped to his left hip, was a true military drum: taut cream calf's skin was stretched across the top and base and tensioned by white-painted rope, which criss-crossed

round the blue, wooden body of the drum. The royal insignia, emblazoned in gold, glowed between the thin, wavy red and white lines beneath the rim.

The drummer's brass badge flared in the sunlight.

'Who are you? And by what authority do you drum in this neighbourhood?'

Was it the sun's reflection which made the boy's eyes glint red, as he mockingly returned the gaze of the angry magistrate?

'Why sir,' he wheedled, 'here is my warrant.' He pulled forth a half-torn document and held it out for inspection. 'I have the authority,' he said with the hint of a sneer in his voice.

'You'll come with me,' ordered Mompesson. 'I want the bailiff to verify this,' and he marched the vagrant drummer to the bailiff's office.

The bailiff examined the warrant, holding it first right up to his eyes to gaze at it through his pince-nez, then out at arm's length, because he had become long-sighted with age. Then he stared at the pitiful spectacle of the lad before him – was he human? The bailiff could

hardly contain a shudder, for the boy looked like some wild creature out of a ditch, with his unkempt hair and filthy hands and the smell about him of something putrid and evil. Yet, there was no denying that he was a skilful drummer who knew all the calls and whose shining drum would pass even the closest scrutiny on the king's parade.

'This warrant is obviously a forgery,' declared the bailiff finally. To the satisfaction of Mr Mompesson, he not only tore it up, but ordered the boy to be arrested and his drum confiscated. The charges, they told him, could be extremely serious; anything ranging from forgery and disturbing the peace, to masquerading as a drummer in the king's uniform and robbing from the dead. How else had he come into possession of the drum? The penalty could be transportation or death.

The howls and curses of the boy rent the air as they stripped him of the drum. His fingers clawed at it. 'It's mine, it's mine!' And he cursed and howled like the devil himself, as they dragged it off his body and tore the remnants of uniform from his back.

A constable was summoned to take the fraudulent drummer boy to the town gaol and the bailiff took the drum and locked it away.

'At last,' thought Mr Mompesson. 'I am free of the drumming.'

For a while, Mr Mompesson went cheerily about his business, until one day he was called to London. On that same day, a man came round from the bailiff with the drum.

'The bailiff said that you were to have it, sir,' said the man. 'The drum is now yours.'

Mr Mompesson looked at the drum. For some reason, his heart missed a beat. 'What happened to the vagrant who caused all the nuisance?' he asked. But the man was vague. 'Why sir, did you not yourself have him transported?'

'Ha, ha, ha.' Mompesson thought he heard laughter.

It matters not to a demon whether he be transported or hanged at the crossroads. He can just laugh, and come back again and again – especially if he wants something!

A sudden, fierce wind seemed to taunt the

weathervane and send it spinning round, and strange
words moaned in John Mompesson's ears:

> *It's not your soul that I require,*
> *But just the drum that I desire.*

John Mompesson shuddered. The man was holding the
wretched drum out to him. He didn't want the thing, but
the man pressed it into his hands. As he took possession
of it, it gave a hollow echo as Mompesson handed it
rapidly to his servant to take indoors. Then he set off for
London, saying he would be home the next day.

That night, when his servants had finally locked and
bolted the doors: when they had dined and cleared
away and settled the fires; when the dogs of the house
had either stretched out in front of the glowing embers
or padded up to the children's bedrooms; when Mrs
Mompesson was deeply asleep in her bedchamber –
there came a low rattling. Mrs Mompesson woke
briefly, listened a few moments, then fell asleep
thinking it must be the wind.

Now the sound came again, this time from the back of the house. Young Barbara, the daughter, awoke. Tap, tap, tap . . . was someone knocking to get in? She sat up curiously. Rappatap tap . . . Rappatap tap . . . A low flame flickered in her bedroom fireplace, casting giant shadows up the walls. 'Who is it?' she whispered. Rat . . . tat . . . tat. The great hound lying on her bed across her legs, who normally would have been the first to leap up with his hair all standing on end, didn't even stir.

The noise got louder and more persistent. First the knocking was on the downstairs back door, but then it came to strike at her windows, where it rapped and rattled so fiercely, that she was sure the panes would break. The girl leapt from her bed with a shriek and ran sobbing to her mother. She told her someone was trying to get into her bedroom. At that moment, her brother Charles also came rushing in, hollering that they were being attacked.

Mrs Mompesson bundled the terrified children into her bed; then she lit the candles, put on her dressing

gown and slippers and taking one of the candlesticks, went on to the landing. The knocking and banging seemed to be all round the house – at first, a rhythmic noise, as if someone rapped out a sequence, but then it turned into such a furious hammering, that it was as if the house had been plunged into the very centre of a battle.

The servants came running – white-faced maids from upstairs and half-dressed grooms from the stables. They carried sticks and clubs and crowded together. But, although the banging and crashing went on all night, nobody gained entrance, and Mrs Mompesson thanked God for their stout oak doors.

No one got any sleep that night.

When Mr Mompesson returned, what a tale every member of the family told him and then every servant.

'Well, I daresay, if they didn't get in last night, we won't be hearing from them again,' soothed Mr Mompesson, though he went round the house and stables with his servants, checking every door and window to see that they were secure.

But the next night a wind seemed to sweep round the house so powerfully that the windows jiggled in their frames, and a high-pitched whistling came down the chimneys and pierced their ear-drums where they lay in their beds. Then came the knocking, the same as before. Ratta tat tat . . . ratta tat tat . . . ratta tat tat . . . The rapping went from door to door all around the outside of the house, getting louder and louder, a giant drum preparing the troops for battle.

'Do you hear?' Mrs Mompesson clutched her husband's arm. 'It's the same noise. The villains have come back.'

'I'll soon deal with this,' roared Mr Mompesson, furious at having his household terrorised in this way. With Mrs Mompesson hovering at his side with lighted candelabra, he dragged on his boots, flung a cloak across his back, and then taking up his brace of pistols, thudded downstairs yelling for the male servants, Harry and George.

Harry and George had already been woken by the banging, and soon appeared, bearing great clubs in

their hands. Wide-eyed and afraid, they looked to Mr Mompesson for instructions.

'Open the door, man!' Mr Mompesson ordered George. George pulled down the great iron bolts, and lifted the wooden bar from across the door frame. Then he took one of the huge keys which hung from a nearby hook, and put it into the lock. Before turning it, he paused, fearfully. 'Why not wait till morning, sir,' he quavered. 'There could be a lot of them out there.'

'Don't be such a coward, George. Open it up.'

The huge door swung open. Only the deep void of night met their eyes. The knocking stopped. There was a great silence. Mr Mompesson stepped outside, his pistols cocked, one in each hand, ready to fire. Harry shuffled forward timidly, holding up a burning branch which he had fetched from the fireplace. Two of the dogs, who had been sleeping upstairs, ambled out stretching and sniffing and wagging their tails. Silently they followed their master all round the outside of the house while, once again, everything was checked. Mr Mompesson himself tried every door and every

window, but all were secure and untouched.

They completed a tour of the grounds and then returned to the front door. 'There's nothing and no one there!' he declared. 'And, what's more, though it's been raining, there isn't a fresh footmark in the mud or any sign of horses or strangers. We're all letting our imaginations run away with us. Look at the dogs! They haven't scented strangers; they don't know what all the fuss is about. It's only the wind!'

But after Mr Mompesson had hustled everyone back to their chambers with reassuring words, he remained downstairs alone, looking suddenly hunched and furtively watchful. He paced up and down, up and down in the hallway, then went and sat at his oak desk in the library, furiously drumming his fingers in a rhythmic tattoo.

He must have fallen asleep, for when he suddenly awoke with a jerk, the room swayed with shadows. The candle had burnt right down to a stub, and was wavering around pathetically as it drowned in a pool of wax. Rappatat . . . tat . . . Rappatat . . . tat . . . it low and

menacing, Mr. Mompesson, low and menacing, knew its parley. It was a drum call to prepare for attack. He felt a chill of horror creep over his body. Rappatat . . . tat . . . Rappatat . . . tat . . . The sound seemed to be near, yet very, very far away – as if in another world. He got to his feet and grasped his pistols in each hand. He went to the window and looked out. It was not yet dawn. There was no moon, but a strange blue light hovered over the stables. Then he saw him – just briefly; just long enough to recognise the tattered scarlet uniform, the blue stockings and the floppy hat on which the badge gleamed like an evil eye. In his hands, he waved a pair of drumsticks and beat the air in a demonic drum roll.

The shrieks of the vagrant drummer were trapped inside Mr Mompesson's head – the same shrieks the wretched creature had emitted when arrested and deprived of his drum; he heard them again. 'I want my drum . . . I want my drum!'

'No, by God! You won't have it back!' John Mompesson was suddenly overwhelmed with anger.

Some time in the night, Mrs Mompesson heard her husband's footsteps clatter furiously up the staircase, but not to stop at their chamber door. Instead, he carried on to the upper rooms, where the children kept their toys. Now she heard his footsteps pacing relentlessly above her head. 'Mr Mompesson,' she went to the bottom of the stairs and called up nervously. 'Won't you retire now and get some sleep? The danger seems to be over.'

'No, no!' were all the words he uttered, though she wasn't sure if they were addressed to her.

The next morning, he was found slumped at the nursery table, sleeping with the drum clasped in his arms.

A few nights later just when the household had fallen asleep, there was a great whooshing sound as if giant objects were being hurled over the house. The knocking started again, fierce as ever; it went from door to door and now up onto the roof, clattering around on the tiles and rumbling down the chimneys.

The household was plunged into terror. Once again the servants rushed out of the house and confronted the

darkness, and again Mr Mompesson raced up the stairs to the nursery, but would not say why. But he knew then it was more than knocking. He understood the language of the drum beating out the advance, the attack, the instructions to rally, or disperse, or retreat.

Night after night, the same thing happened – and with such malice – for it seemed as though whoever made the noise, knew the exact moment that the household had dropped into a deep sleep.

Rappatat tat . . . rappatat . . . tat . . .

'Dammit, you shan't have it,' muttered Mr Mompesson one night, tossing about as if in the middle of a nightmare.

'Have what, sir?' exclaimed his wife, bewildered.

'The drum. The wretched fellow wants his drum. But he shan't have it,' and he flung himself from his bed and stumbled up to the nursery.

The deliberate ratta tat tat of a drummer breaking up the guard was always the sinister finale. Only then would Mr Mompesson emerge from the upper room looking white and exhausted.

'Won't you take us away from here, sir?' pleaded his wife.

'There's been no harm done,' said Mr Mompesson coldly. 'No property has been damaged and no person hurt. I will not be harassed and driven out by any damned spirit of the night.'

'But what about my nerves?' wailed poor Mrs Mompesson, utterly distraught, for she was soon to be delivered of another child.

What is it that can make noises so loud they can be heard across the fields, yet the dogs don't stir? What is it that can pant like a hound, move like a cat, be hot without a fire, ride a horse till lame without it even leaving the stable? What hammers without an anvil and snips without scissors? What can throw furniture about, lift children from their beds and rip up a bible? Who drums against the doors and windows night after night, always ending with the breaking up of the guard?

People said it was the devil.

'Fetch the priest, I beg you,' cried Mrs Mompesson. 'The house is possessed!'

A priest came and went from room to room throughout the house intoning a prayer of exorcism: 'Oh Child of the Devil and enemy of everything that is good, stop perverting the right way of the Lord. *In nomine patrisel filii et spiritus sancti*, I command you to leave this house!' For some weeks after that there was silence – but to Mr Mompesson, it was a mocking silence; a taunting silence. For him, there was no peace of mind. He knew the drum gleamed in the room above as if waiting to be claimed by the drummer and, late into the night, he could be heard pacing restlessly and climbing the stairs to lock himself into the nursery.

A few weeks passed. There had been no disturbance; no knocking of any kind. Gradually, the household became confident that the priest had rid them of the demon. Mrs Mompesson had given birth safely and was lying in her own chamber, with her infant in its cradle beside her bed, where she could reach out and rock it.

One night, in the dead of night, when the whole house slept deeply, the knocking came again. 'Pou . . .

tou . . . pou . . . tou . . . pou . . . tou . . . R.' It was muffled and intimate; it crept into Mrs Mompesson's dreams. 'Pou tou, pou tou . . . R.' Instinctively, she reached out and touched her baby's cheek. It was soft and warm and she felt its steady breath on her hand.

'Pou tou . . . pou . . . tou.'

'Who's there?' called Mrs Mompesson. Nobody answered. 'Poutou . . . poutou . . . R . . . poutou . . . poutou . . . R . . .' the knocking was close by. 'Poutoupoutou . . . pou . . . poutoupoutou pou . . .' It was inside the house. It was at her own chamber door. She wanted to lift her baby from its cradle and hold it to her, but a terrible chill froze her into paralysis.

'Poutoupoutou . . . poutoupoutou pou . . . tou . . . the knocking continued.

'Who's there?' Mrs Mompesson cried in a dread voice. 'Why don't you come in?'

The door remained firmly shut, but the room was suddenly filled with an awful sulphurous smell. The chair in the corner slid forward slowly and the baby's cradle began to rock. Then before the horrified eyes of

its mother, invisible hands lifted the sleeping infant. It lifted it into the air . . . higher and higher . . .

'Please . . .' Mrs Mompesson held out her hands in desperate supplication. 'I beseech you . . .' Slowly, the baby was lowered again, and laid back into its cradle so gently it didn't wake. The cradle rocked.

'In the name of God, who is it? What do you want?' Mrs Mompesson whispered with a shudder.

And a voice answered, 'Nothing with you.' The chair moved back to its place in the corner and the cradle stopped rocking.

One day the people of Tidworth gathered around to watch the Mompesson family leave. It was a strange day for them all, for none could remember a time when a Mompesson had not lived in their district. It was whispered that the demon drummer had finally driven them out. The whole town knew what had been happening in the Mompesson household. Most put it down to the drummer boy, who only wanted his drum back. But Mr Mompesson was a stubborn man. He

would rather leave, than give in to the vagrant drummer boy.

So several huge carts arrived, and were piled high with furniture and chests and all their goods and chattels. It was noted that a military drum was among them. The long procession wound its way to Salisbury – to within the very shadow of the cathedral, where Thomas had prepared a house for them in the Close.

Never had a day seemed more exciting for the children. Just to come into a city like Salisbury – all busy and bustling – and the cathedral bells ringing out, and the streets crowded with people and animals and carriages and hawkers and buskers.

And their house, too, was a most pleasing building – unlike their old one, which had been dark and rambling and draughty and filled with such horror. This one was newly built – in the modern style – a mixture of grey limestone and redbrick with sash windows and hipped roofs. Inside, the rooms were light and airy, each with a view either looking out over the Choristers' Green to the Cathedral, or to the

gardens at the back with their walks and flower beds. Even though they were now in the middle of a city, their new house had such a gentle peacefulness about it. They were sure that not even a demon drummer could disturb this serenity. Gradually he faded like a bad dream.

Two centuries rolled by; the Mompesson family thrived and died out like an old tree and Mompesson House was inhabited in turn by the Longuevilles, the Hayters, the Portmans, the Townsends, and then in 1952, a Mr Martineau moved into Mompesson House.

In a nearby village, a boy was at home for the summer half-term holiday. His father, Mr Hammick, had a new car, and so was looking for every opportunity to drive it.

'Fancy a spin, Philip?' he asked his son.

Mr Hammick put on his tweed jacket and cap, as if he might have been taking out the pony and trap, but instead, they leapt into his latest passion – a bright red MG sports car with shining chrome grid and side lamps.

They climbed the steep wooded escarpments – richly green, and after winding ever upwards through deep-shadowed tunnels of elm and beech trees along empty roads, they broke out into the vast open expanse of Salisbury Plain.

At a crossroads, Mr Hammick slowed down to point out a signpost to Tidworth. 'That's where the demon drummer comes from,' he announced.

Philip hardly noticed when they passed the great, grey slabs of Stonehenge, so intent was he on the strange story of the demon drummer of Tidworth, sometimes known as the Mompesson Ghost, which his father then related to him.

'And is he still around?' asked the boy, excitedly.

'They say he left Tidworth when the Mompessons moved to Salisbury,' replied his father. 'I used to spend my holidays at Mompesson House, in the days when my Uncle Willie lived there, but I can't say I ever heard or saw a thing. It was most annoying – especially as Annie, the housemaid, swore she felt a "presence" in the Green Room and always whistled "We're Soldiers

of the Queen" though she didn't know why.'

'Oh!' Philip sighed with disappointment.

'Why don't we go to Salisbury and look at the house? I haven't seen it since I was a boy,' said Mr Hammick with sudden enthusiasm. 'We're so close to it now.'

Soon, the great spire of Salisbury Cathedral rose before them like a finger, powerful yet delicate, pointing upwards into the pale blue sky. They drove right into the Close and parked the car outside the railings of Mompesson House.

Mr Hammick got out – suddenly overwhelmed with memories. He walked up and ran his fingers along the railings, and lovingly looked all over its stone and brick front. 'Look, Philip, the magnolia – it's still there, and blooming as beautifully as ever! They say it's nearly a old as the house!'

'Shall we go in, Father?' asked the boy.

'It would be rather impertinent, since we haven't made an appointment,' murmured his father, though he looked longingly at the great front door, with its

elaborately sculpted cartouche of the Mompesson coat of arms. 'Oh, to hell with it. They can't eat us, can they? Let's try.' He lifted the catch of the wrought iron gate, walked up to the door and boldly rang the brass bell.

'Yes?' The man who opened the door viewed then with cool reserve, as if mildly annoyed that he had been disturbed.

'Oh . . . er . . . do forgive us!' stammered Mr Hammick. 'Are you Mr . . . er . . . um . . .'

'Mr Martineau,' the man informed them.

'Ah! So you're the new owner of Mompesson House, then,' declared Mr Hammick, his enthusiasm overcoming his shyness.

'Yes, can I help you?' Mr Martineau had not yet opened the door a jot further than was sufficient to see who had knocked.

'Forgive me, sir . . .' Mr Hammick apologised again. 'I know this is grossly impertinent of me, but I couldn't resist calling by as we were passing. You see, I used to visit this house as a child – and loved it so much.'

'Oh, I see, well – perhaps you'd better step inside.'

With conspicuous reluctance, Mr Martineau stood back and allowed father and son into the hall.

Mr Hammick's eyes roamed eagerly around, taking in again, after so long, the beautiful plasterwork, the delicate mouldings and the collections of masks and ornaments. Finally his gaze settled on the elegant oak staircase leading upwards to rooms at the top in which he had once slept and played as a boy.

For a while they talked, or rather, it was Mr Hammick who mainly reminisced about the house: who had lived there and what they did, what changes had been made, and what changes would be made, till finally, his son, Philip, unable to withhold his curiosity any longer, burst out, 'But please, Mr Martineau, sir! Have you seen or heard the ghost?'

Mr Martineau's smile could scarcely disguise the faint contempt he felt for the question. 'I don't believe in ghosts,' he said primly.

Mr Hammick, who was well away now with his memories, insisted that, as the new owner of the house,

Mr Martineau should know the story, even if the ghost is no more.

At first, Mr Martineau stood politely stony-faced but slowly his face took on an expression of intense interest and by the end, the faintest flush of excitement tinged his cheeks.

'Just one moment,' said Mr Martineau, when the story had finally ended. 'Wait here. I think there is something thing you might be interested in seeing.'

He rapidly ascended the staircase and entered the Green Room which was at its head.

Soon he reappeared with something clenched in one hand. 'As you can see, I'm in the process of renovating the house, and I've had the electricians in to re-wire it. Yesterday, one of the men had to lift up the floor-boards of the Green Room. He found this.'

Mr Martineau opened up his hand. Lying on his palm was a discoloured, dusty brass badge.

'Good heavens!' Mr Hammick looked absolutely stunned. He took the badge cautiously, almost as if it might burn him. His fingers stroked the embossed

brass, and he rubbed it to a shine on the front of his jacket. Then he looked at it again, hardly believing what he saw – the image of a drum with crossed sticks and the Royalist insignia.

'What is it, Pa?' asked Philip.

'It's the badge of a drummer boy!'

They stood silent with astonishment.

Then Mr Martineau spoke stiffly. 'Well, now – if you'll excuse me.' His hand trembled as he held it out to take back the badge. Hardly giving it a further glance, he slipped it into his jacket pocket and then opened the front door.

'I'm afraid I must get on. Perhaps you'll call again another time.' But he spoke without any welcoming warmth, and father and son knew that it would be a long time before either of them would enter that house again.

They drove out of Salisbury, back across the plain. and on past the sign-post to Tidworth.

'I wonder what happened to the drum?' murmured the boy.

* * *

How pretty the Close looks at night: the elegant houses round the Green, with their tall windows and looped curtains, where glimpses of crystal chandeliers flicker warmly and the shadows of children bob up and down against the walls. And how safe it feels to see the nightwatchman patrolling the Close – and just to live within the embrace of a house of God, whose tall spire reaches up to heaven. Could such a place be touched by evil?

Mrs Mompesson often toured the house at night, after she had tucked in her children. They had found peace at last. No longer were their nights disturbed. The dark rings of exhaustion had faded from beneath their eyes, and their pale cheeks glowed like winter roses.

Tonight, she went into the Green Room. She did this every night, as if for reassurance, for it was here, along with the children's other toys, that the drum was stored, long ago abandoned by young Charles, who was far more keen on riding his pony.

Placing her candlestick on the table, she gazed out of the window across the Green.

Suddenly, she saw him. A boy; dressed in a scarlet jacket and breeches and sash, and a badge shining on his floppy hat. In his hands he twirled a pair of drumsticks with which he beat the empty air – for he had no drum.

With a dreadful shudder, she realised immediately who it was. The rhythm came hammering into her brain. Rappatat . . . tat . . . rappatat . . . tat . . .

'No,' she whispered. 'Not here, too. Please, not here.'

'I want the drum . . . I want the drum . . .' a voice broke into her thoughts.

Without any hesitation, Mrs Mompesson turned to the far corner table on which rested the drum. Its white ropes hadn't faded, and its body of royal colours gleamed as brightly as if they had just been painted. She picked it up. Her ring struck the calfskin surface and it boomed like a soft heartbeat. She opened the sash window to its maximum, then leaning out, she hurled the drum with all her might – over the wrought

iron railings, beyond the walls with the magnolia. Over the Green it went, spinning towards the drummer boy, and twirled and somersaulted higher than the cathedral spire, higher and higher till it merged with the multitude of stars – and a great shout of joy echoed among the peal of bells striking midnight.

She heard the ratta . . . tat . . . tat of a drum.

She didn't know it was the beat of the retreat, but she heard it receding into the distance – and soon it was gone for ever.

The Bridegroom

'Muni! I saw a bird last night!'

'You did, Didi?'

My dear, sweet, youngest sister immediately stopped what she was doing and turned to me.

'Not now, Muni – don't go listening to her crazy dreams now,' begged my middle sister, Tara. 'We'll be late for school.' She pushed me aside and dragged Muni into the kitchen where mother was preparing breakfast.

I began to wail. I couldn't help it. That's me. I show everything. When I'm happy, I jump and shriek and the strangest sounds squawk from my throat, and when I'm sad, I just stand there with my feet apart and hands outstretched like some kind of stone statue, and it's like

a river bursts behind my eyes, and other strange noises seem to rise from the very pit of my stomach and force my mouth wide open into an appalling grimace, so I look like some frightful temple demon – at least that's how Tara describes me.

Tara hates me. She sees me as the obstacle to her happiness. The trouble is – she's right. I am an obstacle. You see, I'm the eldest girl, and until I'm married, my younger sisters can't marry. And who'll marry me? I blight the whole family. Everybody whispers. People call me the idiot child. They say my parents must have been bad in their previous life to have had me. So no one wants to be associated with any of us. They're afraid they will be contaminated – and their seed also. I often hear my mother wailing. 'We'll never get any offers for our daughters. They'll never marry – not even our beautiful Tara. Oh, what did I do to deserve this!'

Things went wrong when I was born – perhaps even before I was born. My mother nearly died having me – and then when she saw my large head and squashed up face, and small eyes like a pig, and huge nose like the

start of an elephant's trunk, she thrust me away and wouldn't look at me for a month. Then she went to her guru, Narashima, and he warned her that she must have done something very bad in her past life and that I was a test; that if she wanted to be reborn better next time round, she must love and care for me as her most precious child. So she did. She tried as hard as she could. She turned towards me and from then on, never stinted in her devotion. Trouble is, devotion isn't love, and such artificial devotion was a terrible strain on her. Now she has become depressed, withdrawn and wan and sometimes can't get up in the morning and I know it's my fault.

Tara was born almost a year after me – another daughter. Mother and Father felt doubly cursed until it gradually became apparent how beautiful she was. Sadly, it didn't affect the situation. People admired Tara and marvelled at her beauty, but there was no rush to make offers of marriage. Muni was born two years after Tara. A third daughter; pretty, too – though not like Tara. My father was disgusted; another girl? Was he not

man enough to produce sons? He hardly bothered coming home from the office after that, and when he did, he would be blind drunk and we all had to watch out.

No – I had jinxed the whole family, and everything that went wrong, from the curdling of the milk to my father failing to get promoted, was all my fault.

When Tara was old enough, Mother used to beseech her to play with me. But Tara would kick me and pinch me to make me cry. She knew my crying got on Papa's nerves and that sooner or later he would come and shake me and tell me to shut up. I think I'd be dead now, from a broken heart, if it weren't for chota baby – my littlest, sweetest Muni. My life changed when she was born. Now I had a purpose. I carried her about when she was helpless; I fed her and bathed her; I saw her take her first steps and was ready to catch her when she toppled over. It was to me she came when she wanted a cuddle, and it was me she wanted to put her to bed. And as she grew older, she loved me all the more. She doesn't see my ugliness. No complications;

no sense of duty, no persuasion to be nice to me – she just loves me. When she was tiny, she used to have nightmares and scream. It was I who used to go to her, quick as a flash. I would gather her up in my arms and rock her and rock her until she fell asleep again. Sometimes I would crawl into bed with her.

But these days, I too have nightmares, dreams which can send me whirling round the house in a kind of madness, and now she does for me what I did for her – she takes my hand and murmurs softly, 'It's all right, Didi. You're safe at home.' And she'll crawl into bed with me. Papa calls us Beauty and the Beast – and there's no kindness in his voice when he says it.

But Muni and I, we always tell each other our dreams. It became a habit. If I could just tell Muni my dream, and she tell me hers, then I could tolerate the rest of the day, for she would always have an explanation for our dreams.

So there I was wailing at the top of my voice because Tara had dragged Muni away before I could tell her about the bird, and it was important. Very important.

So I screamed even louder. 'Muni! Come and listen to my dream.'

Muni came, a piece of toast in her mouth and one arm inside her blazer sleeve while she struggled with the other.

'Quick, Didi, tell me. The school bus will soon be here.'

'There was a bird, Muni. A huge bird.' I pressed my mouth right up to her ear and whispered, 'And I think he's coming for me, not Tara!'

'What are you saying about me?' demanded Tara barging between us and pushing me roughly aside.

'And Muni!' I tried to go on and tell her how I felt about the strange terror and excitement this dream stirred in me, but outside, the school bus blasted its horn impatiently.

'Tell me when I get home,' she cried.

As Tara dragged her off to the bus I could hear Tara begging Muni to tell her what I had been saying about her. Then the bus revved up and shot off down the road in a cloud of dust.

I stared after it for a long time, until it had become just a speck in the distance. Where the road disappeared into the sky, there hung a huge black monsoon cloud, and my dream came back to me all the more vividly. Yes, I had dreamt of a bird – a night bird, longer than the road. It had come flying out of the pitch black depths of monsoon clouds into a moon-struck, ocean sky, where the stars bobbed like fishing boats. The bird was still far away in the distance, its body seeming to stretch far behind it into the milky way. It was beautiful, yet I was frightened, because its neck was as dark blue as Lord Shiva's, and spiralled like the eye of a tornado, sucking everything up in its path.

Strangest of all – and I *tried* to tell Muni – was that on the end of its outstretched neck was a head. 'It's important, Muni,' I whimpered, 'it had a face, and it was flying straight towards me . . .' My voice trailed away as the bus disappeared from sight.

Why had I said it was coming for me not Tara? Was it because Tara is as beautiful as a goddess, and this face was as handsome and noble as a god prince? That all the

men who ever came to our house only had eyes for Tara? And yet, I was sure that, in my dream, it was me he was flying to . . . I could hardly admit such a silly idea.

Now I heard the servants whispering. 'Tara has a secret lover. Thinks we don't know . . .' they sniggered triumphantly. 'We know everything. Of course, the boy's family won't let him marry her – not with that elephant-headed sister of hers. If they'd been sensible, they would have smothered her at birth.'

I fled from their horrible talk; horrible, horrible . . . I wanted to run to Mother and beg her to comfort me and tell me she loved me and tell her not to worry because everything would be all right when the bird came. But it was no use; when I peered into her bedroom, she was lying like a corpse with her head covered by the sheet, snoring with every breath. 'Mummy!' I whispered, but there was no alteration in the rhythm of her breathing.

I had the same dream again the following night. The same bird, but nearer; that is, its head was nearer but its body still stretched behind all feathery and breaking up into stars as it merged into the land sky of the far

distance. I looked into its face, a human face but with the eyes and beak of an eagle. Suddenly the bird fixed one of its eyes on me, a pale, hazel eye, and it was like being pierced by an arrow. I was filled with terror at the sight of it, yet at the same time had such feelings of . . . love? Could I fall in love?

I awoke, throbbing with disturbances and unexplained excitement.

'Muni!' I lumbered clumsily straight into my sister's bed through the pitch of the night, babbling incoherently. 'The bird! He's coming closer. He is coming to claim me. I'm frightened. Will he kill me or embrace me – I can't tell.'

Muni rolled in her sleep, muttering comforting words and hugged me close. 'Don't worry, Didi – it's only a dream. It won't hurt you. It's only a bird.'

'No, Muni – it has a man's face – it looks at me so lovingly and I know it's coming to marry me.'

That made Muni wake up. 'Marry you, Didi? Marry *you*?'

For a horrible moment, I thought she was going to

laugh – just as Tara would have laughed, or Mother would have sighed, or Father would have thrown up his eyes in despair. My breath halted in my lungs; I stopped breathing; if she laughed . . . if she laughed . . .

But she didn't. She murmured softly, 'But that's wonderful, Didi, I always knew someone would come for you one day.'

'Yet I'm afraid, Muni. No one but you loves me. Everyone else just sees my ugliness.'

'Perhaps your dream bird sees you as I do, the most beautiful person in the world. Of course it loves you.'

I lay there wondering. But can I love? Tara doesn't think so. Tara doesn't see me as human with human feelings. Because no man will ever love me, she thinks I'm incapable of love. But I have my fantasies too. Everyone thinks that because I'm ugly I don't dream of having a wonderful lover; that I don't yearn for a man to circle the flame with me in marriage. I tell Muni about it – and oh how we laugh together and tell each other stories about handsome princes who come riding in chariots, begging for our hands in marriage – and all

the time with an ache in our hearts for it seems that it can never be – and all because of me.

The next day there was no school. Mother and Tara went shopping, so that meant they would be away for hours. As usual, Muni was happy to stay with me and oh, how she teased me about my dream bird. 'Your prince is coming to carry you away for ever. Come on, let's play dressing up. I want to dress you as a bride – from top to bottom. Just to show you how it will be when your day comes.'

'Oh, Muni,' I giggled, though I wanted to cry. 'My day will never come.'

'Nonsense,' exclaimed Muni dramatically. 'You're magic. You see. Only the most special perfect magic person will find you, and then he'll take you away – and . . .'

'And then you and Tara will be free to marry!' I cried.

Muni was bursting with excitement. She rushed into our mother's room and began raiding her wardrobe. She found mother's scarlet and gold wedding saree,

and all her jewellery; gold rings for the fingers and toes, golden bangles, chains, earrings and necklaces; pearls for the hair, mascara and charcoal for my eyes, lipstick and henna for my lips and skin. She gathered it all together and then set about turning me into a bride.

By the time Mother and Tara came home, it was getting dark, but just as we heard the wheels of the car crunching up the drive, Muni finished the last intricate coil of her design in henna on my hands. She sat back on her heels, suddenly exhausted. She had worked so hard. But there I was, looking like a bride, glowing in the crimson saree, glittering with the jewels, my piggy eyes looking round and dark and almost big, outlined as they were with the charcoal, and my lashes swept upwards with mascara. Muni had woven pearls into my hair, outlined my parting in red; my ears and neck gleamed with rubies and gold, making my skin reflect like honey, and in my elephant nose shone a diamond stud. I stared at myself in the mirror, not daring to move. Was that me, really me?

'Oh, Didi, you look beautiful!' breathed Muni, amazed at the transformation.

'What on earth!' A harsh voice lacerated our fantasy. 'Mummy! Just look what Muni and Didi have been up to!' Tara's voice was shrill with scorn and indignation.

'Oh no! Not my wedding saree! Not my very best saree! How could you!'

I felt a ringing stinging slap.

Muni began to whimper. 'Don't hit Didi. It isn't her fault. I made her do it. I wanted her to look beautiful – like a bride. We haven't done any harm.'

Muni's hand reached out for mine, but was dragged from my clasp and I began to shake.

'Make her look beautiful? Like a bride? What kind of stupid ideas have you been putting in her head?'

Mother and Tara raged and sneered in turn, and made such a hullaballoo that even the servants came running.

Then from outside came a dreadful whistling sound. A whistling which became a rumbling which grew louder and louder and louder. The electric lights

dipped crazily in and out and finally out. We were plunged into darkness.

Voices were yelling, 'What's happening?'

'It's a storm coming.'

'More like a tornado,' shouted my father's voice, high with alarm.

'Look, look at the sky . . . What is that!'

My mother and sisters ran outside to see, leaving me still dressed as a bride, staring through the window at the unimaginable sky.

It was my dream, my bird. I could see his great, long body – trailing with clouds and stars and feathery plumes trickling like waterfalls, streaming behind him, spreading across the whole moonlit sky. I could see his dark blue throat twisting and sucking, as if he consumed the universe. Nearer and nearer he came, and now I saw that hazel eye fixed on me and suddenly he was everywhere. I braced myself for pain. I would be drowned, smothered, knocked to the ground, battered and stripped.

I felt something grip my wrist. A grip from which I

could never escape; an eagle's talon with claws of steel, yet as light as a bangle which leaves not one scratch on my skin. I am being lifted; taken; claimed; carried away. All solid things dissolve. I am simply absorbed into light and time and space. I look down on my home and parents and sisters.

Oh, Muni, my dearest sweet younger sister, I can see you running desperately back into the house; running and screaming in terror as you burst into the room where you dressed me as a bride – and you do not find me. You spin in circles, blinded with hysteria, and I beg you to calm down and realise what has happened; that you were right. My prince has come – and you are all free. At last, as you fall weeping to the ground, your hand touches a feather. You look up and the room is floating with feathers.

And now you know.